Journey Toward Home

Includes Bonus Story of
The Measure of a Man

Journey Toward Home

CAROL COX

BARBOUR BOOKS
An Imprint of Barbour Publishing, Inc.

Journey Toward Home ©1998 by Barbour Publishing, Inc.
The Measure of a Man ©1999 by Barbour Publishing, Inc.

Print ISBN 978-1-68322-182-1

eBook Editions:
Adobe Digital Edition (.epub) 978-1-68322-184-5
Kindle and MobiPocket Edition (.prc) 978-1-68322-183-8

All scripture quotations are taken from the King James Version of the Bible.

This book is a work of fiction. Names, characters, places, and incidents are either products of the author's imagination or used fictitiously. Any similarity to actual people, organizations, and/or events is purely coincidental.

Published by Barbour Books, an imprint of Barbour Publishing, Inc., P.O. Box 719, Uhrichsville, Ohio 44683, www.barbourbooks.com

Our mission is to publish and distribute inspirational products offering exceptional value and biblical encouragement to the masses.

 Member of the
Evangelical Christian
Publishers Association

Printed in the United States of America.

Chapter 1

It was unseasonably warm, and a muggy stillness hung over St. Joseph. I sat in the big wicker rocking chair on Aunt Phoebe's front porch and fanned myself. Aunt Phoebe sat facing me, bolt upright in her chair. Her iron-gray hair, pulled into its customary bun, was drawn so tight that I wondered for the thousandth time how she was able even to blink. She pursed her thin lips in disapproval.

"You're a foolish, ungrateful child, Judith. How you can disregard the kindness and generosity I've shown you these past ten years, I cannot imagine. Your mother would never have considered doing such a thing. It is obviously the bad blood you inherited from your father."

I clamped my own lips together to keep silent. We had been over this same ground endlessly in the last two weeks. It would be pointless and perhaps fatal to my plans to open another argument and antagonize my aunt further.

Aunt Phoebe had taken my father and me into her home after my mother died in the influenza epidemic when I was ten. At the time it seemed like the most natural thing in the world, given her autocratic personality and the need to "keep a firm hand" on my father, as she put it.

Papa had been a point of contention between us for years. Gentle, fun loving, and idealistic, his was the complete opposite of Aunt Phoebe's pragmatic nature. Her determination to have us share her large house owed more, I believed, to duty than to affection—an attempt, perhaps, to atone for her lapse in allowing her younger sister to marry him.

"I don't mean to seem ungrateful," I said, choosing my words with infinite care. "But in his letter, Uncle Matthew sounded as though he really needed me to come." I didn't mention how much I longed to go.

"Matthew!" She sniffed in contempt. "Your father's brother,

through and through. A complete reprobate if ever I saw one! Whatever possessed him to write after all these years of silence, I will never know."

I didn't know what had prompted his letter either, but I blessed him for sending it. We had never had the opportunity to know one another well. He had left for the gold fields in 1859. I remember seeing him off, holding my father's hand and waving frantically at his wagon, lettered on the side with PIKE'S PEAK OR BUST. He had waved back jauntily, his merry voice booming out, *"Come and join me when I get settled, Robert. We'll both make our fortunes!"*

After that we received a few sporadic letters, each one from a different gold camp, until finally they stopped coming altogether. Then two weeks ago, another one arrived, a heaven-sent missive addressed to Miss Judith Alder. It read:

Dear Niece,

 Word has reached me that my brother Robert has been dead these three years. I am now the proprietor of a trading post near Taos, New Mexico Territory. I can no longer share my good fortune with your father, but if you choose to join me, I can offer you a home and a share of my future profits. I could sure use your help, as I'm a poor hand at housekeeping and worse at dealing with figures. If you decide to come, anyone in Taos can tell you how to reach me.

Your loving uncle,
Matthew

P. S. I cannot pay for your passage at present, but I am sure that in short order we can build a prosperous business.

My heart had soared as soon as I finished reading it. Here in my hands lay the possibility of escape from dependence on Aunt Phoebe. After opening her home to us, she had never allowed us to forget the debt we owed. I felt gratitude toward her for all she had done, but I yearned to shake off the status of poor relation.

I thought back to my father. He had rarely mentioned his brother in his later years, the time that stood out in my memory being during his final battle with the consumption that had claimed him.

"They tell me that a drier climate in the early stages might have helped," he said wistfully. *"Perhaps I should have followed Matthew west, after all."*

In that moment my mind was made up. I would follow my uncle in my father's stead. All that remained was to convince Aunt Phoebe.

I broached the subject as delicately as I could, but my caution didn't soften Aunt Phoebe's reaction one whit. She alternated between stony stares of disapproval and long tirades in which she took me to task for my ingratitude. I was tempted to answer her sharply, but I held my tongue. I had been left without a cent of my own, and if she refused to help me with the cost of my passage, my adventure would be over before it had begun.

"As I've told you," I said, trying not to let desperation show in my voice, "I promise I'll repay the money for my fare west just as soon as I've earned it in Uncle Matthew's trading post."

Her sharp eyes studied me for a long moment before she spoke. "I have made inquiries and have been informed that it is possible to make a comfortable income from such an enterprise. I am certain, though, that wastrel uncle of yours will squander every dime before you ever lay eyes on it."

I swallowed hard.

"However," she continued, "I can see that you are determined to go." Her eyes misted over. "Just like your mother, you are bent on following the Alder will-o'-the-wisp, probably to your ruin. But, foolish or not, I will not stand in your way."

"Oh Aunt Phoebe!" I cried joyously.

"Just a moment," she snapped, and her eyes were once again hard and bright. "You may delude yourself if you choose, but I will not. You say you will repay the cost of your fare. Very well. I accept your intent, although I do not foresee that you will be able to earn enough in your uncle's care to have more than you need just to keep body and soul together. Nevertheless, I am prepared to finance this venture of yours."

She raised her hand warningly before I could interrupt. "But I refuse to throw away any more money than necessary on a fool's errand. I have looked into the various means of transportation to Taos. The railroad and stagecoach would be the fastest methods, but the fare is over two hundred dollars, far more than I am willing to spend."

I looked at her, puzzled. What on earth did she have in mind?

"I have, however, discovered a way for you to go that should suit us both." She gave me a wintery smile. "As you know, with the advent of the railroad, most of the travel west by wagon has ceased, at least those wagons starting from Independence. It is my understanding that most of those who use that method of travel go as far as possible on the train and outfit themselves at the terminus.

"But I would hardly send a young girl, no matter how headstrong, to choose someone suitable to travel with in that rough environment. Therefore, I have made arrangements for you to leave from here by wagon."

My head spun. A trip by covered wagon, taking weeks instead of days? Surely she wasn't serious! But a look at the grim set of her jaw assured me that she was.

Well, I considered, *why not?* Uncle Matthew had gone that way himself. It would be arduous, I was sure, but what better way of experiencing the country that was to be my new home than to see it at a slow wagon's pace, rather than whizzing by on a train? The more I thought about it, the more enthusiastic I became.

Aunt Phoebe was speaking again. ". . . the Parkers, a family of good character, but without funds to make the journey by train. They will leave St. Joseph on Saturday, four days from now. They have agreed to take you along for a nominal fee and for your help in cooking or any other tasks that should arise. If your desire to go trailing off after your uncle is as great as you say it is, I'm sure you will be willing to employ whatever means necessary to get there."

"I'll do it," I told her, without hesitation. "And I *will* pay you back, every penny."

She might have thought this scheme would discourage me, for my quick acceptance seemed to surprise her; she had little to say after that. The days flew by as I made my preparations, considering what to take, what to leave, packing and repacking as I changed my mind. I decided in the end to take little besides my clothing, toilet articles, and my Bible. I was to have a roof over my head at journey's end, and surely Uncle Matthew would help me secure anything I might need after my arrival.

My trunk was packed and ready early Saturday morning. Aunt Phoebe refused to go with me to the Parkers' home, but did unbend enough to allow Peter, the handyman, to drive me there in the buggy.

At our parting, she surveyed me one last time. "When you've seen the folly of your ways, you may come home," she said, and went back into the house.

Peter and I drew up in front of a run-down house on the edge of town. A gaunt woman was supervising the loading of box after box into a covered wagon already laden with tools and furniture. I stepped down, surprised at my nervousness. "Mrs. Parker? I am Judith Alder."

Ignoring my outstretched hand, she said, "Let's see how much extra weight you've brought."

I signaled Peter to carry my trunk to the wagon. "Put it down!" she ordered. "Just as I thought. You've loaded up with so much finery you won't be leaving any room for us and the things we need."

She hauled an empty box, identical in size and shape to the others being loaded, over to my trunk. "You can take just as much as you can put in that, and no more. These crates will just fit inside the wagon, and I'll not have a big, fancy trunk cluttering things up. I've no doubt you'll all but eat us out of house and home on the trip, but there's no need to start out taking up more than your share of room. We might just as well understand each other from the first." And with that, she went back to bullying the men working at the wagon.

I stared at her retreating figure. So this was the woman of good character Aunt Phoebe had chosen! And we would be spending weeks in each other's company. I groaned inwardly, then squared my shoulders. Life with Aunt Phoebe had increased my immunity to intimidation. I could tolerate a few more weeks of the same if it helped me reach my goal.

Frantically, I transferred as much as I could to the rough box. Some of the clothes would have to be left behind. I picked up my Bible and bag containing my personal items. If I had to, I would carry those myself.

"Are you sure you want to do this, Miss Judith?" Peter frowned, concern in his eyes. "If you want to go back, I can have you home in no time."

I shook my head quickly, before my resolve weakened. "Thank you, but no. If you'll just take my trunk back, I'll be grateful." I gave him a smile that was meant to look confident and walked over to the wagon.

Mrs. Parker barely acknowledged my presence beyond nodding her head in my direction and informing her husband that I was "the girl." He looked me over and grunted. Evidently I had been weighed in the balance and found wanting. A boy who looked to be sixteen or seventeen jumped down lightly from the wagon and wiped his brow on his sleeve.

"I think that's it, Ma." He grinned.

Ma? It was hard to believe that this pleasant-looking youth could be the product of the two sullen individuals I had just met.

Seeing me, his grin broadened. "You must be Miss Alder. I'm Lanny Parker. I'm sure glad you're going to go with us. It'll be real good to have company."

The shock of finding a Parker capable of such a lengthy statement rendered me speechless, but I was able to return his smile with enthusiasm. He might be glad of my company, but he had no idea how profoundly grateful I was for his. At least there would be one friendly face along the way.

The boxes were stowed, the mules hitched. Everything appeared to be set for our departure. I looked around, struck by the fact that I was leaving and how little it mattered to me. In my mind, St. Joseph had already ceased to be home.

Mr. Parker mounted to the driver's seat, his wife beside him. I put up my hands to catch hold of the sideboard and pull myself up and over the tailgate.

"What do you think you're doing?" Mrs. Parker's voice rasped. "You and Lanny will walk. We'll spare the mules as much as we can."

Lanny fell in beside me as I walked with my head bowed, trying to hide my mortification. "Don't mind Ma," he said. "She's got a sharp tongue, but a good heart."

Well hidden, I thought. But the friendly overture had its effect, and soon I was telling him about Uncle Matthew and my hopes for the future.

Mrs. Parker looked back. "Lanny! Come up here and walk by me."

He gave me an apologetic look and trotted off.

I plodded along by myself, staying off to one side to keep out of the dust. *Think about Taos,* I reminded myself. *Just keep that thought before you for the next few weeks. This won't last forever.*

Days later, I questioned that last thought. We had been on the trail for less than a week, but already it had given me a new perspective on eternity. Day followed day with tedious predictability. We awoke before daybreak, ate, and moved on with as little talk as possible. Mrs. Parker, holding steadfastly to her sullenness no matter how pleasant the circumstances, assigned Lanny and me to opposite sides of the wagon each morning, giving us little opportunity for conversation.

I didn't understand her motive for this until I overheard an exchange between her and her husband on our third morning out. I was busy packing the cooking utensils away inside when they stopped just outside, their voices clearly audible through the canvas.

"I never reckoned on making the girl walk all the way to New Mexico." Mr. Parker sounded troubled. "No reason she can't ride a bit. It'll give us a chance to stretch our legs."

"And who would be driving while she rides? Lanny? Can't you see he's got eyes for nothing else? You're a man. You know where that leads.

"We agreed to take her on," she continued, "but she'll keep to herself on the way. And, mind you, keep your own eyes where they belong!"

I pressed my fist against my mouth to stifle a cry of dismay and sat quietly until they moved away. Angry tears mingled with a desire to laugh. Never before had I been cast in the role of a Jezebel! Couldn't she understand that I only wanted human companionship?

Very well, I would walk every step of the way, if necessary. Only a few weeks to endure this, and then I would reach Taos and Uncle Matthew.

Chapter 2

It was a great relief when we arrived at Council Grove and Mr. Parker announced that we would be staying there for a day or two.

"There's three other wagons waiting here already and more expected," he said that night over supper. "We'll form a train and have just that much more protection the rest of the way."

The prospect of being around friendly, talking human beings was encouraging. The wagons clustered together a little way outside town on the banks of the Neosho River. Cordial-looking women approached as we cooked supper over our fire, but a few sharp words from Mrs. Parker soon sent them on their way, shaking their heads.

I started to speak, but Mrs. Parker's warning look made me hold my tongue. I gazed after them wistfully. It would have been refreshing to have had a good woman-to-woman talk. Maybe things would change once we got under way.

Two more wagons arrived during the next day, and the men from the six groups met together to elect a captain, choosing a self-assured man named Hudson. He had had experience with the trail ahead and made the announcement that we would leave the following morning.

I had hoped for more interaction with the others of the train—perhaps with women who, like myself, walked much of the time. But the Parkers discouraged contact and kept our wagon well to the rear of the train. So we made our way across the plains with the wagon train, yet not really a part of it.

The sheer size of this land was staggering. For mile upon mile, I saw a billowing sea of green everywhere I looked. The stems of the grasses reached to the horses' bellies, and many of the seed heads grew well above my eye level.

At Cow Creek we stepped out of that world and into another, as though we had crossed an invisible boundary line. Listening to Mr.

Parker repeating what he had picked up from Mr. Hudson that day, I learned that we had come to the short-grass prairie.

The buffalo and grama grasses grew only inches tall, and instead of the waving softness of the tall grass, the land stretched out in a stark panorama as far as the eye could see.

Moving out of the cover of the tall grasses and into the open made me feel more vulnerable. I was grateful for the protection of the others in our party.

Lanny made things more bearable when he could by talking to me at breakfast and after supper. Once he slipped me a nosegay of wildflowers he had picked, still wet with dew. I smiled at him, grateful for his thoughtfulness, and hid the bouquet before his sharp-eyed mother could spy it.

On the first evening past Dodge, we assembled for a meeting. Mrs. Parker, Lanny, and I sat well away from the rest of the group, but Mr. Hudson's voice carried clearly.

"Folks," he said, "we need to take a vote on the direction we follow next. As some of you know, the trail divides a little way from here. We need to make a choice on which fork we take.

"The easiest way, and the one I recommend, is the Mountain Branch. It's about a hundred miles longer, but we follow right along the Arkansas River like we've been doing, and we're sure of water all along the way."

"What's the other fork like?" asked one of the men.

"The other way is the Cimarron Cutoff. It's sometimes called the *Jornada de Muerte*—the Journey of Death." Prickles ran down the back of my neck as he spoke.

"The first fifty miles are without water at all. You'd have to take all your wagons can carry and pray that it was enough to last you until you reached the Cimarron."

"What then?"

"The Cimarron's a contrary river. Maybe it'll be running, maybe it won't. The decision is up to all of you, but my advice is to take a little longer and be sure of reaching Santa Fe."

The general murmur of assent reassured me even before the vote was taken that the other men saw the wisdom of his advice.

"All in favor of following the Mountain Branch say 'Aye,'" called Mr. Hudson, and a chorus of "Ayes" rang out. "Anyone in favor of the Cutoff?"

"I am," said a lone voice, and I realized with horror that it belonged to Mr. Parker.

A man standing nearby wheeled and stared at him. "Are you crazy, man? I've heard stories about that stretch. We'd all be risking our lives and our families."

"You heard Hudson. It's a hundred miles shorter. I'm in a hurry to get where I'm going."

"So are the rest of us. But we want to get there alive."

"All right, then," said Mr. Hudson. "It looks like it's settled. The majority votes to take the Mountain Branch, and I must say I'm relieved. When we come to the fork tomorrow, we'll follow the right-hand branch."

"Not me." The words fell like a heavy stone into the startled silence.

"He can't be serious," I whispered to Mrs. Parker. "We can't undertake a trip like that alone."

"He knows what he's doing," she replied. "We aim to get this over with as quick as we can."

"But she's right, Ma." Lanny looked as worried as I felt. "We get off by ourselves like that and we're in trouble. If we can't find water, or if we run into outlaws or Indians, we're all alone. There'll be no way to get help."

Mrs. Parker gave him a withering look. "Siding with her against your own parents, are you?"

The men followed Mr. Parker to our wagon, trying to reason with him.

Mr. Hudson grabbed his arm. "Listen to me, Parker. I've been down the trail before. I know the Cutoff. Why, even the jackrabbits carry three days' rations and a canteen of water out there. Think of your women, if nothing else."

"My mind's made up." Mr. Parker's face was set. "The rest of you do as you like. We're taking the Cutoff."

Sleep did not come easily that night. Fragments of conversation tumbled through my mind. *"Fifty miles. . .no water. . .Jornada de Muerte . . .Journey of Death."*

By morning, the rest of the train seemed to have accepted the Parkers' decision, although I saw worried glances cast in our direction more than once. Shortly before we started out, Mr. Hudson came over to our wagon and handed Mr. Parker a sheet of paper.

"If you're bound you're going that way," he said, "at least take this with you." Peering over Mr. Parker's shoulder, I could see that he held a crudely drawn map. "I've marked the route the best I could, and I've circled the places where you'll find springs. You'll need 'em, especially if the riverbed's dry."

Mr. Parker thanked him with a grunt and we waited to hear the order to move out for the last time.

My palms were growing sweaty as we reached the point where the trail forked. Five wagons moved on ahead. Ours pulled to a halt and watched as they became smaller and smaller dots on the landscape.

We forded the Arkansas and headed southwest.

We had taken Mr. Hudson's advice and drunk as much as we could hold before leaving the river. The water barrels were filled to overflowing. I breathed a prayer that Mr. Parker knew what he was doing.

The heat was not the only thing against us. Dust, churned up by the wagon wheels and the mules' hooves, billowed into the air in great clouds. When it settled, it blanketed everything—the wagon, the mules, and us. I gave up trying to brush it off my clothes after the first day and concentrated on keeping it out of my eyes and mouth as much as possible. It made me even thirstier just to see it constantly swirling about.

Our pace had slowed as the heat increased, and by the end of the second day, we were all concerned about whether the water supply would hold out. I sipped my evening ration slowly, savoring every drop.

The mules needed an ample supply to pull the heavy wagon. I felt sorry for the hollow-eyed creatures, but it was hard to watch as Mr. Parker and Lanny poured the precious liquid for them to drink. Mrs. Parker evidently felt the same way about me, for I saw her jealously eyeing every drop I swallowed.

Late in the afternoon of the third day, Lanny spotted trees on the horizon. We pressed on, bone weary, and eventually reached the banks of the Cimarron.

It was dry.

"Where cottonwoods grow, there's bound to be water," Mr. Parker said, and began scooping sand from the riverbed. The sand grew darker as he dug, and finally a chalky white liquid began to ooze into the hole. The mules strained to pull the wagon closer to the water.

Lanny moved a little farther up the riverbed and soon had enough in the hole he scooped out to fill a cup for each of us. It was brackish, and back in Missouri would have been scorned as unfit to drink. But it was water nonetheless, and we drank deeply of cup after cup.

In the morning, Mr. Parker consulted the map he had been given. "I figure we're right about here," he said, indicating a spot with his forefinger. "We need to find one of the springs. Looks like the closest one is here." He pointed to a circle on the map.

"How far?" Lanny asked.

"Ten miles. No more."

"Then how far to the next water? And the next?" Mrs. Parker's voice rose shrilly and I looked at her in amazement. It was the first real emotion that she had shown in all our time on the trail.

"We'll make it," said her husband.

"What about her? She'll use up water the three of us need." She seemed on the verge of hysteria.

"We'll make it," he repeated.

We reached the spring sooner than we expected, before noon. *Now,* I thought, *I understand what an oasis is.*

The water bubbled up, clear and fresh, in the middle of a stand of tall, cool grass. Scattered trees afforded shade from the sun. After blissfully drinking my fill at the spring's edge, I sank down in the grass under spreading branches and felt a light breeze play over my face. I loosened my bonnet strings and let the bonnet slide back on my shoulders so the breeze could stir my hair. It felt wonderful.

The Parkers sprawled around the spring while the mules drank and drank. Relief from the heat and thirst made them seem almost companionable.

We sat like that for a while, enjoying the breeze, the shade, and the freshness of the grass. I hoped we would camp here for the night, but after a time, Mr. Parker got to his feet and nodded at Lanny.

"Give me a hand with the water barrels. We've got to fill up and keep moving."

"Now, Pa?" Lanny's plaintive tone echoed my sentiments. "We're just beginning to cool off a little."

"Get a move on, boy. Your mother and I know what we're doing." Lanny groaned, but rose to obey.

I sighed. At least we would have fresh water for the next leg of the journey. I jumped when I realized Mrs. Parker was standing beside me. I hadn't heard her approach.

"Mr. Parker and I have been talking," she said abruptly. "We're all tired and covered with this awful dust. Would you like a chance to wash here before we go on? We can pull the wagon over beyond those trees so you'll have some privacy."

I could hardly believe my ears, but she looked as though she sincerely wanted me to agree.

"Why...thank you. I'd like that very much." I was touched by this unexpected concern. Perhaps she was trying to make amends for her earlier attitude.

No matter, I thought, as the hoofbeats of the mules grew fainter and I could no longer hear the creak of the wheels. Whatever the reason, I had the opportunity to get clean, and I intended to make the most of it!

I shook as much dust as I could from the folds of my dress and spread it out on the grass to air a little. I had taken a piece of soap from my bag before the wagon moved away, and I carried it with me as I stepped into the spring.

The cold water closed around my ankles with a delightful shock. It was deeper than I had expected, and I squatted down in the center, enjoying the luxury of washing the caked dust from my arms and shoulders.

I scrubbed and scrubbed until my skin glowed, then undid the pins holding my hair and soaped and rinsed it until it lay clean and shining across my shoulders.

I dried off as best I could, feeling revitalized, but somewhat guilty at the amount of time I had spent in the water. Dressing hurriedly, I hastened to the other side of the grove of trees, hoping the Parkers wouldn't be too angry about my prolonged absence.

I needn't have worried.

When I emerged from the screen made by the trees, the Parkers and the wagon were nowhere to be seen.

Chapter 3

I stood facing a vast emptiness, my clothes still sticking in places to my damp skin, and searched vainly for the white canvas wagon cover. Always before on this trip, it could be spotted at a distance, the cloth rippling in the breeze like mighty sails.

Nothing.

They must have gone a little farther ahead. Perhaps they had changed their minds and were finding a place to camp nearby, after all. Even as I considered the possibility, my mind rejected it.

What if the Parkers had fallen asleep, and the mules had wandered off? If they had woken up to find the wagon gone, they might even now be trying to catch up to it. We had entered rougher terrain; the landscape might look flat at a distance, but it held an amazing number of rises and depressions. It would be possible, in this broken land, for a whole wagon train to travel along the bottom of a draw and remain all but invisible save to one at a higher elevation. Yes, it was possible they were only hidden from my sight, in one of the distant ravines.

But the head start needed would surely be greater than any distance covered by an aimlessly wandering mule. I fought down a rising sense of panic and began to follow the wagon tracks.

My legs wanted to betray me at every step and break into a headlong run, but I fought the feeling back. Had I begun to run wildly as I wished, the panic would have overtaken both my body and my reason in short order. I forced myself to walk along the track deliberately and to marshal my thoughts.

I had half expected the wagon tracks to wind deviously to some place of concealment, but to my surprise, they continued openly along the trail. The wagon itself, though, was nowhere to be seen. Not even a cloud of dust marred the western sky.

An idea was creeping into my mind and I made every effort to subdue it. The very thought was enough to give me a chill, even in the noonday heat. But it teased and pulled at the edges of consciousness until it had made its way to the center of my thinking and had to be faced head on: I had been deliberately left behind.

The full implications of that did not strike me all at once, which was a mercy. My first feelings were of disbelief and outrage. I was hardly a piece of excess baggage to be cast aside when its burden became too great to bear! I was ready to march into the nearest town, tell the local constable what had happened, and demand that he take action. So great was my wrath that I had actually taken several steps down the trail before I came to myself and realized that the nearest town was a good many miles away.

I stumbled to a halt, knocking one foot against an object I had not previously noticed in my anger. It took a moment to gather my senses and realize what it was.

It was my box of belongings. In a last uncharacteristic act of charity—or was it merely to drop surplus weight?—the Parkers had stopped their wagon to leave the pitifully few items I had brought with me. My Bible lay on top, along with the bag containing my small personal effects.

The enormity of my situation hit me then, and my knees gave way, dropping me down next to my box. I truly had been left, and I faced whatever perils might come upon me quite alone. Incidents along the journey came to mind—comments and complaints about the amount of space my belongings and I took up, the quantity of food and water consumed, and particularly Lanny's supposed infatuation with me. In Mrs. Parker's mind, I *was* merely an excess piece of baggage and a potentially dangerous one at that.

I recalled her kindness to me, her suggestion that I might like to bathe. Once I had been disposed of, it would have taken them little time to put enough distance between us so that there was no possibility of my overtaking them.

The crate puzzled me. Perhaps a twinge of conscience prompted them to set it by the trail, where it presumably would be found. On a less charitable note, it also gave Mrs. Parker more room to arrange her own belongings.

At least I had my Bible. I reached for it with a hand that trembled and opened it on my lap. A light breeze fluttered the pages. The underlined words in Proverbs, chapter three, caught my attention: *"Trust in the Lord with all thine heart; and lean not unto thine own understanding. In all thy ways acknowledge him, and he shall direct thy paths."*

Papa had always stressed the importance of applying the truths of the scriptures to daily living. *"Do not read God's Word merely for the pride of having read it, Judith. Head knowledge without heart knowledge is an empty thing."* If ever I needed my path directed, this must surely qualify as an applicable time.

I stood up and gazed as far as my eyes could see in either direction. With the sun nearly overhead, east and west looked much the same. For a few panic-stricken moments, I couldn't tell the difference in direction, didn't know which way would take me back to St. Joseph and which would lead me, eventually, to Uncle Matthew. Reason reasserted itself, and I reminded myself that if I waited a short time, the new position of the sun would point me westward.

Nothing in my life up to this point had prepared me for any such turn of events. It was difficult to decide on a course of action without any prior experience on which to base such a decision.

As far as I could tell, only two courses were open to me. I could give way to my feelings, fling myself down upon the trail beside my belongings and weep with abandon, or I could choose to travel either east or west and proceed steadily and rationally in the chosen direction.

The first alternative was by far the more tempting, especially as the shock bore down upon me. But I realized that would only exhaust me and leave me prey to any danger that might arise.

Traveling alone, on foot, and helpless was hardly a thing to be desired, but I determined that even if the end should come soon, as seemed all too likely, it would not find me groveling mindlessly.

Not knowing how long this frame of mind would last, I turned to open my crate before my resolve faltered to see which belongings might reasonably be carried along with me.

I pried up the lid and stared in disbelief. Even in their one act of thoughtfulness, the Parkers had managed to leave me high and dry. The clothes in the crate were not mine, but Lanny's.

I sank to my knees beside the crate. How—*why*—could they have done such a thing? Perhaps it was foolish, but somehow not having even the meager consolation of my own belongings seemed the crowning blow.

I remembered then how, after my morning devotions, I had set my Bible down with my bag on the crate closest to me. I groaned. Mrs. Parker and her look-alike boxes! Being in a hurry, they would have connected my Bible with my box and dumped it all together.

Now what? Pillowing my head on my arms on the edge of the crate, I felt my hair brush against my face. I had left it loose to dry. My hands reached mechanically to smooth it into a coil at the base of my neck and I fumbled in my pocket for my hairpins to make myself presentable.

A sudden shock ran through me. Suppose some other traveler happened along. What kind of woman would they take me for? What sort of woman would be put off a wagon in the middle of nowhere? I could think of only one, and the very thought made me blush.

I had envisioned a possible encounter with kindly people, other emigrants perhaps, who would sympathize with my plight, take me aboard their wagon, and see me safely to Taos. But now—the more I thought over my story, the more unlikely it sounded. If it appeared so even to me, how could I hope to convince others that I was indeed an upright, respectable young lady? And failing to convince them, what would be the dangers of being a woman alone in this wilderness?

Snatches of stories I had heard and put out of my mind came back to haunt me—stories of outlaws, coarse frontiersmen, and rampaging Indians. To be sure, the Indians were supposed to have calmed down, and Uncle Matthew had reported no trouble at his trading post, but mightn't there be renegade bands roaming the plains?

I suppressed a shudder and glanced over my shoulder, half expecting to see dark, hostile eyes peering over a rise.

When loose, my hair rippled over my shoulders, a golden cascade gleaming in the sunlight. It was by far my most attractive feature, and I brushed it faithfully one hundred strokes each night. Now my waist-length tresses seemed nothing but a liability.

Wouldn't such long golden hair be prized as a scalp to hang from a savage's lance? Tears of self-pity stung my eyes. It was all so unfair! Abandoned here through no fault of my own, left to the mercy of hoodlums and renegades far from any form of civilization. I scrubbed at my eyes with the back of my hand.

If I were a man, I thought, *I wouldn't be so lost.* Men always seemed to know what to do. Men carried guns to use for protection. A man alone could travel with relative safety. A man. . .

The idea came with startling clarity, fascinating and repulsive at the same time. It was possible, barely, but surely not dignified. On the other hand, how much dignity was attached to becoming an addition to a warrior's scalp collection?

My mind whirled as I reached into Lanny's box, sorting through the clothes there. Two pairs of sturdy pants lay on top, followed by three shirts, a pair of overalls, socks, and a suit of long underwear. I laid the pants, overalls, socks, and shirts out on the ground; I saw no need to get involved with a man's undergarments.

There were certainly possibilities. Lanny was stockier and taller than I, but with some adjustments, it just might work. I selected the overalls and the cleanest shirt and made my way back behind the trees.

Some time later, a boy stepped out carrying a neatly folded parcel of ladies' clothing. The clothes had not proved to be such a bad fit after all. Granted, the heavy overalls bagged about me, and the cuffs were rolled up to keep them from dragging in the dirt, but that seemed to conceal, rather than emphasize, my figure.

Years before, my father had dressed me in a pair of boy's overalls and smuggled me out to a pasture for a clandestine riding lesson. Sitting astride, he said, was the only sensible way to ride a horse, and his daughter was going to experience that at least once in her life. It was one of many things that would have scandalized Aunt Phoebe, and it was understood without a word being said that neither of us would mention it to anyone.

I remember shrieking with delight as the horse cantered around the pasture. I was able to cling to the mare like a burr and felt that nothing she could do would dislodge me. Overalls or dresses, it made little difference to me in those days. How differently I felt now! Camouflaged or not, I felt undressed and indecent. I nearly changed my mind right then and decided to take my chances dressed as a lady.

Finally, I decided upon a compromise—I would use my new identity only as a protective measure. If I met up with ruffians or hostiles, I would keep quiet, letting my disguise speak for me. If, as I hoped, some kindly people were to pass by and offer to take me with them, I would—if I judged them upright people—disclose myself rather than accept their hospitality under false pretenses.

This decided, I squared my shoulders and prepared to make the best of a bad situation. My hair caused me concern. I debated the wisdom of cutting it off short and was rummaging through the lower layers of Lanny's crate for some sharp implement when, to my delight, I unearthed not only a hat, but a sturdy pair of shoes as well.

I coiled my hair high on my head, pinned it in place as well as I could, and with the hat jammed down over my ears, fancied I could go on my way with little fear of discovery. The shoes were rather large, but strips torn from one of Lanny's shirts and stuffed into the toes made it possible for me to walk without stepping out of them.

I fashioned a sling out of the remainder of the torn shirt, folded my small bag and Bible inside, and fastened it inside the baggy overalls. Then taking a deep breath, I resolutely turned my face toward the west.

Chapter 4

By sundown of that day, my brave resolve had shattered into a million hopeless pieces. Never before had I felt such utter despair. I had no idea how far I had come or how far I had yet to go. The long drink I had taken at the spring before leaving hadn't quenched my thirst for long on the dusty trail. And the oversized shoes had rubbed my feet to a raw, painful mess.

How far did Mr. Parker say we had to go until we reached the next spring? Ten miles? But I had no idea how near the trail it might be. I tried not to think what it would mean if I had already passed it.

Doggedly, I planted one foot more or less firmly in front of the other. Even in my exhausted state, I held fast to the knowledge that the only way to be rescued was to keep moving. The setting sun dazzled my eyes, and I stumbled over a stone.

The fall took every last bit of reserve I had. I pushed myself up on my elbows and tried to gather my knees under me. But my strength was spent, and I pitched forward into sweet oblivion.

The next thought that entered my consciousness was that some large dogs had found me and were sniffing my inert form. I waved an arm feebly, trying to shoo them away, and my hand encountered an enormous wet muzzle. Calculating the size of the beast from the dimensions of its nose, it must have been monstrous.

The realization jolted me into a sitting position. The sky had darkened, and I could just make out huge shapes milling about me, making snuffling sounds.

I rose cautiously. Fright drove all power of speech from me, and I began backing away from the creatures, but they followed me, sniffing ominously.

Hunger, thirst, fatigue, and the sheer terror of being alone to face this peril nearly drove away my reason altogether.

"Never give way to panic." How many times had I heard my father say that? *"Panic will keep you from thinking clearly, and clear thinking is the best weapon you have in a dangerous situation."*

I tried to think as I shuffled backward, wincing as the rough boots rubbed my blistered feet. I had no gun, no knife, not even a stout stick to use as a weapon; I couldn't keep the beasts at bay much longer. I was dimly aware of the blood pulsing in my throat, throbbing in my temples. The throbbing increased to an audible pounding, vibrating through the sand at my feet.

It was several moments before I recognized the sound as the galloping of horses' hooves and a potential rescue. No sooner did that recognition strike me than I had wheeled and was staggering toward the sound with all the strength I had left. Darkness was closing in, and I stumbled over the shadowy ground. The thought that I might come this close to rescue and miss it was too great to be borne.

My throat was so parched from thirst that I was unable to scream. I swallowed painfully two or three times and managed a hoarse cry. Hoofbeats clattered nearer, and a black shape drew up almost on top of me.

"Lookee here!" cried a gravelly voice. I sensed, rather than saw, a figure dismount and step close to me. However, I could pinpoint the location accurately due to the overpowering aroma of tobacco and perspiration.

"Over here, boys!" my rescuer shouted, his breath nearly bowling me over. He fumbled for a moment, then struck a match and held it toward my face. The sudden light hurt my eyes, and I threw a hand up to cover them, stepping backward as I did so.

"Aw, now, if it ain't a kid. Don't be scared, son. You'll be all right. What happened? You wander off from your folks?"

I was saved from answering by a clatter of hoofbeats as two more riders drew up.

"Found 'em, did you, Jake?" asked one.

"Them, and something extra. Look here."

"Where?" spoke yet another disembodied voice.

"Right under your ugly nose," said my protector. "It's a kid. A poor, lost kid."

The moon rose as if on cue, brightening the scene enough to reveal three rough, unshaven men, all staring at me.

"Now don't be scared, sonny," said the one called Jake. "We're not going to hurt you. You just tell us where your folks are, and we'll see you get back first thing in the morning."

I opened my lips to speak, but could only manage a croak.

"Jake, where's your sense?" said one of the mounted men. "Can't you see the kid's dyin' of thirst?"

Jake hurriedly untied a canteen from his saddle, mumbling under his breath. The water tasted as sweet to me as it must have to the children of Israel at Elim. I sipped slowly, letting it trickle down my parched throat, and felt its restoring coolness spread throughout my body.

I used the few moments' respite to compose my thoughts. My original plan, to disclose my identity as soon as I was rescued, did not seem wise at this point.

True, the three men did seem inclined toward kindliness, but they believed me to be a young boy with family nearby. What they might feel about a young woman whose only family was hundreds of miles away might be another matter entirely.

Evidently my disguise was working in the moonlight. But I had no way of knowing how well it would conceal my identity when day came. In the meantime, I decided, I would adopt a cautious policy. I would not deliberately mislead these men by my answers, but neither would I volunteer information unnecessarily, at least not until I was more sure of the type of men they were.

I swallowed again. My voice came out in a raspy whisper. "My parents are dead. I was traveling with another family to go live with my Uncle Matthew, but they left me back down the trail."

"*Left* you?" Even by the light of the moon, amazement was plainly written on Jake's countenance. "You mean they just hauled off and left you in the middle of nowhere?"

It was a difficult question. In my new role, I could hardly say that Mrs. Parker had considered me a threat to her son's virtue.

"I guess I ate more than they liked." That much was surely true. I was saved from closer questioning by a snort from one of the other men.

"Leave the kid alone, Jake. Can't you see he's tuckered out? We'll talk to the boss in the morning and figure out what to do with him. Come on, you take him up behind you. Shorty and I can push these strays back to camp."

Jake spat—tobacco juice, I believed—and mounted before turning to me again. "Come on, kid, climb up here. Those two should just about be able to handle half a dozen steers by themselves."

For the first time since hearing the hoofbeats, I remembered the threatening creatures. Now I saw them standing not many yards distant, long, curving horns clearly outlined in the moonlight.

"Steers," I croaked. "Why, I thought they were some kind of huge dogs." Whatever else I might have said was drowned out by wild roars of laughter, which threatened to unseat all three men. Shorty fairly howled, leaning forward almost double and pounding one fist against his leg.

I could feel an embarrassed flush rise from my neck and wash over my face and was doubly grateful for the darkness. Mutely, I accepted the hand Jake extended between guffaws and scrambled up behind him with as much dignity as I could muster.

As the horse carried us away at a trot, the whoops continued but grew fainter. Jake's shoulders convulsed from time to time, although he at least tried to subdue his mirth.

The day's events had taken their toll, and I found myself struggling to stay awake and upright. Eventually, I managed to balance myself so that I could fall into a light doze without danger of slipping off the horse. I had not asked where we were going or how long the trip would be; I was simply too tired to care. Tomorrow could take care of itself.

At some point we stopped and there were other voices. Hands lifted me from the horse and carried me to a blanket roll beneath a wagon. The last thing I remembered was pulling my hat down securely with both hands.

Morning was heralded by the rattle of tin plates, the creaking of saddle leather, and a general flurry about the camp. These things penetrated my consciousness despite my exhaustion, but I wasn't brought fully awake until a pair of feet flying past the wagon kicked a shower of dirt into my face.

I raised my head and looked about wildly, trying to remember where I was. No one had taken notice of me yet, so I lay peering into the hazy light of false dawn, trying to take stock of my surroundings.

As my field of vision was limited, the closest things I could make out were occasional pairs of boots striding by the wagon. Farther out, other objects were beginning to take shape in the brightening sky. A large group of horses was off to one side; some were being saddled, others rubbed down. Farther along to my right was a vast herd of the cattle that had frightened me so the night before. Evidently the men who had found me were part of one of the cattle drives I had heard about.

A sudden chill crept over me. Did women come along on these drives? I was fairly sure they did not. In that case, I must be the only female among all these rough-looking men, and with no idea how long they would travel until journey's end.

Cautiously, I rolled to my left side, remembering to make sure my hat was pulled firmly in place. I tucked a few stray hairs back up under the crown and peered out. A group of men sat cross-legged in a circle not ten yards away. Most were wolfing down the contents of the tin plates on their laps, while a few slurped their coffee.

Coffee! The aroma made my stomach double up in a hard knot. I had been so tired the night before that even hunger had not kept me awake. But now I was ravenous.

How should I make my presence known? I recognized none of the men whose faces I could see, and I shrank from revealing myself before strangers. Furthermore, my male garb had proven effective last night, but just how much could I rely on it in the light of day?

I was saved from further speculation by Jake, whose head suddenly appeared beneath the wagon's floorboards.

"Well, so you've come around, have you?" The kindness in his eyes belied his attempt to make his voice sound gruff. I nodded, trying to shrink back into the shadows.

"I never saw anyone before who could sleep through Cookie's 'Come and get it.' And right under the chuck wagon, too."

"Jake!" called a stentorian voice. "Is that boy still asleep?"

"No, boss," returned Jake over his shoulder. "He's awake and rarin' to go."

"See that he eats before we pull out. He's probably half-starved." As if in agreement, my stomach gave a loud rumble.

"Look, boy," said Jake, his attention focused on me again, "you roll right out the far side of this wagon. There's some water there, and soap. And after you've scrubbed off some of the trail dust, you come over and get something to eat."

I moved to follow his instructions, but found I had to grasp the wagon wheel to pull myself upright. I could feel the sores on my feet breaking open again.

A basin of water stood on a small shelf jutting out from the side of the wagon. A bar of soap lay beside it, and a grimy towel hung from a nail.

The soap and water felt heavenly, and I wished that I could use them more extensively. My face stung as I dried it on the rough towel. I noticed a small mirror propped up on the shelf, and looked in it to prepare myself for the inspection ahead. I gasped in surprise. If Aunt Phoebe had walked past me on the streets of St. Joseph, she would have gathered her skirts about her and gone by without a second glance.

No wonder the towel had made my face sting. Lanny's hat, while good for disguise, had a much narrower brim than my sunbonnet. My face, with no protection, had been sunburned beyond recognition, and my nose had already started to peel. With the battered hat jammed down on my head, I hardly recognized myself.

The freckles I had treated so diligently with lemon and buttermilk were putting in a fresh appearance, and I wrinkled my nose ruefully. That was a mistake. My face felt as though it would split. I could feel heat radiating from it even in the crisp morning air.

Well, I thought, *sore it might be, but surely not fatal.* And I looked more like a boy than I ever dreamed possible. If I watched myself closely and guarded my tongue, I believed I would be safe for the time being without resorting to overt deception.

Still feeling almost undressed in my rough shirt and baggy overalls, I squared my shoulders, then settled into a slouch, which I told myself looked more boylike, and hobbled around the wagon.

Most of the men had finished eating and were already busy breaking camp, although the first fingers of sunlight were just reaching over the horizon. Three men still sat around the remains of the campfire sipping coffee. One of them was Jake, who motioned me to sit next to him.

He placed a tin plate heaped with beans and biscuits on my lap. "Here you go. Now just set here and eat your fill. We won't worry you till you've had a chance to fill your belly."

I was so hungry that the familiarity didn't even make me blush. At Aunt Phoebe's, we would have been helping ourselves from chafing dishes arranged on the sideboard. The scrambled eggs would have been fluffy delights, the sausages perfectly brown, the toast a delicate gold. There would have been a selection of jams and marmalade in cut glass bowls, and low-pitched conversation would be heard above the soft clinks of silver touching bone china.

Here, a tin plate had been thrust at me, its cargo of beans a towering brown mass. Biscuits dotted the top and their undersides were already getting soggy. But food had never tasted so good.

The beans swam in some sort of broth and I used pieces of biscuit to sop up the last of the juices. The biscuits were surprisingly light. I glanced at the dour-faced man putting things to rights around the chuckwagon. If he was, as I assumed, the cook, then it wasn't necessarily true that it took a merry heart to make a good meal. The conglomeration on my plate hardly had visual appeal, but it was delicious.

After I had bolted the meal, my hunger was assuaged sufficiently for me to give some attention to my companions. I eyed the two across the fire from under the brim of my hat.

One was drinking coffee, holding the tin cup in both hands to take full advantage of its warmth. His profile looked vaguely familiar, and I thought he might have been one of Jake's companions of the night before. His youthful movements as he rose to stir the embers of the fire contradicted the age suggested by his weather-beaten face and hands. His eyes, too, were those of a young man and held a glint that promised a sense of mischief.

I turned my attention to the man standing directly across from me. My eyes traveled up a substantial length of denim-clad leg, took in strong, lean hands holding the inevitable cup of coffee, and came to rest on a face seemingly carved of granite. A firm chin jutted out, the mouth set in a determined line above it.

Suddenly, he glanced my way and his blue eyes looked into mine with an intensity that seemed to bore straight through me. I dropped my eyes and hoped my confusion didn't show. My conscience was pricking me painfully.

I picked up my coffee cup. The steam rose to warm my face as I took my first sip. I gasped and was seized by a fit of coughing. Tears stung my eyes as I tried to catch my breath. I had almost succeeded when Jake began pounding on my back solicitously.

"Are you all right, kid?" he asked, his grizzled face close to mine. I managed to nod and secured my hat, which threatened to fly off under his ministrations.

"Fine," I choked out. Either the coffee or Jake's pounding had made me slightly giddy, and I blinked, trying to clear my vision. "Just fine."

"Coffee's no good to a cowboy 'less it's strong enough to float a horseshoe," drawled the weather-beaten man, rising to his feet.

"You hush, Shorty," snapped Jake. "This young un's had enough trouble without you making fun."

Shorty drew himself up to his inconsiderable height and stalked off with as much dignity as a bow-legged man could muster.

Jake turned his attention back to me. "Now that you've gotten filled up and woke up, you and the boss here need to talk a bit before we head out." He jerked his head in the direction of the man across the fire. "I'll go see to my horse."

I steeled myself to meet that intense gaze again and rose to my feet to reduce somewhat his advantage in height. Even across the fire, I could see that my head wouldn't quite reach the top of his shoulder.

They were broad shoulders. His height was not the gangly awkwardness of some of the young men I had known at home, all arms and legs and lack of grace. He was well-proportioned, and his movements as he set down his cup and turned to study me were smooth and agile. I wished I knew what manner of man lay beneath the exterior.

"What's your name, boy?" he asked.

"Ju—" I caught myself, floundered wildly, and managed to stammer, "Judah." Foolishly, I had been unprepared for the question and came up with the first compromise that entered my head.

"Judah. All right. Don't be frightened, son. We only mean to help." He took a long step over the dying coals to stand at my side and threw a muscular arm around my shoulders.

I caught my breath. There was only kindness in the gesture, but the proximity was unnerving.

"Jake told me how he found you. I know it's tough, being without your folks. Mine have been gone a good many years now, since I was fifteen." His grip on my shoulders tightened as the expression on his face softened. "But we'll see you through till the end of the drive, and then see about finding a way to get you to your—uncle's, was it?" I nodded. He gave a final squeeze and released me, much to my relief.

"How—how long will the drive last?"

"Not long. We're three days at most from the ranch."

Three days alone with all these men! Resolutely I choked down my alarm. This was all the help that was available and I was powerless to change my situation. I would have to make the best of it.

"Let's get moving. It's time to head out." He seemed to be in a hurry, and I tried to match his pace as he strode toward the horses. He noticed my stiff gait and frowned.

"Your feet are raw from all that walking, aren't they? Well, come along, you'd better ride in the wagon."

I limped along behind him to the chuck wagon, where the cook had made ready for departure with amazing speed.

"Cookie, this is Judah," he announced. "He'll be riding with you today." The heavy-set man gave me a sour look and began clearing a space near the wagon's tail. Evidently I wasn't going to sit next to him on the seat.

But that meant less chance of being questioned, I thought, brightening, and it would give me time to reflect on what my next move should be.

The space cleared, Cookie climbed up to the seat and my bene-factor turned to go. "Don't worry, Judah. Cookie's bark is worse than his bite. At least," he said with a sudden twinkle, "I think it is. He hasn't bitten me yet."

I repressed a smile as I scrambled to my perch and raised my eyes to meet his. "Thank you, Mr.—"

"Jeff will do. Short for Jefferson." With that he was gone. Moments later a roar of "Move 'em out!" echoed through the camp, and we were off.

Chapter 5

From my cramped seat I could see the cowboys in position alongside the herd. There was beauty and precision in the way they kept the cattle grouped together, slowing the ones in front who would forge ahead and prodding those who tried to lag behind. From time to time, one of the men would have to veer away from the group in order to head off a stray, and the cooperation between horse and rider was a marvel to watch.

Engrossed in the strange ballet, my spirit soared and I rejoiced in being a child of the God of creation. My throbbing feet soon claimed my attention, however, and I gingerly eased the boots off. Both feet were terribly swollen, as well as being raw and covered with blisters. I winced as the throbbing increased and wished I had a pail of cold water to bathe them in.

Lacking that, I wriggled around sideways so my feet could rest on sacks of flour and my back was propped against the wagon's side.

When I was reasonably comfortable, I leaned back and felt the weight of my Bible pressing against me. I looked around cautiously. Cookie sat hunched over the reins, as unconcerned as if he had nothing more than beans and flour riding behind him. No one was riding near the rear of the wagon, so I reached inside my overalls and drew out my Bible.

I sighed. At least one thing remained constant in my madly changing world. Hardly a day had gone by in recent years that I hadn't begun with time spent reading God's Word. I turned the well-thumbed pages to Paul's epistle to the Ephesians, where I had marked my place—was it only the day before?—and settled back to read.

Chapter four. Paul talks about the unity of believers, their edification, and speaking the truth in love. I was squirming uncomfortably by the time I reached verse 25: *"Wherefore putting away lying, speak every man truth with his neighbor. . ."* There was a distinct twinge in the area of my conscience.

I flipped the page, and a verse fairly flew out to meet me: *"Stand therefore, having your loins girt about with truth. . ."*

The Bible lay open on my lap, but my eyes tried to focus on the sacks of flour, the sideboards of the wagon, anything but the printed page.

Shame swept over me. Deception and falsehood—hardly the path I had committed myself to follow! It had seemed such an innocent thing at first, and the initial goal of protecting myself from marauders had not been a bad one. But now I was becoming more and more enmeshed in the lie I had begun.

The Lord had seen fit to bring me to a point of rescue; could I not then trust Him to provide protection from that point on? Granted, last night's exhaustion had muddled my thinking, but I bitterly regretted not having told Mr. Jefferson the truth this morning.

I resolved I would do so as soon as I saw him. After all, he was the one to whom I had lied directly. This resolution made, I asked forgiveness from the Lord and drifted into an uneasy sleep.

A particularly hard jolt of the wagon woke me. From the sun's position and the heat, I judged it to be about noon. The back of the wagon was stifling. I longed to get out and walk in the fresh air, but my feet were so swollen that I couldn't begin to put the boots back on.

I leaned back and consoled myself with the thought that we would soon stop for the noon meal and I could take that opportunity to confess to Mr. Jefferson.

The wagon lurched along and my stomach began to complain. "Biscuits and some jerky in the box next to you," said Cookie, without turning his head.

I reached into the box and helped myself. The biscuits, I knew, would be good, but I looked skeptically at the strips of dried meat. I tried nibbling at the end of one. That proved fruitless, and I soon found that the only way to take a bite was to grip a chunk firmly between my back teeth and tear it off.

Chewing it was another matter entirely. It took considerable time for it to soften enough to chew at all. It made for slow eating, but surprisingly it was all the more satisfying for that.

The last of my meal gone, I realized I was thirsty and summoned up my nerve to speak to the dour cook.

"Excuse me, will there be coffee when we stop for lunch?"

"Stop?" He snorted. "You just had your lunch. There's water in that canteen in front of you."

There was, although it was tepid and stale. But it did quench my thirst. I began to develop an appreciation for the men who sat on horseback without a break. Some of them were digging into bags behind their saddles and pulling out what looked to be more biscuits and jerky.

I was anxious to have my talk with Mr. Jefferson. Once more I addressed the cook's forbidding back. "When *will* we be stopping?"

He snorted again. It seemed to be his most expressive means of communication. "We will be stopping," he said mockingly, "about an hour before sundown. Boy, if you're in such an all-fired hurry, why don't you hop out and run over to some of them bushes over there?"

I blushed hotly as I realized his meaning. That would be the last time I addressed the man, I vowed. He was exactly the coarse type of person I had been hiding from in the first place.

Hiding. That reminded me of my postponed interview with Mr. Jefferson. Now I would have to wait until sundown! Much as I dreaded the ordeal, I wanted the peace of having it over and done with.

The pile of sacks wasn't as comfortable now as it had been earlier. I rearranged them as best I could and found some empty sacks to place under me, where the floorboards were growing harder by the minute. With that accomplished, I stretched out as far as I could in my cramped quarters and resigned myself to riding out the intervening hours.

The prairie grasses rustled softly in the light breeze. Cattle bawled from time to time, their voices interspersed with yips from the cowboys. The wind shifted, and the breeze played lightly inside the wagon, cooling my hot face. My hair was still coiled on top of my head under my hat. Its weight was oppressive, but I didn't dare take the hat off. . .not yet.

We rolled across the vast prairie, a herd of cattle, a dozen rugged men, and me. Despite our large numbers, we were no more than a speck in that wide and empty land. I dozed off and on during the afternoon, lazily tracking the sun's path as it headed down toward the horizon.

Late in the afternoon, one of the men rode up alongside the wagon and spoke to Cookie. "Got a place spotted?"

Cookie nodded. "Bunch of trees up there. Should be water. I'll go on ahead and set up if it looks good." The team picked up speed and we moved away from the herd.

Apparently there was ample water, for Cookie brought the team to a halt. I was pleased to see that keeping my feet elevated during the day had reduced the swelling, and they were nearly back to their normal size. I tried to slip my socks back on, wincing as they touched the raw places.

Cookie pulled down the tailgate, glanced at my efforts with an impassive face, then reached into a box and tossed me a roll of soft cloth strips. "Bandages," he said.

My feet were still tender when I stepped out of the wagon, although the soft bandages did help a lot. My concern for my feet, however, was dwarfed by the pains that shot through every other part of my body. After a full day of cramped inactivity, my muscles felt as though they had frozen stiff.

Cookie was busy building his fire, but he watched as I staggered around stiff-legged, trying to straighten up. A raspy sound came from his direction, like the wheeze from an organ that has long gone unplayed.

He wheezed again. Why, the man was laughing! My pleasure in discovering that he was capable of such a thing was dampened by the fact that I was the object of his merriment, but it was an encouraging discovery, all the same.

"Boy," he said when he had regained some control, "why don't you go on over and wash yourself?" I was touched by his concern until he added, "You surely look like you could use it." And began wheezing again.

I found a towel in the wagon and went off, reflecting on the strange humor of cowboys.

I returned feeling much refreshed. I had even been able to unwind my hair and brush through it, and the few minutes' respite from its weight on my head had been wonderful.

"Is there anything I can do to help?" I asked Cookie. It was hardly fair to expect to be waited on when these men had so kindly taken me under their wing.

He looked at me appraisingly. "Why don't you scout around for more wood? We'll need enough to keep it going all night long to keep the coffee hot for the night crew."

I stared. For Cookie, this was being positively chatty. I wondered what had brought about the change as I began to gather firewood.

The exercise helped loosen my stiff muscles, and as long as I walked gingerly, I got along rather well. I was proud of the pile I had collected by the time the men had brought the herd up and gathered for supper.

They sprawled around the fire in a variety of attitudes, but none of them displayed the bone-weariness I would have expected after a full day in the saddle. Cookie unbent still further and let me help him dish up the supper. The plates were filled with succulent steaks and the ever-present beans. Coffee that looked strong enough to float any number of horseshoes added its fragrant aroma to the evening air.

I scanned the faces in the group. Mr. Jefferson was not among them. I told myself not to worry. He would surely be in soon.

Taking my own plate, I sat at the edge of the firelight. Some of the men had finished eating and were settling down to talk.

"Good thing Andy got that buffalo yesterday," said one.

"Mm," agreed another around a mouthful of food. "Best steaks we've had the whole trip."

I glanced at the bite on my fork. So this was buffalo and not beef. I took a tentative nibble and found it delicious. There was a lot I had to learn in this new land.

"Anybody seen Jeff?" asked Cookie. "He'd better show up while there's food left."

"He and Jake went to doctor a cow," answered Shorty. "She got a leg tangled pretty bad in some cactus."

So now I would have to wait even longer. I watched idly as Shorty rose and left the circle. He picked up a bedroll and looped his rope around it, then strolled over to a nearby tree. Standing beneath it, he gave the bedroll, rope and all, a toss into the air.

My interest quickened. What new practice of the West was this? The roll fell at his feet, and he threw it again, harder this time. The rope caught around one of the branches about ten feet up and hung in a fork, the bedroll swinging from one side, the end of the rope dangling from the other. I waited to see how he would get the tangle loose, but he walked back to his place in the circle and sat down as if satisfied.

One of the other cowboys shook his head sadly. "Shorty, one of these days, someone's going to dangle a loop over a limb, and it's going to be meant for you."

Shorty grinned. "No chance, Neil. I'm as pure as the driven snow."

Neil grunted. None of this exchange made sense to me, but so far, very little had.

"Here you go, boys." It was Cookie, bearing a tray of steaming pies. "Enjoy the apples. They're the last you'll get on this ride."

I helped him cut huge wedges of the pies and serve them to the men. Shorty looked up as I gave his piece to him. "Well, boy," he said, "what do you think about those three thousand head of big dogs we're herding?"

The chuckles around me revealed that my comment had been repeated and apparently enjoyed. I ducked my head in embarrassment and kept on serving.

"His name's Judah," Cookie growled. I turned to look at him in appreciation and he glared back at me, but this unexpected championship made me feel more protected than I had since Jake had left me that morning.

Shorty, however, wasn't one to give up easily. "Judah, is it?" he asked politely. "Well, that's fine. Judah, are you feeling better today?"

I nodded, sitting down to eat my pie. His face betrayed nothing, but I was confused by his sudden interest, embarrassed at being singled out, and altogether suspicious of his motives.

"That boy don't talk much, does he?" he muttered. I glanced up to see him eyeing me speculatively.

"Shorty?" It was Neil. "Do you think we'll have any trouble with skunks like we did back in Texas?"

"Well, now, it all depends," Shorty drawled. I breathed a sigh of relief. His attention had been diverted from me; he didn't so much as flicker an eyelash in my direction.

"It all depends," he repeated. "I surely hope not. I recollect what happened to poor Lem Harris. You all know that story of course."

"Can't say I've heard it," said a man sitting a few feet from me. "Why don't you tell us all about it?"

"It's a sad and terrible story," Shorty began. "About five years ago, I was on a drive near the Brazos. There were only ten of us, including the cook and the wrangler.

"We'd had trouble all along the way, what with Indians, dry waterholes, and wolves waiting to pick off the stragglers if we gave them half a chance. But the worst problem we had to put up with was the hydrophoby skunks."

I shuddered. Here was another new peril. I listened intently to prepare myself in the event I came across one.

"You've all dealt with hydrophoby skunks, haven't you?" Several of the men nodded solemnly. "For such timid critters, they turn mighty mean when the disease takes them. Cunning, too. They're just itching to bite someone, but they know they don't stand a chance when you're up on horseback."

"What do they do?" asked the man near me.

"Why, they wait around a cow camp, like this one here, and hide in the grass until everyone's asleep. Then they come creeping out and check the bedrolls, one by one. And the amazing thing is how they always check the head end."

"Can't you just cover your head and fool 'em?" asked my neighbor.

Shorty shook his head. "I told you, they get mighty cunning. They have some kind of instinct for finding the head. Maybe it's the sound of breathing. But they'll creep up and pull the blankets right back from your face."

I looked around cautiously, trying to search out the shadows. None of the men seemed particularly concerned, though, and no one took the slightest notice of me.

"Anyway," Shorty resumed his tale, "we'd noticed signs of them hydrophoby skunks for some time, and of course I'd warned all the new men about them. Told them that the only way to keep from getting bit if one comes up to you is to lie perfectly still. You know, they have bad eyesight, and they wait for a body to move so they can take proper aim."

"Tell 'em what happened to Lem," prompted Neil.

Shorty sighed mournfully. "That Lem never was one for listening. One night, we were all layin' in our blankets, when I heard a rustling in the grass. I knew it was some kind of varmint, but it wasn't until it began tugging my blankets away from my face that I saw for sure it was a hydrophoby skunk."

"What did you do?" This from my neighbor.

"Do? Why, I just laid there as still as death, and when he couldn't take a proper aim at me, he moved off to check the others.

"Once he was gone, I kind of eased up on one elbow, and I saw him sizing up old Lem. Lem hadn't taken my warning to heart, and no sooner did the pulling and the tugging wake him than he started up with a yell.

"That was all the skunk was waiting for. As soon as Lem moved, the skunk spotted his target and jumped him."

"How bad was it?" asked one of the men.

"Bit the end of his nose clean off. Lem was up dancing around, whooping and swearing, and in all the excitement the hydrophoby skunk moseyed off and we never saw him again. Lem never did look quite right after that. Them hydrophoby skunks are mean—poison mean."

In the silence that followed, I realized I was holding one hand protectively over the lower half of my face.

The cowboys got up, stretched, and one by one started laying out their bedrolls. Shorty stopped next to me and laid a hand on my shoulder. "I already spread your blankets out for you, boy," he said kindly. "You'd best get some sleep."

The fire had burned down and the night air was chilly. I would roll up in my blankets, I decided, and wait for the return of Jake and Mr. Jefferson.

Shorty had thoughtfully spread my blankets next to the chuck-wagon, and I welcomed its now-familiar shelter. I tossed and twisted, trying to fit my body to the unrelenting contours of the ground.

Overhead, the sky was an indigo blue, with the lighter clouds scudding across it. The moon had nearly completed its circuit and was casting a cheerful glow across our campground. The beauty of God's creation held me spellbound, and it seemed impossible for any but the most friendly creatures to exist in the peaceful setting.

Footsteps sounded on the far side of the fire, and I raised my head to see Jake walk into the circle of light. He looked exhausted. He stood for a moment as if puzzled, then frowned and began pacing around outside the circle of sleepers. "All right, where is it?" he yelled. The cowboys lay undisturbed, apparently sound asleep.

Jake turned away, mumbling, and enlarged his circle. He stopped short under a tree and stared up into its branches. "Hey Shorty!" he roared. "Can't a body come back all tuckered out after a long day's work without finding someone's gone and strung his bedroll up in a tree?"

The bodies around the fire were suspiciously quiet, but I heard a muffled snort of laughter. Until that moment I had forgotten Shorty's strange behavior. The sight of Jake clambering up the tree to untangle his bedroll might have been funny if I hadn't been so tired myself lately and had a fair idea of how he felt.

A movement behind me claimed my attention. On the opposite side of the chuck wagon I could see two pairs of boots and hear the murmur of voices.

One I recognized as Cookie's. "About time you got in. You look about played out. Here, I saved you a plate. It's cold now."

I strained to hear more. This must be Mr. Jefferson.

"Thanks, Cookie. I am tired." It was undoubtedly his voice. My moment was at hand.

"Cow going to be all right?"

"I think so, as long as infection doesn't set in. We'll do the best we can for her."

I drew a long breath and offered a prayer for strength. I was in the very act of slipping from beneath the covers when Mr. Jefferson's next words arrested my movement.

"How's Judah? Did he give you any trouble today?"

I froze, straining to hear Cookie's reply. "You know, that boy's really something. I figured he'd be up beside me, wanting to drive and jabbering in my ear all day. But he sat in the back where I put him and hardly said a word."

"Is he rested up from yesterday? He's had a pretty rough time of it, being deserted like that."

"I'll tell you, Jeff, that boy's got spunk. His feet were worn as raw as anything I've ever seen, but he never once complained. I gave him some bandages, and darned if he didn't come offer to help me! Gathered that pile of wood all by himself. "That boy's game, Jeff. I'll stand by him."

"He must be something special to get you to open up," Mr. Jefferson said, chuckling. "That's more than I've heard you say on the whole drive."

Cookie resorted to his characteristic snort and withdrew into silence. I could see the other pair of boots walk away into the night.

It's said that eavesdroppers seldom hear good of themselves. I wondered how many eavesdroppers heard themselves described in such glowing terms, especially when they knew the praise was undeserved.

I could no more have interrupted that conversation than I could have held the chuckwagon up with one hand. My misery increased— not only had I failed to confess my duplicity, but by my silence I had allowed the two men to form a wholly undeserved opinion of me.

The fire was merely a bed of glowing coals by now. I could not make out Mr. Jefferson's form in the darkness, nor could I call out to him for fear of rousing the camp. My confrontation had been postponed again, at least until breakfast. I rolled up in my blankets, thoroughly disgusted with myself, and went to sleep.

I don't know what startled me out of my sleep, but all at once my eyelids flew open and I knew something was wrong. A tug on my blankets told me I was not alone; someone was gently pulling the blankets away from my face.

A confusion of thoughts whirled through my mind in what must have been only a split second. One of the men, perhaps. Should I cry out? But surely none of our number would come meaning me any harm, not with a dozen strong, armed men sleeping only yards away. It must be Mr. Jefferson, or Cookie, or Jake, come to bring me some message. But then why not shake my shoulder? Why this insistent tugging to uncover my face?

Something in my sleep-numbed brain fought for recognition,

something that lay just beyond my grasp.

Of course! I almost moaned aloud in despair. Shorty's story of the marauding skunks! What had he said to do? Lie perfectly still. That was it. Don't give the poor-sighted brute a chance to take aim.

The blanket inched away from my cheek, my nose, my chin. *Remember Lem Harris,* I warned myself. *Lie still, and it will go away, and you can raise the alarm to warn the others.*

The pulling stopped, although I still felt a vibrating tension on one corner of my blanket, as though the beast were trying to focus on my face, to take aim at my nose. It was almost more than I could bear to lie motionless under its steady, if nearsighted, gaze. The black night hid it well, but I could feel its presence as it waited for a chance to spring.

There was a sudden rustle, and to my terror, a furry body leapt full into my face. I screamed, fighting wildly against both my attacker and the tangle of blankets that held me.

I screamed again and kicked my way free. I caught hold of a fistful of fur and tore it away from my face. There was a roaring in my ears, and I steadied myself. This was no time to faint.

Movement stirred among the bedrolls, and someone threw wood on the fire, sending up a shower of sparks followed by a strong flame that lit up the camp area.

Through my panic, I became dimly aware that the roaring in my ears was the sound of the men's laughter—laughter that died away as they stared at me, openmouthed.

I dropped my eyes before their gaze and became aware of three things. One was the piece of rabbit skin I still clutched in one hand. Another was the rope tied to one corner of my blanket and trailing away toward where the men lay. The third was my hat, lying on the ground.

To pick it up and replace it would have been pointless. My hair had fallen loose during my frantic struggle and now hung down to my waist.

I looked back at the men. They still gaped at me. Only Shorty, absorbed in his hilarity, had failed to notice what had happened. He rocked back and forth, the end of a rope trailing from his hand, whooping and slapping his leg.

"Hear that?" he cried. "Did you hear that? I told you I'd get that boy to talk! I told you—" He broke off, eyes bulging as he finally focused on me.

It was Jake who broke the silence. "My word!" he roared. "He's a girl!"

No one else made a sound. I waited hopefully for the earth to open and swallow me up.

Across the fire, a figure stepped into the circle of light and I found myself looking straight into Mr. Jefferson's eyes.

Chapter 6

The next day found me rocking along in my seat in the rear of the chuckwagon. My feet were over much of their soreness by now, but my pride was grievously tender.

The much-delayed talk with Mr. Jefferson had finally taken place the night before. We had walked to the edge of the firelight while the cowboys rearranged themselves in their blankets. Not one of them had uttered a word following Jake's outburst. Even Shorty had remained silent.

We stopped just before the darkness enveloped us. I was grateful for the effort made to have a private conversation and devoutly hoped that we were indeed out of earshot. I was sure that anything that might be overheard would spread through the group like wildfire. From what I had seen thus far, when it came to passing along scraps of information, Aunt Phoebe's sewing circle had nothing on these cowboys.

Mr. Jefferson turned to face me. He said nothing, but his eyes demanded an explanation.

"I meant to talk to you earlier," I faltered. He raised his eyebrows. I took a deep breath and plunged into my story.

"My name is Judith Alder. That's the only thing I lied to you about. I really was traveling west to help my uncle Matthew at his trading post. The family I was traveling with drove off and left me yesterday morning, just as I said."

"Why?"

"We were running low on food and water. They'd be more sure of getting to Santa Fe if they only had three mouths to feed. And Mrs. Parker. . ." I hadn't planned to elaborate on that portion of the story, but I had made up my mind to make a clean breast of things, and I would, despite my embarrassment.

"Mrs. Parker, the woman I came with, felt I was an...an unsettling influence on her husband and son."

"I can imagine," he said drily. "You've certainly succeeded in unsettling this camp tonight. And did your Mrs. Parker outfit you before she left?"

"Not intentionally. They set out a crate they thought was mine, but their son's clothes were in it. I felt I would be safer traveling alone if I were, ah, incognito."

"I see. But after Jake found you and brought you in...?"

"Please try to understand," I pleaded. "I was so terribly tired and afraid and confused. I had no idea what sort of men you were, and there weren't any other women around.

"After I'd lied to you about my name, I knew I had to tell you the truth and make it right, but I didn't see you anymore today. And after I got in bed, I heard you come in, but then I heard what you and Cookie were saying about me, and I just couldn't bring myself to do it then.

"And then," I gulped, my emotions getting the upper hand, "when you went away, I decided I'd tell you at breakfast, but Shorty played that horrible trick about the hydrophobia skunk, and...and..." For the first time since being left, I gave way to tears, and they came in abundance.

I covered my face with my hands to muffle the sobs that shook me. Never had I felt so alone and so ashamed. Not only had I purposely deceived the kind people who had taken me in, but I had failed miserably at following the example of Christ.

Mr. Jefferson shuffled his feet. Apparently he was as uncomfortable as most men around feminine tears. Wiping my eyes with the backs of my hands I choked back the sobs and waited for whatever censure was to come.

"You're tired, Ju—Miss Alder. You'd best go get what sleep you can. If we push ourselves, we may be able to make the ranch by sundown tomorrow, and you can have a decent bed." His lips tightened.

"And a change of clothes."

"Thank you," I said meekly. He stretched out an arm as if to throw it around my shoulders as he had that morning, but drew it back abruptly.

"Go get some rest," he said.

After the evening's turn of events, I expected to lie awake for hours. Instead, I slept dreamlessly, noticing nothing until Cookie's "Come and get it!" roused the camp. I elected to stay close to the wagon to eat the plate of biscuits and beans Cookie silently handed me rather than join the men around the fire.

Now it was nearing noonday, and I helped myself to biscuits and jerky. Cookie made no effort at conversation, but then, no one had spoken a word to me all day. I felt a twinge of self-pity.

You've only yourself to blame, I scolded myself. I wondered, though, if I would be ostracized like this once we reached the ranch. If the story was passed along to the owners. . . If! How could I doubt its being told, and with suitable embellishments, at that.

But they would have to talk with me at least long enough to let me know how I was to reach Uncle Matthew. I sighed. Being passed from hand to hand was growing tiresome.

Late in the afternoon, one of the men rode up next to Cookie. "Jeff said to tell you we're making better time than we thought. He's scouted on ahead and he says we ought to be at the ranch in an hour or so."

"Good," Cookie said. "It'll give me a chance to unload in the daylight."

Yes, unload, I thought wearily. *Unload the food, unload the equipment, and unload me.* I pulled out my bag and found my comb, then set to work on the snarls in my hair. If we were getting back into civilized country, I had better make myself presentable. Well, as presentable as possible. I fervently hoped that the rancher's wife wasn't another Aunt Phoebe.

At least I could make a reasonably fresh start there, and I would be free of the cowboys' scrutiny, Shorty's practical jokes, and the look in Mr. Jefferson's eyes in which I was sure I had read disappointment and reproach. Once I was safely inside the ranch house, I need not see any of them again.

I found a small handkerchief tucked away in my bag, soaked it with water from a canteen, and used it to scrub my face and hands. The trail dust, I knew, would settle and cling again almost as soon as I had washed it off, but it boosted my morale to make the effort.

There was little that could be done about my clothes. I slapped dust from the overalls with my hat as I had seen the men do. Thank goodness I wouldn't have to wear it again! I smoothed my hair as best I could into a coil at the back of my neck, thinking how good it would feel to have it clean once more.

The wagon rocked more slowly now. I tried to peer out the front, but could see nothing beyond Cookie's broad back. He seemed to be maintaining his cold-shoulder treatment to the end. I had tried to apologize earlier, but he had gone about his business as though I were not even there.

Cookie drew the team to a stop and jumped off the seat, not bothering to glance back at me. I was sorry to leave him on such a cool note.

Jake's face appeared at the back of the wagon. "Miss Judith, we're at the Double B now. Come on out and I'll take you to meet the Bradleys."

He helped me down with such courtly manners that I almost laughed in spite of my nervousness. "Jake," I said, "I want to thank you for rescuing me. And I'm sorry—very sorry—that I deceived you as I did. Please forgive me."

To my surprise, he turned as red as a beet. "Don't you worry about that, Miss Judith. I've been talking to Jeff and he explained it all to me. You kind of bowled us all over last night, but I think you're one spunky little lady."

My spirits soared. "Thank you, Jake. You don't know what it means to have one friend left among you."

"*One* friend?" His eyes widened, then narrowed. "Miss Judith—" He broke off at the approach of a tall, smiling man.

"Jake! It's good to see you here. Jeff tells me you have something to show me."

My embarrassment returned full flood. Some*thing*, indeed! Jake reached out eagerly to pump the man's hand. "Yep, we rounded up more than our share of strays this trip. Miss Judith, may I present Mr. Charles Bradley, owner of the Double B Ranch. Charles, this here is Miss Judith Alder, late of St. Joseph, and on her way to live with her uncle over in Taos."

Mr. Bradley took my extended hand and immediately endeared himself to me by ignoring my strange garb entirely.

"Miss Alder, I am pleased to make your acquaintance. I hope you will do us the honor of being our guest for some time." He turned at the sound of approaching footsteps and smiled. Two women were walking toward us. The younger woman, slight and fair-haired, leaned on the arm of the older one, whose sharp, disapproving glance took in the group and focused on me.

"Allow me to present my wife, Abby," said Mr. Bradley. "Abby, Miss Alder." His wife was as gracious as her husband, smiling and completely overlooking my unconventional arrival. She released her hold on the older woman's arm and took a step toward her husband, who smiled and put a supporting arm around her waist.

"I'm glad to meet you, Miss Alder." Her voice was soft and her speech bore evidence of a southern origin.

The older woman stood as stiff and straight as if she had swallowed a poker. Her eyes had not left my face since she had first seen me, and they glittered now with animosity.

The Bradleys seemed to recall her presence. "My apologies," Mr. Bradley said, smiling. "Miss Alder, this is Mrs. Styles."

Her sharp eyes looked me up and down. I tentatively offered a hand, which she ignored. "And your family, Miss Alder? Are they stopping here also?"

Somehow I felt instinctively that the Bradleys wouldn't blink at my strange situation, but I hated to explain in front of Mrs. Styles. "I am not traveling with my family. I was on my way west when the people I was with deserted me. These trail drivers were kind enough to bring me here until I can make arrangements to finish my journey."

"And how long have you been in their company. . .alone?"

I made an effort to speak evenly. "I have been with them for two nights and two days, and all of them have behaved as perfect gentlemen." I put as much dignity into this speech as I could, considering that I was hardly dressed as the perfect lady.

Mrs. Styles sniffed and looked me up and down. "I shall be on my way, Abby. I will return to see you and Charles at a later date." She gave me a final scathing look and walked to a buggy standing in front of the house.

The four of us—the Bradleys, Jake and I—let out a collective sigh of relief and looked at one another guiltily.

"Please, Miss Alder—may I call you Judith?" said Mrs. Bradley. "And you're to call us Charles and Abby. Things aren't nearly as formal here as they are back east. Don't be too upset by Lucia Styles. It's just that she has exceptionally high standards and so few of us manage to live up to them." Her pale cheek dimpled as she smiled mischievously.

"Won't you come in and sit with me? I believe I need to rest a bit." She certainly looked it. The hand resting on her husband's arm was trembling.

"I'm sorry, dear," he said in a stricken voice. "I'll take you in at once." And with that he swept her up in his arms. He turned to me. "She only came out to greet the drivers. She isn't supposed to be up for long periods. Please do come in. You must be exhausted."

I took my first look at the ranch house as I followed them inside. It was huge, a long, low, rambling affair of stone. Off to the west, the sun was setting in a glorious array of pink and gold, its last brilliant rays picking out the soft hues in the stone walls. Different styles of building seemed to be represented, as though several additions had been made to the original structure, but all in all the effect was one of strength and permanence.

The house stood on a level area at the top of a low hill, commanding the view for miles in all directions. In the distance, cattle dotted the slopes.

Inside, the house was furnished elegantly and with taste, making one feel at home immediately without any hint of pretentiousness. Charles laid Abby gently on a couch, arranging cushions at her back to let her rest comfortably.

I sank gratefully into a deep chair he pointed out to me. It was my first taste of comfort in many days, and I felt as if I could sit there forever.

A plump woman in a gingham dress brought in a tea service, and Charles poured out steaming cups for the three of us.

"Now, Judith," he said, "you say your party deserted you along the trail?"

I retold my story for what seemed the thousandth time while we sat sipping our tea. I went back to Aunt Phoebe's choice of the Parkers to take me along and omitted nothing along the way, including my decision to wear Lanny's clothes. Abby's dimple deepened at that, but she said nothing.

"And so they brought me here, and it appears they have decided I'm to stay with you until I can contact Uncle Matthew to make further arrangements. But I don't want to impose."

Abby laughed softly. "Judith, if you only knew how I welcome your company! Of course you must stay with us. Charles, please show her to a room and have Vera bring her plenty of hot water. I still have some dresses that haven't been taken in. She can try them on." She added to me, "I think you're much the same size I was before I lost weight."

I followed Charles down a long corridor to my room. He stopped at an open doorway. "Please make yourself at home, Judith. I'll see

Vera about the water and Abby's dresses."

The room carried the same stamp of elegant simplicity that I had noted before, nothing lavish, but everything comfortable and lovely. The bed drew my attention first, and I settled myself gingerly on a corner. It was a wonderfully soft mattress, especially tempting after so many days of bedrolls on the ground. I didn't dare lie upon it now, or I was sure I wouldn't move until morning.

A small overstuffed chair sat in one corner next to the stone fireplace, and there were a wardrobe and dresser on the other side of the room. The bed, chair, and floor had been covered with bright rugs, which I guessed were Indian in design and added a warm glow of color to the room.

There was a knock on the door, and the plump woman came into the room, carrying an armful of clothing. She was followed by two young boys, one bearing a bathtub and the other buckets of steaming water. The boys set down their cargo and left, but the woman lingered behind.

"Charles said to bring you dresses, but I figured you'd need more'n that, so I brought along some necessaries, too." She grinned and produced an array of undergarments from beneath the pile of dresses.

"That's very thoughtful." I smiled back at her. It was easy to relax in the face of her good humor.

She hefted the buckets as though they weighed nothing and poured them into the bath. "Soap's over there." She nodded toward a small table next to the dresser that also held a basin and pitcher.

"After you get all clean, I'll come if you want me to and help you try on the dresses. If they need some taking up or letting out, I can do that, too. But they should be pretty close. Abby used to be just about your size."

"Is she. . ." I trailed off, not knowing exactly how to ask about my frail hostess.

Vera understood. "No one's sure what's ailing her. She just started wasting away about six months ago. Nobody knows why, but Charles is worried sick about her."

"But surely a doctor could help."

"Honey, we don't have a doctor handy. There've been a couple passing through, though, and neither one of them could find a thing wrong." Her eyes misted over. It was plain to see that she was as worried about Abby as anyone.

"But what you need right now," she said briskly, "is a long soak, some supper, and bed. I'll quit talking, and you get on with it."

Left to myself, I peeled off Lanny's shirt and overalls and the rest of the clothes I had worn, now filthy. Bless Vera for having thought of the "necessaries"!

The hot water felt heavenly. I soaked and scrubbed and rinsed, then scrubbed some more. I lathered up my hair and washed it until it squeaked and my scalp tingled. When the water began to cool, I got out and wrapped myself in one of the huge, fluffy towels Vera had brought. I used another to get as much water as I could out of my hair.

I sorted through the clothes on the bed. They were all well made, with the attention to detail that transforms an ordinary garment into one of distinction.

I had just finished putting on clean undergarments when Vera tapped on the door and came in.

"My land, there was a pretty girl under all that grime," she said with a chuckle.

Together we held up the dresses and Vera helped me into one that took my fancy. It was a pale blue, simply made, which brought out the blue in my eyes that my father had always called cornflower. Vera provided a supply of hairpins and we dressed my still damp hair into a simple style low on my neck.

"I need to see about supper," said Vera. "You come back to the parlor with me so you don't get lost your first night here."

Back in the parlor, I realized that despite the hearty helpings of beans, biscuits, and more beans that I had eaten the last two days, I was famished for a home-cooked meal served at a table.

No one else was in the room, so I wandered around, admiring several of the different objects. My skirts rustled and swayed as I moved, and it was a welcome feeling after having been encased in boy's clothes.

I sighed. Being clean again, wearing a dress, and once more looking like myself would have been enough, even without the Bradleys' kind hospitality. Their warm welcome, this lovely home, and the tempting smells that were finding their way from the kitchen made the Parkers' perfidy and my masquerade fade away like a bad dream.

And I would not have to face the shunning of the cowboys any longer. I had known them only a short time, but I still did not like the thought of losing their respect.

I turned to see Charles Bradley standing in the open doorway, a pleased smile on his face. "You look refreshed, Judith. And that dress suits you admirably. Supper is ready now, but if you don't mind waiting a few moments more, my brother will join us."

I smiled back at him. "Thank you. I'm sure I can last a few more minutes. Is Abby feeling better?"

A shadow crossed his face. "She is having her supper on a tray in her room. I shouldn't have let her stay up and get so tired. But she was so excited about the rest of the cattle arriving safely that I thought it might do her good." He smiled again. "For all of her frailty now, Abby loved being involved in the ranch and the life that goes with it."

"I can see how she would. You have a beautiful home and a perfect setting for it. I want to thank you for your hospitality, especially to an unexpected guest. I do hope I won't need to impose on you for more than a short time."

"Please feel free to stay as long as you like. Both Abby and I are delighted to have you. So now, you see, you're an invited guest and don't need to consider your stay an imposition."

"I'll try not to. But is there some way of sending a message to my uncle? He'll be expecting me soon and I need to let him know where I am and ask him to arrange for some kind of transportation for me."

"Of course. I know you must be concerned for him and anxious to finish your journey. If you'll write out your message tonight, I'll send it with one of my men to the stage station tomorrow morning. And now," he said, turning, "I believe I hear my brother coming."

Footsteps sounded in the corridor, and a tall man stepped into the room. I gasped and felt the warm blood rush to my cheeks.

"I believe you're already acquainted with my brother, Jefferson," Charles said.

Chapter 7

His brother! Our eyes met and held while I struggled to keep from gaping and to make some sense of this new development.

Charles looked confused. "I'm sorry. I thought you two had met. Miss Alder, my brother, Jefferson Bradley."

"No, you're right, Charles. We have met," said his brother, the corners of his mouth twitching. "But it appears neither one of us made our identity quite clear."

Charles's brow furrowed again and Jeff laughed. "Don't worry, I'll explain later. Right now, I'm sure Miss Alder must be as hungry as I am. Let's go in to dinner."

The aroma that had drifted to me from the kitchen had awakened a delicious anticipation of the supper to come. But after meeting Mr. Je—Bradley, I corrected myself—I could not have told what we ate.

The brothers were clearly delighted to be together again, but made every effort to include me in their conversation. I appreciated their attempt to smooth over the awkwardness we all felt and soon became caught up in their discussion of the ranch.

"Something puzzles me," I ventured. "I always thought cattle were driven *from* the ranch *to* the market. But you brought thousands of them here."

Charles answered my question. "You're right, Judith. This is a little out of the ordinary. You have to understand that we grew up ranching in Texas and built up quite a herd. But times aren't easy in Texas these days. Abby and I moved up here a little over a year ago and brought half our herd with us. Jeff kept the rest in Texas in case the experiment failed.

"But this New Mexico Territory is open and fresh and ready for new blood. The cattle thrive here. And best of all, the railroad will extend this far west in just a few years, and we'll be able to drive cattle to a railhead in just a few days, instead of taking them all the way up the trail to Abilene."

"So now you've brought all your livestock up here?"

"That's what we've done. We're sure now that the land will support the cattle, and Jeff and the hands we had left drove the rest of them here. Your arrival along with them was a pleasant surprise, eh, Jeff?"

"She was certainly a surprise," Jeff replied drily.

I chose not to rise to the bait.

After dinner, Charles excused himself to check on the new stock. Jeff walked with me as far as the parlor.

"It's a little different, seeing you like this," he said, smiling.

I ducked my head in confusion. "I'm really sorry about the mix-up. I never meant to—"

"I didn't mean that as a criticism," he said. "It's a nice difference."

"Thank you."

"You said you overhead me talking to Cookie last night?"

I nodded. "I couldn't help it. I don't eavesdrop as a rule."

"I just want you to know that. . .all the things Cookie said about you. . .I still think they're true." He cleared his throat. "Good night." And then he was gone.

I floated down the corridor to my room. Trying to think sensibly, I told myself that a total stranger had said I had spunk, that I was game. It should hardly have produced such a heady sensation. I climbed into bed feeling ridiculously happy.

Next morning, after eating the breakfast Vera brought to my room on a tray, I dressed in another of Abby's dresses, a flowered print this time, and sat down to compose a note to Uncle Matthew, explaining my plight. With that done, I managed to find my way to the front of the house.

Charles was at one end of the broad porch, talking to his brother, while Abby lay in a hammock at the other. I felt my cheeks grow warm at the sight of Jeff and hurried to a chair next to Abby, hoping the others had not noticed.

She smiled. "That dress looks charming on you. I'm so glad you are able to wear it."

"It was good of you to lend your dresses to me. I'll return them once I've reached my uncle and can make more."

"No, don't worry about that. I'd like for you to have them. I have plenty for myself now, and I'm not likely to need that size again." A swift shadow crossed her face, to be replaced by her gentle smile.

"Don't look so distressed, Judith. Vera said she had told you about my illness. I would like to grow well again, of course, but I know the Lord as my Savior, and I'm sure of a home in heaven if I don't recover." Her gaze rested on her husband lovingly. "It's Charles that concerns me most. Charles and the children."

"Children?" I don't know why that should have surprised me, but I had seen no evidence of them, and it only seemed to compound the tragedy.

"We have two," she said, laughing, "although they get into so much mischief that sometimes it seems like more.

"Charles is so busy running the ranch that he can't spend as much time with them as he'd like, and Vera has all she can handle managing the house. Since I've been ill, I'm afraid they've run rather wild." The shadow crept into her eyes again. "It's for them that I mind most."

I tried to think of something to say. Surely there were words of comfort, but they eluded me. Her faith touched me deeply, and I was grateful that she knew the Lord.

Would I be able to face death as calmly as she, even though it meant leaving a beloved family? I wondered.

She seemed to sense my distress, for she smiled again and tactfully changed the subject. "Tell me," she said, her eyes twinkling, "how did the men react when they found out you were a young lady instead of a boy?"

I groaned. "It certainly wasn't what I had expected. I was prepared for all kinds of recriminations, but when it came down to it, I don't believe one of them actually said a word. Except Jeff of course. Even Jake kept away from me after that until we arrived here.

"They must have been even more embarrassed than I was, but I still felt bad that they were all so angry they wouldn't even speak to me."

"Angry?" Abby raised an eyebrow. "Judith, is this your first trip west?" I nodded. "Well, brace yourself, my dear. I think you're in for a surprise."

Before I could ask what she meant, Charles and Jeff had come up behind us. Charles smoothed his wife's hair tenderly. "Did you write your message to your uncle?" he asked me. I took the note from my pocket and handed it to him. "One of the men is leaving for town soon. I'll send it along with him," he promised.

Abby looked up at Jeff and smiled. "Welcome home," she said. "I didn't get a chance to greet you last night. I hope you were comfortable."

Jeff grinned back at her. "After all those nights on the trail, anything would have been an improvement. But my bed felt wonderful, Abby. The place already feels like home."

"Did Charles tell you the news?"

"Nothing but news since I got here. Was there any particular thing you had in mind?"

Abby made a face at him, and I gathered that the light-hearted banter between these three was of long standing. I wondered if this was too tiring for Abby, but her color seemed improved and her manner more relaxed.

"Why *the* news, of course. Just in time for your arrival, we have acquired a minister at Three Forks."

Jeff whistled and a grin broke out on his face. I felt my heart quicken and told myself it was due to the news and his infectious grin. I would surely be here at least throughout the weekend. How wonderful it would be to attend a worship service again before traveling on!

"How did you manage that?" Jeff asked.

"Really, he just fell into our laps," answered Charles. "He had to give up his church in the east because of ill health and traveled out here under his doctor's orders. If the climate suits him, he may stay permanently."

"Wouldn't that be fine!" Jeff's eyes glowed with a happiness that—I checked myself. I was becoming all too interested in the moods of a stranger, even one who had rescued me. I would be gone in a few days to a new life filled with new people. The thought should not have left me feeling so bleak.

I forced my attention back to the conversation. ". . .only had time to shake his hand and say hello," Charles was saying. "But this western air should make a new man out of him, if he'll stay long enough to give it a chance."

He broke off and frowned, sniffing. There *was* a peculiar smell, sweet and cloying, even though we were outside. We were all looking for its source when Shorty and Neil stepped around the corner of the house, bringing an even stronger cloud of the scent with them. They stopped before us and shuffled their feet.

"What on earth!" sputtered Charles. "Did you two tangle with a skunk this morning? Back away so the rest of us can breathe, won't you?"

Shorty looked hurt. "Aw, Boss, you ain't making fun of my cologne, are you?"

"Cologne?" Charles stepped down off the porch and circled the pair slowly. "Hair combed," he said in awe. "Clean shaven, and, I declare, I believe those shirts have been washed sometime within the last six months. What's gotten into you boys?" Behind me, I heard Abby giggle.

"Why, Boss," said Shorty, with an attempt at wounded dignity, "we just came in off the trail and wanted to make ourselves presentable. Right, Neil?"

Neil, his eyes fastened on the toe of his boot, mumbled assent.

"And being naturally kindhearted, we thought we'd come and see how Miss Judith was doing this morning. We wanted to see if there was anything we could do for her. Right, Neil?"

Neil gulped and nodded.

"I see," Charles said kindly. "I appreciate that, boys, and I'm sure Miss Alder does, too. As a matter of fact," he continued, "there is something you could do, but it's a job for just one of you."

Shorty stepped forward. "I'm your man," he announced.

"Good for you," Charles said. "Take this message to the stage station at Three Forks. It's on the trail, about fifteen miles southwest of here. You can't miss it."

Shorty stared, crestfallen, as Charles handed him the note and gave him a hearty clap on the shoulder. He looked mournfully at the paper, then shook his head and started toward the corral.

Charles turned his attention to Neil. "Well, what's keeping you from your chores?"

Neil turned brick red and stared intently at his boot. "Begging your pardon, Boss, but I twisted my ankle something awful this morning, and I thought maybe I ought to sit down and give it a chance to heal." He raised his eyes hopefully. "Like maybe on the porch?"

Charles rolled his eyes skyward. Neil heaved a sigh and walked away with a pronounced limp I was sure had not been evident earlier. Jeff and Charles watched him go, then walked off toward the corral, chuckling.

I had sat wide-eyed through this performance, unable to utter a word, but now I turned to Abby. "Was that really for my benefit?"

She nodded, still trying to control her laughter. Evidently, her illness had not dampened her sense of humor. "Oh Judith!" she burst out, "I knew your coming here would do me good, but what havoc you've wrought on these poor cowboys!"

I sighed. If nothing else, my presence here seemed to be highly entertaining to everyone else. No, I shouldn't feel sorry for myself. If I could do anything at all to lighten Abby's spirits, I would do so.

We talked on in the warm sunshine. A light breeze stirred from time to time. Abby told me of her girlhood in Virginia as the youngest daughter of a wealthy plantation owner and of her family's dismay when she married and left with Charles, who had been visiting relatives nearby.

"They told me I would regret marrying 'beneath me,'" she said. "But I've never regretted one instant with Charles. Judith, I hope that when the time is right, you will find someone who will make you as happy as I have been." Her eyes sparkled with mischief. "You realize, of course, that you have only to say the word to have the pick of any of the cowboys on the ranch."

I pretended to consider the matter. "Shorty, perhaps? No, I don't think I'd care to go through life wondering if a skunk was going to creep up on me in my sleep." We both laughed.

When Abby felt she could walk a bit, she showed me around the house. The arrangement was much less complicated than I had thought. The house was made up of four wings forming a hollow square, in the center of which was a spacious courtyard.

Nearly all the rooms in the house opened onto the courtyard, except for a few, including mine, which were located in a sort of annex that projected beyond one corner of the square. The annex itself was connected to the courtyard by means of a covered walkway that separated the north and west wings.

A tall cottonwood tree grew in the center of the courtyard, with a bench encircling it. Bright flowers bloomed near a well, and two sets of hitching rails flanked a large gate set in the east wall.

"How lovely," I breathed. "It's like having your own little world."

"It is peaceful here," Abby agreed. "It started out as a trading post, and they had to build it almost like a fortress for protection. The fur trade started to die out, so it was sold several years ago to an Englishman. He had a substantial amount of money, but, as a younger son, no hope of inheriting property in England. So he bought this place and transformed it from a trading post into a showplace.

"He added onto the original building. I rather imagine he planned to build more on bit by bit and create his own 'ancestral home.' By the time he had finished the annex, he'd grown lonely and bored and went back to England where he could spend his money in a more populous area."

"And then you moved here?"

She nodded. "When we first saw it, it seemed like home. Charles and Jeff were determined to leave Texas so we could have a better life, and it seemed this place was here just waiting for us."

We were interrupted by Vera's call to lunch. Today, I joined Abby for the meal, which she ate in her room. She seemed to have enjoyed the conversation and walk, but she tired so quickly, she explained, that it was easier for all concerned if she could eat and go immediately to bed for a midday rest.

The next few days fell into a pattern. I would spend the morning visiting with Abby, then eat lunch with her and help her to bed. I usually took a brief rest at that time myself, then the rest of afternoon was mine to use as I wished, exploring the immediate area or relaxing on the bench in the courtyard with a good book.

The fellowship with Abby was sweet, and I was grateful that the Lord had given me this oasis of calm in the midst of the upheaval in my life. I wished, though, that Uncle Matthew would hasten his reply. Despite the Bradleys' glad acceptance of my company, I had no wish to be a burden.

It was during my third afternoon on my own that I became acquainted with the Bradley children. I had ventured out the gate and had walked for some distance, reveling in the view and the pure air. Surely, I felt, in such vast surroundings, a person ought to expand in character to match it.

I had made my way back to the house and was passing through the wide gate when something hard was pressed into my back.

My knees went weak. Abby's words came back to me: fortress,

protection. This was still wild country. How could I have forgotten?

A voice behind me piped, "Hands up, and don't try anything."

Piped? Either I had been accosted by a soprano ruffian, or. . .I took a chance and turned my head. I had to drop my eyes to come in contact with those of my assailant, who was holding a stick rifle in the small of my back and trying to maintain a stern expression.

Another small figure moved from behind the gate and stood beside the first. Both wore rough clothing, a miniature replica of the cowboys' garb. Both wore hats several sizes too large pulled down over their eyes and held wooden rifles. And both glowered at me.

The smaller one spoke first. "See, Lizzie, you spoiled it! If you hadn't gone and talked, it would've been fine. She turned just as white as a sheet."

I knelt down in front of them and raised their hat brims so I could look into their faces. "What on earth were you two doing?"

Again, it was the smaller one who broke the silence. "We were bein' outlaws. And if Lizzie here hadn't of opened her mouth, I bet we could have gotten all your money. You were really scared, weren't you?"

"As a matter of fact," I admitted, "I was. How did two youngsters like you learn to be outlaws?"

"Aw, we hang around the bunkhouse a lot," said my young informant. "They tell real good stories, and they don't mind us bein' there, as long as we keep quiet. They even let Lizzie stay around, and she's a girl." He lowered his voice conspiratorially. "Even if she don't dress like one."

At this, Lizzie found her voice. "I don't have to dress any different if I don't want to!" she shouted. "Shorty said I look fine just like I am. He said it didn't matter if I didn't want to wear girl clothes. He said... he said there was a lot of it going around," she ended defiantly.

It was time to change the subject. "All right. I know you're Lizzie. My name is Judith." I looked over at the other aspiring outlaw. "Now, what's your name?"

"That's Willie," Lizzie answered. "He's my little brother. Our last name is Bradley. What's yours?"

"Alder," I said, trying to come to terms with the fact that these little hoodlums belonged to Charles and Abby.

I wondered if Abby was aware of just how wild they had become. I had been under the impression that they were cared for during the day in a part of the house where their noise wouldn't disturb her rest. Apparently they ran loose, unattended. Hanging around the bunkhouse, indeed! I could imagine the kind of stories they were likely to overhear.

This, I realized, could be a way to repay Charles and Abby in part for their kindness in letting me stay. If I could do nothing else, I could at least look after the well-being of their children while I was here.

"Why don't you both come with me," I said, rising. "We'll see about cleaning your hands and faces, and then we'll try to find something for you to eat while you tell me about those outlaws you seem to like so well."

To my surprise, they each took one of my hands and walked along docilely to my room, where I poured water into the basin and scrubbed their hands and faces until they fairly shone.

"Underneath all that dust, you were hiding some very good-looking children," I said, surveying my work with satisfaction. Willie was a miniature of his father, with a naturally cheerful expression not even his assumed scowl could hide. Lizzie had her mother's fair hair, but along with that went the determined Bradley chin I had noticed on her uncle.

They both stood and stared at me. I thought of how their lives must have changed over the past few months, with their mother suddenly unable to care for them and their father busy building up a new ranch. Everyone was so occupied with their own duties that the children were, for the most part, forgotten.

The poor things were trying to adjust to the upheaval without any consistent guidance. They had been passive enough about doing as I had bidden, but it was little wonder that they were reluctant to open up to a stranger.

"How about something to eat?" I asked.

Vera had been in the habit of bringing a late-night snack of cookies and milk to my room, and I had some leftover cookies wrapped in a handkerchief in a dresser drawer. When they saw what I was offering, their faces lit up, and in no time the three of us were munching away at our impromptu tea party.

My heart went out to them. How long had it been since they had had a bit of fun, I wondered. I discounted story hour in the bunkhouse. From my acquaintance with the cowboys, I felt certain that it was not the sort of entertainment the children needed.

Lizzie, having finished her cookies, eyed me steadily. "That's my mama's dress," she announced. I nodded, wondering if she felt I had no right to be wearing it and whether I should explain. "It still smells a little like my mama," she said, and to my surprise, snuggled up next to me. I put my arm around her and blinked to keep back the tears.

"Wouldn't you like to go with me to your room, Lizzie, and pick out a dress for you to wear?" I was totally unprepared for her reaction. "No!" she shouted. "I won't! If I wear a dress, everyone says I'm just like my mama. And I don't want to get sick like she is. I don't!" With that, she burst into sobs and buried her face in my lap. I stroked her fair hair and let her cry. She had to have some way to turn loose of the pain she had been carrying.

Willie looked on with a stoic expression until I tentatively held out a hand to him. Then he, too, snuggled into the circle of my arm and the three of us huddled together in a tight little knot while Lizzie's sobs racked her small body and even Willie sniffled occasionally.

Poor little things! I held them even closer to me. Lizzie couldn't be more than nine years old, and Willie looked to be six or seven. I tried to picture the family as they must have been, with Abby caring for her children and Charles romping with them, before this wasting illness took its toll. Abby was right; she was not the only one to suffer.

I promised myself to bring up the subject gently with her at the first opportunity. She had told me that the children ate their meals in the kitchen and that she seldom saw them until they were brought to her room at night, freshly scrubbed and ready for bed. I was sure she believed they were being properly tended to, for I could not believe for a moment that she would rest easy if she had any idea how much time they spent on their own.

The shadows were growing long by the time the emotional storm had subsided. I washed the children's hands and faces again and sent them along to the kitchen for their supper. I was touched by their reluctance to leave me and promised them we would spend more time together during my stay.

The next day was Saturday, and Abby took a turn for the worse. Charles turned full responsibility for the ranch over to Jeff and spent the day hovering over her. Vera, solemn-faced, rushed to and from her room with supplies and tonics I gathered had been left by the doctors she had mentioned.

I felt utterly useless. I tried to find the children, but was informed they had been taken for a ride in order to spare them the tension of the day. So I found myself empty-handed and restless.

I decided to take a walk. Maybe the exercise would work off some of my own tension. How long had I been here? Was it only four days? And yet these people had become so dear to me that I hated the thought of being separated from them.

I sank down under a spreading cedar tree and prayed, first for Abby's recovery, then for my own situation. Would there ever again be a place where I truly belonged and had a right to stay?

The smells of summer were all around me, the scent of the scrub brush and the dusty ground where I sat. The land rolled away from me, the grasses waving in the gentle wind. Off in the distance I could see groups of cattle, and here and there a rider appeared against the skyline. It was a calm, pastoral scene, belying the worry in the house and the tumult within me.

I stayed under my cedar until most of the afternoon had passed, alternately praying and wondering what the future held in store. When the sun was well down in the sky, I stood, dusted myself off, and turned back toward the house.

Jeff's figure loomed in the open gateway as I approached, and I hurried toward him, fear mounting within me. "Abby," I faltered. "Is she. . . ?"

"She's resting," he said, and I sighed with relief. His mouth curved in one of his slow smiles. "I didn't mean to frighten you. I wondered where you were, and nobody had seen you for some time, so I thought I'd make sure you were all right."

"I wanted to stay out of the way, and I was worried about Abby, so I went for a walk," I said, lowering my eyes to hide my pleasure at his concern.

"It's been rough on you, hasn't it? Have you had any word from your uncle?"

I shook my head and raised my eyes to search his. "Shouldn't I have heard something by now? It seems that a stagecoach would have had time to get there and back."

"That would be cutting it pretty close. And if there were any problems at all, it could delay your message, or his, or both."

"What kind of problems?"

"This is still new country. A lot of things can happen. But I wouldn't be too concerned just yet. Give it a few more days."

He walked with me to the door of my room. "I'll have supper sent to you. What with all the worry over Abby, our routine is a bit off today."

"Of course. Isn't there something I can do? Maybe sit with her tonight?"

He shook his head. "Charles will insist on doing that himself. They're devoted to each other, as I'm sure you've noticed. I just hope this doesn't last too long. He's about done in, what with trying to handle the ranch alone and worrying about her on top of it. I wish you had known her before she got sick."

He seemed lost in thought for a moment, then pulled himself together. "Well, I'll see you tomorrow," he said. He turned as if to leave, then hesitated. "Judith? I know Charles and Abby won't be up to going into town for church in the morning. But if you'd like to go, I'd be happy to drive you."

"All right," I said. "I'd love to go." I entered my room before he could see the foolish grin that spread across my face. It wasn't until I was almost asleep that I realized he had called me by my Christian name for the first time.

Chapter 8

By the next morning, it was clear that Abby was going to rally, and I readied myself for my first church service in weeks. Was it really possible that only a week before I had been rolling along in a wagon with only the Parkers for company?

I hummed a happy little tune as I tried to decide which dress to wear. Truly, there was a great deal to be thankful for on this Lord's Day.

I chose a sprigged muslin with ruffles at the wrists and throat. Vera had thoughtfully provided a number of hairpins, so I was able to dress my hair more elaborately than usual.

I looked in the mirror for a final appraisal and saw a sparkle in my eyes and a pink flush on my cheeks, due, I assured myself, to the excitement of going to a church service. How wonderful it would be to worship in company with other believers and hear the Bible taught by this learned man from the East!

Muffins and coffee were waiting in the kitchen. Everyone was too tired from the strain of the day before to care much about a formal meal.

A glance out the window showed a team and wagon approaching the house, so I gathered up my Bible and a light shawl and hurried outdoors. Jeff sprang down to help me up to the wagon seat and handed me my shawl.

"We'll be all set as soon as our other passengers are ready," he said, smiling up at me. Good heavens! Up to then I had completely forgotten the need for a chaperon. I smiled to cover my confusion and said a silent prayer of thanks that he was gentleman enough to have thought of it as a matter of course. After my experiences on the trail, I knew I would be perfectly safe with him or any of the cowboys, but we were heading for civilization of sorts, where tongues would wag if given half a chance.

I turned at the sound of footsteps and drew a quick breath in astonished delight. Lizzie and Willie stood beside the wagon, scrubbed and dressed in their Sunday best.

Willie looked gentlemanly, if uncomfortable, with his stiff collar and slicked-down hair. And Lizzie was the very picture of an angel with her hair neatly combed and in, wonder of wonders, a dainty ruffled dress. Jeff lifted them into the back of the wagon, where they scooted up behind the seat and looked at me shyly.

"One more and we'll be off," said Jeff. I looked at him in surprise. Neither Abby nor Charles would be in any condition to stir today. Perhaps Vera was coming. A broad smile broke out on Jeff's face and I followed his gaze to see Jake emerge from the bunkhouse and walk our way.

His hair was plastered as close to his head as Willie's, and he wore what must have been his best pair of work clothes. I hoped he hadn't felt it necessary to borrow Shorty's cologne.

His expression, his walk, his every move showed resignation rather than pleasure at the prospect of going to church. I couldn't quite suppress a smile at his hangdog look.

"Hurry up, cowpuncher," called Jeff. "We're ready to roll!"

"So help me, Jeff, I don't see why you needed someone to come along to play nursemaid," Jake muttered, his eyes gloomily fastened on the ground. "Seems to me you ought to be able to handle a couple of half-pints by yourself."

"Why, Jake," Jeff said, all innocence, "I asked for one of you boys to volunteer to come along this morning. Do you mean you aren't here by choice? I really do need you. You see, I have three on my hands, instead of two."

"Three?" Jake looked up at his employer for the first time, then glanced around. His eyes lit on me and his jaw dropped ludicrously. "Excuse me, ma'am," he sputtered. "I surely didn't know any young lady was going or I wouldn't have talked so."

"Good morning, Jake," I said demurely. "I've missed your company."

He peered up at me, squinting, then his eyes grew round in surprise. "Will ya look at that!" he exclaimed. "If it ain't Miss Judith!"

If I had needed any gratification for my feminine vanity, I couldn't have asked for more than Jake's reaction. He climbed silently into the back of the wagon and sat, shaking his head from time to time.

It wasn't until we had driven a mile or so that he began to chuckle softly. The chuckles increased until he was leaning against the side of the wagon, his head thrown back and tears streaming down his cheeks.

"All right," said Jeff. "Better tell us what it is before you hurt something."

Jake pulled a bandanna from his back pocket and mopped at his face. "It's. . .it's seein' Miss Judith up there lookin' like that," he said, gasping for breath. "Won't Shorty be sore when he finds out who I'm goin' to church with?"

"I don't understand," I said. "Why should Shorty be angry?"

"He's the one that slipped me the short straw when we were deciding who was going to 'volunteer'!" And he went off again into gales of laughter.

Jeff looked at me as if wondering how I would react to learning I was the loser's lot. When our eyes met, we both laughed heartily. The children, too, joined in the general merriment, and the slight tension that had been present dissolved.

The drive into town took about three hours in the wagon, and we whiled away a good bit of the time singing hymns. Jeff had a pleasant baritone and started us off on song after song in seemingly endless procession.

I was pleased to find I knew most of the hymns he sang and could join in with him. What Jake's voice lacked in quality, he made up for in enthusiasm on the songs he knew, and on some he didn't. The children, I noted with approval, knew a good many of the hymns. I made a mental note to teach them one or two more before I left.

The settlement was small, not much more than a store, a warehouse, two saloons, and a dozen houses along a wide, dusty street.

Jeff drew the team to a halt in front of the store and checked his watch. "Thirty minutes to spare," he announced with satisfaction. "That gives us a chance to look the place over."

Jake stared wistfully at the nearest saloon. "I don't suppose. . ." he began.

"Not today," Jeff answered. "Today you are coming to church. Take Lizzie and Willie in and find us *all* a place to sit, will you?"

He grinned as he lifted me down from the seat. "This is hardly the way Jake planned to spend his Sunday. He's a good man—one of the best—but he relies too much on his own merit. Hearing a real man of God may be just what he needs to realize that no one can be 'good enough' on his own.

"Tell me," he went on, tucking my hand under his arm, "what kind of miracle have you worked on Lizzie and Willie? They've always had a mischievous streak, but as soon as they heard you were coming to church with me, they were wild to come along. They look positively angelic this morning. Vera tells me it's the first time Lizzie's worn a dress in months."

As I related my meeting with the children, his face sobered as he realized the depth of their feelings about their mother's illness. "Poor kids! I guess we've all been so busy that they've been 'out of sight, out of mind.'" He gave my hand a gentle squeeze. "It looks like your coming has been good for all of us."

I floated into the store where the service was to be held and had to make an effort to respond sensibly to the people I met. I shook hands with people whose names I barely heard and could not remember, until a familiar face loomed before me, and I recognized Mrs. Styles.

"Mr. Bradley," she said archly, "I am pleased to see you here this morning. Is Abby better? I drove out yesterday to visit her, but was turned away most abruptly by one of your hands."

Jeff nodded politely and said, "She seems to be better today, thank you," and was about to walk on to our seats when she stopped him.

"Come now, aren't you going to introduce me to your charming companion? We don't see many fresh young faces around here, you know."

"But I thought you had already met her. This is Miss Judith Alder, Mrs. Styles. She's a guest at the ranch." The smile froze on her face and she peered at me more closely.

"Oh," she said. "Oh!" She withdrew the hand she had extended toward me, turned stiffly and marched to a seat on the front row of chairs.

The encounter brought my feet back to earth with an effective thud. We spotted Jake. He had found seats for all of us on the last row, which suited me fine. I sat between the children, leaving the two men to flank us.

Jake leaned across Lizzie and whispered hopefully, "The place is fillin' up, don't you think? Maybe I ought to slip on out and give other folks a chance to sit down."

Jeff responded with a look that made him sit back in his chair, shoulders slumped. It would have been funny if I hadn't felt so mortified. Mrs. Styles had obviously formed a most unflattering opinion of me. I would have to be careful to behave in an exemplary manner around her.

A hush fell as a middle-aged man stood and led the congregation in singing hymns. I tried to recapture the joy of worship I had anticipated, but the mood wouldn't come.

You're being ridiculous, I scolded myself. *Letting yourself get caught up in romantic notions when you're only going to be here a short while! If you're not careful, Judith Alder, you'll appear to be just what Lucia Styles thinks you are.*

That was enough to settle my thoughts in preparation for the sermon. Wasn't this why we had come—to hear a man of God bring a message from the Word?

I deliberately focused my attention on the man who now stood at the front of the worshippers. He was younger than I had expected, probably around Charles Bradley's age, and the black frock coat he wore accented the pallor of his skin. He had come west, I remembered, for his health.

"Welcome, my friends," he intoned. "As many of you good people know, I am the Reverend Thomas Carver from Philadelphia, Pennsylvania. I have come to this savage land seeking a climate conducive to recovery from a wasting illness and have agreed to preach in your quaint settlement this Sunday. If we find each other satisfactory, I will consider lengthening my stay to help you profit from the knowledge I have acquired."

I felt a stab of disappointment, though I could not pinpoint the cause. His preaching style was different from what I was accustomed to, that was all.

He was quite slender, as might be expected of one who had recently been ill. His face was long and narrow, the features almost delicate. His hair was a very light blond, and his eyebrows and lashes must have been as well, for from my seat I could not distinguish them. He was, I judged, in his early thirties—still a young man, but old enough to have had experience in the pulpit.

I heard the rustle of pages and realized that he had announced the scripture text for his sermon and I had not been paying attention. I peered over Willie's head at Jeff's Bible, trying to see what page he had turned to. Isaiah 61. I hastily turned there myself.

" 'The Spirit of the Lord God is upon me; because the Lord hath anointed me to preach good tidings unto the meek; he hath sent me to bind up the brokenhearted, to proclaim liberty to the captives, and the opening of the prison to them that are bound; To proclaim the acceptable year of the Lord. . .' "

The words lingered in my mind as Reverend Carver stood for a moment, surveying the congregation. He sighed as if disappointed in what he saw, then took a deep breath and began.

"Brethren," he said, "I see unhappy faces here among you. I see faces lined with bitterness and despair. Why? Why are you discouraged? Why do you feel you have failed in some way? Because, my friends, you have succumbed to the philosophy of many that there is no inherent goodness in man."

There was a stirring among those present, whether of interest or antagonism I could not tell. I was having a difficult enough time trying to concentrate on what he was saying rather than on the rise and fall of my emotions.

Really, I chided myself sternly, *whatever is troubling you can wait until after the service. An opportunity for spiritual feeding may not come often in these parts.*

"Certainly there are those who do not treat others as they should, those who are bad neighbors, those who fall into crime. But why are they this way? I tell you, it is not due to any evil within themselves, but to the lack of love given them from parents, friends, society itself!

"Friends, no one ever bothered to look for the good that was in them, to bring it out and nurture it. And how could they love others if they did not love themselves first and foremost? Therein lies the key to the evils in this world. Many have failed to look for the good."

Even my wandering attention was held by this. The sermon went on interminably in the same vein, seeking to point out man's innate goodness.

I wondered if anyone else was bothered by the lack of concern with sin and man's unrighteousness. A quick glance to my left showed Jeff's mouth set in a thin line. I relaxed a little. So it wasn't only my own perception.

It was an effort to stay awake until the end of the service, too much effort for Lizzie and Willie, who slumped against me and slept.

After the final prayer, people rose and milled around, talking quietly. Reverend Carver positioned himself at the door to greet the worshippers as they left. As I tried to wake the children, I couldn't help but notice that while the preacher's comments were enthusiastic, the responses he got were lukewarm at best.

By the time we were ready to leave, there were only a couple of men left in the store putting away the chairs. I took a drowsy Lizzie by the hand and started for the door, wishing there were another exit.

Reverend Carver smiled at Lizzie, who glared at him. He then turned to me. "Ah, Miss Alder, is it not?" he asked with a wonderful display of white teeth. I managed a nod. "Mrs. Styles has told me a great deal about you."

I hope you told her to look for the good, I thought rebelliously.

He went on without bothering to lower his voice. "I believe you were stranded alone on the trail and arrived here under the, ah, protection of a group of trail drivers. Is that correct?"

I looked around frantically, not wanting my experience to be overheard and misinterpreted by the whole town. "As I told Mrs. Styles," I said in a low voice, "they were kindness itself and absolute gentlemen."

Behind me, Jake and Jeff had given up trying to rouse Willie, and Jake was carrying him out. "These are two of the men who helped me," I told the minister, turning gratefully to Jeff, who was by this time at my elbow. "This is Mr. Bradley. I believe you have met his brother."

"Of course, of course. Good morning, Mr. Bradley. I hope you enjoyed the service." I didn't hear Jeff's reply, as I had propelled Lizzie toward the wagon at the first opportunity and now stood leaning against it.

The morning had started out with such promise; now even the brightness of the noonday seemed to have dimmed. Mrs. Styles alone had been bad enough, but knowing that she had spread her version of my arrival made me want to crawl under the blanket on the wagon bed and remain there until we were out of town.

The pastor's inflection had left no doubt in my mind as to the picture that had been painted of me. I thought of the people I had met before the service. My head had been too much in the clouds at the time to take note of their reaction, but now I wondered. Had there been a hidden meaning behind the smiles and friendly words? Suddenly, I couldn't wait to get away.

I hoisted Lizzie to the wagon bed, gave her orders to sit quietly, and scrambled to the seat. If only the men would hurry! I imagined curtains being drawn back furtively to take a look at the questionable newcomer.

To my intense relief, Jake and Jeff came striding toward the wagon at that moment and arranged a comfortable place in the back for Willie, who was snoring gently.

Jeff was just settling onto the seat beside me when a man ran out of the store, waving at us.

"Miss Alder?" he said. "I'm Fred Kilmer. I run the general store. I have a letter here for you, but I didn't realize who you were until Reverend Carver pointed you out."

My cheeks burned as I envisioned the scene, but I reached for the letter with hope rising in my heart. "Thank you," I said as we pulled away.

Joyfully I tore at the envelope. I need not stay here to suffer further humiliation. Soon I would be heading west once more to begin my new life. I read:

> *Dear Judith,*
> *Sorry to hear of your delay, but it may be for the best. There was a fire at the trading post. Burned the place clear to the ground. I don't have the money to rebuild and restock, so I'm off to find greener pastures. Glad to hear you have found a place where they're good to you. Stay put until I send for you. Don't know how soon it will be.*
>
> *Your loving uncle,*
> *Matthew*

I stared at the paper. *"Stay put"?* Tears stung my eyes and blurred the landscape. How could I stay? I could not presume indefinitely on the Bradleys' hospitality. I had no money to pay for my board, either there or in town. And the thought of remaining, to be an object of community scorn, filled me with dread.

The only course that seemed open to me was one I dreaded as much as Mrs. Styles's wagging tongue. I could wire Aunt Phoebe, throw myself on her mercy, and beg for forgiveness and passage back home.

I knew that would end any further hopes of going west to be with Uncle Matthew. My rebellion in doing so once would never be forgotten.

We were over halfway back to the ranch when Jeff spoke. "Have you had bad news?" he asked softly. I handed him the brief letter, which he scanned and handed back.

"I'm sorry," he said. "You've had a hard time of it lately." I nodded, too miserable to speak.

He turned his head toward the back of the wagon. I followed his gaze. Lizzie had curled up next to her brother, and Jake leaned against the wagon's side, head back and eyes closed.

"Do you want to talk about it?"

I struggled to force words past the obstruction in my throat. "I guess the only thing for me to do is to go back to Missouri, to my aunt."

"And try again when your uncle has relocated?"

I shook my head and managed a small laugh. "No. I'm afraid this will be my first and last trip west. Once I go back, my aunt will see to it that I never leave St. Joseph again."

He stared straight ahead. "Will that really be so bad? It isn't civilized out here yet, at least not in the way you're used to."

"But I like what I've seen. There's a wildness here, a bigness that's almost frightening, but I want—wanted—to be a part of it."

"Then why go back?"

"It's the only thing I can do. I have no choice." A warm breeze rustled the grasses and played with loose strands of my hair, but the beauty of the day was lost on me as I stared at the rolling hills through tear-filmed eyes.

When we reached the ranch, Jeff took the children to see their mother and I closeted myself in my room. I lay facedown on the bed, trying to adjust to the idea of returning to a way of life I thought I had left forever.

My brain was numb, unable to deal with the blow I had received. Could I go back again to being the poor relation, tolerated only because of a blood tie? My whole being rebelled at the thought, but what else was there?

The return of the prodigal. That's how Aunt Phoebe would see it. But there would be no joyous welcome, no fatted calf. It would be back to life as usual, dancing attendance on Aunt Phoebe and being the object of disdain among the ladies of her circle. They would have plenty to fuel their imaginations as they tried to figure out what I had really been up to during my absence.

The tidy streets of my aunt's neighborhood would be the same, yards neatly trimmed, picket fences faithfully whitewashed. It was the scene from my growing-up years, constant and unchanging since the day we came to live with Aunt Phoebe.

I closed my eyes wearily. In my mind's eye I could see the vast land outside the courtyard walls. It, too, had remained the same, and for much longer than St. Joseph. But here, there was openness and freedom. The very landscape had a life of its own as it responded to the wind, rain, and sun. One could spend a lifetime here getting acquainted with the country, always discovering something new.

A figure appeared on my imaginary landscape, a figure who turned and looked at me with smiling blue eyes, called out a glad welcome, and waited with open arms for me to come. I shook myself back to reality and noticed how far the sun had moved across the sky. I must have been dozing.

I poured water into the basin and scrubbed at my face. I wanted to stay. But how? Resolve began to stiffen my drooping spine. I didn't know how, not yet. But for once in my life, I would fight for something I wanted.

Pacing the floor of my room, I began to make my plans. Surely I could find a job in town and a place to stay. Since I'd planned to help Uncle Matthew in his trading post, perhaps I could get a job helping Mr. Kilmer at the general store.

The more I mulled over the possibilities, the more enthusiastic I became. Even the thought of Mrs. Styles and her venomous gossip could not dampen my mood. I knew I had done nothing wrong, and it was high time I started holding my head up.

For the first time in days, I felt sure of where my path led. Yes, I would stay, I determined. There would be no slinking off, no whimpering in defeat. This was where my heart lay. This was where I belonged.

I patted my hair into place and headed for the parlor, bursting with the need to tell someone of my plans. I nearly collided with Charles in the doorway. He looked tired, and I remembered how much sleep he must have lost caring for Abby. Perhaps because of that, he was quick in coming to the point.

"Jefferson tells me you're leaving us," he said without preamble.

"Yes, but—"

"Don't do it," he interrupted. He seemed to realize how brusque this sounded and made a visible effort to collect himself. "I mean, don't do it, *please*."

Still bubbling with my newly devised strategy, I didn't see at first what he was getting at. "Charles, I appreciate so much the hospitality you've shown me, but I can't abuse it. That's why I've decided—"

"Have you talked her out of it yet?" This time the interruption came from Jeff, who strode into the center of the room and stood clenching and unclenching his fists.

I stared from one brother to the other, trying to understand. Jeff seemed to sense my bewilderment.

"Charles, do you mean you haven't asked her yet?"

"You haven't given me much opportunity," Charles said mildly.

"Ask me what?" I nearly shouted. "Will someone please tell me what's going on?"

Jeff looked at me, then at his brother, turned on his heel and was gone. I stared openmouthed at Charles.

He smiled and shook his head. "Please forgive us both, Judith. We've both been under a great strain.

"I talked with my children a little while ago. Talked *and* listened for the first time in longer than I care to admit. I had no idea they'd been allowed to go unsupervised all this time.

"That leaves me in a dilemma. My time will be fully taken up for some time. Abby is in no condition to do anything but rest, and I have no people here whose work will allow them to take on the added responsibility for the children.

"Would you consider staying here to care for them, at least for a while? Until we send some cattle to market, all my transactions will be on credit, so I can't offer you more than room and board for the time being. But the children seem to like you a great deal, and you'd be doing us all a great favor—myself, Abby, and Jefferson."

"Jeff?"

"My brother is not ordinarily a highly strung person," he said with a smile. "But you saw him just now. And I've never seen him in as excitable a state as when he told me you were leaving and ordered me to find a way to keep you here."

I looked at him in surprise and he grinned back. "If Abby and I hadn't already decided to ask you to stay, I would have had to create a reason, just to pacify him.

"So what do you think, Judith? Could you put up with us all a little longer? Would you like some time to consider the matter?"

"No! I mean, yes. I mean. . .I'd be very happy to stay on. Thank you." I managed to contain myself until I got back to the privacy of my room, where I spun about with wild abandon. Jeff had demanded that Charles ask me to stay!

I could hardly contain my joy. He wanted me here!

Chapter 9

It was with a light heart that I was able to pen a letter to Aunt Phoebe, telling her of my safe arrival in New Mexico Territory, the unfortunate fire at Uncle Matthew's, and my temporary position at the Bradley's. I was sorely tempted to give her my opinion of her carefully chosen chaperones, but I could so easily picture her deriving a perverse sense of satisfaction from my plight that I focused only on the positive aspects of the situation.

I placed the letter with others that would go out as soon as someone made a trip to town. Knowing Aunt Phoebe, I expected no reply but felt better having discharged that obligation.

The speed with which news traveled among the widely scattered inhabitants of the territory never ceased to amaze me. No sooner had I announced my intention to remain than a trickle of would-be suitors began showing up on the Bradley doorstep.

In the weeks that followed, the trickle became a steady stream. I was puzzled at first, then amused, and finally driven to seek Abby's counsel.

"What have I done to make myself fair game?" I cried in frustration. "Abby, I promise you I have never given any of them an indication that their attentions would be welcome. But just yesterday a total stranger rode in out of nowhere and asked me to *marry* him! When I turned him down, he just shrugged and rode off again. What am I to do?"

Abby pushed herself higher on her pillows and managed a weak chuckle. Her strength seemed to diminish a fraction with each passing day, but her good humor and interest in events at the ranch never wavered. The crisp fall air had brought a tinge of color to her cheeks, and she looked at me now with a hint of the old sparkle dancing in her eyes.

"Why, Judith, what you've done is very serious," she said, attempting to sound stern. "You've become a permanent resident. An attractive, single, *female* resident. It's started every one of those lonely cowboys thinking how good it would be to come home to a wife and a place of his own.

"In a way," she said, laughing softly, "you really can't blame them. I guess they feel there's no harm in trying."

She became suddenly grave. "None of them have tried to force their attentions beyond decent limits, have they?"

"No," I admitted. "I have to give them credit for that. Nearly all of them have given up after the first 'no.' And the rest have gotten it through their heads after two or three tries. . .all except Shorty."

"Shorty! I should have guessed."

"I can't go anywhere or do anything without that man popping up. Just yesterday, the children and I were out walking. I would have sworn there wasn't anyone but the three of us around, but all of a sudden, there he was, all big soulful eyes and deep sighs, come to 'walk with us a ways.' Is this going to go on until I've exhausted every single man in the territory?"

"Well, there is one thing you could do."

"What?" I asked eagerly.

"You could take one of them up on his offer."

"Oh Abby! I thought you were serious."

"I am. You're not planning to stay single all your life, are you?"

"Of course not. It's just that. . .well, the right person hasn't asked me yet."

"I was afraid of that. I don't know why Jeff's dragging his feet so." She laughed at my expression. "Don't worry. You don't make it terribly obvious, if that's what you're afraid of. Sometimes we women are just quicker to read the signs, that's all. Don't forget that I fell in love with a Bradley man myself."

"Maybe it's more one-sided than I thought. Maybe there's someone else?" She averted her eyes, and my heart sank. "Abby, please!

You've got to tell me. There is someone, isn't there?"

"No, dear," she said, meeting my eyes again. "At least, not now. It happened a long time ago, and I hadn't thought of it for some time."

"Please. Tell me anyway."

"I hate to. No," she added hastily, "not for the reason you think. A member of my family was involved, and I suppose I feel responsible.

"It was while we lived in Texas," she continued. "A distant cousin of mine came to visit. I hadn't seen Lorelei since we were children, and she had grown into the most beautiful woman I have ever seen. She had skin like fine porcelain, with dark curls and deep blue eyes, and a way about her that could make you feel you were the only other person on earth.

"Jeff was much younger then and was absolutely captivated by her. It was a whirlwind courtship, and I'd never seen Jeff in such a fever. He had plans to expand the ranch, add stock, build a house. He seemed to be everywhere at once. . ." Her voice trailed off.

"What happened?"

Abby sighed. "She left. Just up and left one day. Charles told me later that she'd laughed at Jeff, told him it was foolish to think she would consent to live in a barren wasteland where she couldn't have the social life she was accustomed to.

"Jeff was devastated. It was his first love, and he'd believed it would last forever, that Lorelei felt as deeply as he did. We were terribly worried about him, but time seemed to heal the wounds, and he has never referred to her again. But now. . ."

"Now?" I prompted.

"I wonder if he's afraid of being hurt again. This country is terribly different from what you've been used to, and he knows you have family in Missouri you can return to if you choose."

"Oh no," I moaned. "If he only realized! I sometimes think that if I had to choose between an Indian raid and Aunt Phoebe, I'd take a chance on the Indians. But even if things had been better back there, it's not home to me anymore. I can't explain it, but I feel that I belong here, that I was made for this place. It's never seemed barren or desolate to me."

"Does Jeff know that?"

"I've barely been able to speak to him the last few weeks. He's spent so much time out on roundup, and when he is at home I seldom see him, except at supper. That's hardly the place to start that kind of conversation, with Charles and the children there, too. It's almost as though—" Sudden panic gripped me. "Abby, you don't think he's changed his mind, do you? That he's avoiding me?"

Abby laughed softly. "I don't think you need to worry about him changing his mind. As to avoiding you, he may need time to come to grips with himself and realize you won't change your mind and leave. Can you be very patient, if need be?"

"I can wait as long as it takes, as long as I know he cares for me!" The heavy weight that had oppressed me lifted, and I felt light, free, and capable of all patience. "Now if I can just convince Shorty that I'm not refusing everyone else to leave the way clear for him!"

We both laughed, and I went off to collect the children for their lessons with a lighter heart than I'd had for many a day.

Both Lizzie and Willie had bright, inquiring minds, and with the help of books I chose from Charles's library, I was trying to channel their curiosity in a more acceptable direction. Although I had no training as a teacher, I was pleased with the progress they were making.

We were sitting on the porch, reading aloud from *Ivanhoe*, when Reverend Carver drove up in a rented buggy. I stood and went to greet him, assuming he had come to call on Abby. It was rather late for that, I thought peevishly, as he had not been to the ranch before in all the time he had been in the territory.

Reverend Carver had been the topic of many a puzzled conversation among us. He had indeed stayed on, "to bring light into our dark corner of the world," as he put it, but his idea of being a shepherd seemed to stop at preaching a lukewarm sermon once a week on the goodness of man and the ills of society.

He turned a deaf ear to complaints that he ignored the sick and ailing of his flock. Attendance at the Sunday services had dropped to a pitifully low level.

Jake and the other cowboys had had their fill early in the minister's tenure. Once, during a time of sharing testimonies, Shorty had stood up and announced that he wished to speak.

"Preacher," he had drawled, "it seems you do a powerful lot of talking about bein' good and kind to one another, and that's all well and good. But me and the boys have been comin' to hear you for three weeks now, and you haven't said anything different from one time to the next. I've never even heard you mention the Good Book.

"Beggin' the pardon of everyone here, but if this is all there is to your brand of religion, I guess the boys and me can save ourselves the trip and talk to each other about how good we all are."

And with that, he, Neil, and two other men stalked out, leaving the congregation and Reverend Carver in stunned silence. Even the Bradleys and I had not attended a service in several weeks. I had spent much time reading my Bible, finding in it the guiding truths Reverend Carver's sermons had lacked. And now, after all these months, he had come to call.

I said a quick "good day" to him and turned to lead him through the house to see Abby. I was anxious to get back to Lizzie and Willie and their reading lesson. To my surprise, he laid his hand on my arm and whispered, "Please, may I speak with you alone?"

Annoyed at the delay, I showed him to a seat in the parlor, hoping Charles, Vera, anyone would come along to take over. His face shone with beads of perspiration, and his hands shook. I wondered if he were becoming ill himself. I was about to offer him a drink of water when he spoke.

"Miss Alder." He cleared his throat nervously. "Judith. I. . .I hardly know how to begin."

It was all I could do to keep from tapping my foot impatiently. This was usually a busy area of the house. Why didn't someone come?

"I find great gratification in my work here," he went on. "But some days the time does lie heavy on my hands, and I begin to think."

I thought to myself that if he would spend more time visiting the sick and tending to other pastoral duties, he would have less of it on his hands.

"A man gets lonely, Judith," he said, and I realized with a sick feeling where this conversation was leading. "He begins to realize his need for a companion, someone to share the lonely times, the bleak moments, as well as the joys of success."

"You hardly paint a happy picture of married life," I said tartly. To my relief, I heard footsteps approaching from the hallway. Rescue was at hand!

"Your smile, your sweet disposition, all lead me to believe you would make an ideal companion."

Hurry, I willed whoever was beyond the door. My heart leaped as it opened and Jeff stood framed in the doorway. He opened his mouth to speak, but at that moment, Reverend Carver flung himself on his knees before me and cried, "Judith, I am asking you to be my wife."

The three of us remained frozen for what seemed an eternity. It was Jeff who finally broke the silence.

"Excuse me," he said. "I seem to be interrupting." He turned on his heel and was gone.

"Jeff, wait!" I cried, utterly ignoring the Reverend Carver, who still knelt on the floor. I ran to the doorway, but Jeff's long strides had already carried him out of sight. I turned in exasperation to find my suitor standing immediately behind me, hands clasped in pleading.

"Judith, please. What is your answer?"

"My answer is no!" It came out sharper than I had intended, but I was too vexed to care.

"I see." He drew himself up with far more dignity than he had shown up to now. "I have tried to bestow upon you the greatest honor a man can give to a woman. You have refused me most abruptly. May I hope that, after you have had time to give the idea due consideration, you may change your mind?"

"Please," I said, fighting to keep my temper in check. "I appreciate your kind proposal, but you must accept my answer as final."

"Very well," he said stiffly. "Then I will not trouble you again." He stopped at the door and turned. "Judith, this was intended as much for your good as for mine. Considering the. . .unorthodox manner of your arrival here, do you think you can ever truly be accepted by the people? Come away with me, and we'll start a new life together."

My temper was slipping its restraints. "You're quite mistaken about my acceptance here. The Bradleys have opened their home freely and have entrusted their children's care to me. Surely they wouldn't do that for anyone whose morals might be suspect.

"Any other notions about my respectability come from the fevered imagination of Lucia Styles. I am not concerned about her malicious gossip, and I beg you not to be either."

His lips tightened and he closed the door behind him with more force than was strictly necessary. I breathed a sigh of relief and ran to look for Jeff. Not finding him in the house, I hurried outdoors toward the corral, where I found Jake leaning against the rail.

"You wouldn't be lookin' for Jeff now, would you?" he asked, a twinkle in his eye.

"Have you seen him, Jake? Where is he?"

"He came stormin' out of the house a few minutes ago, threw a saddle and some gear on his horse, and said he was going to check the stock up on the north range. Said he'd be back in about a week."

"A week!"

"Uh-huh. Kept mutterin' something about women while he was gettin' ready. Any idea what he meant?" he asked, with an air of innocence a child could have seen through.

I was beyond answering. I turned and scanned the horizon. He must have ridden like the wind; the gently rolling hills held no sign of him.

A week to live through before I could see him and explain. A week for him to imagine all sorts of mistaken situations. I forced one foot in front of the other and made my way back to the front porch to finish the interrupted lesson.

"Did the minister come to see Mama?" Lizzie asked.

"Why was he so mad when he left?" Willie wondered. "He jumped in his rig and took off like he was gonna run that horse to death."

"He did seem upset, didn't he?" I murmured. "Let's see, what page were we on?"

"I'll bet he didn't come to see Mama at all," Lizzie said. "He wasn't here long enough for a real visit. And besides, Mama doesn't make people mad like that."

"Here we are," I announced brightly. "Page thirty-eight. Lizzie, I believe it was your turn to read."

"You're right," Willie said, as though I weren't there. "Mama doesn't make anybody mad." He eyed me speculatively. "But *she* does."

"I. . .I what?"

"Make people mad," Willie answered solemnly. "I heard Jake say he never saw any woman in his life that got people stirred up more."

"Willie!" scolded his sister. "You're not supposed to say things like that."

"But it's true, Lizzie! You know it's true. Like when you told Shorty he ought to ask her to marry him—"

"Willie, don't," Lizzie warned.

"—and he did, and she said she wouldn't."

"Willie!" Lizzie shrilled.

"Remember how mad he was before you told him he ought to keep trying and not give up?"

"*Willieee!*" Lizzie screeched, leaping upon her brother and trying to cover his mouth with her hands.

By this time, I had recovered sufficiently to pry them apart, and the three of us stood looking at one another.

"Lizzie," I panted, "you didn't really tell Shorty to. . .to. . ."

"Sure she did," Willie bragged. This time Lizzie silenced him with a look.

"But why?"

"Well," she said reluctantly, "Vera said you looked sad one day, and she thought it was because you were pining for someone. So I thought if you got married, you'd be able to quit pining and be happy."

"I see. Uh, Lizzie, you didn't say this kind of thing to anyone besides Shorty, did you?"

"Well. . ."

"Oh, she told lots of people," put in the helpful Willie. "Lots and lots. *Lots* and *lots* and. . ." Catching sight of both our faces, he trailed off. "We just didn't want you to pine," he mumbled.

"Children," I said, "our lesson is over for today. Go to the kitchen and see what Vera can find for you." They scampered off in relief, and I sagged limply against the porch rail.

Chapter 10

Much to my surprise, the week flew by in spite of Jeff's absence. I had fully expected to "pine," as Lizzie put it, worrying about his frame of mind. Instead, the week was so full of activity that I had little time to dwell on my problem.

Charles had given a steer to an old settler and his wife in the next valley. The man had broken his leg on a hunting trip and had been laid up for weeks, unable to work or hunt. Pride had kept the couple from asking for help, and by the time one of the Double B cowboys noticed their plight, they were subsisting mostly on apples from their orchard.

In gratitude, they had sent over a wagonload of apples, and Vera and I fell heir to the task of putting them up.

We peeled and cored and sliced all week long. Some went in the canning kettle to be added to the glistening rows of jars already lining the pantry shelves. Others, Vera baked into pies.

The smell of their baking brought more than one cowboy to the kitchen, where Vera had them sweep the floor, carry out ashes, or bring in wood for the stove before she served them a generous helping.

"Baking takes extra time," she said, grinning, "but this way we have a lot of chores taken off our hands."

I laughed and agreed that it wasn't a bad trade.

Most of the apples were cored and sliced, and the slices strung to hang over the woodstove to dry. These would keep almost indefinitely and could be taken along by the men when they rode out on the range or be used by Vera for baking as the winter progressed.

Lessons were suspended for the time being; Lizzie and Willie sat on low stools in the kitchen and strung the slices as we cut them. I was touched to see how seriously they took the task, carefully spacing the rounds so they didn't touch and the air could move freely around them.

Willie was impressive, going through his bowl of slices nearly twice as quickly as his sister. I noticed, though, that we didn't hang his strings over the stove any more often. I was about to comment on this when he let out a horrible groan.

I looked to see what was wrong. He had turned a light shade of green and was doubled over, clutching his stomach.

"Willie!" I cried, kneeling beside him. "What's wrong?"

"Oooh, it hurts. It hurts!" was all he could say before he went off into a series of pathetic moans.

Vera felt his forehead. "He's cold and clammy," she told me. "No fever. Help me get him to bed."

Between us, we carried him to his room. By the time Vera was turning down the covers on his bed, beads of perspiration were standing out on his forehead.

We laid him between the sheets, still moaning, and I found I was trembling almost as much as Willie.

"What is it, Vera? Do you know?" Memories of a child back in Missouri whose appendix had ruptured rushed into my mind, and the memory of the tragic consequences chilled me.

"I have an idea," she said. "You go on back and tend to Lizzie. She looked almost as scared as you do."

I marveled at her calm as I ran back to the kitchen where Lizzie sat, white faced. I sat in the big rocker and held out my arms, and she came readily. We took comfort in each other's presence as we rocked silently, waiting. I was debating whether or not to disturb Abby with the news when Vera appeared in the doorway.

"Is it serious? Should we call his parents?"

"How's my brother?" Our words tumbled over one another as we scrambled out of the rocker.

Vera settled herself comfortably in her chair and mopped her forehead before she spoke. "Willie's just fine," she said.

"But his stomach. . . I'm sure he was really in pain. . ."

"Oh, he was in pain, right enough," she agreed as she picked up her paring knife and another bowl of apples.

"Vera!" I cried in exasperation. I was astonished to hear her chuckle.

"Now, didn't you notice how fast Willie strung those apples?"

"Yes, but what—"

"And didn't you think it was peculiar that with all that speed, he had only finished as many strings as Lizzie?"

"Yes, I wondered about it. But what does that have to do with it?"

"That little scamp was eating a slice for every one he strung." She grinned. "He must have popped one in his mouth whenever he figured we weren't looking."

I looked at the strings festooned over the stove. Half of them were Willie's, and to eat that many apples at once. . . "Good heavens! Why, that would. . ."

"Uh-huh. Young Master Willie had a good old-fashioned bellyache."

I laughed in relief. "But you're sure he's going to be all right?"

"Let's just say that nature has taken its course," she said drily. "He'll feel a mite puny the rest of the day, but by morning he'll be looking for new mischief to get into."

"Thank goodness." We settled back into our routine. Lizzie seemed rather subdued, which could have been expected after the scare we had just had. But I had noticed that many of her quiet spells were followed by some type of prank, and I wondered uneasily what we might be in for next.

Vera broke into my reverie. "Have you decided how you'll decorate your box?" she asked.

"What box?"

Her hands flew to her face. "Mercy! Don't tell me I clean forgot to tell you?"

"Tell me what?" I asked, bewildered.

"About the box supper social this week." She sighed. "I must be getting old. I didn't say a word about it, did I?"

"I guess not. I'm still not sure what we're talking about."

"There's to be a get-together in town next Saturday night to raise money for a school. People will be coming in from all over this part of the territory."

"Oh. That sounds nice."

"Honey, haven't you ever *been* to one?"

"No," I admitted. "Are we going to this one?"

"You'd better smile, we're going! All of us except Charles and Abby and the children. And you'll be a little more excited once you hear what it's all about."

"All right." I laughed. "Satisfy my curiosity. You've certainly stirred it up."

Vera took her time removing the core from the apple she was working on. "Well," she began, "all the single ladies cook up the best supper they can and pack it in a box. Then they decorate their boxes real fancy and take them along to the supper.

"When it's time to eat, the men bid on the boxes. The highest bid gets the box, the supper, *and* the company of the lady that fixed it."

"You mean they auction them? But how do they know whose box they're bidding for?"

"It's all supposed to be a secret," she said. "And some of the fellows don't care so much about whose it is as they care about getting a good home-cooked supper and some female companionship while they're eating.

"But the ones who really want to sit with a certain young lady usually have some way of finding out ahead of time." She eyed me slyly. "Might be worth your while."

I shot her a sharp glance. "What is that supposed to mean?"

"Nothing," she replied airily. "Just that when a man and a woman are having trouble getting off on the right foot, a long conversation over a good meal sure can't hurt."

I bit off a tart reply and peeled apples with fervor, hoping Vera would think the flush I could feel on my face was due to the heat of the stove. She wouldn't be fooled for a minute though. She seemed to have a sixth sense when it came to human relationships.

Well, why not take her advice? The way to a man's heart might not really be through his stomach, but it might help to pave the way.

The more I thought about it, the more my spirits rose. Jeff's initial reaction to the scene he had witnessed with Reverend Carver was understandable, but he'd had nearly a week to think about it. Granted, he hadn't heard my refusal, but surely he realized I wouldn't accept.

If he returned on time, he should be home tomorrow. I built up the scene in my mind. I would go to meet him and simply explain what had happened. He would have regained his good humor during his week away, and we would laugh together over the incident.

With the ice thus broken, the box supper two days later would give us the perfect opportunity to iron things out. Maybe reach some kind of understanding. Maybe even. . . I took a firm hold on my soaring imagination before I became positively giddy. There would be a lot of planning to do over the next few days—what dress to wear, what food to prepare—but it would all be worth it in the end. Vera was right, I was sure. It would all work out.

That evening I sat on the porch, watching a harvest moon rise above the hills. Its brightness washed the countryside with a silver glow. It was a pity, I thought, that its beauty would be waning by the night of the social. I consoled myself by thinking of Jeff lying in his bedroll under the stars, staring at the same moon. Was he thinking of me at this moment?

Next morning, I took special pains with my appearance before hurrying to help Vera finish the last batch of apples. Both the children worked with us again, Willie having recovered according to Vera's prediction. I noticed that today he conscientiously strung every slice. It would be quite some time, I suspected, before he was tempted to gorge on apples again.

With the last of the strings hung over the stove, I put the children through their lessons at a rapid pace, and sent them, protesting, to straighten their rooms. I gathered up some mending and stationed myself on the porch, where I could watch the horizon. Today was the day.

The sun was nearly at its peak when a shout from one of the stablehands drew my attention to a rider coming from the north. I leaned against the porch rail to watch, turning over in my mind exactly what I would say. It was silly to have let silence come between us when a few words of explanation could have smoothed the way.

The rider drew closer, and as he neared the bunkhouse, I could see that it was Jeff. Just the sight of him astride his mount made me catch my breath with love and pride. He reined in his horse and swung down from the saddle.

I drew a deep breath and started toward the stable to greet him. Jeff had his hat off now and was mopping his brow. The boy who had come to take his horse looked past me and gestured toward the road. I glanced over my shoulder and saw a buggy coming. It looked like the Styles's.

I nearly laughed out loud. Let Lucia Styles come, disapproving glares and all. This was my moment, my turning point. All the busybodies in the world couldn't take it from me.

Following the gesture, Jeff, too, had seen the buggy, but now his eyes were fixed on me. I stopped under a cottonwood and waited for him, trying to remain calm. He smiled, and there was only warmth and tenderness in his glance. It was just as I had imagined; soon we would be laughing over the incident together.

I stretched out my hands to him. "I'm glad you're back. There's something I want to explain." My hands remained suspended in the air as he stood stock-still in front of me, his eyes riveted on a point somewhere over my shoulder.

Turning to locate the distraction, I found that the buggy had drawn up behind us. It was indeed the Styles's buggy, but alighting from it was the most beautiful creature I had ever seen. Finely chiseled features, raven hair, and a porcelain complexion combined to give an impression of exquisite loveliness and fragility.

She smiled radiantly. "Jefferson, dear. It's been so long."

I wheeled around to face Jeff. He gaped at the newcomer as though seeing a ghost and choked out one word: "Lorelei!"

Chapter 11

I stared at the array of frills spread across my bed. Scraps of fabric and colored paper, bits of lace, ribbons, and buttons of assorted sizes, all donated by Vera to decorate my box. I moved different items around in various combinations, without finding one that suited me. But then, nothing seemed to please me lately.

The entire household had felt the strain of the last two days. Lorelei, it seemed, had heard of Abby's illness through the family grapevine and had taken it upon herself to come out to "care for dear cousin Abby through these last trying days."

My own feeling was that the days hadn't been nearly so trying before Lorelei arrived, but I took care to hold my tongue. She was, after all, a member of the family.

She took up residence in the room next to Abby's to be available whenever she was needed. I couldn't help noticing that Abby's periods of rest came more frequently and lasted longer, and I wondered whether her condition was worsening or if this was her only means of gaining some moments of privacy.

Whatever the case, it gave Lorelei ample time to explore the ranch, in Jeff's company, more often than not. During the children's lessons on the porch, we often saw them strolling arm in arm.

Lizzie and Willie didn't seem to be any happier about her coming than I was. She had made overtures to them both on the day of her arrival but soon retreated under their sullen glares. I chided them for their lack of courtesy, but the rebuke was halfhearted on my part, and they seemed to sense it.

My own conversations with her had been as brief as I could politely manage. I could see that she was curious about me. She approached me shortly before supper on her first evening at the ranch.

"I can't tell you what a relief it is to see that the children are being cared for properly," she said with a bright smile. "That was worrying my poor mother to death. And here they are with a regular. . . governess, would you call yourself? What an asset you must be! Did Charles advertise back east?"

Knowing full well by then that she had met Lucia Styles upon her arrival in Three Forks and had prevailed upon her to drive her to the ranch, I confined my answer to a simple no. She would have already heard the Styles's version of my arrival, and I had no intention of trying to defend myself.

"Jefferson has told me what a help you are with the little dears." She lowered her voice to a confidential tone. "Jefferson and I are old, old friends, you know."

I clenched my teeth and displayed them in what I hoped would be convincing as a smile. Vera came to call us for supper at that moment.

"Well, dear," Lorelei said, "I'll see you after supper, and we'll have a cozy little chat." She looked surprised as I followed her to the dining room. "Oh, do you eat here with the family? Why, how very . . .democratic!" And with a flash of dazzling white teeth, she swirled away to her seat.

Despite the addition of a guest, dinner that night was not a festive event. The children stared steadfastly at their plates. Charles, usually the perfect host, made several attempts at conversation, then trailed off, at a loss for words. Jeff was apparently still in shock from her unexpected arrival and alternated between staring at Lorelei and pushing food aimlessly about on his plate. My appetite, too, had vanished.

Only Lorelei seemed unaware of the lack of conviviality. She chattered on and on about her journey by train and stagecoach, about the relatives in Virginia, and how wonderful it was to be with dear Charles and Abby and Jefferson.

By the time dessert was ready to be served, I pleaded a headache and went to my room.

Things continued in much the same fashion over the next two

days, with Charles struggling to be courteous, Jeff in a daze, and Lorelei either attending Abby or attaching herself to Jeff.

"Like a. . .a leech," I complained bitterly to Vera on the morning of the box supper. Deprived of Abby's counsel, I had turned to Vera with my doubts and frustrations. Knowing that she was well aware of my feelings for Jeff, it had been a relief to unburden myself to her.

"Just when I thought it was all working out, she comes along and everything falls apart."

"Well, for heaven's sake, girl," Vera snapped. "If something's worth having, it's worth fighting for, isn't it? She's with Abby most of the time, isn't she? Get out there when you've got a chance and talk to the man."

"It's not that easy. He's away from the house so much of the day, and when he is around, Lorelei's free and needs him as an escort." I slumped miserably against the kitchen counter. "And what would I say now, anyway? 'Make up your mind, Jeff, and choose between us?' I couldn't do that."

Vera sniffed. "I didn't say it was going to be easy. Nothing worth having ever is. All I know is, if I cared about someone as much as you care about Jeff Bradley, you can bet I'd be willing to put up a fight!"

I had to smile at the thought of Lorelei and me dueling over Jeff in the courtyard. But Vera's talk had its effect. I didn't have to resort to punching and jabbing, but neither did I have to crawl away like a whipped pup, handing Lorelei the victory by default. There were more ways to win a fight than with a clenched fist.

Under Vera's guidance, I soon had an apple pie in the oven, with biscuits to follow. Crispy fried chicken, potatoes, and gravy would complete the meal, which Vera assured me was Jeff's favorite.

Lorelei came to the kitchen in the afternoon while Vera was finishing her own box supper, to fix, as she put it, "some fancy sandwiches for that quaint little social." We watched in astonishment as she cut bread into elaborate shapes and filled the sandwiches with bits of ham.

I had been on the ranch long enough to know what a hard day's work did for a man's appetite. Any one of the cowboys could easily have devoured the entirety of Lorelei's meal without batting an eye and then looked around for the main course. I felt a stab of sympathy for her and hoped that whoever bought her supper would be gentleman enough not to complain too loudly.

Watching Lorelei's lovely form while she worked at the counter, I was assailed by a flood of doubt. I had looked upon her as an interloper, but what if Jeff honestly did prefer her to me? He had loved her once; had he really gotten over it, as Abby thought?

Now the time had come to decorate my box, and I was busy wrestling with my feelings. "All right," I said aloud. "Suppose the worst happens. Do you love him enough to want him to be happy? Enough to be glad to let him go to Lorelei if that's what he truly wants?"

I did, I realized with a mixture of pain and relief. I had done nothing to be ashamed of in loving him. I would do nothing now to embarrass him or hurt him in any way. It was his choice; he would have to make up his own mind.

I picked up a length of red ribbon. A milliner had once shown me how to fashion a rose out of ribbon. Did I still remember how? A fold, a few twists, and while the end result wasn't of professional quality, it was at least recognizable. Jeff and Charles had mentioned once how much they missed the roses that grew at their Texas ranch. I would give him a garden of roses.

I twisted ribbon after ribbon, forming roses of varied sizes and hues, enough to nearly cover the top of my box. I wrapped the box in soft green cloth as the base of my "garden," then carefully fastened the roses to it. Lizzie and Willie burst through the door when I was nearly finished.

"Oh, it's beautiful!" Lizzie cried, and I basked in the warmth of her praise.

"Green, with flowers," muttered Willie to himself, as if committing it to memory.

"We were hoping you had it finished," Lizzie said.

"Yeah," said Willie, " 'cause someone's been asking us what it looked—ow!" He broke off as a well-aimed kick caught him on the shin.

"Well, now you've seen it. But you know," I added virtuously, "that no one is supposed to know who made which box."

"We know," Lizzie agreed cheerfully. "And we wouldn't tell. . .not just anybody, anyway!"

I hugged myself in delight as they left, giggling. *"Not just anybody,"* indeed! I hadn't imagined his feelings for me, after all. Of course Lorelei's coming had stunned him; that was only natural. And it was just as natural that he could not avoid her. After all, she was a guest at the ranch, and Jeff would have to be gracious out of courtesy.

But tonight—tonight when the bidding was going on for the supposedly anonymous suppers—it could hardly be considered neglect of Lorelei to fail to bid on hers. I fastened the last few ribbon roses to the box with tender care. It did look lovely, if I said so myself.

I realized with a shock that I had spent so much time preparing the box that I had left barely enough time to get myself ready.

The dress I had chosen was pale blue with a tight bodice and puffy sleeves. It had seemed too lovely to wear before, even to church, and I wondered about the wisdom of subjecting it to the long wagon ride into town. But I was determined to shine, this night at least.

The dress fit as though it had been made for me, and for the hundredth time I blessed Abby for her generosity. She must have looked stunning in this dress, I reflected, and turned to study myself in the mirror. Excitement and the mounting anticipation had brought a pink flush to my cheeks and an expectant sparkle to my eyes. I smoothed a stray wisp of hair into place and grinned at the girl in the glass.

Vera had found a dark blue cloak for me to use as a wrap, and I was glad of its warmth when I stepped out to the waiting wagon. The rays of the late afternoon sun didn't do a thing to combat the crisp chill. Autumn was definitely in the air.

Vera was waiting just outside the kitchen door. "Here, give me your box before anybody sees it," she said. She set it carefully inside a covered basket next to two other boxes of similar size. One was wrapped in calico, the other in a cloth of delicate blue which had a wide ruffle of lace around the edge and a large velvet bow on the top. It wasn't difficult to decide which box was whose.

"You did a nice job." She smiled approvingly. "The roses were a nice touch." She gave me a sly wink as she closed the basket. I laughed happily, letting the mood of the evening take over.

Shorty and Neil had placed a box at the end of the wagon for us to use as a step and stood ready to assist us as we climbed in. Shorty was wearing his cologne again. The aroma wafted over us as he helped me step to the wagon bed, and I hoped it would not cling to my hair or clothes.

Vera shook off their hands and stepped up herself, carefully balancing the basket as she did so. Neil reached out to take it from her, but she slapped his hand away.

"Keep those hands to yourself," she snapped. "You're just dying to lift that lid and see how those boxes are done up. But you're just going to have to wait your turn like everyone else!"

Shorty hooted at Neil's discomfiture until Vera wheeled toward him and said, "And you, you'll do us all a favor if you'll stay downwind."

I sat on one of the blankets that had been laid over fluffy piles of straw, carefully smoothing my skirts to avoid as many wrinkles as possible. Vera sat opposite, guarding her basket jealously.

A strangling noise from Shorty made us turn. He and Neil were gaping at a vision of loveliness framed in the doorway. Lorelei had a knack for making an entrance a grand event. She had only to stand, as she did now, looking helpless and appealing, and every man in the vicinity would fall all over himself to go to her aid.

Shorty and Neil sprang forward, each trying to be the first to reach her. They collided, bounced apart, and stumbled to her side together.

"Looks like a tie," Vera muttered.

Lorelei appeared to regard it as such, for she favored each contender with one of her brilliant smiles and allowed each of them to tuck one of her dainty hands in the crook of his arm. They led her to the wagon in state, the picture of well-trained footmen, and helped her tenderly into the wagon as though she might break.

"I never saw anything like it," Vera said to me in a low voice. "All she has to do is stand there." We watched, fascinated, as she seated herself upon the straw as though it were a throne. She smiled graciously at her courtiers, dismissing them, and turned to us.

Evidently, Lorelei was not immune to the excitement of the evening, for she seemed as inclined to giggle and chatter as a schoolgirl.

"Isn't this quaint?" she gushed. "It'll be such fun to tell everybody back home about it. Imagine. . .taking a chance on spending the evening with a total stranger!" She shivered in delicious anticipation.

"Appears to me that it's the men who are taking the risk," Vera said drily. "They're buying two pigs in a poke—the company and the meal."

"Why, what an unflattering comparison, Vera dear!" Lorelei laughed gaily.

Vera opened her mouth as if to make a retort, and I was relieved when Jake's sudden arrival interrupted them. "Your driver at your service, ladies," he announced grandly. "And there's no one who'll be driving any lovelier ladies to the supper."

"I'm inclined to agree," said Jeff, stepping out of the doorway.

"Jefferson!" Lorelei exclaimed. "Don't you look fine!" He stood tall and straight in his black frock coat and striped pants.

"Thank you," he said, stepping easily into the wagon and settling himself between us. "May I return the compliment?" While Lorelei fluttered happily, he turned to me and said softly, "You look lovely tonight, Judith." His smile was like a caress. I found myself suddenly unable to speak, but smiled back at him with my heart in my eyes.

Jake stepped nimbly to the seat, shook out the reins with a flourish, and we were off. Neil and Shorty had mounted their horses and rode beside the wagon. The evening's excitement was infectious, and good-natured banter flew back and forth between the wagon and the riders. Even Neil shook off some of his shyness and ventured an occasional comment.

Lorelei dominated the conversation, batting her eyes first at one cowboy, then another, archly accusing all the men of trying to find out which basket belonged to which girl.

Shorty's and Neil's mounts proved unexpectedly susceptible to injury, Neil's bruising its foot on a stone and Shorty's acquiring a limp perceptible only to Shorty himself.

Both tied their horses to the tailgate and climbed into the now crowded wagon. As the only available space was along Vera's side, it placed both of them opposite Lorelei, which seemed to satisfy them admirably.

Vera grumbled and held on to the basket. Jake remarked loudly that there was plenty of room next to him on the seat, but no one seemed to pay any attention.

With Lorelei holding court and the cowboys eagerly competing for her attention, the rest of us were left to amuse ourselves. This suited me well enough; it was pleasant just to sit close to Jeff without having to say anything.

The sun had slipped behind the mountains and there was a chill in the air. I drew my cloak around me and shivered.

"Cold?" Jeff reached around me to tuck a blanket about my shoulders.

At that moment, one of the rear wheels hit a hole, and the wagon lurched violently. I was thrown back against Jeff, whose arm tightened protectively around me. It took a moment to recover my balance sufficiently to right myself. Recovering my composure took longer. Fortunately, everyone else had been similarly thrown about, and no one seemed to notice.

"I'm sorry," I whispered, dismayed to find my breath coming in little gasps.

"I'm not," he said quietly. His smile had faded, and he looked at me intently in the twilight.

We said nothing more during the ride into town, but that moment hung between us like a promise.

Chapter 12

Lights spilled out of the windows of the warehouse and painted yellow squares on the darkened street. Jake let us out at the door and went to find a place to leave the wagon.

We moved through a swirling throng of gaily laughing people, only a few of whom I recognized. I followed Vera as we threaded our way to a long table already covered with decorated boxes. I looked them over quickly, but none resembled my "rose garden." My breath whooshed out in a sigh of relief. There shouldn't be any doubt as to which was mine.

Vera handed her basket to one of the women presiding over the table, and we retired to a corner, out of the crush.

"I had no idea there were this many people to be found around here," I said, panting slightly.

Vera produced a handkerchief from her sleeve and dabbed at her forehead. "They've come for miles in all directions. Anything like this happens so seldom that it brings them right out of the woodwork. Those who aren't in on the auction brought potluck suppers and will donate money, anyway. And the thought of having a school and a good teacher for their youngsters—the bidding ought to go high tonight."

I looked at the children scampering around the room and felt a momentary pang of regret for Lizzie and Willie. How they would have loved playing with them! But no, they needed a quiet evening alone with their parents even more. There had been little enough time for them as a family lately.

A tall, lean man stood up on a platform behind the long table and tried vainly to get the crowd's attention. He called, he whistled, he clapped his hands, but even though I was watching him, I couldn't hear him over the din.

Finally, a husky, square-shouldered fellow motioned him off the platform, mounted it himself, and let out a screeching war whoop. The effect was almost miraculous. All eyes turned toward the man, who bowed, stepped down with a grin, and pushed the tall man back up again. "They're all yours, Sam," he announced.

"All right, folks," said the one called Sam. "It's about time we got started. Ladies, please have a seat on the benches over there along the wall. Gentlemen, you line up here on this side so you can all see what you'll be bidding on. I'm your auctioneer for the evening, and I hope you men all brought good appetites and full wallets so we can raise plenty of money for the new school!"

A cheer rose and died away as we all moved to find our places. I had begun to feel guilty about leaving Lorelei to her own devices, but as we made our way toward the benches lining the far wall, I saw her talking animatedly to a group of young men. Even here, she was the undisputed belle of the ball.

Her admirers escorted her to one of the benches and left, reluctantly, I thought. I sat between her and Vera and scanned the group of men opposite. Jeff leaned comfortably against the wall. His eyes met mine and a smile lit his face.

"Isn't this exciting?" Lorelei whispered delightedly. I nodded, in complete agreement with her for once.

"Ladies and gentlemen," intoned the auctioneer, "the auction will now begin!" He held up a box covered with yellow paper cutouts of the moon and stars. "What am I bid for this box, which promises to contain a heavenly feast?"

A ripple of nervous laughter swept the room, but no one seemed inclined to open the bidding.

"Come, come," the auctioneer chided. "No need to be shy, folks. Let's start the bidding at twenty-five cents. Who'll be first?"

A hand went up across the room. "That's more like it! Now do I hear thirty cents? Thirty cents for the new schoolhouse?"

"I'll bid thirty."

"Thirty-five."

The bidding began to grow more spirited, and a final bid of fifty-five cents brought the auctioneer's gavel crashing down on the table.

"Sold!" he cried. "To Eb Winters for fifty-five cents. Step right up, Eb. Claim your dinner and your partner."

Eb Winters, a tall gangly youth who looked to be barely out of his teens moved forward, grinning sheepishly. He handed over his money amid good-natured catcalls, took his box, and turned to look hopefully for his dinner partner.

A pleasant-faced woman of about fifty stepped out of the crowd and went to join him. Eb made an obvious effort to control his disappointment and escorted his companion to a table with dignity.

I began to wonder just how enjoyable the evening would be for most of the participants. My concern must have shown on my face, for Vera patted me on the knee and said, "Don't worry, honey. She's one of the best cooks around. By the time he eats his fill, and she gets finished mothering him, he'll feel like he got more than his money's worth."

Sure enough, Eb was tucking into his supper as though he hadn't eaten for a month. His partner watched with pleasure, smiling maternally and urging him to take even more. Looking at it from Vera's point of view, it made sense. In fact, judging from the crowd's reaction, a good deal of the fun was in the unlikely matches that occurred.

More of the tables were filling up as the boxes went to their various buyers. I became interested in watching the reactions of the girls and women around me as the tension mounted as to whose box would be offered next.

The auctioneer held aloft a box wrapped only in brown paper, with birds drawn on it. It was easy enough to see that it belonged to a young girl sitting back near the wall by the wave of crimson that spread over her face. The bidding started slowly, to the girl's obvious embarrassment.

A flurry of activity on the other side of the room caught my eye.

A boy of about the same age as the girl was sidling along the wall, stopping first at one man, then the next. Some of the men slipped something from their pockets into the boy's hand, while others shook their heads. The boy reached the end of the line and hurriedly examined his collection.

"Forty cents," said the auctioneer. "Are there no more bids? Going once. . .going twice. . ."

"I bid seventy-eight cents!" cried the boy. The auctioneer swept his gavel down, and the girl, still blushing, walked away with her hero.

There were now no more than half a dozen suppers on the auction table, Vera's, Lorelei's, and mine among them. The men left waiting to bid began to take special notice of the boxes being presented.

Once Jeff offered a bid on one of the suppers, and my heart stopped. Again it was Vera who reassured me. "See the 'RT' down in the corner? Everybody knows that's Rose Taylor's box and that she's sweet on Bill Carson," she said. "Bill doesn't want anyone else to have her, but he's one of the biggest skinflints you ever saw. Jeff just wanted to make him pay what the supper's worth, that's all."

As usual, Vera was right. After giving Jeff a baleful look, a glowering man with shaggy black hair made the final bid and led Rose away.

Vera's box was the next to go. She was calmer than I was as we watched the bidding mount. I wanted to cry out with pleasure when the gavel rang out on the final bid of a dollar. She squeezed my hand and gave me an encouraging wink. "It won't be long now," she whispered as she left.

And it wasn't. In no time at all, only two boxes remained—my garden of roses, and Lorelei's lace-trimmed confection. I was glad now that most of the room was engaged in eating; the strain of waiting was bad enough without being the center of the whole group's attention.

Lorelei wore the look of a contented, cream-fed cat. She was actually enjoying the suspense, I realized. The whole thing couldn't be over soon enough for me.

The auctioneer paused dramatically and made a show of deciding which box to pick up next. His hand moved from one to the other and back again before finally settling on mine.

He held the box under his nose and inhaled deeply. "Aaah," he sighed. "Gentlemen, I won't tell you what is in here, but I guarantee that if it tastes as delectable as it smells, it contains a meal fit for a king!" I felt pleased despite my nervousness, but I wished he would get on with it. I was interested in only one particular bidder.

My eyes sought out Jeff. He was lounging casually against the wall, a slight smile on his face. I was glad that he, at least, could relax, but did wish he would show a little more enthusiasm.

"Men," cried the auctioneer, "if you're hungry, you'd better wake up and bid. This is almost your last chance. Let's hear an opening bid."

"Twenty-five cents."

"Thirty."

"I'll go thirty-five."

Something was hurting my arm. It was Lorelei, gripping it tightly with both hands. "Who do you think it will be?" She looked unaccountably anxious.

"The highest bidder, I suppose," I replied, trying to keep my voice steady. I laced my fingers tightly together and willed my hands to lay calmly in my lap, hoping no one would notice the white knuckles that betrayed my nervousness.

Now that the moment had come, I was assailed by sudden fears. What if something went wrong? But how could it, barring fire, flood, or imminent collapse of the roof? My lungs ached for air, and I realized I had been holding my breath.

"Forty-five cents," called out a cowboy.

"Sixty!" I recognized the voice as Shorty's. I started, then smiled shakily as I remembered Jeff's ploy with Bill Carson. Jeff would want to make a nice contribution to the school fund—evidently he was using Shorty to drive the price up.

"Seventy-five." I breathed a sigh of relief. Jeff was joining the bidding at last.

"Eighty-five," sang out the cowboy, getting into the spirit of things.

"One dollar," called Jeff, grinning.

Shorty looked irritated. He was playing his part well. He felt in one pocket, frowned, and explored the depths of the other. His face cleared. "I bid two dollars," he announced. We had everyone's attention now. A jump of a dollar in the bidding was unheard of.

"Two fifty," Jeff said.

The cowboy sat down resignedly. Silence fell, and the auctioneer raised his gavel. "Two fifty," he announced. "I have two fifty. Will anybody make it three?" He paused hopefully, scanning the men's faces. "Going once. . .going twice. . ."

"Three dollars!" shouted Shorty, his face as red as mine felt.

"Three dollars," echoed the auctioneer. Silence again.

"Going once. . ."

"Hurry, Jeff," I breathed.

"Going twice. . ."

"Please. Just get it over." I fidgeted, exasperated. This charade had gone on more than long enough to suit me.

"Sold!" The gavel rang out on the table. "Folks, let's hear it for Shorty Nelson, the highest bidder so far tonight!" Enthusiastic applause rocked the room. Lorelei gave my arm another squeeze.

Shorty swaggered to the table and counted out his money with a flourish. I sat in stunned disbelief. Could Jeff possibly have run out of money? He stood watching, with a broad grin stretched across his face. He didn't look at all like a man disappointed.

I rose woodenly and somehow got to Shorty's side. I didn't dare risk another look at Jeff.

How Shorty managed to get himself, the three-dollar supper, and me to a small table in a corner of the room, I never knew. The whole evening seemed like a bad dream. I had to make a determined effort in order to be aware of anything at all.

It struck me then that Shorty was fumbling with the wrapping on the box and I roused myself to help him. It was hardly fair to him to be penalized for making such a gallant gesture. Three dollars, I knew, was the equivalent of several days' wages to the cowboys—hardly a sum to be dismissed lightly.

My fingers moved mechanically, trying to disturb the ribbon roses as little as possible. The room began to come back in focus again, and I realized that Lorelei's box, the last of the evening, was being bid on.

Evidently the remaining group of hungry men was being spurred to new heights both by Shorty's high bid and by the realization that Lorelei and the last box must go together. Pockets were being turned out, money hastily counted, and enthusiasm was at a fever pitch.

"A dollar seventy-five." Apparently the bidding had been going on for some time before I had come out of my stupor.

"Two fifty." Jeff spoke clearly.

"Two seventy-five." I looked at Jeff, tall and remote across the room. He had stopped at two fifty before. Would he do it again?

"Two eighty." To my relief, the voice was not Jeff's. The momentum of the bidding was slowing down.

The auctioneer scanned the men as if to draw out any more prospective buyers.

"How about two ninety?" he called. "Do I hear two ninety?"

"Three dollars and fifty cents." Every head swiveled to see from whom the bid had come, but I didn't need to look. I knew that voice well enough.

I watched Jeff pay for his supper after the auctioneer's gavel had descended for the last time. Lorelei stood and swept toward him, grace and elegance in every line of her bearing. I could picture her moving the same way down a curving staircase at a lavish ball. She would always be queen of whatever group she chose to rule.

They did make a handsome couple. It wasn't hard to see how any man could lose his heart to Lorelei. I just wished it hadn't been the one man to whom my heart would always belong.

Pull yourself together, I reminded myself. *If you love him, love him enough to let go. Remember?*

"Anything wrong, Miss Judith? You're not feeling sick or anything?" Shorty still beamed triumphantly, but a touch of concern crept into his voice.

I forced a smile, although my face felt as though it would shatter. "I'm sorry, Shorty. I guess I was just woolgathering."

A smile of relief brightened his face still more, and I felt ashamed of myself. I hastened to take two plates from the box and fill one of them with pieces of fried chicken, fluffy mashed potatoes, biscuits, and gravy. I wouldn't have thought Shorty's face could have gotten any brighter, but now he fairly glowed.

I took smaller portions for myself and bowed my head to say grace. Shorty looked at me quizzically for a moment after my amen, then began tucking into the food. He concentrated solely on eating for several minutes, and when he finally stopped to catch his breath, his face wore an expression of pure satisfaction.

"No lady's cooked a supper just for me since my ma died when I was fifteen."

"I'm glad you like it." And to my surprise, I found that I meant it. To keep the conversation going I added, "That was quite a bid you made."

He grinned, then his face darkened. "I thought for a moment ol' Jeff was going to bid me clear out of the running, but he stopped just in time."

That was an area I didn't care to explore. "Tell me about your mother," I ventured.

I had found the right tactic for keeping the talk away from dangerous subjects. Shorty told story after story about growing up as the son of a sharecropper in Arkansas. His father had died when he was ten, and he and his mother had barely managed to keep going by taking in laundry and doing odd jobs. When she passed away five years later, he decided to head west.

I felt an unexpected softening toward Shorty. I could understand his feelings on the loss of his parents, and the West had seemed to me, too, the door to a brighter future. The realization that we had so much in common brought me up short, and I looked at him with new eyes. When he wasn't devising practical jokes or begging me to marry him, Shorty could actually be pleasant company.

When he saw the apple pie, he set to with relish, polishing off all but the narrow slice I had cut for myself. Remembering Willie's experience, I hoped Shorty wouldn't fall prey to the same malady.

He leaned back in his chair and sighed blissfully. I returned the empty dishes to the box and wondered what came next. I steeled myself and glanced covertly at the table where Jeff sat with Lorelei. They were smiling and chatting merrily, and Jeff was devouring her little sandwiches with every bit as much enjoyment as Shorty had shown with my meal.

People around us were beginning to stir, clearing away the remains of their suppers and shoving chairs and benches back up against the tables. Evidently the evening was over. I dreaded the long drive home.

I swept the last of the crumbs off the table and brushed them into the box. Shorty looked up at me and said, "You know, I really didn't think it would be like this, me actually getting to eat with you and all. I guess I've been pretty hard to be around. Can we kind of. . .start over, do you think?"

I sighed. "Shorty, I just don't know. Right now, I need some time. But. . .I would like for us to be friends, if that's all right."

"Well," he said, pushing away from the table and helping me with my cloak, "it's better than nothing." He grinned and held out his arm.

The crowd had thinned out by the time we made our way to the door. Outside, Jake had drawn the wagon up. Shorty boosted me easily to the wagon bed and said, "Thanks for tonight."

"Thank you for buying my supper," I managed. "And thank you for being my friend." He nodded and gave me a cheerful wink, then went to mount his horse, which had apparently recovered from its limp.

A wave of weariness and misery engulfed me, and I was grateful to be able to settle myself in a front corner before the others got aboard. I pulled the hood of my cloak up so that it shaded my face.

The rest of the party came out on a wave of Lorelei's prattle. I was too tired and heartsick to rouse myself to greet them, even when Vera laid a solicitous hand on my shoulder.

Neil joined Shorty on horseback, which left only the four of us and Jake in the wagon.

Once, Lorelei directed a remark to me, but before I could make the effort to reply, Vera intervened.

"She's asleep," she snapped, in the manner of a hen defending her only chick. "Just keep your voices down and leave her be."

All I remember of the endless ride home was that we seemed to float on a stream of Lorelei's constant chatter. Even when I didn't catch her words, her tone indicated that she was immensely pleased with herself.

After what seemed an eternity, we pulled up before the ranch house. Charles had left lamps burning low for us, and I was glad as I stumbled to my room that I didn't have to carry a candle.

I threw the cloak and the lovely blue dress over the back of my chair, flung myself across the bed, and slept.

Chapter 13

The following days went by in a blur. My senses were numbed by my emotional upheaval, and I was content for the time being to go along in that unfeeling state. I knew that at some point in the near future I would have to face the prospect of my future and make plans. But for now a sort of protective cocoon enveloped me, and I welcomed it.

Avoiding the other adults on the ranch became an obsession. The children made a good excuse, and I took them on long walks on the pretext of getting in as much exercise as possible before the snow fell.

Lorelei unknowingly aided me by monopolizing as much of Jeff's time as possible. "I guess I'm just not cut out for full-time nursing," she declared. "If I spend too much more time in that stuffy little room, I'll be laid as low as Abby. You don't mind giving me a little break now and then to get fresh air, do you?"

Actually, I didn't. Vera agreed to keep Lizzie and Willie under her watchful eye while I was with Abby, so I was able to spend nearly all my time either alone with the children or in the sickroom. Abby slept for a good part of each day, which left me free to brood. I found myself with more time to do this as Lorelei discovered an increasing need for fresh air.

"That woman is acting like she owns the place," reported Vera, setting my lunch tray down in Abby's room with a muffled thump. "She actually had the gall to ask me if she could rearrange some of the furniture in the parlor!"

I knew her words were intended to rouse me to action, but I had tried Vera's philosophy of "stand up and fight" and had been defeated soundly. Right now, all I wanted was to lick my wounds in peace.

Charles came to Abby's door every evening and said he would relieve me for supper, but I always insisted he go instead. I was grateful for the excuse not to have to face Jeff or watch Lorelei's possessiveness. It was cowardly, I knew, but it was hard to care about that or anything else from within my protective cocoon.

But little by little, small things began to work their way through unsuspected chinks in my carefully constructed armor, fanning to life sparks of feeling I thought would never surface again.

Lizzie and Willie dogged my steps every time I set foot outside their mother's room. They had been models of good behavior ever since the night of the box supper social, and it was evidence of my numbed state of mind that that alone didn't send me flying into a panic.

During one of our long walks, we stopped to rest in the shelter of an enormous cedar. The children arranged themselves on either side of me, each holding one of my hands. We sat like that, listening to the wind stirring the branches, until I felt their small bodies slump against me. I eased them down so that their heads could rest in my lap.

Lizzie stirred and reached for my hand again. Taking it, she pressed it against her cheek. A lump formed in my throat. Willie slept contentedly, a soft snore escaping his lips from time to time. Lizzie, however, whimpered repeatedly and squirmed in her sleep, squeezing my hand as though for reassurance.

The lump in my throat grew until it reached the bursting point, and by the time both children's eyelids flickered open, slow tears were coursing down my cheeks. Uncharacteristically, they didn't say a word all the way back to the house.

I left them with Vera and fled to the sanctuary of Abby's room, thrusting an astonished Lorelei out into the hallway. I sat straight in the bedside chair, lips pressed together, hands clasped in my lap, feet arranged just so, as if by holding my body in rigid alignment I could calm the tumult that raged within.

"Abby," I whispered to the sleeping form through lips all too inclined to tremble, "I wish you could hear me. I thought things would be so different by now. I'm so confused. Jeff and Lorelei are together all the time now, and ever since the social, he's seemed like a total stranger.

"Right up until that night, I was sure there was something wonderful between us, but I guess I was wrong. Maybe he never really did get over Lorelei, after all. I turned it over to the Lord because I. . .I love Jeff and I want him to be happy. I thought that would solve everything—but then, why am I so miserable?"

I put my face in my hands and wept, trying to stifle the sound so that Abby wouldn't be disturbed. If only she were well again! I needed her counsel and friendship now more than ever.

A gentle touch on my knee made me bring my head upright with a start. To my surprise, I found myself staring into Abby's calm gray eyes.

"What is it?" she asked gently.

"Oh Abby!" I cried. "I didn't mean to wake you."

"Why are you crying, dear? Can I help?"

"It's. . .it's not important," I answered, trying to keep my voice level. Much as I longed to share everything with her, the burden of my problems was the last thing she needed to bear.

"But, Mama dear, you seemed worried over something."

I stared uncomprehendingly as the impact of her words sank into my consciousness.

"Mama?" I repeated blankly.

"Is it about Charles? I know you think I'm making the wrong choice in marrying him, but I love him, Mama, truly I do. And I know he'll make a kind and wonderful husband."

The gray eyes held mine steadily, but there was no doubt that the face she saw was from another place and time.

I drew the covers up over her gently, patted her hand, and murmured sounds that were meant to be comforting. I withdrew from the room, closed the door softly, and bolted down the hall in search of Charles, Jeff, Vera, anyone who could dispel this nightmare. My own troubles were, for the moment, firmly thrust aside.

Worried days and wakeful nights followed each other in a seemingly endless procession. Abby went from delirium to lucidity and back again while we all performed what tasks we could for her comfort and chafed at our helplessness to do anything of significance.

Vera, Lorelei, and I took turns watching at her bedside during the day, while Charles took the night watches himself. Consequently, Jeff shouldered full responsibility for the ranch. He was away from the house all day, except for supper, the one time we all gathered for a meal.

I alternated between helping Vera in the kitchen and minding the children when I was not on duty in the sickroom.

"What do you think?" Vera asked me as we peeled potatoes one morning. We tried to keep enough food available during the day so that any of us could eat whenever we had a free moment.

"About Abby?" I asked.

She nodded, her brow furrowed with worry. "I thought she looked like she'd gained a little this morning, didn't you?" She looked at me hopefully.

"I honestly don't know what to think," I replied cautiously. "Sometimes she seems as if she's almost back to normal. Then she starts talking like she's a girl in Virginia again."

"I know." Vera sighed. "I'm so afraid for Charles and those little ones." She paused in her work to wipe the back of her hand across one cheek.

"Isn't there anything we can do? There must be something! It's unbearable to sit by and watch her waste away like this."

Vera shook her head wearily. "There's not a thing more that any of us can do. . .except pray."

"I've been praying for her almost constantly. We all have."

"Then I guess we'll just have to leave it in His hands, won't we?"

I nodded. A feeling that a turning point must soon be reached pervaded the house, and the resulting tension spread over us like a pall.

Everyone felt the strain, but I ached especially for the children, who were denied even the satisfaction of performing little duties for their mother. Charles had ordered that they be allowed in the sickroom only when Abby was asleep. I knew they missed her company, but had to agree that they needed to be protected from the shock of realizing that their own mother didn't always recognize them.

The nightly gathering at the supper table was primarily for their benefit, to preserve a sense of normalcy, but it served to give the rest of us an anchor as well. I had resumed eating with the family, finding that the sense of unity gave us all added strength.

It was at the dinner table one evening that Jeff had a piece of astonishing news. "I had a long visit with the Reverend Carver today," he said, helping himself to slices of roast beef.

I winced and fastened my eyes on my plate. I hadn't seen the pastor since the day of his proposal, nor did I care to.

"And what did the good reverend have to say?" asked Charles, with a sarcasm I knew would not have been present if not for his anxiety.

Jeff took a moment to swallow his food. "I think I've discovered the reason his sermons have seemed so far off the mark. The man doesn't know the Christ he preaches."

I stared at Jeff in spite of myself.

"Do you mean he's here under false pretenses?" asked Charles. "He isn't even a Christian?"

"I should have said he *didn't* know Christ," Jeff replied. "He met the Lord this afternoon."

"I don't understand," put in Lorelei. "How could he be a minister and not be a Christian?"

Jeff looked at her thoughtfully before replying. "I had business in town this morning," he said, "and as I was about to head back home, I bumped into him on the street. He asked me about Abby, and I told him she wasn't doing well at all."

"As he'd know if he ever bothered to call out here." Charles snorted in disgust.

"Yes, we touched on that topic," Jeff said with a crooked grin. "I told him that it was hard to see her this way, that if it weren't for knowing the Lord, it would be more than any of us could stand.

"And do you know what he did?" He shook his head, remembering. "He coughed and spluttered and said, 'Yes, I'm sure Mrs. Bradley has led an exemplary life. And if her days should be drawing to a close, her works will precede her and open the way to paradise.'"

"He actually said *that*?" I gasped. Jeff didn't even glance in my direction.

"He did. So I sat him down in front of the store and asked him just exactly what he did believe."

"I'll bet it has something to do with 'the inherent goodness of man,'" Charles quipped.

"That, and a lot besides," Jeff said. "It seems his grandfather and two uncles are ministers at churches back east. When it came time for him to decide on his life's work, he just figured he'd follow in the family tradition."

"And what's wrong with that?" Lorelei challenged. "It's a noble and respectable calling."

"Yes," Jeff answered slowly, "if it's the Lord who's doing the calling. But Carver never saw it that way. He just looked on it as a job like any other.

"Apparently he got in with some progressive-thinking church that thought his brand of religion was fine. Then when his health failed, he decided he'd spread the light of all his knowledge to the poor, backward souls in the west while he recuperated. He never could understand why he got such a cool reception here."

"Until today?" Charles prompted.

"That's right. We took a long walk through the Bible he was carrying, and he found out that man has no inherent goodness and that our works don't mean a thing if they're not based on faith in Jesus Christ as Savior and Lord."

"You mean he was converted right then and there?"

"Right where we sat. Once he got past the idea that he was able to make himself good enough for heaven, he asked me, 'Then how can I be saved?' Just like the Philippian jailer," he chuckled.

"It was wonderful to see. He bowed his head and repented and asked the Lord to save him. He's a new man in Christ!"

"That is wonderful," Charles agreed. "Will he stay on and preach, then?"

"No." Jeff shook his head. "He said he thought he'd spend some time in study to see what he really is supposed to be saying. I think that in time the Lord will have a fine spokesman in him."

"What does 'repent' mean?" Lizzie asked. I jumped a little. The children had sat so quietly through supper that I had almost forgotten their presence.

"What does it mean?" she repeated, wide-eyed.

"Well, honey," said Charles, "it's kind of like when a man realizes he's been going down the wrong trail and he needs to turn around and go back the right way. It's when you decide to turn back from going your own way and go God's way instead. Understand?" She nodded, and Charles rose from his seat and gave her a warm hug.

We all prepared to go our separate ways—Charles to sit with Abby, Jeff to a final check of the ranch for the night, me to see the children to bed, and Lorelei to her beauty sleep. I dipped a corner of Willie's napkin in his water tumbler and was using it to scrub his face when I heard a cry behind me. Lizzie had laid her head down on the white tablecloth and was sobbing wildly.

Charles and Lorelei had already gone. Jeff looked at me with as much astonishment as I felt.

"What is it, Lizzie?" I asked, giving Willie's cheek a final rub.

Her sobs turned to wails and I hurried to quiet her.

"I. . .I. . .I repent!" she choked out.

"Of what, honey?" I stroked her hair.

"I lied to Uncle Jeff, and I knew it was wrong, and I want to repent!"

"Lied to me?" Jeff knelt beside her, eyes full of concern. "What about?"

Lizzie sat up, her face swollen and tear streaked. I handed her one of the napkins and she blew her nose thoroughly. Her breath came in quick little gasps as she turned to her uncle.

"It was the day of the box supper social," she gulped. "Remember when you asked Willie and me to find out what Miss Judith's box looked like so you could bid on it?"

Jeff nodded. I stirred uneasily, thinking that this was a line of thought neither of us would wish to pursue.

"I remember," he said. His voice betrayed nothing.

"And remember I told you she said that her box and her dress would match?"

I drew a quick breath, remembering my blue dress and Lorelei's blue box.

He nodded solemnly.

"Well—" she faltered, "I lied. I knew her box was the green one with the pretty flowers."

Jeff glanced up at me. Our eyes met and held, but neither of us spoke.

He looked Lizzie squarely in the eye. "Then why? Why tell me something that wasn't true?"

Her shoulders shook as the sobs took hold of her again. "I thought it would be funny," she said. "A good joke. But it wasn't funny at all. I never thought about you getting that old Lorelei's box by mistake, and now she says she's going to marry you, and Mama's so sick, and, oh, Uncle Jeff, everything's going wrong!"

She threw her arms around his neck and he held her close. "It's all right," he said, rocking her in his arms. "Everybody does wrong sometimes. But now you've told me about it, and I forgive you. So it's over. You don't need to worry about it anymore."

Instead of being soothed by this, Lizzie's agitation increased and she clung to him all the more tightly. "But I want to be clean," she wailed. "I want to be all new, like Reverend Carver."

A joyful smile broke out on Jeff's face. "Well, Lizzie," he said, "that's a real easy thing to arrange. Let's go find your father." And he carried her out of the room in search of Charles.

I let out a pent-up sigh of relief. It looked as though two new children would enter the Kingdom of God that day. I turned to the wide-eyed Willie and herded him off to bed.

I lay awake for a long time, thinking over Lizzie's confession. How different things would be right now if she had not unwittingly fabricated a story that would play right into Lorelei's hands!

Or would they? I wondered.

On the one hand, Jeff had not denied Lizzie's statement that he had intended to buy my box at the social. I had not, then, been mistaken about the warmth of his manner toward me on the way to town that night.

But, I reflected, there had been opportunity since then to explain the mix-up if he had wanted to. Had the mistake turned out to be a favorable one for him, rekindling his feelings for Lorelei? If what Lizzie had quoted Lorelei as saying was true, it would certainly seem that the social had acted as the catalyst that brought them back together.

I tossed and turned, pummeling my pillow into a myriad of shapes as I examined the pieces of this puzzle and tried to fit them into a meaningful pattern. Finally admitting defeat, I breathed, "Lord, it's all Yours. I can't begin to understand what's happened." And with that I promptly fell asleep.

Chapter 14

I awoke well before daybreak, feeling fully rested and ready for action. No matter how hard I tried, I could not go back to sleep, nor could I convince myself to burrow under the covers against the chill morning air.

I dressed quickly and crept down the hall to the kitchen. Even Vera wasn't up and about yet. I pulled one of her shawls from a peg near the door and stepped outside.

If I hadn't been fully awake, it would have taken only that first moment of contact with the frosty air to make me so. Even the warm shawl couldn't stop the icy fingers from raising gooseflesh along my arms.

I paced up and down the porch and filled my lungs with the invigorating air. A light frost crunched beneath my feet, and I reveled in having this moment to myself.

The indigo hue of the sky was fading to gray. One by one, the stars were lost to sight. It was impossible, I felt, to witness all this beauty without being aware of the One who made it. I brought my concerns to Him one by one: Abby's failing health; Lizzie and her new life in Christ; Jeff, Lorelei, and their engagement; and direction for my own future. In this time alone with God, even that uncertainty paled in significance.

Back inside, I had biscuits mixed and in the oven by the time Vera walked in. "Well, aren't you bright-eyed this morning!" she said, blinking in surprise.

I smiled at her. "I couldn't sleep. I've been getting some things straightened out between me and the Lord."

"Good for you." She squeezed my shoulders. "I've been worried about you."

"I'm sorry. I guess I've been feeling so sorry for myself that I didn't think how my attitude might affect anyone else. It won't happen again. We all have enough to worry about without my adding to it."

"Well, it's over now." She eyed me critically. "You're feeling a lot better, aren't you?"

"I feel fine," I said, laughing. "Ready for anything." And it was a good thing, because Vera kept me flying from one task to another until well after lunchtime.

We were standing on the porch, taking a few moments to catch our breath, when Neil rode up.

"I had to go into town yesterday. They were holding a bunch of mail. It was late when I got back, so I held on to it till today." He tossed a bundle of envelopes to Vera and loped away.

Vera glanced through the envelopes quickly, then went back to examine each one more thoroughly. She pulled one, grimier than the rest, from the pile. " 'Miss Judith Alder,' " she read, holding it gingerly by one corner. "Looks like the dogs delivered this one." She handed it to me, and I accepted it with quickening breath.

A glance at the handwriting verified that it was from Uncle Matthew. No one else I knew used quite the same slapdash scrawl.

I stared at the missive. There was something awe inspiring about receiving word from him only a few hours after praying for guidance.

The confusing whirl of thoughts from the night before renewed their dance through my mind. Jeff had been ready to buy my box. So, buying Lorelei's instead hadn't really been his intention. He had to dance attendance on her that evening, but certainly no one had forced him to do so since. All he had to do was say the word, and I would be willing to stay forever. Abby had said he was through with Lorelei. But Lorelei said. . .

Impatiently, I wedged my finger under the flap and ripped the envelope open. All I was doing was indulging in idle speculation. I had prayed for direction; was I willing to accept it?

"Would you look at this!" Vera exclaimed. "Charles! *Charles!*"

"What is it?" I asked, almost glad of the interruption.

"What is it?" Charles echoed, striding onto the porch, followed by Jeff.

"Look at the return address." Vera waved the envelope under his nose. "Isn't that the name of one of the doctors who came through last spring?"

Charles had to grab it from her to hold it still enough to read the name. "I think so," he agreed. "Jeff, come take a look at this."

As the two men moved farther down the length of the porch, I pulled my own letter from its envelope and read:

Dear Niece,

There have been a few problems with creditors since the trading post burned down. I have decided I'd be healthier in a different climate. By the time you get this, I'll be headed for greener pastures. Your aunt always said I was a shiftless no-account, and I guess maybe she was right. You'll be better off staying where you are or going back to Missouri.

Your affectionate uncle,
Matthew

I stared at the paper, willing it to say more. Was this the divine guidance I had sought? All it did was close one door and leave me as much in the dark as before. Stay or go back east—those were my choices. My heart was here. But was there a reason to stay? The reason I hoped for?

"Praise the Lord." I looked up at the sound of Charles's voice. He and Jeff stood grinning at each other. "Praise the Lord!" he repeated, and the brothers slapped each other on the back.

"Well, are you going to share it with Judith and me," Vera snapped, "or are we going to have to take that letter from you and read it ourselves?"

Charles looked from one of us to the other as though he didn't know where to begin. Jeff clapped him on the shoulder and laughed. "You'd better tell them before they come after you."

His brother grinned and shook his head as if to clear it. "You're right, Vera. This is from Dr. Anderson." He turned to me and explained, "He was out in this area last spring and examined Abby while he was here. He was just as puzzled as anyone and had no idea as to what was causing her illness.

"However, he writes that on returning to Boston, he has learned that promising work is being done with patients who have symptoms similar to Abby's. He believes that if we take her back east, there is every hope that she'll recover."

This time I was able to add my heartfelt praise to the others'. To think that Charles and the children might not lose Abby after all! Truly, this was a day of answered prayer.

"When will you start?" Vera demanded.

"Just as soon as possible," said Charles. "This week, if we can. Even though her mind wanders, it seems to me that she's rallied physically the past few days. I want to do it soon, before she loses any more ground. There's no point in starting for Boston if she can't stand the trip."

"What about the children?"

"I think they should come with us. Abby's mother would be glad to take care of them, I'm sure. Jeff will have to run the place alone, and he'll be busy enough without having to watch out for them."

Jeff chuckled. "You sound as though you've been planning this for weeks instead of five minutes."

Charles smiled. "The Lord must have been laying the ground-work for this in my mind all along. The ideas just seem to be falling into place." He stopped abruptly. "Except for one thing." He looked at me intently.

"Judith, I know it's presumptuous of me to ask this of you, and I wouldn't except for Abby's sake. I know how much it means to you to be able to join your uncle. But we'll need someone to care for the children on the trip back. Could you possibly consider postponing your plans long enough to help us?"

Uncle Matthew's letter seemed to burn in my hand. Little did they know how my options had narrowed. I thought rapidly. If Abby and Charles were going to leave, I could hardly remain here. Unless... I looked at Jeff, hoping he would step forward and give me a reason to stay.

He didn't make a move.

This was, then, evidently the guidance I had looked for, though hardly in the form I had hoped. I looked at Charles, squared my shoulders and said, "Of course I'll go."

The days of preparation flew by as the details for the trip were worked out. Vera and I starched, ironed, and packed clothes for the five of us who would be traveling, took turns tending to Abby, and tried to maintain some semblance of control over Lizzie and Willie, who were wild with excitement at the prospect of the journey.

Charles ran himself ragged trying to get all the travel plans in order before Abby's slight increase in strength waned. We would go by wagon to Raton, where we would rest overnight before taking the eastbound stagecoach to Dodge and the train to Boston.

He had wired Abby's mother, who had replied that, rather than having the children stay with her, she would take rooms in Boston. That way she could be near her daughter, and the children wouldn't have to be separated from their parents.

And Jeff—Jeff worked as though driven, trying to live up to the responsibility placed upon him, consulting with Charles to be sure they were in agreement over what should be done during the coming winter. If our time together had been scarce before, it was all but nonexistent now. We didn't exchange more than a few words during the days of preparation.

I told myself it was just as well. There was nothing left to say.

I, too, pushed myself to the limit through the long days of activity, trying to stay busy enough to ignore the growing sense of loneliness. Not since the Parkers had slipped away, leaving me on the prairie, had I felt so utterly alone. The fact that I was in the midst of people only made the emptiness more difficult to bear.

I knew well that once we arrived in Boston, with Abby's mother at hand to care for the children, my usefulness would be at an end. They would all expect me to make my way back and join Uncle Matthew.

Charles had generously insisted on paying my way back to New Mexico, and I hadn't been able to bring myself to tell him, or anyone, that I was even more adrift now than when I had first climbed out of the chuck wagon at their doorstep.

I knew the Bradleys well enough by now to realize that if they had any inkling of my true situation, they would feel obligated to help me. I could no longer presume on such generosity when I could in no way repay them.

"Fight for what you want," Vera had advised. I had fought, in the only ways I knew how, and had come out the loser. I was completely at loose ends, totally dependent upon the Lord to show me the next step to take.

In due time, I supposed, I would get over Uncle Matthew's betrayal and would be able to look back on my months in New Mexico as a lovely interlude, a memory to be treasured through the remainder of my life. I wondered dully if time would also heal the aching void I felt when I thought of leaving Jeff forever.

One day, in the midst of all the preparations, Vera and I were folding clothes and arranging them in a trunk with Lorelei's indifferent help. After Vera had to refold a third dress that Lorelei had carelessly wadded, she told her to sit on the bed and watch.

Lorelei moved instead to the mirror and occupied herself with twisting already perfect ringlets into shape around her lovely face.

I was smoothing the folds of the sky blue dress I had worn to the box supper social when Charles looked in through the open door.

"Everything going all right?" We assured him that it was. His eyes lingered on the dress in my hands and grew wistful. "I'm glad you're taking that dress, Judith. Abby would want you to consider all the clothes she gave you as yours to keep."

"I'm not taking this for myself," I told him. "This is for Abby to wear when she's well." His eyes misted over, and he turned abruptly and left.

"Do you know," said Lorelei, still primping, "I believe I'll travel back with you all. All this nursing has just about worn me out, and I think I need a change."

I stared at her, dumbfounded. "But what about the wedding?"

"Oh, that," she murmured vaguely and swept out of the room.

"Well, forevermore!" Vera exclaimed. "What on earth's gotten into her?"

I had no answer for her. The question in my mind was how Jeff would feel, being turned down twice by the same woman.

Somehow we all managed to complete our assigned tasks, and the day of departure came. I hurried outside at dawn to have a few minutes to myself. My eyes swept across the landscape, taking in the shrubs and trees close at hand as they emerged from the dark folds of night and moving on to the vast reaches of prairie that swept out to the horizon.

I felt a part of this land. It was home to me in a way that the once-familiar streets of St. Joseph never had been. It drew me now, and I stepped back almost involuntarily, as if to break the spell.

"Good-bye," I whispered, knowing that a part of me would always remain here.

Saying good-bye to Vera was nearly impossible. Poor Vera! She had taken care of Charles, Abby, and the children for so long that it was almost as if part of her was being physically torn out to see them go. If she had her way, she would have gone all the way to Boston to be sure her charges were properly cared for. But Charles had convinced her that she needed to stay and keep house for Jeff.

I waited until she finished tucking Abby in, making sure she had done everything possible for her comfort. She stood back from the buggy, biting her lower lip and blinking rapidly.

Finally the last piece of luggage had been loaded, and we were ready to go. Charles had hired a buggy for Abby to ride in to Raton, and he was to ride with her, with Jeff driving them. Lorelei, somewhat miffed at being left out of the more comfortable arrangements, was seated next to the driver of the wagon carrying our luggage. Lizzie and Willie were waiting for me in a second wagon.

I turned to Vera, trying for her sake to keep the parting on a steady note. "Good-bye," I said. "You'll never know how much your friendship has meant to me. I'll never forget you." I heard my voice climbing higher, nearly breaking, and it proved Vera's undoing.

Her face working, she drew me into her arms and we clung to each other, letting the tears flow. Then we stood facing each other, mopping our cheeks with sodden handkerchiefs, and Vera tried to speak, but the words would not come. No matter. I knew how she felt and knew that her friendship and respect were things to be valued highly.

I sat between Lizzie and Willie and we waved until the house and Vera were out of sight. "Thus ends the pioneer life of Judith Alder," I murmured.

The nip in the air made the horses lively and anxious to be moving, but even so the ride into Raton lasted the whole day. Charles hurried into the hotel to secure rooms for all of us, and I helped him settle Abby for the night after he had carried her upstairs. The long drive had not fatigued her as much as we had feared, and I prayed her stamina would hold throughout the trip.

We gathered in the dining room adjacent to the hotel lobby. The food was well prepared and plentiful, and it was a relief not to have to cook and help clean up after the meal.

Tired as we were, no one spoke much except Lorelei, who managed to find something to criticize about her room, the food, and the service. When Lizzie and Willie all but fell asleep at their places, I used the excuse to take them upstairs and put them to bed in the room we shared. Lorelei's constant faultfinding was more than I could bear just then.

Chapter 15

Once again I rose before the sun. Dressing quietly in the dark, I managed to slip out without waking the children. The stage did not leave until midmorning, and I wanted to come to terms with myself on my last morning in New Mexico Territory before I had to face the others.

I dared not go too far away in case someone should need me, but I walked softly along the boardwalk until I was several buildings away from the hotel and stood facing the east, awaiting the sunrise.

So much had happened; so many changes had taken place. I was not the same person I had been when I left Missouri.

I could just make out the building across the street. The telegraph office. I wondered if I should wire Aunt Phoebe when it opened to let her know I would be returning soon.

Everything within me rebelled at the thought. Even though I was no longer the same person, I was limited in what I could do on my own. I wondered idly what positions might be available in Boston for a Christian young lady of moderate education and no experience.

"Good morning."

I gasped and whirled, a hand at my throat. So engrossed had I been in my thoughts that I hadn't heard him approach.

"G—good morning," I faltered, fighting for composure.

Jeff looked down at me through the graying light. "I didn't mean to frighten you," he said gently.

Caught off guard like that, I couldn't think of a thing to say. The lines around his eyes were more deeply etched than before, and his face looked thinner. I thought angrily of how much damage Lorelei had done and with what little feeling.

I longed to trace the contours of his face with my fingertips. Instead, I laced my fingers tightly together so they would not betray me of their own accord and turned away slightly, feigning interest in the telegraph office across the street.

"Planning to send a wire?"

I shook my head yes, then no, then shrugged. "I don't know. I thought I might let my aunt know that I'd be coming back soon." The prospect seemed no less dismal when voiced aloud. I placed my hands around a post and held on for support.

"I guess you'll be glad to get back to your family and civilization again."

Splinters from the post bit into my fingers as I gripped it to keep from crying out that what I wanted was to stay with him, wherever he might be.

He didn't seem to notice my lack of response. "Seems like the people you care about the most always leave," he said, almost to himself.

"Maybe they don't always want to." The words were out before I could stop myself.

"You mean Lorelei?"

"I wasn't talking about—" I wheeled to face him. "What do you mean?"

"I mean," he said slowly, "that Lorelei wasn't any too happy when I sent her away."

I must have been even more tired than I thought. Nothing was making sense this morning. "You *sent* Lorelei away?"

He nodded. "I told her we had found out long ago that we weren't meant for each other. No use raking up dead coals. She didn't take it well. I think she's been used to being the one who's called it quits."

I thought back over the last few days. "Then that's why she's acted so strangely lately." A thought was trying to penetrate my fog-enshrouded brain, but I couldn't quite grasp it.

Jeff seemed to be having the same difficulty. "If you weren't talking about Lorelei. . .what *did* you mean?" I started to turn away again, but he placed one hand on each shoulder and looked squarely into my eyes. "What did you mean?" he repeated.

"I just meant that. . .that people who leave don't always go because they want to." My voice shook. I wasn't saying it well at all.

He wet his lips and spoke carefully, as if searching for the right words. "Do you mean, Judith, that *you* don't want to go?" I nodded mutely. "Then why—?"

"What choice do I have? Uncle Matthew wrote that he couldn't take me, and I couldn't very well stay on at the ranch with Charles and Abby gone. And I thought that, well, you and Lorelei. . .I mean, I didn't think there was a reason for me to stay."

The next thing I knew, his arms were around me, holding me close. One hand pressed my head tight against his chest. His breath stirred my hair as he whispered, "To think I was almost fool enough to let you get away!"

I drew back a little, still remaining within the circle of his arms. The lines in his face had disappeared and he looked boyishly exuberant. I found that my arms were wrapped around him and clinging as though I would never let him go.

His work-hardened hand caressed my cheek. "It's been tearing me apart to think of you leaving, but I know how hard life can be out here. I didn't want to take you away from the comforts you'd known, when I had so little to offer."

"Little!" Tears stung my eyes. "Everything I'd ever want is right here." I searched his face. "You're sure you want me to stay?" I asked, and his response was more than enough to convince me.

The dawn broke then, bathing us in a golden haze. Joy welled up inside me and bubbled over into a spring of delight. Let Uncle Matthew and others like him search for hidden riches. It was enough for me to have the treasure of Jeff's love.

"We'll have to make some plans," he said softly.

"Plans?" I repeated dreamily. Then awareness jolted me back to reality. "Why, I suppose—Jeff! What about Abby? What about the children? What about—?"

He stopped the flow of words effectively with a kiss that left me breathless. "What did you have in mind?" I asked meekly.

"I suggest," he said, tucking my hand into the crook of his arm as we walked back toward the hotel, "that I send word to the ranch that I won't be back for a while. Jake and Shorty can hold the fort for a couple of weeks.

"Then I can ride along with you on the train as far as, oh, say Missouri. If you like, we can go ahead and wire your aunt from here and ask if she'd like to attend the wedding.

"And then," he said, cupping my cheek in his hand, "we'll travel back to the ranch—back to our home—on our honeymoon."

I sighed in blissful contentment. Once again, though, duty reared its stern head. "But what about the children?"

One corner of his mouth turned up in a crooked grin. "We'll let Charles put Lorelei in charge of them. It will be a good experience for her."

I turned back to face the sunrise. The golden glow was giving way to a rosy hue. It was a new dawn, a new day.

A new beginning.

The Measure of a Man

Enjoy Your
Bonus Story

Chapter 1

Scattered clouds moved slowly across the sky, casting broad shadows on the grassland below. Occasional gusts of wind tugged at the red-checked cloths covering the tables set up end-to-end in front of the sprawling ranch house, but the weather didn't seem to dampen the spirits of the crowd gathered in the yard.

Hearty laughter burst forth from one end of the line of tables, where a group of weather-beaten cowboys sat. The high-pitched voices of children punctuated the buzz of conversation. Everyone seemed perfectly in tune with the lighthearted spirit of the day.

Everyone but the young girl seated near the head of the first table.

Lizzie Bradley toyed with her food, pushing bits of mashed potatoes, baked beans, and shredded beef around her plate with her fork. It didn't make an appetizing combination, but if the food was disturbed enough, she reasoned, maybe no one would notice that she had barely touched her dinner on this special day.

Overhead, the clouds gathered and thickened, marching in formation across the sapphire sky. The same procession had occurred daily for over a week now, but so far the summer rains had not materialized. Lizzie glanced up, trying to decide if these clouds meant business. She sighed inwardly. *It's hard to know about so many things,* she thought.

All around her she could hear the happy chatter of her family—her parents, her brother, her young cousins and their parents—and, in deeper tones, the good-natured banter of the ranch hands, who were always an important part of the annual barbecue at the Double B. Usually this cookout was a high point of Lizzie's existence, reinforcing the sense of security in their way of life on the ranch that her father and uncle had built. This year, though, try as she might, she couldn't force herself to get into a festive mood.

What's the matter with me? she wondered. But she had no answer.

Her father rose to his feet and the buzz of conversation gradually stilled. Charles Bradley's gaze swept over the gathering, and Lizzie felt a familiar twinge of pride at his ability to speak to a large group while making each person present feel that Charles was speaking directly to him or her.

"Folks," he began in a strong, clear voice, "we've come a long way since we first set foot on this land eleven years ago. We came here with three thousand cattle and our hearts full of dreams. God has been faithful beyond our hopes. The Double B is now running more than twenty thousand head of cattle on some of the finest range in New Mexico Territory. And we have working for us, without question, the best ranch hands in the country."

Hearty whoops of approval from the cowboys greeted that statement, and Charles, grinning now, waited for the roar to subside before he continued. "Abby and I have been blessed to watch our two children grow strong and healthy in this land."

Lizzie shot a quick glance at Willie, wondering if her younger brother felt as embarrassed as she suddenly did. Probably not, she concluded wryly. It took a lot to disturb Willie's sunny equanimity.

Her father was still speaking. "We've also been blessed to have my brother, Jeff, and his wife, Judith, as our partners, and to watch their family expand." Lizzie covered a quick smile with her hand as she saw her aunt Judith blush at this reference to her obviously pregnant figure. True to form, her father went on smoothly, only a twinkle in his eyes betraying his amusement at Judith's discomfort.

"All in all, God has blessed us richly over the years, and we thank Him for His goodness. This fellowship meal is a very small way to express our gratitude for all of you who have worked so hard this past year."

Jeff rose to stand beside his brother. "I'm not the speaker Charles is," he said, "but then, few people are." He grinned as laughter quietly rippled among the tables. "But I want to add my appreciation to his for what you've done, all of you. The success of the Double B wouldn't have been possible without your help and loyalty, and we thank you." The brothers raised tall glasses of cider in salute just as a rumble of thunder clapped overhead loudly enough to rattle the silverware, and huge drops of rain spattered on the table.

Excited squeals from the children added to the commotion as chairs were quickly scooted back and everyone scrambled to lend a hand grabbing dishes, bowls, and utensils and hurrying them into the house.

The shock of the cool drops snapped Lizzie to attention, and she hastened to stack the dishes closest to her into two large serving bowls and gathered the whole load in her arms. Willie, enjoying the unexpected excitement, grinned broadly as he approached her, swiftly rolling up the tablecloths and whatever utensils that remained on them.

"Look out, sis!" he called as he hurried past her. "You almost wound up in there with the forks and spoons!"

They dashed together onto the broad porch and into the kitchen where Vera, the Bradleys' long-time housekeeper, directed the sudden rush of volunteers. "Willie," she cried, "I hear something clinking in those cloths. Don't you dare walk off and leave them all balled up in the corner that way."

"Yes ma'am," Willie responded, giving her a cheeky grin and a wink as he moved to obey.

Lizzie set down the bowls on the countertop, carefully removing the dishes and stacking them neatly next to the sink. Vera declined offers to help clean up and shooed everyone outside to continue visiting, giving Lizzie a sharp look as she went by.

The flush of excitement ebbed away, and Lizzie felt as listless as before. She joined the rest of her family and some of the ranch hands out on the porch. Eddies of conversation swirled around her as she passed by happily chattering clusters of people and stood alone at the end of the porch, her head resting against the corner post.

The much-awaited rain was coming down in earnest now, the

large drops pelting the dusty ground as if eager to make up for their long absence. Lizzie closed her eyes and sniffed, enjoying the pungent smell of rain-dampened earth. Thunder rumbled in the distance, and the wind whipped some of the drops toward her, splashing her cheeks.

Instead of drawing away, she remained pressed against the post, enjoying the sensation of the wind tumbling her hair and tugging at her skirt. She squeezed her eyes shut even tighter, willing the wind to blow away the confusing thoughts that had beset her lately, so that she might feel like herself once more.

A tug on her arm roused her from her reverie. She looked down to see her cousin Rose, her face smudged and hair ribbons dangling limply. "Lizzie, aren't you listening? I've been talkin' and talkin', and you won't answer me."

"I'm sorry, Rose. I guess I was daydreaming."

"You must always be daydreaming anymore," the little girl complained. "Half the time when someone talks to you, you don't even hear 'em."

Stung by the justice of Rose's remark, Lizzie made an effort to pull herself together. She knelt in front of the eight-year-old. "I'm listening now," she assured her. "What's the trouble?"

Rose's lower lip jutted out belligerently. "It's Sammy," she said, referring to her twin brother. "He and Travis are being mean to me."

Lizzie tried to smother a smile. The squabbling of the three siblings was legendary. "You know who you and your brothers remind me of?" she asked. Rose shook her head solemnly. "You remind me of what Willie and I were like when we were your age."

Rose's eyes grew round with wonder. "You and Willie?" she asked suspiciously, as if doubting whether anyone who had reached the advanced age of nineteen could once have been eight herself.

Lizzie nodded emphatically. "We were either the best of friends or at each other's throat," she said. "Either way, it seemed like we were always getting into trouble."

"Willie's still in trouble a lot of the time," Rose said solemnly.

Lizzie managed a small smile. "Not as much as he used to be," she told her cousin. "And he's only sixteen. He's still growing up."

Rose eyed her gravely. "But you're all growed up, aren't you?" she asked. "You hardly ever get in trouble." She sighed. "I hope I grow up real fast, so I don't have any more problems."

Lizzie winced. How could she tell the little girl that growing up brought more problems than she had ever dreamt of? She couldn't, she decided. She didn't even know specifically what her problems were—only the vague unsettled feeling she'd had lately that things were changing faster than she could keep up with them.

"Tell you what," she said, scrubbing at the little girl's cheek with her handkerchief. "Let's get your ribbons tied and your face and hands washed, and then you can go back and play with Sam and Travis some more." When Rose seemed ready to protest, she added, "It really will get better someday. I promise. Boys go through stages like this."

"Okay," Rose agreed. She reached out to give Lizzie an enormous hug. "Thanks, Lizzie. I'll be glad when I'm grown and know all the right things to do, like you."

Like me? Lizzie watched the little girl scamper off and felt a wave of despair twist at her heart. *Honey, if you only knew! Half the time, I don't even feel like I know who I am anymore.*

Willie appeared at the front door and scanned the crowd on the porch until he spotted Lizzie. He made his way smoothly through the small knots of people, grinning and making lighthearted comments as he passed. He paused for a moment to give his aunt a hug and bent to peck a quick kiss on his mother's cheek. Both women shook their heads and smiled indulgently as he moved past.

His lively blue eyes lit up as he reached Lizzie, showing a familiar mischievous twinkle. He lounged against the porch rail, trying his best to look nonchalant. "Have I got a great idea!" He spoke softly from the corner of his mouth. A slight frown crossed his face when Lizzie didn't respond immediately. "I said I've got a great idea, sis—one of my best. Don't you want to know what it is?"

Lizzie stirred uneasily. Willie's "great ideas" had gotten them into a ton of trouble during their growing-up years. Well, to be honest, she'd had just as many ornery ideas as Willie, maybe more. Only last summer, in fact, it had been her notion for them to sneak into the bunkhouse when the cowboys were absent and move all the mattresses up into the rafters. Now, though, the prospect of mischief didn't even begin to appeal to her.

"I don't think I feel up to pulling any pranks today, Willie."

Willie's brow furrowed. "What's the matter, sis, you sick?"

"No, I'm not sick," she answered impatiently. Then, seeing his dejected look, she gave in. "Okay, what's your brilliant idea?"

Willie's face lit up at the chance to share his stroke of genius. Casting a sidelong glance at the chattering crowd on the porch to make sure no one was paying attention, he slid one hand under his vest and pulled out a stout stick that had been cut in half. One end of each piece had the point of a hat pin protruding from it.

"You know that new gray Stetson Bert's so proud of?" he asked, referring to the favorite headgear of one of the cowboys. Willie's eyes gleamed. "Well, all we have to do is stick these pins in his hat, one through each side, and it'll look like someone jammed the whole stick through. It won't hurt the hat any, but Bert will have a fit!" He stopped, looking immensely proud of himself. "What do you think?" he asked.

A cold weight seemed to settle in Lizzie's stomach. "I don't think so, Willie. It just doesn't seem. . .right."

"Not right? What do you mean, not right?" Even Willie's crestfallen expression couldn't motivate her to give in and get involved, as it surely would have only a few months ago. She shrugged in irritation.

"It just seems. . .I don't know. . .childish, I guess. Go ahead if you want to. I just don't feel like doing it, that's all."

Willie's disappointment turned to vexation. "I don't get it, Lizzie. We've always done everything together. You've always been my best friend. But lately, you don't want to do anything but moon around all over the place. You go around like you're walking in your sleep, and you don't hear half the things people say to you. If you're not sick, then what's wrong with you?" He turned on his heel and stomped away in disgust.

Lizzie watched his retreating figure as he wove through the crowd. "I don't know, Willie," she murmured softly. "I just don't know."

Returning to her previous position at the post, she closed her eyes and let the breeze tug at her hair, savoring the welcome chill of the raindrops that made their way past the eaves to splatter on her skin.

From the opposite end of the porch, Adam McKenzie watched the loosened tendrils of hair play around Lizzie's face, feeling the familiar longing stir within him. *She looks like an angel,* he thought. *A dreamy, gray-eyed angel.*

Adam leaned back, bracing his hands against the porch railing. Charles and Jeff had declared this a ranch holiday, with only absolutely essential work to be done. Today he could take a guilt-free break and indulge himself in feasting his eyes on the most beautiful sight in northern New Mexico.

Lizzie swept a finger across one cheek, capturing a lock of golden hair and tucking it behind an ear. Adam wished he could caress that cheek, stroke that hair, whisper his feelings into that ear.

He swallowed, trying to dislodge the lump in his throat. Unable to do it, he cleared his throat loudly and turned resignedly toward the barn. No matter how pleasant the distractions, the horses still needed to be fed.

Chapter 2

"Mama! Lizzie's comin'!"

Lizzie heard Rose's shrill yell long before her horse reached the barn at her aunt and uncle's home. She rounded the corner of the building to see her little cousin skipping to meet her.

"Can I take Dancer, Lizzie? Can I tie him up for you?"

Lizzie dismounted with an easy grace born of countless hours in the saddle and started to hand the reins to Rose when another high voice broke in.

"Don't you touch Dancer, Rosie! It's my turn!" An eight-year-old whirlwind with Rose's chestnut hair and blue eyes burst through the front door of the white frame house and into the yard.

"Is not!" Rose countered.

"Is, too! You got him last time."

Lizzie tried to suppress a smile as Rose's eyes narrowed at her twin and her foot began tapping an ominous tattoo in the dust.

"Samuel Austin Bradley, you know that's not true," she accused. "Last time Lizzie was here, you got to brush Dancer and feed him and water him and everything, 'cause I was in the house helping Lizzie and Mama. You're just trying to sneak an extra turn."

Young Sam's eyes bulged and he opened his mouth to make a hot retort. Lizzie decided she'd better step in before fists started flying.

"All right, Sam, that's enough," she said, trying to sound stern. "Rose is right. You did get to take care of Dancer last time, so it's her turn today." Noting his mutinous expression, she went on. "My saddle got awfully dusty on the ride over today. Do you think you could un-saddle Dancer and wipe it down for me?"

Sam puffed out his chest and answered, "Sure, Lizzie. I'll polish it up real nice!"

She watched the two walk away—Rose leading Dancer, Sam following along and keeping a proprietary eye on the saddle—with a sigh a relief, hoping the uneasy truce would last. Tapping on the partly open front door, she let herself in at Judith's call. "You saw?" she asked Judith, who was seated at the quilting frame near the large window.

Judith nodded. "And heard. That was a nice touch, making Sammy feel useful."

Lizzie sagged into a chair across from Judith. "Do they ever let up? How do you manage it?"

"Well, in addition to relying on a lot of prayer and the Lord's wisdom, I have one secret weapon."

Lizzie's eyes widened. "You do? What is it?"

Judith's eyes twinkled as she leaned toward Lizzie and lowered her voice conspiratorially. "I had a lot of prior experience with some rambunctious Bradley children," she confided.

Lizzie stared blankly for a moment, then felt her face redden as she realized her aunt was referring to her and her brother in their younger days.

"Oh no!" she protested. "Willie and I may have been a handful, but we were never. . ." Her voice trailed off at Judith's look of amusement. "All right," she conceded. "I guess we were every bit as rowdy as those two."

"At least!" Judith laughed in remembrance. "If you weren't pretending to be outlaws plundering the West, you were plotting to nail the outhouse door shut. Sometimes I used to wonder what was more dangerous—a full-scale Indian raid, or the two young Bradleys."

"But you did say it gave you experience," Lizzie reminded her with an impish grin.

"That's true," Judith replied. "So count your blessings, Lizzie." At the younger girl's puzzled expression, she continued, making an obvious effort to maintain a straight face. "The experience you're gaining now with Rose and Sam will be excellent training for you when you're trying to deal with your own children."

CAROL COX

"My own?" Lizzie sputtered. "Oh no. I'm not having any like that!" She clapped both hands across her mouth, appalled at what she had just said. Then, seeing one corner of her aunt's mouth twitch upward despite her best efforts, she amended sheepishly, "I guess I won't have much choice in the matter, will I? Is that one of those cases of 'sowing and reaping' do you think?"

"No doubt about it," Judith answered. Her tone was solemn, although her eyes sparkled with mischief. "Somewhere in the Bradley makeup is a strain of pure orneriness. The only consolation for those of us who have to deal with it is that it's sure to come back upon them when they become parents themselves. What do you think keeps me holding on with Sam and Rose?" she added mischievously.

A laugh welled up inside Lizzie and burst forth in a delighted gurgle. "So that's your secret? You can stand it now because you know they'll have to go through the same thing later?" Her aunt nodded, and both women burst into gales of laughter.

"What's so funny?" demanded Sam, who had just come into the room.

"Nothing, dear," answered his mother, wiping her eyes. "Just thinking ahead to the future."

"Oh," Sam said doubtfully. "Can I use some of those rags you cut up to clean Lizzie's saddle?" At his mother's nod, he left again, shaking his head over the mysteries of women.

Judith followed him with her gaze, smiling tolerantly. She rubbed her swollen belly, slowly tracing large circles with the flat of her hand.

"Are you all right?" Lizzie asked, concern coloring her voice.

"Fine," Judith reassured her, shifting to a more comfortable position. "I think all our silliness woke up the baby. He'd been resting quietly, but now he's awake and raring to go. Here," she said, reaching over to grasp Lizzie's hand and place it on her protruding abdomen. "See for yourself."

Startled, Lizzie stiffened for a moment, then relaxed. She could make out a solid form beneath the taut fabric of her aunt's dress.

"That's the baby?" she whispered hesitantly.

"That's him," Judith affirmed. "Now just keep your hand still for a moment and see what happens."

Keeping her arm in position, Lizzie hooked one foot around the leg of her chair and scooted it closer to Judith's. She waited, trying not to move or make a sound. Her eyes widened as she felt the form shift beneath her hand. "He's moving," she breathed, just loud enough for her aunt to hear. "He's really moving!"

Judith smiled serenely. "Keep your hand right there. He's just getting started."

The movement ceased as she spoke, and Lizzie started to remove her hand. Judith stopped her with a quick shake of her head. Suddenly, rapid fluttering erupted beneath her palm. Judith grinned as Lizzie's gaze met hers in disbelief then lowered again, watching the frenzied movements that were clearly visible.

"I can't believe it," Lizzie said in awe when the baby's performance had ended. "It's what it might be like if I could put my hand in a pot of boiling water and feel the bubbles churning all around. But that felt a lot more solid than bubbles would!"

"It did, indeed!" Judith replied, laughing. "Here, let me show you what you were feeling." She moved her own hand across her abdomen, probing with her fingertips at intervals, then told Lizzie to place her own fingers on top of hers. "Press right there," she said, slipping her fingers out from underneath Lizzie's. "No, don't worry. You won't hurt me. Do you feel that hard, rounded spot?"

Lizzie, utterly entranced, could only nod. She moved her fingers gently back and forth, tracing the outline of the little lump beneath them.

"That's a knee," Judith told her. "And over here, I think. . .yes." She pressed against another spot. "Move your fingers over here. See if you can feel another hard spot, only smaller and sharper."

Lizzie complied, fascinated. She nodded when she located the tiny object her aunt had described. "What is it?"

"An elbow."

Lizzie noted the relative positions of the elbow and knee, then continued to probe, following the baby's outline. "Then that must be the back. And is that the head?" She gasped and drew her hand away at the realization she had been shamelessly prodding her aunt's midsection. "Oh, I'm sorry! I didn't mean to get so carried away."

"Don't worry," Judith said, squeezing her hand. "I understand how fascinating it is. Here I am, getting ready for my fourth child, and I'm just as intrigued by it all now as I was the first time with the twins. Except," she reflected, "that the twins were twice as lively as this little fellow."

"You can't mean that!" Lizzie protested. "Why, it was one thing to feel him kick like that from the outside, but to have that going on inside you, and then with two, instead of just one. . ." Her voice trailed off and she shook her head. "I can't imagine it. Is it awful?"

"Awful? No, not at all. Even when my babies were kicking their hardest, it was a reassurance to me that they were strong and doing fine, and a reminder of the precious mystery that was taking place. Now," she said, taking up her needle and leaning over the quilting frame as far as her protruding middle would allow, "let's get working on this quilt. I want to have it finished before the baby comes. If we don't, it'll be a while before I'll be able to help you with it again."

In a daze, Lizzie moved her chair to the opposite side of the quilting frame and picked up one of the threaded needles Judith had prepared. Concentrating on taking tiny, even stitches across the bright colors of the Wedding Ring quilt helped steady her thoughts, but she couldn't help thinking again and again about the baby and the miracle that was taking place inside her aunt's body. To distract herself, she began talking.

"Do you really think Mama will like this quilt?"

"For the hundredth time, she'll be thrilled. She honestly doesn't know you've learned to quilt?" Judith shook her head in amazement. "It's a wonder you've managed to keep this a secret. Not too many secrets last around here."

"I think after she tried so hard to teach me to sew when I was younger and not at all interested, she finally gave up," Lizzie answered. "I was such a tomboy that all I cared about was spending time around the bunkhouse with Willie and the ranch hands and learning to ride. I pestered them half to death to teach me to rope, but I didn't care a lick about anything to do with a needle."

She reached the end of her thread, fastened it, and picked up another needle. "With Mama being such a lady and knowing how to do all the right things, I think it's been hard on her that I cared about so many of the wrong things and didn't care at all about the right ones."

Judith frowned. "What do you mean?"

Lizzie faltered, trying to find the right words. "I'm really not sure. It's just that I sometimes think she'd rather I was more like her instead of the way I am."

Judith stopped abruptly in midstitch. "Lizzie Bradley, do you think for one minute that your mother isn't proud of you?"

"Well, not that exactly, I guess." Lizzie squirmed uncomfortably, wishing she had not brought up this subject. "But she's so feminine and ladylike, and I'm so. . .so. . ." Words failed her, and she shook her head in frustration.

"What I started out to say was, thank you for teaching me how to quilt. When I finally realized how much it would mean to Mama for me to learn something like this, I thought it would be fun to surprise her, that's all. I really appreciate all the time you've taken, helping me with this." She kept on with her stitching, eyes focused determinedly on the bright pieces of fabric.

Judith still hadn't resumed stitching. "Honey," she said gently, her voice taking Lizzie back to earlier years when she had nestled happily on her aunt's comforting lap, "I want you to understand something."

Lizzie, stitching busily, made a sound to indicate that she was listening.

"Your mother and I have talked a lot about our growing-up years, about how both of us were brought up. I've only heard about the Virginia plantation where your mother was raised, but you've actually been there and seen it, haven't you?"

Lizzie nodded, memories of the large white house with its graceful verandahs and sweeping lawns springing into her mind. Her mother's upbringing had been suitable for a proper Southern young lady, and she apparently had taken to it with her usual style and grace. Lizzie knew she would never have been able to measure up to the standards her grandmother had set, nor would she have wanted to.

"It was a different world," Judith continued. "A world your mother fit into quite well, but not the world she wanted to stay in."

Lizzie's head snapped up, her hands stilled for once, the beginnings of hope flaring up as she searched her aunt's face, trying to read the true meaning of her words.

"Your mother loved her parents, of course, and I know she appreciated all they did for her. But when your father came along, she was more than ready to make her life with him, in spite of their disapproval."

"Disapproval?" Lizzie echoed, her mind whirling. "They didn't like my father?"

"It wasn't so much that they disliked him, I think, as the fact that they felt she'd be marrying beneath her if she accepted his proposal."

Lizzie straightened indignantly, jabbing the point of her needle into one finger. She yelped, and popped the throbbing finger into her mouth, trying to soothe the pain.

"I can't believe anyone could think that about my father," she mumbled around her finger. "Look at this ranch. Look at what he and Uncle Jeff have built here. Look at the time he spends in Santa Fe with all those politicians. Why, he's been there all this past week. People respect him and his opinions. He's an important man!" she finished indignantly. "How could they ever feel that way about him?"

Judith smiled gently. "When your mother and father first met, he didn't have any of this," she reminded Lizzie. "He and his family still

lived in Texas, and as far as your Virginia grandparents were concerned, he was just a shirttail relative visiting one of their neighbors.
Your mother was the one who could see past the inexperienced youngster he was then to the fine man he could become."

Lizzie pulled the finger out of her mouth and inspected it, gri-
macing at the coppery taste of blood in her mouth. "Thank goodness
for that!" she said tartly.

An all-too-familiar knot in her stomach made her forget the pain
in her finger. "But after all those years out here, Mama's still such a
lady. How can she not be disappointed in me?" Her throat tightened
and she lowered her eyes once again to the quilt, hoping her aunt
hadn't seen the sudden tears that stung her eyes.

"What I'm trying to say, Lizzie, is that your mother sees not only
the girl you are now, but the woman you're becoming. She doesn't
see you as failing to meet some standard your grandmother set. She
sees you as a wonderful, unique person with a special life planned for
her by the Lord. Watching that person unfold is an adventure, not a
disappointment."

Nothing broke the silence as the two women stitched steadily.
Intent on keeping her lines straight and her stitches even, Lizzie
found that one part of her mind was still free to ponder what her
aunt had said.

If only it were true! As a child she'd been much more interested
in tomboyish activities than matters of propriety, but back then she
hadn't cared what anyone else had thought. At nineteen, the difference
between her perception of herself and the accomplishments proper
young ladies were supposed to have achieved was something she felt
keenly.

She could hardly believe her lovely, well-brought-up mother
could be satisfied having a daughter like her. But if Aunt Judith said
it was so. . .

"It really is all a mystery, isn't it?" Lizzie asked abruptly.

"What is?"

"Oh, life and growing up and all. Sometimes I feel like your baby there." She flushed when Judith glanced up and raised her eyebrows questioningly, knowing she wasn't saying it the way she wanted to. "I mean, he's there inside you, a real, live person, with his own identity. But he's still developing and growing so he'll be ready to be born when the time comes. He's still becoming the person he's supposed to be.

"That's kind of how I am," she went on, feeling that she was beginning to express some of what she felt. "I've lived for nineteen years now, and as far as the calendar's concerned, I'm an adult. But I don't feel like it. I think I'm still not finished. I'm growing and developing like your baby, trying to become the person I'm supposed to be. But I don't even know who that person is!" she ended in a wail.

"I look at other girls my age, girls I've known growing up. Most of them are already married. A couple of them are at finishing schools back east, and the rest at least have some sense of who they are. But me—all I am is confused!" She flung her hands out in frustration, connecting with a vase full of marigolds and pansies and knocking it to the floor with a crash.

She stared at the jagged crockery fragments and sodden petals, stunned by what she'd done. "Oh Aunt Judith, I'm so sorry!" She knelt to pick up the broken pieces. "See what I mean? I'm just a mess!" The tears poured from her eyes in earnest, blurring her view of her aunt pushing herself to her feet and moving heavily into the next room. By the time she returned, Lizzie had disposed of the ruined vase, mopped up the soggy mess, and dried her eyes, although they felt puffy and swollen.

Judith carried a tray with two steaming cups and set it on a low table near the settee. Lowering herself slowly onto the seat, she patted the cushion next to her. "Come over here and have a cup of tea. It'll do wonders for you."

Lizzie complied, wiping her nose surreptitiously as she did so. Judith slipped one arm around her shoulders and pulled her close.

"Listen to me, Elizabeth Bradley. There is nothing in the world wrong with you. God has a special timetable for each one of us, and you're no different. Quit worrying about what other girls your age are doing and start concentrating on being the person He created you to be. You're on a voyage of discovery—enjoy it!" She gave Lizzie a squeeze and handed her one of the cups.

"Thanks, Aunt Judith." From the time Judith had come to be a part of the Bradley family, Lizzie had turned to her for refuge in times of confusion. For the first time in a long time, she felt like she had regained a sense of being acceptable. "I'm so glad you married Uncle Jeff," she blurted out impulsively.

"Well, so am I," her aunt replied, and they both laughed. Lizzie tried to remember—didn't the Bible say something about laughter being good like a medicine? It seemed like today's dose had gone a long way toward helping to heal the way she'd been feeling lately.

She glanced at Judith with affection. "Was it like this with your aunt? The one you grew up with?"

Startled, Judith looked as though she didn't know whether to burst into laughter or tears. Then a resigned smile curved her lips. "You mean being able to talk things out like this?" She shook her head slowly. "No, it was nothing like this. When I went to live with my aunt, I was the same age you were when I came here to New Mexico. My mother had died not long before, and my aunt offered my father and me a home. He accepted, trying to do what was best for me, I suppose, and probably felt having a woman's influence would be good for me."

She stared into the distance for a moment, apparently lost in her memories. "Aunt Phoebe was nothing like my mother, even though they were sisters. I think she cared for me in her own way, but she wasn't a very demonstrative person. I was never able to take my problems or questions to her." She blinked, then seemed to return to the present and looked at Lizzie. "At one time, I felt terribly sorry for myself over the way she treated me. But now I can see how it all worked into God's plan."

Lizzie shook her head doubtfully. "Being treated badly was part of God's plan? How?"

"If I'd been comfortable and content back in St. Joseph," Judith responded, "I never would have come out west to start a new life. And if I hadn't done that, I never would have met your Uncle Jeff and become part of this wonderful family.

"You see?" she continued. "Those growing-up years were hard. They weren't what I wanted. But if I hadn't gone through them, I wouldn't have what I do now."

Lizzie nodded, trying to see things from this new perspective. "So maybe what I'm going through now will all work out in the long run?" she asked eagerly.

"Absolutely," her aunt said with conviction. "God promises that in His Word. The Lord is the hope of His people, Lizzie, remember that."

"Hope," Lizzie breathed. "That's exactly what I need." She gave her aunt a warm hug. "I'm sorry you didn't have a good life with your aunt, but I'm glad, too, since it brought you here." She drew back a bit in concern. "That sounds awful, doesn't it?"

Judith chuckled. "I know what you mean, and I couldn't agree more."

Lizzie hugged her again, relieved. "I'd better be getting back now. I'm sorry we didn't get more done on the quilt."

"Don't you worry," Judith said, smiling. "Sometimes more important things come up. Besides, we're close to being finished. Two or three more sessions ought to do it. Can you come again next week?"

"Maybe even before then," Lizzie assured her. "For now, though, I'd better get going and take Dancer for a good run before I go home. As far as Mama knows, I'm just out for my daily ride, and Dancer had better look like he's done more than stand in your barn munching hay."

With her aunt's reassuring words echoing in her mind, she guided the buckskin gelding in a wide loop on her way back to the ranch house.

Everything would work together for good, she reminded herself. Aunt Judith had said so, and God Himself had promised it.

Chapter 3

When Lizzie led Dancer into the barn, she was delighted to see her father's big black stallion contentedly munching grain in his own stall. She unsaddled Dancer quickly, giving him a hurried but thorough grooming, and closed him in his stall with a full ration of oats.

Hurrying to the house, she paused to smooth her hair before she entered. Her father stood before the fireplace addressing her mother, Uncle Jeff, Willie, and Adam McKenzie who stood in the back of the room, leaning casually against the wall. Charles's face creased in a delighted grin when Lizzie entered, and he broke off in midsentence to sweep his daughter up in a bear hug. Lizzie returned his hearty squeeze and thought for the thousandth time how much she loved and admired her father.

"It's good to have you back," she told him. "I missed you."

Charles smiled affectionately and cupped her cheek in his hand. "I'm glad to be home, honey. It's good to have a part in territorial affairs, but it's even better to be back with my family."

"How was Santa Fe?" Lizzie asked as she took a seat on a footstool next to the chair where Willie sat. "Did I miss hearing all the news?"

"Hardly," her father replied. "I just got started."

"Actually," her uncle Jeff said dryly, "he started a while ago, but he's just now working up a good head of steam."

Everyone laughed, including Charles. "All right," he said, looking a bit sheepish, "I'll admit I get a little worked up over all that's going on in the capital—"

"A little!" Jeff whispered loudly, winking broadly at Lizzie and Willie.

Charles shook his head in mock exasperation, cleared his throat, and began again. "As I was saying, the state of the territory is precarious, with all the trouble that's still going on down in Lincoln County," he said, referring to the conflict between two factions over contracts for military supplies that had escalated into bloody violence two summers earlier.

"I thought all that was over," Lizzie's mother said with a worried frown.

"It was supposed to be," Charles replied grimly. "But things never settled down completely. Lately there have been more outbreaks of lawlessness—everything from small-time rustling to open raids on some of the outlying ranches."

"What about the law?" Her mother asked. "Aren't they doing anything to stop it?"

Charles snorted in disgust. "A good number of the undesirables the Rangers ousted from Texas have made their way into the territory, and some of them have decided to give themselves the appearance of being law-abiding citizens by joining the posses. The very ones who are supposed to uphold the law are often no better than the ones they're chasing!

"Governor Wallace is doing his best to resolve the situation," he continued. "He's offered Billy the Kid a full pardon if he'll turn himself in. If that young killer will give himself up, maybe some of his gang will see the light and settle down. Short of that, I don't know what it will take to bring peace to New Mexico."

Lizzie looked around the room. Every face wore a grim expression, with the exception of Willie's.

"How can you say Billy's bad?" he blurted out. "Haven't you heard the story about how he rode all night to get medicine for that little Mexican girl? She almost died! She would have died, too, if Billy hadn't done that."

As the company gaped at him, Willie leaned forward in his seat, warming to his subject. "Folks talk about the people he's killed. Well, maybe he has killed some. But it's only been to defend himself, or protect women or someone else. Billy and his friends are more like knights than outlaws. It's all been blown up bigger than it really is!"

Jeff spoke softly. "Better get all your facts straight, boy, before you go taking someone's part."

Willie opened his mouth to protest, but at a stern glance from his father he slumped back in his chair, a look of disgust on his face.

Lizzie studied her brother out of the corner of her eye. Surely he couldn't be defending that notorious killer! Willie might be fun-loving, even ornery at times, but there wasn't a truly mean bone in his body. She turned her attention back to the group listening to her father.

"There's grave concern among those in the territorial government that this will have an adverse effect on our hopes for state-hood," he said. "If we can't manage our own affairs successfully, why should they admit us into the Union?"

Jeff's brow furrowed in concern at his brother's words. "We've come too far to have all our hard work destroyed now."

Lizzie's mother spoke, her voice pleading as she searched her husband's face. "Aside from the effect it may have on the statehood issue, will the trouble stay in Lincoln County? You don't think it will affect us here, do you, Charles?"

Her father's gaze softened as he regarded his wife tenderly. "I hope not, Abby. I truly hope not. It's a hard thing to have put in so many years of effort, only to have all our work placed into jeopardy by the actions of a few desperadoes."

Lizzie crossed her arms and hugged herself tightly. *Please, God, don't let the trouble spread here.* There had been so little unrest at the ranch in all the years they'd been there that the idea of something like this rocking her secure world was unthinkable.

Next to her, Willie stirred. "I don't believe they're desperadoes," he declared hotly. "But even if it's true, maybe if they came up here, we'd have some excitement for a change!" He stood and stalked out of the room, slamming the door behind him.

Silence gripped the room as the group stared after him in shock. Charles recovered first. "What in the world has gotten into that boy?" he demanded.

Adam straightened from his place in the back of the room. "I remember how restless I was when I was his age. I wanted to lick the world and had no doubt I could do it. A boy that age needs heroes, but Willie's picking some bad ones if he's looking up to the likes of that crew."

Lizzie started at the sound of Adam's voice. He had stood so still and been so quiet, she had forgotten he was even in the room. It had always been that way, though, she reflected. She had heard other girls giggling over his brawny physique, the sandy hair that would never quite stay in place, and his dark brown eyes. But for her, Adam had been a part of the place for so long that he seemed a natural part of the background—like the furniture, the wallpaper, or the scenery outside.

She watched her father glower at the closed door as though he could see Willie right through it. Then he exchanged a troubled glance with her mother. "They all have their growing pains, I guess. I hope that's all this is." He turned his head and smiled at his daughter. "At least we've never had a reason to worry about Lizzie."

Lizzie flushed with surprised pleasure at the general murmur of agreement from the others. Had they always felt like this? she wondered. And if they had, why hadn't she realized it before now? The glow she felt at her family's approval was dimmed only by the niggling worry that goaded her when she remembered Willie's uncharacteristic attitude.

She must remember to pray for Willie, she decided. Maybe he was going through the same type of uncertainty she herself had been experiencing. She would pray that God would work things out according to His will in Willie's life, too.

Chapter 4

Lizzie walked toward the barn, the glory of the bright summer day matching her lighthearted mood. Life always seemed more unsettled when her father was gone on business. Having him home again the past week made her feel that the pieces of her life were back in their proper places.

Small clouds like white puffballs were scattered across the sky, but she knew they would soon begin gathering, massing into thunderheads that would bring the afternoon rains. Lizzie loved the feeling of anticipation that came before a rain and looked forward to her daily ride, knowing Dancer would be as eager as she was to work off excess energy before the storm broke.

Far off to the west, a rider appeared as a dot on the horizon. One of the cowboys heading in for some reason, she supposed. Nearer at hand, Bert was mending a hinge on the corral gate, and Hank prepared to mount a green-broke horse in the breaking pen.

Even though she had lived on a ranch all her life, the process of breaking a horse to ride—that contest of wills between man and animal—still fascinated Lizzie. She slowed her pace, her attention riveted on the drama about to take place.

The horse, a rawboned dun, stood stiff-legged, ears laid back flat against his head. Hank stroked the horse's neck and spoke in a soothing tone. Lizzie respected the way their long-time ranch hand treated the green horses, trying to win their confidence instead of attempting to master them by brute force. The dun snorted nervously, and Lizzie could see the muscles bunch in his neck.

Hank carefully placed his foot into the left stirrup and swung smoothly into the saddle. The horse's nostrils flared when he felt a man's weight on his back for the first time. His eyes flared so wide that Lizzie could see a ring of white around each dark iris.

Hank sat easy in the saddle. He looked completely relaxed, but Lizzie knew he was on the alert, ready for a blowup.

It came without warning. With a shrill squeal of rage, the horse exploded into motion, like a spring compressed to its limit, then released. Leaping and twisting, he slashed the air with his forefeet, then lowered his head and thrust his hind feet high above him. Hank hung on gamely, shifting his weight to maintain his balance on the frantic animal's back.

Bert trotted over from the corral and stood on the lower rail of the breaking-pen fence. "Ride him, Hank!" he shouted. Dangerous as it was, this raw action never failed to thrill Lizzie. She moved closer to the pen, her eyes never leaving the spectacle.

"He has a lot of spirit, doesn't he?" she said quietly.

"That's for sure," Bert answered eagerly. "Look at him—full of fire and vinegar! He'll make a good cow pony when Hank's finished with him. Plenty of stamina in that one."

Hank's skillful handling seemed to be having the desired effect. The horse no longer lunged with his original violent force, and Hank was smiling, apparently confident the battle was nearly over.

The dun stopped abruptly in the center of the pen, head down and breathing hard. Hank, still wary, relaxed a bit. As if he had been waiting for that very response the horse burst into action again, with all of his former determination.

Caught off guard, Hank was thrown slightly off center. Encouraged, the horse redoubled its efforts. Hank hung on grimly, although each jarring landing knocked him further off balance.

"Don't let him throw you, Hank!" Bert yelled. Lizzie held her breath, knowing a fall was inevitable.

The dun gave a mighty leap, twisting in the air as he did so. Hank threw himself as far from the pounding hooves as he could, landing hard. He lay still for a moment, and Lizzie felt her heart pounding heavily in her chest as she willed him to move. The horse, free of his load, ran toward the fallen cowboy, snorting vengefully.

"Get up, Hank! Get up!" Lizzie shrieked, aware that Bert was vaulting over the top rail even as she shouted.

Hank raised himself on his elbows and started to rise but grimaced with pain and sank back to the dust. With one eye on the raging animal he began dragging himself away, using his arms to propel himself toward the edge of the pen and safety.

The horse whirled and glared at Bert, who skidded to a halt midway between the dun and Hank. Lizzie raced around the outside of the pen and dove under the fence near Hank. "Come on!" she screamed, grabbing him under his arms and pulling for all she was worth. "You've got to get out of here before he kills you!"

"I think my leg's broke," Hank ground out through clenched teeth. He dug the toe of one boot into the ground and thrust himself forward. "I'm making it okay, but you'd better get back under that fence before you get hurt."

Lizzie continued to tug at Hank, glancing desperately from him to the fence, which seemed impossibly far away. Bert stood frozen, looking for an opportunity to gain control of the enraged animal, which shifted its malevolent gaze back and forth.

Out of the corner of her eye, Lizzie saw Adam appear in the doorway of the barn, holding a partially mended bridle. "What's going on, Hank? Can't you keep your seat in that saddle?" he called cheerfully. Then he spotted Hank's prone figure, and his smile disappeared.

Dropping the bridle, he backed through the doorway again and reappeared with a lariat in his hand. "Easy, Bert," he called softly. "Don't make a sudden move and spook him."

"I'm not plannin' on movin' much at all," the cowboy replied. "Not until the situation changes a mite, anyway."

"Lizzie?" Adam's voice was sharp with concern. "You and Hank freeze, too. Let me ease over there and get a loop on him."

Knowing Adam's skill with horses, Lizzie obeyed without question. Hank, too, ceased his struggle to reach the fence.

Lizzie's breath stilled as she watched Adam approach the breaking pen, shifting his weight from one foot to the other and advancing so gradually that it hardly seemed he was moving at all. "Easy, boy," he said in a calm, low voice. "Settle down, fella." In the same soothing tone, and without raising his voice, he said, "As soon as I get this loop over his head, all of you get out of there in a hurry."

The dun's nostrils flared as he evaluated this new threat. His front hooves beat a nervous rhythm on the hard-packed earth, and his ears flicked back and forth as he tried to concentrate on all four humans at once.

Without warning, he pivoted on his hind legs and rushed madly toward Lizzie and Hank. Lizzie heard Adam's hoarse cry as she flung herself toward the fence and wriggled under the bottom rail. She could feel the vibration of the horse's pounding hooves as she pressed herself flat against the earth.

Rolling over quickly, she saw Adam's muscular arm whirl and straighten as he flung the loop toward the horse's head. The dun swerved abruptly just as Adam released the rope, avoiding the noose by a fraction of an inch.

Adam immediately began to retrieve his rope for another try. Bert had made his way out the other side of the pen and was going for his own lasso. Only Hank was left inside with the infuriated animal.

Before Adam could prepare for another throw, the dun turned and headed for the side of the pen at breakneck speed. With a powerful thrust of his haunches, he cleared the top rail and bolted away.

Bert threw down his rope in disgust. "That's going to be one tough horse to catch again," he muttered.

Lizzie and Adam ran to Hank's side. "That was close," Hank said, grinning weakly. "I thought I was a goner there, for a minute."

"How bad are you hurt?" Adam asked.

"It's his leg. It may be broken," Lizzie told him. She raised her eyes to look at Adam and was stunned at the intensity of his gaze as it locked onto hers.

"And you! What did you think you were doing?" he demanded.

Lizzie blinked and lowered her eyes before the force of his glare. Then she bristled. What right did he have to speak to her this way?

She opened her mouth to make a sharp retort, but a whoop from Bert interrupted her.

"Look! Look at that! I never seen anything like it!" Bert was staring, mouth agape, at the scene unfolding to the west.

The rider Lizzie had seen earlier had set his horse on a course that intercepted the escaping dun. When the dun swerved to evade him, the rider spurred his mount, gaining on the runaway with incredible speed. A thin line snaked out from the rider's hand and a loop settled gently around the dun's neck. Rather than jerking the animal to a stop, the rider gradually guided him in a wide arc back toward the waiting group.

"If it ain't too much bother. . ." Hank's strained voice broke into the awed silence.

Lizzie started guiltily. "Oh Hank, you poor thing!" She knelt beside the injured man. Adam hunkered down across from her.

Adam scanned the cowboy's leg. "I'm afraid you're right, Hank. Legs don't bend quite like that on their own. I'll get Bert to help me, and we'll get you inside and send for the doctor. Bert!" he called.

Bert tore his gaze from the advancing rider and hurried to help move Hank. "Did you see that?" he sputtered, bending over his injured friend. "Beats anything I ever did see. Why, I didn't know anyone could rope like that."

His voice trailed off as he and Adam disappeared inside the bunkhouse, carrying Hank between them. Lizzie watched them, anxiety for Hank clouding her expression. The sound of approaching hoofbeats caught her attention and she turned to greet their unexpected champion.

The man on horseback guided his mount to the breaking pen, where he opened the gate without dismounting, swung it wide, and shooed the recalcitrant bronc inside. Securing the gate, he rode back toward Lizzie and tipped his hat courteously.

He was, Lizzie judged, about twenty years old, with dark brown hair framing a narrow face. Deep-set eyes flashed a dazzling blue gleam her way and he gave her a winning smile. "Tom Mallory at your service, miss."

Lizzie, suddenly aware that she was gaping at the stranger like a codfish, tried to recapture some semblance of dignity. "Welcome to the Double B, Mr. Mallory, and thank you for your help. We're in your debt."

Tom Mallory leaned forward in his saddle. "Well, miss, I'll certainly keep that in mind."

Lizzie felt herself blush furiously. What on earth was wrong with her? She had been around cowboys and ranch hands all her life, and none of them had ever affected her this way.

"If you'll excuse me, I'll go get my father," she said, trying not to sound as flustered as she felt. "I know he'll want to thank you himself, and I need to let him know one of the men needs a doctor." She turned toward the house, willing herself not to give in to her desire to break into headlong flight.

❧

After checking on Hank and summoning the doctor, Charles strode over to the newcomer and held out his hand. "Mallory, I'm obliged. I understand you made a pretty impressive showing out there." He swept his hand toward the range.

Lizzie, at Charles's elbow, couldn't seem to focus her eyes on anything but Tom Mallory. He was of medium height, smaller than her father, with the slender build and narrow hips of a rider. She took in the long, tapering fingers that gripped the belt of his chaps.

When he grinned boyishly at Charles, she saw how the cleft in his chin deepened. An unfamiliar tingling sensation began in her stomach and spread outward in a warm glow. What in the world was she doing, noticing so many details, and why were they affecting her this way? She clasped her hands in front of her, hoping no one would notice they were trembling, and tried to concentrate on the men's conversation.

". . .really wasn't much," Tom was saying. "Glad I could help out. I was riding in this way to see if there were any jobs open. Are you hiring?"

Charles beamed at him. "If you're looking for a job, it's yours. Hank will be laid up for a good while with that broken leg, and if I needed a recommendation, your actions out there tell me all I need to know about your qualifications. Put your gear in the bunkhouse and tell my brother, Jeff, you've signed on." He turned to introduce Lizzie. "This is my daughter," he began.

Tom Mallory swept his Stetson from his head with a flourish. "I've already had the pleasure," he said. He turned the full force of his dazzling blue eyes on Lizzie and she felt as though she'd been struck by a thunderbolt.

"We're pleased to have you with us, Mr. Mallory," she managed.

"I'm honored, miss," he replied. Lizzie followed him with her gaze as he shouldered his bedroll and headed toward the bunkhouse.

Inside the bunkhouse, Willie was helping Adam plait reins when Tom strode in. Tom stopped, taking a casual stance in the doorway.

"Where do I put my gear?" he asked.

Adam nodded toward a bunk in the corner. "Over there." He turned back to his leather work.

Willie dropped his end of the reins and moved ahead of Tom to sweep some tack off the bunk. "Glad to have you on board," he said, beaming.

Tom smiled in acknowledgment and set his belongings down on the bunk.

"Bert told me what you did out there," Willie continued. "He said he'd never seen anything like it. I guess it was really something, wasn't it, Adam?" Adam grunted noncommittally, holding the dangling ends of the reins Willie had dropped.

"It wasn't much," Tom responded. "Glad I could help."

"Wasn't much! Why, you should hear Bert tell about the way you

174

rode that horse and threw that rope! Where'd you learn that, anyway?"

Tom's eyes crinkled at the corners as he grinned at Willie. "Oh, I've been around a bit, that's all."

"I'd sure like to learn how to do that," Willie hinted.

Tom clapped him on the shoulder and started for the door. "We'll see what happens. I'd better tend to my horse now and make sure he's fed." He strode on out in the direction of the barn.

"Isn't he something?" Willie's eyes glowed with delight. "What do you think, Adam? Maybe I can learn some things from him while he's here. Do you think he'll have time to teach me?" Without waiting for an answer, he hurried out the door in pursuit of his new-found hero.

Adam exchanged a wry glance with Hank. "So what do you think of your replacement?" Adam asked the older man.

"I didn't exactly get a good view of all the goings-on," Hank replied dryly, "being face down in the dirt and all. But it sounds like he's 'really something,'" he added, mimicking Willie's unconcealed admiration.

Adam snorted. "Sounds like it, doesn't it?" He frowned when he saw Hank wince. "How bad's the leg?"

"Not so bad if I lie still." Hank shifted slightly on the bed, trying to get comfortable. "Talking helps keep my mind off it some." He watched Adam toss the unfinished reins down in disgust. "What's the matter? You look worried. Do you know Mallory from somewhere?"

Adam shook his head, annoyed with himself for not hiding his feelings better. "Nothing's wrong, Hank. At least, nothing I can put my finger on. I just feel uneasy. I don't really know why."

"It wouldn't have anything to do with him being the big hero instead of you, would it?" Hank chuckled when Adam gave him a hard stare.

"What's that supposed to mean?" Adam demanded.

"Oh, nothing much," Hank answered with an obviously contrived air of innocence. "Just that it must be awful hard to have them big gray eyes staring at this Mallory fellow instead of you."

"It's not like they stare at me all that often," Adam muttered. He felt a surge of alarm knot up inside his stomach. Just how much had Hank guessed? And if Hank could read his feelings as easily as that, how many other people knew?

"It's nothing real obvious," Hank said, as if reading Adam's mind. "I just happen to be what you'd call observant. I had three brothers, and whenever one of them got lovestruck, he had the same hangdog expression on his face you have on yours whenever a certain young lady comes into view."

"You're imagining things," Adam said, trying to sound casual. "You better just lie still until the doctor gets here."

Hank snorted and gave Adam a knowing look, but kept quiet.

Adam walked to the door of the bunkhouse. Fifty yards away, he could see Lizzie seating herself gracefully on the porch swing. He leaned against the doorframe, watching her push herself gently back and forth with one dainty foot. His lips curved into a smile. Her hair gleamed like gold in the sunlight, even at this distance.

Adam was too far away to see her eyes, but he was fully aware of their gray depths. When he was a small boy, his father had taken him to the Atlantic Ocean. Adam still remembered the swelling gray waves, exactly the same shade as Lizzie's eyes. *A man could drown in those eyes,* he thought. *And it wouldn't be a bad way to go.*

A quick movement off to one side caught Adam's eye and he turned to see Tom Mallory standing at the corner of the corral, staring intently at Lizzie. *That's a hungry look if ever I saw one,* Adam thought, his mouth hardening into a thin line. *The look of a coyote watching a defenseless rabbit. Or would I resent any good-looking man looking at Lizzie?* he wondered, trying to be honest with himself.

Willie wheeled around the corner of the bunkhouse, nearly colliding with Adam. "Tom's going to teach me to rope," he announced, skidding to a stop. "Do you want to come, too, Adam? Maybe you can pick up a thing or two."

Adam clenched his teeth together, heard them grate. "Not today, Willie," he said through tight lips. "I've spent too much time working on those reins already. I'm heading out."

He turned on his heel and went to saddle his horse.

Chapter 5

Three days later, Adam stood before the door of Charles Bradley's office. He took a deep breath to calm himself, realizing he was on edge after several nights with little sleep.

The advent of Tom Mallory at the Double B had been met with mixed responses. Charles and Jeff both appeared to be relieved to have a capable hand turn up just as Hank was injured, and seemed pleased with Tom's ability. Hank watched Tom and Adam carefully in the bunkhouse, but didn't share his thoughts with anyone, as far as Adam knew.

Willie had a full-fledged case of hero worship, spending as much time with Tom as he could manage, and turning every conversation into a discussion of what Tom had said or done that day and what Willie had learned from him.

And Lizzie. . . Adam's eyes clouded, remembering how often she had shown up unexpectedly around the corrals the last few days. When Tom hadn't been there, she had sighed and gotten ready for her daily ride without further dallying. Adam was aware that in all the years he had been at the Double B, Lizzie had never shown the slightest interest in any particular man.

Adam shook his head helplessly. His own reaction had been to ignore the feelings churning inside him during the day, and spend the night hours in a futile effort to sort out his thoughts. Tom Mallory awoke a response in him he had never experienced before. There was, as he had told Hank, no specific thing he could point to, nothing he could pin down. He just didn't trust the man. Or was it simply a case of out-and-out jealousy? He honestly didn't know. Maybe it was his own perceptions he didn't trust.

All this speculation didn't get the job done, he knew. He had set his course and he needed to follow it. He raised his hand and knocked on the heavy door.

"Come in," Charles called.

Pushing the door open, Adam saw both Charles and Jeff seated at the massive oak desk, studying a map of the Double B and the surrounding area.

"Do you have a minute?" Adam asked.

"We can always make time for you," Charles answered with a smile.

Jeff stood and stretched. "It's about time someone rescued me. I was stiffening up, sitting and listening to all the plans my brother has," he said, grinning. "Do you want to talk to both of us, or just Charles?"

"Both of you, if you have the time," Adam said. "I have some ideas, and I'd like to get your reactions, too."

"More plans, huh?" Jeff shook his head in mock despair. "Looks like I'm outnumbered today."

Adam grinned, relaxing for the first time in days. Both Bradley brothers were men he respected, and he valued the advice they'd given him in the past. He felt he'd earned a measure of respect from them in the years he had worked for them.

"I'm glad you have that map out," he began. "I wanted to ask your opinion on a piece of property."

"Really?" Charles raised his eyebrows in pleased surprise. "You're ready to get started on your own place?"

"That's what you get for being gone from the ranch so much," Jeff said, teasing his brother. "Adam's made a lot of progress over the last few months."

Adam felt a warm glow of pleasure. To have the support of these two men meant a great deal to him. He walked over to the desk and pointed to an area on the map. "I know you're familiar with the Blair place," he said, tracing the property adjacent to the Double B with a work-hardened finger.

"Of course," Charles replied. "Wait a minute, is old Thad putting it up for sale?"

Adam nodded. "He says he's getting along in years and he wants to take what he's made and spend the time he has left with his sister in Denver. Personally, I think he wants company more than anything."

"Ranching isn't an easy way to make a living," Charles agreed, "and it's got to be hard not to have a family to share both the good and the bad times with.

"But," he continued, his eyes sparkling, "you're just a young fellow getting started. By the time you get the place built up a little, you ought to be the most eligible bachelor in these parts." He chuckled as Adam's face reddened. "He's sure come a long way from that scrawny kid who came out of nowhere all those years ago, hasn't he, Jeff?"

"I'll say," his brother agreed, settling himself on a corner of the desk. "You looked like a strong wind would blow you away back then. How long has it been, anyway? Eight years? Ten?"

"Ten years next spring," Adam confirmed. "I was only fifteen, and as wet behind the ears as any newborn foal. The only things I knew were how to work with horses and that I wanted to see the West."

"It took a lot of gumption, a youngster coming out on his own like that, with no family to fall back on," Jeff said.

"Wasn't much family left," Adam reminded him. "My folks were gone, and the owner of the horse place where my dad had been head trainer didn't have any use for a young pup like me. My older sister had married, and there wasn't much reason for me to stay around. All I ever wanted to do was have my own place where I could raise some good stock. Now it looks like that's going to happen, but it wouldn't have without your help."

"Don't take credit away from yourself," Charles said. "You've worked hard for us here, and you've earned every bit of what you have."

"Not everyone would have been willing for me to build my own corrals on their range and take time off to catch wild horses to break and sell."

"Which you've turned into some of the finest stock in the territory, and which we're able to buy at a cut rate," Charles put in with a smile.

"If I can interrupt the meeting of this mutual admiration society," Jeff said, "what do you say we fine, noble souls listen to whatever it is this upstanding young fellow has to say?"

Charles laughed out loud, and Adam grinned self-consciously. It wasn't often he opened himself up to others this way, and he hoped he hadn't overstepped any boundaries. He enjoyed the good-natured banter between the brothers and appreciated them treating him as an equal.

Adam directed their attention to the map once again, telling them the asking price of the property he wanted to buy and outlining his plans to set up his own horse ranch. He pointed out future locations of catch pens, breaking pens, and hay barns, his voice growing increasingly animated.

"So what do you think?" he asked at length. "Is this as good a proposition as I think it is, or have I just talked myself into something because I want it so much?"

The two brothers were silent for a moment. "Let's hear from Jeff first," Charles suggested.

Jeff cleared his throat. "The price is fair, so if you've got enough saved up, that's not a problem. The location is prime and your ideas for setting things up sound like you've put a lot of thought into them." Adam nodded in wholehearted agreement. No one else knew how many hours he had spent planning the operation down to the last detail.

"To be honest, I can't see a thing wrong with it," Jeff concluded. "What about you, Charles?"

"I'd have to agree," his brother said. "For what you're planning, I can't think of any place around here that would be more suitable. Everything about it sounds ideal. I think you're getting yourself a set-up with a lot of potential, Adam. Congratulations."

Adam's shoulders slumped in relief. He'd thought long and hard about taking this step and had hoped he'd covered all the angles. Hearing such enthusiastic support from the Bradleys confirmed that his ideas were sound. He took a deep breath and let it out slowly, facing the idea that soon he'd be his own boss, running his own spread.

Charles heard his sigh and chuckled. "Need a little fresh air? Let's move on out to the porch.

"You know," he continued when they were positioned comfortably against the porch railing, enjoying the sweet summer air, "the location is ideal in more ways than one."

Adam looked at him with a questioning frown.

"It borders the Double B," Charles explained, "which means you'll still be close by. It's selfish of me, I guess, but I'd hate to see you move out of the area. You're practically part of the family, you know."

Adam shifted uncomfortably, hoping Charles couldn't read his mind as well as Hank had.

"Last time I was over at the Blair place," Jeff said thoughtfully, "the buildings all looked like they were in pretty fair shape. Have you taken a good look at them?"

"I went over all of them," Adam said. "Everything's solid—the house, barn, outbuildings, corrals. Old Thad has really done a good job of keeping the place up. The only thing I'd change," he said, his eyes focusing on a point in the distance, "is the house. It's a little on the small side. I thought I'd enlarge it pretty soon, or maybe build a new one."

The brothers exchanged curious glances. "I remember Thad's house pretty well," Charles said. "It's no mansion, but it seems to me there was plenty of room for one person." He nudged Adam with his elbow and asked, "Do you have plans we don't know about?"

Adam hated the way he turned a bright red when he was flustered, and he could tell by the way the heat flushed over his face that he was doing it right now. The gleeful grins of the brothers confirmed it.

"It was just a thought," he muttered. "Nothing to get excited about."

The front door closed and all three men turned their heads to see Lizzie heading toward the porch steps, dressed for her ride. Her lustrous hair was caught in a braid that hung down her back, and Adam knew that if she came closer, he'd catch the scent of the rose water she always wore.

"Hello, Papa. Hello, Uncle Jeff," she called brightly. The two men voiced their greetings.

"Afternoon, Lizzie." Adam tipped his hat as he spoke.

She gave him a brief smile and a nod before she descended the steps.

Adam watched her walk away, noting her free, swinging gait and the sway of her heavy braid. He was so absorbed that he didn't notice Jeff's speculative glance, didn't see the slow grin that spread across his face.

As Lizzie neared the barn, Tom Mallory appeared in the doorway. Adam watched as she looked up, apparently startled to see him, and spoke. He saw Tom flash a smile at her and move aside so she could enter the barn, then turn and follow her inside.

Adam knew his jealousy of Tom Mallory was unreasonable. He didn't have any outward claim to Lizzie, only the inner commitment of his heart. He'd never spoken of his feelings for Lizzie to her or anyone else; he couldn't, until he had a home to offer her—a home far better than a mere cowhand could afford. That, however, didn't prevent the feeling that a strong hand had reached into his stomach and given it a twist. He mumbled an excuse to the Bradleys and strode to the bunkhouse before they could see his dark expression.

Lizzie gave a little jump when Tom's lean frame appeared, blocking the doorway to the barn. Flustered, she gave a little laugh, hoping to cover her embarrassment.

Tom's bright blue gaze seemed to shoot right through her, and if that wasn't enough to unnerve her, he followed it up with a smile that seemed to be meant just for her. He moved aside just enough for her to pass, but not so far that she couldn't feel the spark that passed between them. Instead of going on out to the corral as she expected, he turned and followed her inside.

Lizzie, who had spent much of her life in that very barn, looked around her as though at a totally unfamiliar place. She pressed a hand against her stomach, trying to calm the fluttering that had begun when she walked past Tom. Glancing nervously in his direction, she saw he still stood there, watching her with an enigmatic smile.

"I–I'm just going to get my horse," she stammered, hating the way her voice quavered. She turned and started toward Dancer's stall, both relieved and disappointed when Tom didn't follow.

Slipping the bridle over Dancer's head, Lizzie paused a moment with her arms around the gelding's neck, pressing her face against his warmth. Here, the familiar smell of horse, straw, and grain soothed her jangled nerves, and she breathed deeply, steadying herself.

When she led Dancer back down the aisle, Tom was waiting, lounging against the wall. And when she tied Dancer and started to brush him, Tom grabbed another brush and began working on the other side. Lizzie swallowed, trying to maintain her composure. What was it about Tom that made his nearness so unsettling?

Lizzie turned to reach for Dancer's saddle blanket, but Tom moved past her and got to the rack first. "This one?" he asked, his eyes twinkling.

Lizzie nodded dumbly. Tom settled the blanket on Dancer's back, adjusting it for the horse's comfort, then turned back to Lizzie. "Which saddle is yours?" he asked. Lizzie pointed and watched as he swung it smoothly into place, wondering at the constriction in her chest.

Finding her voice at last, Lizzie stepped forward and took hold of the cinch strap. "Thank you, but I've been doing this for most of my life," she said. "I really don't need any help." Her fingers responded like blocks of wood as she tried to thread the strap through the cinch ring, refusing to respond with their usual competence. She ground her teeth, wishing with all her heart that she didn't feel like a gawky twelve-year-old every time this man came near.

Tom smiled and stepped back, seeming to take no offense. He hooked his thumbs in his pockets and watched quietly as Lizzie completed her preparations, giving Dancer's glossy black mane a final brush, adjusting the bridle, and checking the cinch once more because Dancer had a habit of puffing up when he was first saddled.

Lizzie grasped the reins under Dancer's chin and turned to lead him outside. Tom stepped back slightly, but not enough to allow her to pass without practically brushing against him. Lizzie timidly tilted her chin to look up at him, feeling spots of color rise in her cheeks as he held her gaze. They stood there, not moving, as though the moment was frozen in time.

Lizzie was vaguely aware of the sound of footsteps approaching the barn, sounding on the doorstep. The steps paused, stopped. Then the door slammed shut with a crash, jolting her out of her trance. She sprang forward, dragging Dancer, avoiding Tom's amused gaze.

Bert swung open the door, which now hung slightly out of kilter. "What'd you say to Adam, Lizzie?" he asked.

"N-nothing," she stammered, feeling herself blush furiously. "I didn't say a word."

Bert stared back over his shoulder across the corrals. "Wonder what got into him, then. He slammed the door and took off looking like a thundercloud."

"I really have no idea," Lizzie murmured. She hurriedly led Dancer from the barn, mounted, and set off, with Tom's low chuckle echoing in her ears.

Chapter 6

The recent rains settled the dust and lent a clean freshness to the air. Lizzie breathed deeply, savoring the scent of grass, sage, and cedar. Little by little, she felt as though she were regaining her equilibrium. She closed her eyes, simply enjoying the sensation of moving as one with Dancer's rolling gait.

Opening her eyes, she took in the vast landscape that had surrounded her for most of her life. To some, she supposed, the open grassland and cedar-studded hills punctuated by mountains in the distance might seem lonely, even barren. But Lizzie saw only the beauty, the wide expanse inviting her to measure up to her surroundings.

It was a perfect summer day. Heavy white clouds cast purple shadows, shielding her from the sun's heat. A light breeze stirred, bending the heads of the grasses. *Lord, when You created this land, You made it a very special place. Thank You for putting me here.*

Her thoughts turned to a verse she had read that morning. Ever since her conversation with Judith, Lizzie tried to spend time each day reading her Bible, instead of being satisfied with her typically sporadic efforts. If God had plans for her life, she reasoned, surely she should make an effort to know more about Him and His wonderful promises.

She had begun reading the book of Psalms. Remembering the book was supposed to contain a great many promises, she decided it was the perfect place to begin her search. That morning, the fourth verse of Psalm 37 had fairly leaped off the page. *"Delight thyself also in the Lord: and he shall give thee the desires of thine heart."* She caught her breath even now at the memory of how the words seemed to have been intended just for her.

Lord, You really do care about me, don't You? She hugged the precious knowledge to herself with a sense of wonder. It was easy to break into conversation with the Lord out here, away from the bustle of the ranch headquarters.

Tentatively she began again, speaking aloud this time. "Father, I really need to know what You think about my feelings for Tom. When I'm around him, he makes me feel special. Nervous, maybe, but special, too.

"I look at how Mama and Papa love each other and love You. Uncle Jeff and Aunt Judith are the same way. That's the kind of marriage I want to have, with someone who will love me like that."

She reined Dancer to the right to avoid some prairie dog holes, knowing the area beneath them would be honeycombed with tunnels and could cave in under Dancer's weight. The holes, she reflected, were like a sign pointing out an area of possible danger. *That's what I need from God,* she thought. *Something to show me which way is safe, and where the danger lies.*

"Lord," she prayed, "You said in Your Word that You'd direct my paths. I need You to show me the right path now. The feelings I have for Tom feel so natural, so right. If he truly is the one You've chosen for me, then show me. Show my family, show Tom, show everyone that this is Your will. In Jesus' name, amen."

Feeling a renewed sense of hope, Lizzie touched Dancer's sides lightly with her heels and the buckskin loped across the range. The wind whipped at her face, blowing away the clouds of confusion and doubt and leaving peace in their place.

The sun emerged from behind the clouds and Lizzie, her eyes dazzled by the sudden brilliance, pulled Dancer back down to a trot, then a walk. It wouldn't do to guide him over hazardous ground while she was unable to see clearly. Dancer walked on contentedly, seeming happy with the slower gait after his brief run.

A rider appeared, merely a speck in the distance. Still trying to adjust to the sun's intensity, Lizzie found it impossible to tell who it was. Dancer's step never faltered, but Lizzie felt unaccountably nervous. She had never before felt uneasy about riding alone on the Bradley range, but she knew the Double B riders should all be occupied elsewhere.

She glanced around. The grassy plain afforded no hiding place, and she was certain the rider must have already seen her. The only possible place of concealment was a clump of cedars a short distance to the north. *I'll just have to brazen it out*, she decided.

Lizzie squared her shoulders, then leaned forward to pat Dancer on the neck. "We'll be okay, won't we, Dancer? You're all loosened up now, and you can run like the wind to get us home safely if you need to."

The rider raised an arm and waved in her direction. Lizzie's stomach tightened into a knot. Determined not to show fear, she timidly raised her hand in return. At that, the rider broke into a lope, heading straight toward her.

Lizzie's knees tightened against Dancer, prepared for flight if necessary. As the other horse drew near, she squinted against the sun's glare, trying to make out the rider's identity.

"Lizzie!" The voice sounded reassuringly familiar, and Lizzie realized with delight that it was Tom. A wave of relief washed over her, and every one of her muscles seemed to go slack. She pulled herself together with an effort, telling herself sternly that this time she would make a better showing with Tom. This time she would behave as an adult, not a clumsy, fumbling child who deserved Tom's amusement.

Tom cantered up, pulling his mount to a sliding stop at Dancer's side. "Well hello there." He grinned, and sparks of blue fire seemed to shoot out of those amazing eyes.

Lizzie, one hand pressed to her throat, was unable to answer. She scolded herself. Was she never going to act like a mature woman around this man?

"You look a little tired," Tom told her. The words were solicitous, but laughter glinted in his eyes, and Lizzie had the feeling he knew exactly how his presence affected her.

"I'm all right," she said. "I just needed to catch my breath."

"Uh-huh," he replied dryly. Lizzie shot a sidelong glance at him, but his expression was innocent. *Too innocent,* she thought. She had spent too many years around Willie not to recognize the signs.

Tom swung his horse around to walk beside Dancer. "You heading anywhere in particular?"

Lizzie shook her head. "Just riding. I haven't been over this way in a while."

They rode for several minutes before Tom broke the silence. "Getting a little hot, isn't it?" He pulled out his bandanna and wiped the back of his neck.

Lizzie thought the day was surprisingly pleasant, but then, she'd only been out for a casual ride. She didn't know how quickly Tom had covered the distance between the ranch and here. *Maybe he was hot,* she told herself.

"How about taking a rest in those cedars?" he asked suddenly. "I could use some shade, and I wouldn't mind some pretty company to go with it."

Lizzie hesitated, wondering if that was wise. *Grow up,* she told herself impatiently. *You don't want him to think you're a baby, do you?* "All right," she said softly. "Just for a little while."

Tom's horse led the way into the cedar grove. The trees rose thirty feet above them, spreading their limbs to form a sheltering canopy. *It's almost like entering another world,* Lizzie thought. The welcome shade both refreshed and protected them, screening them from the view of anyone outside while allowing them to see out quite clearly.

In silence, Tom helped Lizzie dismount. Accustomed to fending for herself, she was unused to this kind of attention, and the warmth of his hands at her waist threatened to unnerve her completely. She clamped her lower lip between her teeth as he ground-tied the horses, wondering if she had made a grievous mistake.

Tom led Lizzie to a fallen log and seated her upon it with a gallant bow, then took his own seat on the ground nearby. Lizzie fidgeted nervously, twisting her hands together and keeping her eyes fixed on the toes of her boots. What was she thinking, putting herself in a situation like this? She did nothing but look like an absolute fool every time she was around Tom, and this time would be no different. She might just as well get on Dancer and—

"Lizzie," Tom spoke softly, his voice caressing her name.

She raised her gaze as far as his top shirt button, unwilling to meet his eyes.

"Lizzie, look up. Look at me," he said.

Slowly, reluctantly, she obeyed. His eyes glowed an even deeper blue than usual. Unable to tear her gaze away, she stared back, her heart beating wildly.

"I'm glad I saw you," he said. "I've been wanting to talk to you alone ever since I met you."

"You—you have?" Lizzie's voice came out in a timid squeak.

His smile made her shiver inside. "Is there something I do that makes you nervous? You seem skittish every time I come around."

Lizzie groped for the right words to say. Yes, he made her nervous. Yes, she totally lost her composure whenever he was near. But she could never admit that to him!

She managed a weak smile. "I'm fine," she said, not altogether truthfully. "I'm glad you came along, too." The words were out of her mouth before she could stop them, and she was appalled at her boldness.

To her relief, Tom seemed to accept her answer and he leaned back, relaxed. "That's good," he said, and added, "Are you hungry? I've got some lunch in my saddlebags."

Lizzie nodded. "I could eat something," she admitted. She watched Tom carry his saddlebags to the log and unpack a blanket and several packets of food. Spreading the blanket before her, he set out ample quantities of bread, cheese, and fried chicken. Lizzie looked at the food, realizing it was more than one cowboy, even a hungry one, would bring along just for himself. Her heart beat faster, and she wondered if this meeting might not have been accidental after all.

Tom sat cross-legged at the far edge of the blanket, and after a moment's hesitation, Lizzie slid off the log and sat on the ground facing him. She bit into a drumstick, trying to pretend they were on an outing her parents knew about and approved of.

"Tell me about yourself," she ventured, surprising herself again.

Tom looked pleased at this sign of interest. "There's not a lot to tell," he began. "I was born in east Texas. My pa died of cholera, and my ma ran off with a dry goods drummer when I was twelve. I've been on my own ever since."

Lizzie gaped, trying to imagine what it must have been like. "How awful!" she exclaimed. "How did you manage?"

"I hired out to a neighbor at first, wrangling horses. Then I went to Fort Worth and trailed a herd over to Chisum's ranch. One time or another, I've done a little bit of most everything. I've met a lot of people and seen a lot of country while I was doing it. Now I'm here," he drawled, his eyes glinting at Lizzie. "And it's a mighty pretty place to be."

Lizzie blushed furiously, warning herself not to take his words personally.

"What about you?" Tom asked.

"Me?" She stared at him blankly.

"I know you're the boss's daughter. I know that you go out riding nearly every day, and that you've got the prettiest gold hair I ever laid eyes on, but that's all I know. I want to know more." He leaned toward her intently. "Lots more."

Lizzie crumbled some cheese between her fingers and racked her brain for something, anything to say that would begin to equal Tom's colorful life. By comparison, her own experiences, which up to now had filled her with such contentment, seemed flat and dull.

"Well," she began, "I was born in Texas, too, but we came here when I was eight, so I've lived here most of my life. I've spent a lot of time riding, and doing things with my brother, but I've never been much of anywhere except for one trip back East when I was a little girl. I guess there isn't much to tell," she concluded wistfully.

Tom regarded her thoughtfully. "I think there's a lot more than you know," he said. "And I intend to find out what it is." His voice, warm and husky, melted her nervousness like the snows in spring.

She realized with a start of surprise that, for the first time, she felt comfortable in his presence. Tom stretched out, propping himself up on one elbow, and Lizzie leaned back against the log, enjoying the companionable silence and watching the canopy of branches overhead sway in the wind.

Why have I been so skittish around him? Right now I feel like I've known him all my life. With a burst of energy accompanying this realization, Lizzie got to her feet and began clearing away their picnic, shaking out the blanket and folding it ready to be packed away. Tom stood, too, and took the blanket from her. Their fingers met and Lizzie felt the tingling sensation that sometimes came with a lightning storm. Tom opened his mouth as if to speak, but at that moment both Dancer and Tom's horse threw up their heads and whinnied, their ears pointing toward the south.

Tom instantly looked in that direction and stiffened. "Someone's coming," he said in a low voice. "Stay here while I go out to meet 'em. If they don't get too close, they'll never know you're here." He shoved the blanket and food wrappings into his saddlebags, threw them on his horse, and mounted. Gathering the reins, he turned to Lizzie and said, "Thank you. It isn't often I get to spend time in the company of a fascinating woman." He touched his horse with his heels, and Lizzie was left alone.

She watched as he trotted out to meet the newcomer, who she now recognized as Bert. The two men talked for a moment, then rode off together.

Lizzie watched their retreating figures, pressing her fingertips to her lips and reflecting on the way Tom had kept her presence a secret. The simple, chivalrous gesture touched her deeply.

She looked around the place where they had eaten, committing every detail of their time together to memory. How much had changed in that short time!

When she judged enough time had passed, she went to get Dancer. Holding the reins in her hand, she closed her eyes and whispered, "Father, thank You for hearing my prayer and giving me this sign. Please keep on showing me the way."

Chapter 7

Lizzie stood with her face only inches away from her bedroom mirror, looking intently at the girl who stared back at her. Large gray eyes fringed by dense lashes widened as she realized with a sense of wonder that not an ounce of baby fat remained on the delicate oval face. Her fingertips lightly traced the reflection from the curve of the brow to the small but determined chin.

Stepping back, she could see her fair hair, loosened for the night, cascading past her shoulders like a waterfall. She brushed the golden waves behind her shoulders and looked critically at her camisole-clad figure. When had she developed that trim waistline? And there were curves evident when she looked at her profile that she hadn't noticed before.

She caught her breath in a ragged gasp. *It's true. I'm not a little girl any longer. I'm a woman—a "fascinating" woman,* she thought, hearing Tom's remark again in her memory. Flinging her arms wide, she exuberantly spun around her room, delighting in her discovery.

She changed quickly into her nightdress, blew out the lamp, and slipped between the sheets, hugging the newfound knowledge to her in the darkness.

An hour later, sleep still had not come. Rising, Lizzie pulled on her robe and stole barefoot down the corridor and into the courtyard.

The ranch house was made up of four wings forming a hollow square. The center of the square was the courtyard, which had always been Lizzie's special haven.

Tonight she crept across the patio, its flagstones still warm from the day's heat, and picked her way to the enormous cottonwood tree that stood sentry in the courtyard's center. Seating herself on the bench that encircled the trunk, she drew her knees up under her chin and leaned back against the rough bark. She tilted her head upward, gazing in delight at the stars overhead.

There they were—the North Star, the Big Dipper, and other constellations she had known since childhood—beaming down on her like old friends.

And somewhere, she knew, even bigger and brighter than these glowing points of light was the One who had created them all. The same One who had created her and loved her, and was even now working out amazing things for good in her life.

"Lord," she breathed, her voice no louder than the whisper of night air that rustled the leaves above her, "it's hard to realize sometimes that in Your whole, vast creation You can look down and find me, but I'm so glad You can. Thank You for loving me and guiding me and bringing me to this point in my life. I'm so happy right now. So very happy!"

Lizzie sat like that for some time, the sounds of the night creatures whispering their own songs of praise in harmony with the melody in her heart, before she returned to her bed. This time she slept.

Shrill whinnies pierced the air, punctuated by the staccato beat of nervous hooves on packed earth. Adam hooked one boot heel over the bottom rail of the corral and rested his elbows on the top rail as he watched Charles study the select group before him.

Charles eyed first one horse then another, looking them over with an expressionless face. Finally, he pushed himself away from the corral fence and stared straight at Adam.

"There's a problem," he said bluntly.

Adam felt knots form in his stomach. He straightened slowly, as if waiting for a blow.

"What do you mean?" he asked. The horses he had brought up today for Charles's inspection were his finest stock.

Charles looked at him thoughtfully and narrowed his eyes before he spoke. "Yep, a problem. They're all so good, I can't make up my mind which ones to take." He guffawed in delight when Adam finally absorbed the meaning of his words, his jaw dropping in relief.

Adam sagged back against the top rail. "You had me going there," he admitted. "I'm glad you like 'em."

Charles shook his head in admiration. "It beats me how you can take those sorry-looking broomtails that eat up our range and turn them into good cow ponies. You really have a gift for this, Adam. Once the word spreads, it won't surprise me a bit if you become one of the top horse breeders in the territory."

Adam turned to look at the horses, as much to hide the emotion that gripped him as anything. After all the years of planning, the long, grueling hours of work, this affirmation was sweet indeed. Having the praise come from the man who was not only his employer, but the father of the woman he loved, made it doubly sweet.

He cleared his throat, hoping the rising emotion wouldn't be evident in his voice. "You still haven't said which ones you want."

"Pick out the best three, Adam. I trust your judgment."

The sound of light laughter reached them, and the two turned to see Lizzie and Willie approaching the barn. Willie was saying something to his sister, and she responded with more laughter.

Charles watched his children with a fond smile, and Adam noted the way the sunlight glinted off Lizzie's hair. She looked even lovelier than usual.

Someday, he promised her silently, *someday soon, I won't just be one of your father's hired hands. I'll have a place that's fit for you, and I'll be able to tell you what's in my heart.*

As the pair drew nearer, Charles waved to them, and, laughing, they waved back. Willie grinned at Adam and called out, "Not a bad-looking bunch you brought in."

"Thanks," Adam responded dryly. And then, "Afternoon, Lizzie."

Her gaze passed right by him to a point over his shoulder; Adam turned to see Tom Mallory emerge from the barn leading Dancer, who was saddled and ready to go.

Lizzie swept by Adam without a word.

Charles frowned. "What's gotten into her? That was downright rude." He started to go after her, but Adam laid a restraining hand on his arm.

"Don't worry about it," he said, his lips tightening in frustration. "She just has her mind on other things."

&

Lizzie accepted Dancer's reins from Tom and mounted her horse, a slow flush suffusing her cheeks at Tom's look of frank admiration. He held the horse's headstall a moment longer than necessary. Moving so Dancer stood between him and the two men by the corral, he whispered, "Are you going to take the same route you did yesterday?"

Lizzie nodded, hardly daring to hope that he might mean what she thought he did.

Tom gave only a smile and a swift wink in response. He bent as if to check Dancer's front hoof, then straightened and patted the gelding on the shoulder. "Looks okay to me," he said. "You should be just fine." He touched two fingers to his hat brim in salute and sauntered off toward the bunkhouse.

Lizzie tried not to let her excitement show as she waved to her father and rode off. Following her path from the day before, she wondered if Tom had truly meant to imply that he planned to meet her again. If so, where would it be? And when? How she wished he had made his meaning clear! The trees, she decided. He would make a point of meeting her at the same place as yesterday.

But when? How could she know when to be there?

In the end, she decided to go just where she had gone yesterday. If Tom knew where she'd been and when, and wanted to intercept her elsewhere, she should stick as close as possible to yesterday's schedule.

Lizzie fidgeted as she rode, wishing she were already at the trees and hoping she had chosen the correct course of action. What if he were already there, waiting? What if he had gotten tired of waiting and left before she got there? It would be horrid to have spent all this time determinedly following yesterday's course, only to find she had misunderstood Tom.

She brooded over the possibility as Dancer continued along in his smooth, easy gait. Was it only the day before that she had taken such pleasure in the scene around her, reveling in its beauty? Now she felt only irritation as the scenery passed by far too slowly to suit her.

By the time the cedars came in sight she was a nervous wreck. She stood in her stirrups, straining to make out every detail, willing herself to spy Tom or his horse.

Only the trees, the scrub brush, and the gently waving grasses marked the landscape. Tom was nowhere to be seen.

Lizzie stifled a sob, fully realizing only now just how much she had longed to meet him again. *What a ninny you are!* she scolded herself. *He was probably only trying to be friendly, and you've made a big thing out of nothing. Serves you right to be disappointed!*

She swiped the back of her gloved hand across her eyes, dashing away angry tears. The day, which had started out with such glorious promise, now seemed cold and dismal, even though the sun was shining brightly.

She kicked Dancer into a lope. She was angry, she told herself, nothing more. Angry at Tom for not speaking plainly, angry at the day for holding out such empty promise, and most of all, angry at herself for her naive assumption that Tom was interested in her.

And that cold, empty feeling inside her was only hunger, she told herself unconvincingly.

She decided to stop at the trees after all. She would eat some of the biscuits she had brought along and enjoy the cool shade, all on her own. There was no reason to feel the day was wasted, no reason at all.

It wasn't until she was sliding off Dancer's back that she caught sight of Tom's mount, tethered farther back among the trees. Suspended halfway between the saddle and the ground, she dangled in midair, looking anxiously about for Tom.

His breath tickled the skin behind her ear at the same instant she felt his hands circle her waist and lower her to the ground as easily as if she weighed no more than a sack of oats. A warm flush burned its way up her neck to stain her face, and she felt utterly ridiculous. What a sight she must have made, hanging there gaping!

She whirled around the moment her feet touched the ground, determined to regain some of her lost dignity. But with Dancer immediately behind her and Tom still clasping her waist, she suddenly realized there was nowhere to go. Nowhere at all.

She attributed the uncontrollable pounding of her heart to her surprise at his appearance, and to the relief at his being there. A relief, she realized, that was so overwhelming it was almost frightening.

Tom slowly, lazily removed his hands from her waist and placed them against Dancer's saddle, on either side of her shoulders. Apart from her father and Willie, and an occasional hug from her uncle, Lizzie had never been this close to a man. She found the experience unnerving.

Unnerving, and not altogether unpleasant.

Her glance traveled up the front of Tom's shirt, past the bandanna tied at his neck and the cleft in his chin that deepened as his lips curved in an amused smile, to the fiery blue gaze that held her like a rabbit hypnotized by a snake.

"I thought you'd never get here," Tom said, his breath stirring the loose tendrils of hair at her temples.

Lizzie shut her eyes, fighting for control. Her knees had turned to jelly and threatened to give way at any moment. "I wasn't sure where you wanted to meet me," she said, hating the way her voice quavered.

Tom straightened, pulling away from her at last. Lizzie couldn't decide whether she was disappointed or relieved. He gave a low chuckle, as if satisfied.

"I knew you'd be smart enough to figure out what I meant." He placed a finger under her chin, tilting her face up toward him. "Don't feel bad," he said gently. "I've only been here a little while. It just seemed like hours, waiting for you to show up."

He turned and waved toward the log where she sat the day before. "Come over here. I want to make the most of the time we have."

As he walked beside her, Lizzie willed her trembling legs not to betray her. Was this what love did? Did everyone have this uncontrollable, shaky feeling?

Lizzie was touched by Tom's obvious attempts to make the setting attractive. He had swept the dirt smooth with a cedar branch and cleared away the broken limbs and twigs that had littered the ground. *Yesterday must have meant as much to him as it did to me,* she thought happily. *Otherwise, he'd never have taken such pains.* The knowledge gave her a warm inner glow and a newfound confidence.

She accepted the sandwich Tom handed her, enjoying the tingling sensation she felt whenever their fingertips touched.

Look at him, she told herself, thrilled with her new ability to meet and hold his gaze without dropping her own. *Here we are, all alone. He could have taken advantage of me a dozen times already, if he'd had a mind to. But all we're doing is sitting here, eating and talking. What a perfect gentleman!*

Their conversation went along much the same lines as the last time, with each filling in gaps in their personal histories. Finally Tom turned, shielding his eyes with one hand and gauging the height of the sun. "I'm afraid it's time to pack it in for today," he said, turning back to Lizzie. The regret in his eyes mirrored her own.

Swallowing her disappointment, she helped him clean up the area. *Maybe,* she thought, *just maybe, this won't be the last time.*

She waited for Tom to bring Dancer to her and wasn't surprised when he grasped her at the waist again to boost her into the saddle. He paused before lifting her and stared intently into her eyes. Lizzie felt her heart race and knew for certain that this time it was due to pleasure and not surprise.

"Will you meet me here again tomorrow?" he asked.

She nodded, afraid to trust her voice.

"Good." Tom smiled, and the glow she felt seemed to rival the sun for its warmth. "I don't always know what I'll be doing from one day to the next, so I can't promise to be here every day. But I'll make it as often as I can, and try to let you know when I can't. Is that all right with you?"

Lizzie nodded again, too happy to speak.

"Good," he said again, and this time he did lift her onto Dancer's back. "You go first this time," he told her, squeezing her hand. She could see him standing in the same place, watching her as she rode away.

Lizzie marveled at the way the day had improved. Only a short while ago it had seemed so dead and dismal, and now it was positively radiant. And while she'd been willing to settle for biscuits alone under the cedars, instead she had enjoyed another interlude with Tom.

She laughed softly to herself. This had been better than biscuits. Much, much better!

Chapter 8

Two weeks later, Lizzie saddled Dancer and turned him toward Judith's house. Tom wouldn't be able to meet her at the cedars today, so she planned to use the time to work on her mother's quilt. Maybe she'd finish it today. It would be nice to have it done and out of the way.

She knew Judith was anxious to finish it before the baby's arrival, and realized with a twinge of guilt that it could have been done earlier if only she'd gone to Judith's more often. But she'd been too busy.

Busy with Tom, she reminded herself dreamily, still hardly able to believe he cared. He had shown her, though, shown her time and again.

They had met nearly every day at what Lizzie now thought of as "their" place. Sometimes she would find Tom already waiting and seeming as anxious for their time together as she was. Other times she would arrive first and wait with delicious anticipation, hoping against hope his duties hadn't taken him elsewhere.

On the days when he was unable to meet her and hadn't been able to let her know in advance, she spent the time moving from spot to spot, letting each one spark its own memory. Even now, miles from the grove, she could picture it clearly in her mind's eye.

There was the log where they sat most often, with Tom pleasantly close beside her as they talked and dreamed together. Tom gradually told her more about himself, opening up more, she sensed, once he realized he could trust her not to judge him too harshly for some of his actions.

He had been involved in several gun battles, he had confided, and at first she had been shocked and disturbed by the news. But when he explained the circumstances, how each time it had been in defense of himself or someone weaker, she found herself more in love with him than ever.

Over near the tallest cedar was the spot where she had tripped over an exposed root and would have fallen if Tom had not moved quickly and caught her. She closed her eyes a moment, savoring the memory of being supported in his arms. He had held her longer than strictly necessary, but not too tightly, and had released her before she became uncomfortable with the proximity.

And there, by the spot where the horses waited. . . Lizzie breathed a sigh of pure wonder as she remembered their last parting. They had spent a perfect hour together. Tom's gaze, always intense, had burned with a fire that left her breathless. When it was time for her to mount Dancer, he moved to help her as he always did. But this time, instead of taking hold of her waist to boost her to the saddle, he had gently grasped her shoulders and lowered his head toward hers.

She caught her breath now in memory, even as she had when it had dawned upon her that he was about to kiss her. Her eyelids had fluttered closed of their own accord, and she scarcely dared to breathe, not knowing what to expect. When his lips pressed against hers, she had felt as though she were rising through the air, spinning in the sky to dance among the clouds, and thought it was the most perfect moment of her life.

She could still feel the warm pressure of his lips and the hard muscles of his shoulders as she had shyly wrapped her arms around his neck. For a moment, she wondered uneasily what her parents would say about this, but assured herself they would understand when the time came for Tom to talk to them.

And that time would come soon, she knew. Tom had hinted at it only moments after that beautiful, perfect kiss. He had looked deep into her eyes until Lizzie felt he was examining her very soul. Then he whispered, "Not much longer, Lizzie, my sweet."

Right now, Lizzie thought, *life seemed almost too wonderful!*

Once again she rode into the yard, handing Dancer's reins to Sam this time. She watched him strut proudly toward the barn, with Travis, his tow-headed younger brother, following in his wake.

Rose waited for her in the open doorway. "I'm helping Mama clean the house today," she announced importantly. "She'll be with you in just a minute," she said, ushering Lizzie inside. "Just as soon as she freshens up. She's been lying down." Her voice lowered and she whispered conspiratorially, "She really needs her rest these days, you know."

Lizzie nodded with what she hoped was an appropriate show of understanding and took her place at the quilting frame while Rose, dust rag in hand, went off to her chores. She could tell at a glance that Judith had worked on the quilt alone since she'd been there last, and felt another pang of remorse. Judith had enough on her mind right now without having to carry Lizzie's responsibilities as well. Then she remembered their earlier conversation about God working things out for the best in her life. Since Tom was her answer to prayer, surely Judith couldn't argue about her spending time with him.

Lizzie picked up one of the threaded needles and set to work. Back and forth, in and out, the tiny stitches accented the colorful pattern. *How pretty this will look on Mama's bed!*

Lizzie was on her second needle when Judith entered the room. "Hello, stranger," her aunt greeted her, smiling. Lizzie flinched a little at the mild rebuke.

"Hello yourself," she replied brightly, determined not to let anything ruin her beautiful day. "Thank you for the extra work you've done." She took a second look at her aunt and frowned. "Are you feeling all right? You look pale."

Judith waved her hand, dismissing Lizzie's concern. "It's just getting close to time, that's all. It'll all be over soon, and then I'll really look pale after all those sleepless nights taking care of the baby."

Her words were intended to be soothing, but they had just the opposite effect on Lizzie. "Just how close is it? Should you be up and around right now?"

This time Judith laughed. "If babies came exactly on schedule, it would make everyone's life easier. Unfortunately, they seem to have a sense of timing all their own, no matter what date we decide they should arrive." She shifted in her chair, sitting even farther away from the quilting frame than she had the last time.

"As to whether or not I should be up and around," she continued, "if I went to bed and stayed there until the baby came, I might wind up lying around for the next month." Judith grinned, watching Lizzie's wide eyes stare at her bulging midsection in disbelief. "Or he might make his appearance today. Either way, I'd rather be up and going about my business until he comes, instead of sitting on pins and needles the whole time."

Lizzie shook her head and went back to her sewing, wondering if she would be able to show the same energy and fortitude when it was her turn to become a mother. Lost in happy speculation about whether her children would have her blond hair and Tom's cleft chin, she didn't catch Judith's next remark.

"What's that?" she asked when she realized her aunt had spoken.

"I just asked if you'd been all right yourself," Judith answered. "I was a little concerned when you didn't come back to work on the quilt for so long, but Jeff said you weren't ill."

The unspoken question hung in the air between them, and Lizzie searched for a way to satisfy her aunt without telling her too much of her cherished secret.

"I've been fine," she said slowly, "just very busy lately." The answer sounded weak even to her, and she glanced up to see Judith's reaction.

To her surprise, Judith looked as uncomfortable as Lizzie felt. "Lizzie," she began, "may I ask you a personal question?"

"I guess," Lizzie answered, flustered.

"Have you been spending time with Tom Mallory?"

The question caught Lizzie completely off guard and she floundered, trying to find a way to answer truthfully without saying too much. "I've talked to him some around the corrals." That at least was true, if not the whole truth. She decided to take the offensive and ask a question of her own. "Why do you ask?"

Judith rubbed her hand slowly across her abdomen several times before she spoke. "I'm not sure how to say this, dear, and I don't want to give offense. It's just that Jeff—well, Jeff has some real concerns about him, and we hoped you weren't. . .getting involved with him, that's all."

Lizzie's eyes widened, and Judith fluttered her hand and laughed nervously. "That didn't come out quite the way I meant to say it." She took a deep breath and started again. "Jeff was out the other day and heard some shooting. When he rode over to investigate, he found Tom Mallory practicing a fast draw." Her expression grew sober. "Jeff said he was good. Very good."

Lizzie felt giddy with relief. "Is that all?" she asked lightly. "It sounded like you thought he was a criminal of some kind," she explained, seeing her aunt's startled look.

Judith opened and closed her mouth several times, as if choosing and discarding the words to say next. "But Lizzie honey, law-abiding people don't go around practicing a fast draw. That's for gunfighters and ruffians."

"No, really, it's all right," Lizzie countered. "Tom's told me all about it. He got involved in a gunfight when he was fifteen. Some drunken bullies were tormenting a poor old man, and Tom stepped in to stop them. They pulled their guns and threatened both him and the old man, and Tom managed to wound the leader and scare the rest of them off before they fired a single shot. He did all that when he was only fifteen. Imagine that!

"Since then there have been other times when the same kind of thing happened. Tom says it's like a gift he has. He's just good with a gun. If he hadn't been there, goodness knows what would have happened.

"And as far as practicing goes," she went on, "once someone gets the reputation of being fast on the draw there will always be others who come along, trying to prove they're faster. He has to practice, just to make sure he keeps his speed up. He does it to protect himself."

Judith, looking unconvinced, bent over her needlework once more. After a moment, Lizzie followed suit. Doesn't she understand? she wondered. It's really so simple.

They stitched in silence for a time, with part of Lizzie's mind focused on the job at hand and part wondering whether she would see Tom again the next day.

Judith broke the silence. "Is he anything special to you, Lizzie?" she asked quietly, gaze still fixed on her moving needle.

The need to share her news with someone overcame Lizzie's caution, and the words fairly gushed forth from her.

"I think he is," she confided, trying to maintain some degree of calm. She searched her aunt's face but couldn't gauge her reaction.

"He's kind, he's a gentleman, and. . .and he really seems to think I'm special, too," she said softly, remembering his kiss with a blush. "I guess you could say he's pretty special." She wondered if the joy that welled up inside her at the opportunity to speak of him showed in her eyes. She felt as if it lit up her whole being.

Judith drew a long, cautious breath before she spoke again. "What about the gunfighting?" she asked. "Doesn't that concern you?"

Lizzie sighed impatiently. "I told you, it's all been to help other people. Kind of like the knights of old in the books we read together when I was a little girl. They had to fight, too, but it was always to help someone else. People looked up to them then; why can't they appreciate Tom now?"

Judith nodded slowly, as if trying to understand. "Has he ever. . .made advances to you?"

"No!" Lizzie responded hotly. "I told you, he's been a perfect gentleman." The kiss, she told herself, didn't count. Tom hadn't forced himself upon her at all. "A gentleman in every way," she said emphatically.

"All right, honey," Judith said gently. "I didn't mean to imply anything else, or pry, for that matter. It's just that Jeff and I care so much for you, and we don't want you to be hurt. You've led a pretty sheltered life here all these years, you know."

" 'Sheltered' is right!" Lizzie replied with a vehemence she hadn't known she possessed until that moment. "I've hardly been anywhere or done anything, and Tom's done so much!"

"I wouldn't say you haven't gone anywhere," Judith argued. "There have been quite a few trips with your father to Santa Fe, as I recall, where you've met some pretty influential people. And what about your trip back East? You certainly saw a lot then."

"Oh, that," Lizzie said airily. "That doesn't count. I was only a child then, Aunt Judith, a little girl! And I'm not a little girl anymore," she said firmly. "When I hear about the places Tom's been—and on his own, not traipsing along holding on to a grownup's hand—it makes me realize how little I've done with my life." She sighed. "I want to do more, and I don't want to wait much longer to do it."

Judith sat staring at her for a long moment, then pressed her lips together and glanced down at the quilt. "Look at that," she said, fastening her thread and breaking it off. "It's finished!"

"Let's spread it out and look at the whole thing," Lizzie said eagerly, forgetting her restlessness. Together they removed the quilt from the frame and carried it into Judith and Jeff's bedroom, where they spread it lovingly across the bed.

"It's beautiful," Lizzie said with a happy sigh. Then she looked up at her aunt, frowning. "Isn't it?"

Judith laughed as though the earlier tension had never been. "It is indeed. Your mother will love it. Do you want to take it home with you today?"

"If it's all right with you, I'd like to leave it here until Mama's birthday. We've kept it a secret so long, I'd hate for her to find out about it ahead of time by accident."

Judith nodded her agreement and they folded it carefully and placed it inside Judith's cedar chest.

"Would you like a cup of tea?" Judith offered.

Lizzie shook her head. "I'd better start for home," she said, eyeing the clouds through the window. "I don't want to get caught in the rain."

Judith walked her to the door and stood sniffing the rain-scented breeze. "I don't think you're leaving a minute too soon," she agreed. "I'm glad we've finished that quilt. Now I can let the baby come with a clear conscience."

Lizzie laughed. "As if you had much choice in the matter!" She started to leave, then turned back and hugged her aunt fondly. "I want you to know you were right." Judith's eyebrows shot up in surprise.

"About what you said about God working out His plan for my life," Lizzie explained. "I read my Bible and prayed, and it's all coming together, just like you said. It's like my own little miracle!" She gave Judith a swift kiss on the cheek and trotted off to the barn to retrieve Dancer, unaware of the troubled look that clouded her aunt's eyes.

Chapter 9

Adam and Jeff leaned over the papers strewn across Jeff's dining table, talking in low voices and making occasional corrections to the sheets full of figures and diagrams. At the end of an hour, Jeff gave a mighty stretch and stood, rubbing the back of his neck. "How about a break?" he suggested. "I'll go see if Judith's got some coffee on the stove."

Adam nodded agreement, but continued adding to the sketch on the sheet before him. He kneaded the bridge of his nose between his thumb and forefinger, as if he could rub away his exhaustion.

He was pleased with his plans, and even more pleased that Jeff had volunteered to help him work on them. Being able to bounce ideas back and forth had given him confidence in most of his thoughts, and had shown him how to shore up the weaknesses in others. He'd be glad when this particular phase of the project was over though. He was made for physical action, not this paper and pencil business.

He laid down his well-chewed pencil and walked across the room to look out the window, massaging the tight muscles in his neck. Was this all going to be worth it? Would it be everything he anticipated? He surely hoped so. God seemed to be giving him the go-ahead, so all he knew to do was keep on until he sensed a check in his plans.

Turning, he surveyed the room with pleasure. The heavy wood table, flanked by six sturdy chairs, dominated the center of the room. Knickknacks on the equally heavy sideboard and a pair of framed paintings on the wall provided a balance. It wasn't too frilly and feminine, but neither was it overwhelmingly masculine; it was a thoroughly well-designed room, he decided.

Jeff had built this home for Judith when they were first married, wanting, in spite of his close relationship to his brother and Abby, to keep enough distance between them that his own family could flourish on their own. He had done a good job, Adam thought with approval. It was a home large enough to house a growing family, along with all the love and laughter they could produce. The kind of home he wanted to make for Lizzie. . . .

And that's what it all came down to. Adam brushed a wave of hair out of his eyes and scooped up the notes and drawings, arranging them in neat stacks and wishing he could bring similar order to his thoughts.

He had known how he felt about Lizzie Bradley for ages. He'd worked and saved his money like a miser, waiting for the time he could have something good enough to offer her. Until the prospect of owning his own ranch had opened up, the likelihood of achieving that goal had seemed like a distant dream.

Now that his long-held goal looked as if it were about to become reality, he had to remind himself that Lizzie needed time to catch up to his desires. Adam was painfully aware that Lizzie had long considered him a comfortable part of the background—always there, but of little personal interest to her. Up until recently, though, he had thought his chances of catching her interest would be pretty good when the time was right.

Up until the intrusion of Tom Mallory, that is.

Now Lizzie was more distant than ever. Distant, dreamy, and to all appearances, utterly captivated by Tom. Adam clenched his teeth together. Why did he have to show up now? And why here, of all places?

Jeff appeared in the doorway, holding a fragrant mug of coffee in each hand and balancing a plate on one arm. "I raided the pantry and came up with some of Judith's oatmeal cookies," he said, grinning as he maneuvered plate and mugs onto the table.

Adam took his mug and sipped gratefully, savoring the feel of the scalding liquid coursing its way down his throat. "That wife of yours sure knows how to make coffee."

Jeff nodded smugly. "I trained her well."

"I heard that!" Judith's voice rang out from the kitchen, and Jeff moved to close the door, grinning sheepishly.

Adam enjoyed watching the byplay between these two. It was just the right blend of tenderness and playfulness. Just what he hoped for himself in a relationship with a wife. In a relationship with Lizzie.

❧

"You okay?" Jeff looked at Adam over the rim of his coffee mug.

Adam shook himself mentally, aware he had slipped into a daze. *Keep your mind on the business at hand,* he cautioned himself. *Time for daydreaming later.*

"I'm fine," he said with a rueful grin. "Just too many things on my mind, I guess."

"Uh-huh." Jeff shot a shrewd glance at him, then stared into the depths of his mug.

Now, what did that mean? Adam felt unaccountably defensive. He gestured toward the stacks of papers on the table. "I've been concentrating pretty hard on this lately."

"Hmmm." Looking unconvinced, Jeff leaned his elbows on the table and rested his chin on his fists. "Seems to me that this afternoon is the first time I've seen you really concentrate in quite a while."

Adam straightened his papers once more and reached for his pencil, hoping to avoid Jeff's speculative gaze. Jeff hadn't helped build this ranch into a showplace by being unobservant.

When he looked up again, though, Jeff was still staring at him, an amused grin playing around the corners of his mouth. "Is something funny?" Adam asked edgily.

"I'm just trying to put two and two together and see what I come up with," Jeff said, leaning back lazily in his chair. "Let's see. . ." he held up an index finger. "You're in a real fever all of a sudden to get this place of yours fixed up and in operation."

"I've been dreaming of this for years. You know that," Adam protested.

Jeff held up another finger beside the first. "You walk around like you're in some other world, and don't see half of what goes on around you."

"Like I said, I've had a lot on my mind, trying to pull all this together." Adam frowned. "You aren't saying I've been slacking off on my work, are you?"

Jeff continued unperturbed, raising his ring finger as he spoke. "When Tom Mallory comes anywhere near you, I can hear your teeth grinding."

Adam flushed and made a conscious effort to relax his jaws. "You've had your own doubts about him. You've told me so."

"And last," Jeff concluded, waving four fingers in the air, "you're uncommonly edgy around a certain Lizzie Bradley." Leaning across the table, he fixed his gaze on Adam's. "You tell me if that doesn't add up to four."

Adam spluttered and started to protest, but gave it up as wasted effort. *Who am I trying to kid? He's figured it out, anyway.* "Okay, you've got me," he admitted, his shoulders slumping in defeat. "And I might as well level with you, it feels good to finally be able to talk to someone about it."

Jeff threw back his head and let out a delighted whoop. "I knew it!" he yelled. "I knew it!"

Judith's head appeared in the kitchen doorway. "What's all the commotion, Jeff? Is everything all right?"

Jeff, still crowing, seemed about to pour out his discovery, but after a look at Adam's stricken face, he relented. "Everything's fine, honey," he said. "I just came up with the answer to a mathematical problem, that's all. Sorry if I scared you."

His wife gave both men a quizzical look, then shook her head and disappeared behind the swinging door.

Adam eyed Jeff warily. "Are you finished trying to announce this to the world?"

"I guess I did get a little out of hand," Jeff said, chuckling. "But why all the secrecy, man? This is great news. Have you spoken to Charles yet?"

"I haven't even spoken to Lizzie," Adam confessed. At Jeff's astonished look, he went on, "I wanted to get everything in place first, have a decent home to offer her before I said anything."

"I can understand that. But you're well on your way now. Why not go to her?"

Adam hesitated before answering. "The timing just doesn't seem right."

"It's that Mallory fellow, isn't it?"

"He's part of it." Adam fought down the jealousy that always rose up in him at the very thought of the man. "He seems to be around whenever she is, helping her with her horse, offering to clean her tack for her. He knows what he's doing around women, all right. She can't help but be impressed."

"So get out there and do the same thing. Show her you can be impressive, too."

Adam shook his head. "That's just not me, Jeff. I'm not a flashy show horse, just steady and reliable. And I'm not sure that's what she wants."

"It's the steady ones that go the distance. Lizzie knows that."

"But it's the show horses that get noticed. I've been around here so long that to her, I'm just part of the scenery."

"Hmmm." Jeff stroked his chin as he thought. "You might be right, there. Seems to me that what you have to do is make yourself flash a little bit, just so you get her attention."

Adam shook his head stubbornly. "I won't try to be something I'm not, just to get her to notice me. I've put this in God's hands. If it's His will, she'll love me for who I am. If not. . ." His voice trailed off. "If not, then I'll have to go on, that's all."

Jeff came around the table and clapped the younger man sympathetically on the shoulder. "Then I'll pray with you that God will work it out the way He wants it to. Now, let's get back to work."

❧

Lizzie sat at the supper table with her family. Jeff and the three children had joined them, Jeff explaining that Judith had begged off at the last minute.

"She's tired, mostly," he said in response to Abby's anxious query. "Plus, she said food just doesn't sound good right now, and that's no slur on Vera's cooking," he added with a grin. "She hasn't had much appetite at all with this one. I figured I'd give her an evening alone to rest and not have to put up with all of us."

Lizzie watched her cousins eagerly attack Vera's roast beef and potatoes. Their appetites didn't seem to be affected, she thought in amusement. She looked at her own plate ruefully, noting the barely touched food, and picked up a bite with her fork.

The lively conversation faded to a muted buzz as she thought dreamily of Tom and their last meeting. It had been brief—too brief—but once again he had held her and touched his lips to hers at parting. What would it be like, she wondered, when the days of secrecy were over and they could meet openly, with her family's consent? That moment couldn't come soon enough to suit her.

She looked up several times during the meal to find Jeff's eyes on her. *What is he looking at?* she wondered, raising her napkin to her mouth to wipe away any traces of food that might be lingering there. That didn't seem to be the problem, though, for he continued to stare at her thoughtfully from time to time.

Talk around the table drifted easily from politics to ranch business to local news. During one lull in the conversation, Jeff cleared his throat and began to speak.

"Guess what I spent the afternoon doing?" he asked, speaking to the group in general. When no one ventured a guess, he went on. "Adam McKenzie brought over his plans for his horse ranch, and we worked on them for several hours."

"How are things working out for him?" Charles asked with interest.

"He's really coming along. I can't remember when I've seen anyone work so hard to make a dream come true. He's a fine man, Adam is."

"I couldn't agree with you more," Charles replied. "He has the drive and the ability to make quite a name for himself. I'm proud to have been able to help him get started."

"Will he be moving onto his own place soon?" Abby asked with a trace of concern. "I'll hate to see him leave anyway, but especially now when we're short-handed."

"I don't think he has any immediate plans," Jeff answered. "I think he's just getting things together so the place is ready whenever he is.

"Has he talked to you about what he's doing?" Jeff asked, looking directly at Lizzie.

She straightened quickly, startled at the sudden question. "Me? No. I mean, why would he?" She looked around the table in confusion. "Adam's a good worker, I guess, but why would he want my opinion? I mean, he's just there."

"Not like some other people, huh?" Willie's teasing eyes glinted at her, and she blushed hotly, hoping the rest of the family wouldn't pick up on his meaning. Willie had already made it clear he'd noticed her interest in Tom and considered it fair game for any amount of teasing.

To her relief, the conversation turned to other matters and she was no longer the center of attention.

They were cleaning up the last bites of apple pie when hooves clattered up outside and the sound of heavy boots on the porch was followed by a knock on the door.

"Dan Peterson!" Charles cried with delight when he admitted his long-time friend. "What brings you here? I haven't seen you in a month of Sundays."

"I wish it was something better," replied the weathered rancher, twisting his hat in his hands. "John Pritchard's boy rode down to White Oaks on some business for his pa, and stayed over for a dance. A bunch of those wild cowboys who're trying to ape Billy the Kid started raising a ruckus. John's boy took a bullet in the thigh."

Abby's hand flew to her mouth, and Lizzie sank back into her chair.

Charles frowned grimly at the news. "This is bad business, Dan. It doesn't look like things are settling down after all. Man, you must be beat, riding all that way. Come sit down and have something to eat."

Dan shook his head. "I've got to keep moving. It's another couple of hours yet to Pritchard's place. Young Jack will pull through all right, but I need to let his folks know he'll be out of commission for a while. I just thought I'd swing by and tell you the news, Charles. I knew you'd want to know."

Abby hurried from the kitchen with a packet of food which she pressed into Dan's hands. He thanked her and was gone, putting an effective end to the light-hearted evening.

"So much for your hero, Willie," Charles said, giving his son a dark look. Willie responded by throwing his napkin on the table and stomping out the door, leaving his parents looking worriedly at each other.

Lizzie excused herself and went to bed early, a jumble of ideas whirling through her head.

Chapter 10

Lizzie's thoughts continued to be muddled over the next few days. Tom had gone to the south range, sent there by Charles to determine whether enough water remained in the water holes to get them through the summer. Lizzie tried to console herself with the thought that it showed her father's trust in Tom and would prove valuable to them in making their case to her parents when the time came, but such hopeful thoughts did little to ease her mind.

She hadn't realized how much of her time had been spent trying to meet with Tom until he was nowhere nearby. For the first time in her life, she felt absolutely at loose ends. The quilt was finished and she had no other projects to occupy her time.

Willie found her mooning by the corrals late one morning. "What's the trouble, sis?" he asked in his old easygoing manner. Lizzie was encouraged by this, since Willie had grown increasingly sullen and withdrawn over the past few weeks.

"I was trying to decide what to do next, that's all," she said, making the effort to sound cheerful. Willie had been her companion all her life, and she didn't want to lose that closeness.

"Would it perk you up any if I gave you this?" His eyes held their old familiar sparkle as he took a folded piece of paper from his shirt pocket and dangled it before her.

Lizzie's forehead crinkled in confusion. "What is it?" she asked. "Where did you get it?"

"Let's just say that it's a note that's supposed to be handed to you, dear sister. I'm not going to tell you where it came from." He held the paper tantalizingly above her head, moving it just out of reach as she made a grab for it.

"Willie, give that to me!" she cried in exasperation, jumping up to try to snatch the note. "You may be sixteen, but you don't act like you've grown up one bit!"

Willie only grinned at her own childish behavior and flicked his wrist, sending the note spinning through the air and fluttering into Lizzie's outstretched hands. She started to unfold it eagerly, then remembered his curious gaze and creased it shut again. "All right, you've delivered your note. Now get on back to whatever it is you're supposed to be doing." She gave him a little push to start him on his way, and after one last knowing look, he sauntered off, grinning smugly.

Lizzie fumbled at the edges of the note with unaccountably trembling hands and smoothed it open.

Dear Lizzie,

I've missed you and our time together these last few days.
It's shown me how important you are to me. I can get away for
a little while today. Meet me at our special place at noon. There's
something I want to ask you.

Tom

Her hands weren't the only things shaking now. She was trembling all over, like the time she'd had a high fever. It wasn't fever that affected her now though.

She breathed a happy sigh as she traced her finger across his name and went over the note again, more slowly this time, trying to read the meaning between the lines. He had missed her, just as she had missed him! She savored that delicious thought as she continued reading.

"There's something I want to ask you." What could he mean by that? What could he possibly mean, except... She caught her breath, hardly daring to allow herself to believe that he might be ready to declare himself this very day. *Settle down,* she told herself. *You'll find out soon enough. Just wait until noon.*

Noon? She checked the position of the sun and gasped. She had barely enough time to reach the grove by then if she started right now, and Dancer wasn't even out of his stall yet.

Lizzie raced into the barn, where Willie sat braiding a lariat. He glanced up idly when she rushed past him. "What's chasing you?" he asked.

"Leave me alone, Willie," Lizzie panted. "I need to get Dancer saddled, and I'm in a hurry." She rushed to the end stall, wrenched the door open, and hustled the startled Dancer back down the aisle.

Willie met her, brush and saddle blanket in hand. "Let me help," he offered, performing the grooming and saddling chores with effortless efficiency. Lizzie swallowed her surprise at his offer and used the time to catch her breath and try to regain her composure.

"Thanks, Willie," she said, accepting the reins he held out to her. Swinging into the saddle, she looked down on her brother with a warm surge of affection. "I really appreciate it. You're always there for me when I need you, aren't you?"

Willie just waved and returned to his braiding. Lizzie urged Dancer into a lope and galloped away.

Approaching the grove, Lizzie let out a sigh of relief when she realized Tom was nowhere in sight. She had ridden hard, harder than she preferred to, but it was worth it, as she had apparently beaten him to their meeting place. She was glad she would have a few minutes to calm down. It wouldn't do to meet him looking flushed and anxious.

Lizzie slowed Dancer to a relaxed pace and walked him the rest of the way, taking the time to look around carefully. This was a day she was certain she would remember for the rest of her life, and she wanted to commit every last detail of the scene to memory.

Had the sun ever shone more brightly or the scent of the rain-washed cedars smelled sweeter? The wildflowers, having received the life-giving summer rains, stood proud and erect, showing themselves to their best effect. Even the clouds drifted lazily overhead today, not in threatening clusters, but scattered in light patches across the sky. *The day could not be more perfect,* she decided. *Except for one thing. I only need Tom here to make it complete.*

Lizzie tethered Dancer and nervously patted at her hair, wishing she had a mirror and comb. On this day of all days, she wanted to look her best.

The sun was now directly overhead. *Straight up noon,* she thought. *He'll be here any minute.* She craned her neck, scanning the horizon in all directions, but no rider appeared.

She paced anxiously back and forth within the shelter of the trees, casting an envious look at Dancer, who was contentedly munching on clumps of grama grass. "Look at you," Lizzie told him. "As long as you have food in front of you, you're not worried a bit." She pressed a hand to her own stomach as it rumbled at the mention of food. "See what you've done?" she scolded the horse affectionately. "You've gone and made me hungry. How can I even think about food at a time like this?"

Maybe Dancer had the right idea, Lizzie thought, after another spell of fidgety pacing. She needed something to keep her mind off her nerves and the fact that Tom was overdue. Glancing around for inspiration, her eyes lit on some wildflowers, covered with blooms after the recent rains. Splotches of white, yellow, and purple dotted the ground. They would make a lovely bouquet, she decided, and she began to gather an armful.

Carrying her prize back under the trees, she sat on a smooth, flat rock and began to sort through the flowers, discarding any that were broken or even slightly wilted. She wanted to keep only the perfect specimens. When she got home, she could press a sample of each kind of flower as a reminder.

Lizzie looked up again at the sun, measuring its movement across the sky with a practiced eye. She had been there for at least an hour. Where could Tom be? She curled up under a cedar and continued to wait.

In the next hour, Lizzie wove a chain of wild asters, made herself a garland, and stripped all her discarded blooms of petals while reciting, "He loves me, he loves me not." The last petal made it come out "he loves me not," and she flung it away in disgust.

The sun was now a bright ball dropping lower in the sky, and Lizzie was forced to admit that Tom wasn't coming. Angry tears stung her eyes. He had cared enough to send her the note; how could he have changed his mind so quickly? If he had lost his nerve, the very least he might have done was ride by and make sure she was all right, instead of keeping her waiting, hungry, and alone.

The tension and anticipation that had filled her ever since Willie gave her the note had built up like a summer thunderstorm and needed some release. Lizzie mounted Dancer and started home without a backward glance, trying to keep her pent-up emotions in check. She succeeded until she was almost in sight of the ranch buildings. Then tears of humiliation pricked at her eyes and she felt their hot sting as they coursed down her cheeks.

Lizzie bit her lip to keep from sobbing aloud. If she could just make it to the barn without meeting anyone! There, alone in its concealing shadows, she could let her tears run freely. No one need know of her disappointment.

No one stirred as she rode closer. Her whole attention was focused on reaching the barn unseen. Only a few more yards now, and still no one appeared. . . .

She had made it. Slipping from the saddle, she gathered the reins in her hand and hurried inside the barn. Dancer nuzzled her shoulder from behind and she turned to bury her face in his silky mane. Relief at reaching her goal made her weak, and she clung to the horse for strength to remain upright.

"Why?" she whispered in an agony of spirit, as though the horse could understand and answer. "Why did he send that note and then not come?" Sobs rose in her throat, and with no reason now to hide them, she let them come, great racking sobs that shook her whole body.

The scrape of a boot sole against gravel warned her she was not alone. Swiftly she dashed the tears from her face with the back of her hand and busied herself undoing the cinch strap.

"Hi, sis." Willie lounged against the partition behind her. "Just getting back?"

Lizzie flickered a quick glance his way, then turned back to her work, determinedly keeping her face from him. "Mm-hm." Her voice came out as a tiny squeak, and she had to clear her throat and try again. "Yes," she said flatly. "I'm just now getting home." She slid the saddle from Dancer's back and began brushing his coat vigorously.

"Where were you heading in such an all-fired hurry anyway?" Willie continued to lean against the wall as if he didn't have a care in the world, but Lizzie could detect a speculative gleam in his eye.

"I—I had to meet someone." Lizzie hoped her voice was steady enough to fool her brother. She placed her hand on Dancer's rump and circled to his off-side, working to remove the crust of sweat.

Her concentration was broken by a rasping sound, and she swung around to see Willie, lips pressed together, trying to stifle a laugh. When he saw her puzzled expression, he threw his head back and burst into a loud guffaw.

"You believed it!" he cried delightedly. "You swallowed the whole thing, hook, line, and sinker!"

Lizzie felt the blood drain from her face and she stared in disbelief at Willie, now convulsed in laughter.

"What do you mean, I 'believed it'?" she asked slowly, unwilling to accept the dreadful idea that was forming in her mind.

"The note!" Willie chortled. "I thought you'd see right through it, but there you went, tearing out of here like a nest of hornets was after you. I bet you've been out there waiting for him to show up all this time, too, haven't you? Whew, I thought you'd fallen for him, but you've got it even worse than I thought!"

Lizzie tried to speak, but her numbed brain couldn't seem to form any words.

"Do you. . ." she managed, "do you mean the note didn't come from Tom after all?"

"You should have seen your face when I gave it to you," Willie gasped, so engrossed in his mirth that he didn't see the murderous look Lizzie turned on him. "I thought you'd figure it out in the first minute or two, but no, you went ripping out of here and then you spent half the afternoon sitting out there waiting for him. That's got to be the best joke I ever—oof!" he grunted as Lizzie launched herself straight at him.

Lizzie, unable to think clearly at this point, knew only that her anger must have some object, and the only object at hand was Willie. She flailed at him with both fists, something she hadn't done since they were children.

Caught off-guard and off-balance, Willie was unprepared for the whirlwind onslaught. He threw up his hands, trying to protect himself from the blows, but the force of Lizzie's attack threw him backward and he landed in the corner in a heap.

"All right, sis. Enough!" He caught at her wrists, but Lizzie, empowered by unreasoning rage, had the upper hand. One wild swing caught Willie on his nose, which spurted a crimson stream of blood.

"Ouch, Lizzie! Cut it out; this is getting out of hand." Willie, caught in an awkward position, couldn't regain his feet, and the blows continued to rain down on him unabated.

"Stop it, Lizzie! I'm serious now." Willie sounded concerned. "Come on, you've always been a good sport. Where's your sense of humor?"

Lizzie, blinded by tears, was deaf to his pleas. She was focused on only one thing—to hurt Willie as much as he had hurt her—and to that end she was giving her all.

Her attack was interrupted when a pair of muscular hands encircled her waist, lifted her off of Willie, and set her firmly on the ground. Her arms pummeled the air for a few moments before she fully realized she no longer had a target. She covered her face with her hands and heaved in great gulps of air.

"What's going on here?" asked a bewildered voice, and she looked up to see Adam McKenzie's worried face looming over her.

Lizzie risked a look at Willie, just getting to his feet. Streaks of blood were smeared across his face and shirt and a large welt was beginning to rise on one cheekbone. If his betrayal hadn't left such a raw wound, she might have felt sorry for him.

Willie glared at her in return, wiping his nose with one arm and adding another streak of blood to his shirt sleeve. "What's the matter with you, anyway?" he demanded. "It was just a joke."

"Just. . .a joke." The words were forced out through clenched teeth. Lizzie had no desire to do anything but be alone with her own misery. She turned and stumbled toward the house, oblivious to Adam's voice calling her name.

She reached her room without meeting anyone else, and flung herself face down across her bed, wishing the floor would open up and swallow her whole.

❧

Adam stared out the barn doorway, wondering what exactly had happened. Just after Lizzie stormed out, Willie had left, shrugging off Adam's restraining hand as well as his questions. Willie had then mounted his horse, which had been tied to the corral, and rode off north.

Adam felt as though he had been caught in a hurricane. He had tried to give himself time to calm down and think clearly by putting the barn back into some kind of order. He finished grooming Dancer and put the uncharacteristically nervous horse into his stall, giving him an extra measure of grain as a consolation.

The extra time did not help clarify the situation. He had seen those two get into scraps before, but this. . .

He shook his head, glancing in turn from the house to the direction Willie had taken. This was like nothing he had ever seen before, and completely out of character for both of them.

Something needed to be done, that was obvious, and no one else had witnessed the scene. It looked like he was the one to get to the bottom of things. He looked once again toward the house. He could hardly go barging in there, demanding admittance to Lizzie's bedroom. He nodded, his mind made up. It would have to be Willie who gave him the answers.

Lord, I could sure use a good dose of wisdom about now, he prayed, heading off to saddle his horse.

Nearly an hour later he was still on Willie's trail. *The boy must have ridden like the wind,* he mused. *He knows better than to—* He drew his mount up sharply at the sound of rapid gunshots.

The shots had come from just beyond a nearby rise, and Adam immediately swung out of the saddle and ran uphill, crouching low as he neared the top.

Cautiously he peered over the crest. Willie stood below him, gun in hand, and Adam, with a hand on the butt of his own pistol, looked around wildly to locate the attacker.

Willie, however, seemed unconcerned. He thumbed another round of cartridges into the cylinder and replaced the gun in its holster. Spreading his feet to shoulder width, he crouched into a gunfighter's stance.

Suddenly his hand whipped the pistol from the holster and raised it, aiming at a row of bottles Adam could now see were set up fifteen yards away. The gun bucked in Willie's hand, and Adam counted five more shots fired in quick succession. No bottles were left standing.

The worry, tension, and utter confusion that had built up inside Adam whirled into an explosion of anger. Springing to his feet, he descended the hill with giant strides and grabbed Willie roughly by one arm, swinging Willie around to face him.

"What in the world do you think you're doing?" Adam bellowed.

Willie's whole being registered panic at first. Then, recognizing Adam, he relaxed into an attitude of proud defiance.

"Not bad, huh?" he asked, nodding toward the scattered shards of glass.

Adam let go of Willie's arm and raked his fingers through his hair in exasperation, knocking his hat to the ground in the process. "Have you and your sister both gone crazy?" he demanded.

Willie moved away, swaggering slightly. "Tom's been teaching me." He refilled the empty cylinder. "I think I've got the hang of it."

"Tom," Adam repeated. "And just why does Tom think you might need to know how to do this?"

Willie shrugged. "A man's gotta know how to protect himself. If I ever get in a tight spot, I'll know what to do."

Adam's eyes flashed. "One of the easiest ways to protect yourself from trouble is not to get into tight situations in the first place. Or didn't Tom mention that?" he added, biting the words off one by one. He picked up his hat, slapped it against his leg to knock off the dust, and turned to leave.

"You don't like him, do you?"

Adam turned back to see Willie eyeing him belligerently. He took a slow, deep breath. "No," he said truthfully, "I guess I don't."

"I thought so," Willie said, with some satisfaction. Adam turned again to leave, and once more Willie's words stopped him. "Lizzie does though."

Adam wanted to walk away as quickly as he could, but his feet brought him to an unwilling halt of their own accord. The truth he longed to avoid was being driven home to him with hammerlike blows. He turned back to Willie. "I guess I knew that," he said evenly. "What was wrong with her today, anyway?"

"Oh, that." Willie snorted. "She can't take a joke, that's all. I gave her a note from Tom, asking her to meet him. Only it wasn't from Tom; I wrote it myself. I thought sure she'd catch on, but she rode out as soon as she'd read it. She spent a good bit of time out there, too, waiting for him to show up," he said, chuckling in remembrance. "Then when she got back and found out I'd set her up, she jumped me like a wildcat." His fingers touched the welt on his cheekbone gingerly. "I don't know what the problem was. It was just a little joke."

Adam held himself firmly in check, not following the impulse to close the distance between them and throttle Willie. Only his hands, clenching and unclenching at his sides, betrayed his thoughts. Instead, he turned without another word and strode away.

Chapter 11

Adam's thoughts whirled on his way back. "Has the whole world gone crazy?" he muttered to himself. Willie, whom he had always looked on as a younger brother, was sure acting like it, with his cocky new attitude and his admiration for Tom.

Lizzie, too, had been acting like a madwoman when he pulled her off her brother earlier. He shook his head ruefully, remembering how he had hesitated to take hold of her, not knowing if she would turn on him next. Yes, Lizzie was definitely acting unbalanced, and the cause for that, too, was tied to Tom Mallory.

And what about himself? Adam snorted derisively. He was definitely crazy. Crazy to get involved in Willie and Lizzie's brawl, crazy to try to straighten out a kid who obviously didn't want straightening out, and crazy—definitely, absolutely, certifiably crazy—to have fallen in love with a woman who was smitten with someone else.

Lord, what's going on? Things have always been so peaceful and straightforward around here, but lately it seems like everything's turned upside down. Show me the way so I can know what You want me to do.

Topping a low hill, he spotted Tom Mallory, who was back from the south range and riding in to headquarters. Adam spurred his horse into a lope and set his course to intercept Tom's.

Tom seemed surprised to see Adam bearing down on him, and pulled his horse to a stop. He tilted his hat further back on his head and met Adam with an inquiring grin.

Adam reined in beside Tom and spoke abruptly. "You've been teaching Willie to fast draw."

Tom's grin widened and he leaned back lazily in his saddle. "The boy wanted to learn," he said. "No harm in it."

"Don't you think you should have checked with his father first?"

Tom chuckled. "He's almost a man. When I was his age, I'd been taking care of myself for years. He's got to grow up sometime, and if his daddy won't let him, he'll find a way to do it on his own." He tipped his hat mockingly and rode away.

Adam watched him through slitted eyes. This was beyond anything he could handle alone. He needed help, and he needed it now.

❧

"I've been afraid something like this would happen." Jeff hooked a boot heel on his porch railing and looked at Adam with troubled eyes. "I've seen Mallory shooting." He shook his head. "This is a bad business, Adam."

The younger man nodded his agreement. "I guess I'm a coward. By rights, I should have gone straight to Charles, but I didn't know how to tell him. I was almost hoping you'd tell me I was overreacting."

"I wish I could." Jeff straightened reluctantly. "Let's go get it over with," he said. "We'll tell Charles together."

Adam wished he could be anywhere else at the moment that Jeff tapped on the door of his brother's study. When Charles called for them to enter, he wished it even more. Instead of its usually amiable expression, the older brother's face wore an exhausted frown.

"What is it, Jeff?" His weary tone matched his countenance. The man looked like he carried the weight of the world on his shoulders already, Adam thought. And they were about to add to his concerns.

"Nothing good, I'm afraid," Jeff answered, waving Adam to a seat and closing the door behind them. "I'll get right to it, Charles. How much do you know about Tom Mallory?"

Charles's eyes narrowed. "Only what I saw the day I offered him a job, and what I've seen since, which is that he seems to be a hard worker who knows what he's doing and does it well. Why?"

"Have you noticed the way Willie's been following him around?"

Charles threw his hands in the air and shook his head. "What that boy is thinking lately is anybody's guess. It's sure beyond anything I can understand. He needs someone to look up to, and if Tom Mallory can be a good influence, I suppose I can't complain."

"Even if he's teaching your son to be a gunfighter?"

Utter quiet blanketed the room. Charles froze, his gaze darting between Jeff and Adam. "What are you talking about?" he demanded.

"I've seen Mallory out in the hills, practicing. He's good, Charles, and fast—really fast. And Adam here had an encounter with Willie today. Tell him what you saw, Adam."

I'd just as soon be roping rattlesnakes as this, Adam thought, recounting the scene. He watched Charles's eyes take on a stony glint and his lips tighten into a thin, hard line. Charles started to rise, ready to take decisive action.

"Simmer down." Jeff spoke quietly but firmly. "There's more." Charles gaped at him and slid back into his chair with a thud.

"Lizzie came over to visit Judith the other day," Jeff continued. "It seems the subject of one Tom Mallory came up, and Lizzie went on and on about him. I've talked to Judith about my concerns and she tried to help Lizzie see what kind of person he is, but no luck. Lizzie has stars in her eyes where the fellow's concerned."

Charles groaned and buried his face in his hands. "I've been worried sick about the political situation. Looks like I should have been worrying about things closer to home instead."

He slammed a fist on his desk, sending a bottle of ink skittering perilously close to the edge. "What's he trying to do, corrupt my whole family?" He rubbed a weary hand across his face, the picture of dejection. "If we weren't so short-handed, with Hank laid up, I'd fire him on the spot. As it is, I'll have to keep him on until after roundup. But you can count on me putting him on notice. There will be no contact—none—between him and any member of the family except Jeff and me. And woe unto him if he tries to defy me!"

The door swung open just wide enough to admit Lizzie's head. "Oh," she said dully when she saw the three men talking. "I didn't mean to disturb you. I'll come back later."

"Stop right there," Charles commanded. "I need to talk to you, and now's as good a time as any. No," he said as Adam and Jeff moved to leave. "You both know what's going on. You might as well stay."

Those rattlesnakes are looking better and better, Adam thought. Lizzie entered the room hesitantly, and Adam studied her face closely, seeking a clue to her present condition.

Traces of the emotional storm still lingered. Her eyes were puffy, and red blotches stood out against her pale skin, hinting at the earlier tears. A faint bruise was beginning to show along the knuckles of her right hand. Adam figured that must have been where she'd connected with Willie's cheekbone.

Lizzie stopped just inside the room and pressed her back against the wall. Her look flitted from Charles to Jeff to Adam and back to Charles, reminding Adam of a trapped bird facing a group of hungry cats.

"I just came in to borrow a book," she said uneasily. "I can wait."

"What I have to say can't wait." Charles fixed his daughter with a long, measuring look. "Sit down," he ordered without further preamble.

Moving mechanically, Lizzie slid into the leather chair facing Charles's desk. She sat warily, shoulders tensed and hands clasped tightly in her lap, making the resemblance to a trapped creature even more pronounced. She hunched her shoulders slightly and lowered her head, as if awaiting a blow.

Adam's heart went out to her. If he could, he'd sweep her up in his arms and carry her out of there, regardless of her father's presence. But he didn't have that right, he reminded himself bitterly.

"What's this I hear about you and Tom Mallory?" Charles demanded. Lizzie flinched as if a blow had indeed been struck.

Her face ashen, she raised her chin and met her father's angry gaze. "I don't know what to tell you until I know what you've heard," she said with a touch of defiance.

Charles let out a deep breath that was almost a growl. "It has come to my attention," he said, measuring his words, "that you're sweet on Mallory. It has also come to my attention that this swain of yours is no better than a common gunfighter, and he's teaching your brother to follow in his footsteps."

"That's not true!" Lizzie leaped to her feet and faced her father across his desk.

"You don't care for Mallory, then?" Charles asked, eyeing her steadily.

"No! I mean. . .I mean. . ." Her voice trailed off as a hot red wave swept up her neck and suffused her face.

Adam could feel her humiliation at having her feelings laid bare in front of the three of them. *Oh, my sweet Lizzie, I hate to see you suffer like this. But you're too good to throw yourself away on someone like Mallory!*

"I think we can see what you mean," her father said grimly. "Just how far has this infatuation gone, Lizzie? Hasn't it occurred to you that a man like that is only interested in—"

"How can you say that?" cried Lizzie. "You don't know anything about him or what he's really like. How can you sit in judgment like this without any proof?"

Charles, making an obvious effort to control himself, steepled his fingers and waited a moment before he spoke again. "It seems to me," he began, "that an honorable man, the kind of man I'd consider as a son-in-law, would have come to me openly, instead of sneaking around behind my back and encouraging you to do the same. Just how much more proof do I need?

"And that's just the part that has to do with you," he went on. "I have it on good authority he's been teaching your brother the art of gunfighting. Is this really the kind of man you expect me to approve of?"

"Don't talk to me about Willie," Lizzie put in. "If he's the one who's been filling your head with these wild stories, I wouldn't believe them for a minute. Willie's word isn't always to be trusted."

Her self-control was dangerously close to slipping away completely, Adam thought. He watched the scene uncomfortably, wondering if he'd witness a repeat of the previous explosion. *I'd just as soon not, Lord.*

One rescue a day is about all a man can deal with.

"Let's get back to the main issue," Charles said. "In this case, you and Mallory. I don't understand, Lizzie," he said, his voice betraying his hurt. "If you honestly felt something for him, why didn't you talk to your mother or me? Why slip around like this?"

Lizzie drew herself up with what dignity she had left. "It's true. I care for Tom, and he cares for me. We planned to tell you soon. As for why we didn't say anything earlier, just look at the way you're behaving now." Her voice warmed with passion. "Look at the way you've already judged Tom, without ever talking to him yourself. Can you honestly say that if he—one of your employees—came to you and said he wanted to come calling on me, you'd welcome him with open arms?"

It was Charles's turn to look uncomfortable, and Lizzie, seeing this, pressed her advantage. "Can you?" she repeated.

"I don't know, Lizzie," he admitted. "Perhaps not. But that doesn't make your own underhanded behavior any more acceptable."

"My behavior has been just fine all along," Lizzie stormed. "So has Tom's." She strode to the door and yanked it open, pausing to turn back for a parting shot. "You go ahead and believe all the lies you want to. I know Tom's a fine man—and you'll find out the truth some day!" The crash of the door reverberated through the room.

Charles slumped in his chair and let out a long sigh. "I sure put her in her place, didn't I?" he asked ruefully.

Adam excused himself and walked back toward the bunkhouse, deep in thought. That Tom Mallory was wrong for Lizzie was certain. That Lizzie fancied herself in love with him was equally certain. Adam had heard her admit her feelings for Tom with increasing despair, each word hitting him like a hammer blow.

He had halfway expected it, although hearing it stated in such unvarnished terms had wounded him more than he'd anticipated. What he hadn't been prepared for was Charles's admission that he might not approve a mere ranch hand as a suitor for Lizzie.

Adam tried to console himself with Charles's wholehearted enthusiasm for his ranch. Owning his own spread would mean he would no longer be a hired hand, but a solid businessman.

At least that was how Adam looked at it. But would Charles see it the same way?

Chapter 12

R ider comin'," Bert announced.

Adam looked up from pounding a new rim into place on a wagon wheel and shaded his eyes with one hand. The sun was nearly straight overhead; its brilliant light dazzled his eyes. "Can you tell who it is?" he asked.

"No one I know, far as I can tell," Bert replied.

The rider on the tall chestnut gelding drew up fifteen yards from them. "Mornin'," he drawled, dismounting in one fluid motion. "Or is it afternoon?" He smiled, an engaging grin turning up the corners of his mouth and brightening his face.

Adam removed his hat and wiped his forehead with his sleeve. "Whichever it is, it's close enough to time to break for lunch," he said, returning the stranger's grin. He thrust forth a hand. "Name's Adam McKenzie."

The other man gripped his hand firmly. "Henry Antrim."

"Are you looking for work, or just passing through?"

Henry mopped the back of his neck with a bandanna. "Actually, I'm looking for a friend of mine. I was told he was working here. Tom Mallory—you know him?"

Adam narrowed his eyes and examined Antrim more closely. He didn't seem like a bad sort, but Tom Mallory was definitely a wild one, and any friend of his might bear watching.

"Mallory's out doctoring cattle," he said cautiously. "He's not due in until evening."

A voice hailed Adam and Bert from the direction of the ranch house, and they turned to see Willie waving to them from the porch.

"Jeff needs to talk to you both about something," he told them when they met him halfway to the house. "He'd like you to have lunch with us, if you're ready to eat."

Bert grinned. Vera's cooking put their usual bunkhouse fare in the shade. "That won't take much persuadin'," he said. He hesitated and glanced back over his shoulder. "Fellow out there just rode in looking for Mallory," he told Willie. "Maybe we should feed him at the bunkhouse and come see Jeff after lunch."

Adam winced inwardly. Knowing how Willie idolized Tom, he feared the boy would immediately claim any friend of his hero's for his own. He wasn't disappointed. Willie's face lit up as soon as he heard Tom's name, and he went at once to ask Henry Antrim to have lunch with the family. They were too far away to hear Antrim's response, but Adam could see him shake his head and shuffle his feet, seemingly reluctant to accept the invitation.

Adam watched Willie turn on all his persuasive powers, waving his hands for emphasis. Finally, Antrim laughed, clapped Willie on the shoulder, and accompanied him to the house. "I sure hope this is okay," he said quietly to Adam while they washed up on the back porch. "I don't want to push my way into a family meal." Adam reluctantly chalked up one point in Antrim's favor. Tom Mallory, with his overly confident ways, would never have considered turning down an opportunity to have himself included in the family circle.

Jeff, Abby, and Lizzie stood waiting in the dining room when they entered. Vera placed the last steaming serving bowls in place and chuckled when Adam and Bert inhaled the aroma gratefully.

Adam cast a quizzical glance at Charles's empty chair. Abby hastened to explain. "Charles had planned to be here, too, but Matt Chambers is talking about selling off his place, and Charles had to go meet with him at the last minute. We were already looking forward to the idea of having you and Bert for dinner, though, so Jeff agreed to play host. The addition of Mr. Antrim is a welcome surprise."

"Thank you, ma'am," the newcomer responded politely. He still seemed somewhat ill at ease, Adam thought, but his reserve appeared to be melting away at the sight of Vera's cooking.

Watching Jeff help Abby into her chair, Adam realized Willie had not made a move to help Lizzie, and he moved toward her. But he had hesitated too long, and Jeff performed that task as well. Adam berated himself. Here he'd had a perfectly good opportunity to catch her attention while Tom Mallory was nowhere nearby, and he had muffed it.

On second thought, he wondered if Lizzie had any idea who had held her chair for her. She sat silent, her eyes fastened on her plate, not seeming to know or care who else was in the room.

Jeff led the family in saying grace, then waited until the platters of food had been passed around to begin talking to Adam and Bert about his idea for fencing a portion of the range.

Following a spirited discussion of the pros and cons, Abby glanced around the table and asked, "Is anyone ready for seconds?" She laughed gently at Bert's haste in taking advantage of the opportunity. "What brings you to the Double B, Mr. Antrim?" she asked, turning to her unexpected guest.

Henry Antrim wiped his mouth with his napkin and took a swallow of water from his tumbler before replying. "I was just passing through, ma'am, and thought I'd look up a friend who works here."

"How nice!" Abby said brightly, looking at the other two ranch hands. "Was it Adam or Bert you came to see?"

"Actually, ma'am," he replied, looking embarrassed once more, "it wasn't either one of them. Tom Mallory's the friend I'm looking for."

Lizzie's head snapped up, her face brightening for the first time since they had entered the room.

"You know Tom?" she asked eagerly.

"I should smile I do," Antrim answered, giving her a thoughtful look. "Known him for years. We've been through a lot together."

Lizzie's face grew even brighter, and Adam laid his fork down on the table. Vera's famous apple pie, which had been so tempting only moments earlier, had suddenly lost its appeal.

"Tell us about him," Lizzie requested.

"He's a good man," said Henry Antrim. He forked up a generous bite of the flaky pastry and chewed thoughtfully. "I'm not sure what all you want to hear, but I can tell you he's helped me out of more than one tight spot, and he's as loyal a friend as I've had."

Lizzie lifted her chin and cast a challenging look at both Jeff and Adam. It was obvious to Adam that she was gathering ammunition to use in a future round with her father.

"That's so nice to hear," she answered sweetly.

Henry Antrim shifted in his chair as if sensing there was more to this conversation than appeared on the surface, but not knowing what it was. He scooted his chair away from the table.

"Ma'am," he said, nodding to Abby, "I've enjoyed this meal more than anything I've had in a long while, but I don't want to impose on you any longer. If you'll excuse me, I'll mosey on now and see if I can't run across Mallory on my way."

Abby returned his smile. "It's been a pleasure to have you, Mr. Antrim. I'm only sorry my husband wasn't here to meet you. Feel free to stop in again any time you're passing this way." She rose to escort him to the door, and the rest of the company followed them out onto the porch.

Adam had to admit that Antrim wasn't so bad. *If I didn't know he and Mallory were friends, I'd be tempted to partner with him myself. He is one likable fellow.*

Adam stretched, trying to make himself believe he hadn't over-eaten. Vera's cooking was way too good to pass up, and he'd done his share to keep it from going to waste. He leaned against the porch railing while the women and Willie returned to the house, and watched idly as Henry Antrim checked his cinch and mounted his horse.

Jeff, looking similarly stuffed, watched, too. Beyond Antrim's horse, they saw Charles emerge from the barn. He looked up curiously at Antrim, who touched his hat brim in a casual salute and rode off.

"I wonder when Charles slipped in?" Jeff said idly. "He sure missed a good meal."

"You aren't getting enough home cooking these days?" Adam joked.

Charles stared curiously after the departing guest and walked slowly to join them. "Who was that?" he asked when he reached the porch. "He looked familiar, but I can't place him."

Jeff's mouth quirked up in a half-smile. "An unexpected dinner guest," he answered. "He also happens to be a friend of Tom Mallory's."

Charles halted in midstride. "He ate at my table?"

Jeff nodded in wry amusement. "He showed up at mealtime, and Willie wouldn't take no for an answer."

Charles compressed his lips and shook his head. His eyes followed the horse and rider, growing smaller in the distance. "What was his name?"

"Antrim," Adam answered. "Henry Antrim." Charles swung around to gaze at him in disbelief, then pivoted to stare after Antrim's retreating figure.

Jeff looked as startled as Adam felt. "Something wrong, Charles?" he asked his brother.

Charles looked from Jeff to Adam and back again. His lips were drawn in a thin line and the skin around his eyes was taut. "I thought his face looked familiar," he stated in a harsh voice. "Henry Antrim also goes by the name Billy Antrim. Also by William Bonney. But he's best known as Billy the Kid."

Jeff and Adam watched in silence as he stormed off, calling for Abby.

◈

Lizzie slipped into her riding skirt with a sense of elation. The unexpected arrival of Henry Antrim at lunch and his championship of Tom had buoyed her sagging spirits for the first time in days. The altercation with Willie had been bad enough; the rift between herself and her father was worse. Being dressed down by him in front of Uncle Jeff and Adam had been one of the most humiliating experiences of her life.

Now, though, she had her own ammunition. Mr. Antrim had endorsed Tom's character in no uncertain terms, and in front of witnesses, no less! When her father heard about that, he would have to withdraw his objections and give Tom his approval.

He wouldn't like it, she knew, but he was a fair man and would do the right thing. She adjusted her skirt with a smug grin, thinking of how Uncle Jeff and Adam had been present for both scenes, and would have to lend support to her story.

Thank You, Lord. You really are making my way plain. She was amazed at how easy it had been to find answers since she'd started asking God for guidance. It was just like she'd heard in sermons all her life. Why had it taken her this long to put it into practice for herself?

The pounding on her door put an abrupt end to her reflections. "Lizzie?" her father bellowed. "Are you in there?"

Lingering resentment from their earlier blowup flared for a moment, and Lizzie wondered nervously what he wanted. Then she remembered her newfound strategy and strode confidently to open her door.

"Come to my office," her father ordered brusquely. "I need to talk to you."

Lizzie followed him along the hallway, hating the feeling that she was a little girl again, about to get a lecture. She was a woman, she reminded herself, and was prepared to conduct herself accordingly.

The sight of her mother seated in front of the heavy desk gave her a moment's pause. Abby's face was strained and her hands were clasped tightly in her lap. Lizzie wondered if this was indeed about Tom, or if something awful had happened. Not Willie! A surge of fear clutched at her heart. Infuriating as he was, she didn't know what she'd do if something terrible happened to her brother.

She had intended to remain standing, even after her father jabbed a finger toward one of the heavy wooden chairs, but her mother's presence and her concern for Willie weakened her resolve, and she found herself sinking obediently into the seat.

"Young lady—" Charles began, halting as Abby raised a hand in protest.

"Not that way, Charles, please," she said. She turned to Lizzie and searched her face carefully. "You remember Mr. Antrim of course."

The perfect opening! Lizzie sat up straighter and tilted her chin, looking past her mother into her father's stormy eyes. "Of course! Did you tell Papa what he said about Tom?"

"I started to," her mother replied. "But it turned out he had something to tell me, instead. You see, dear, Mr. Antrim wasn't quite who he appeared to be."

Lizzie looked from one parent to the other in confusion. "What do you mean? Are you saying he isn't a friend of Tom's?"

"Oh, I have no doubt he's a friend of Mallory's," Charles said, rejoining the conversation. "That's just the problem."

Lizzie glanced at her mother for illumination. Abby cleared her throat and gave her daughter a sympathetic look. "It appears we've just broken bread with none other than Billy the Kid."

Lizzie sat a moment in stunned silence before she found her voice. "He—Mr. Antrim, I mean—"

"Is the same outlaw who's been causing nothing but trouble throughout the territory."

"I don't believe it!" Lizzie cried hotly.

"Here." Her mother spread a large sheet of paper on the desk. "Your father has a copy of a wanted poster. Look at the picture."

Lizzie looked closely, hoping against hope it was only a superficial resemblance. But even she couldn't deny that the face on the poster was that of their recent guest.

"Even so," she protested, rallying, "it doesn't change all the fine things he said about Tom. It's Tom's character we're concerned with, not—"

"Exactly," her father interrupted. "If he's a close friend of a notorious outlaw, what does that say about his character?"

"Mother, will you make him listen to reason?"

Abby's usually calm voice quavered as she spoke. "I'm afraid I agree completely, Lizzie. If this is the kind of companion Mr. Mallory chooses—"

Lizzie wheeled and dashed out of the office. Nearly knocking Willie over as they collided in the front doorway, she ignored his startled yelp and headed straight for the barn. She saddled Dancer in record time and rode off like the wind.

Tears blinded her, and she dashed them away angrily. Conflicting thoughts whirled through her mind. Henry Antrim couldn't be Billy the Kid! She rejected the thought, remembering his polite behavior at dinner. But there was no doubt in her mind the picture on the poster was his. Maybe Willie was right in his assessment of Billy. No, she had heard too many stories to believe that, even for a moment. Maybe Tom didn't know what his friend really was. But she had to dismiss that notion, too. They couldn't have been friends for such a long time without Tom knowing all about him.

God, where are You? her soul cried. *I thought You were on my side!*

Lizzie galloped into Judith's yard without bothering to cool Dancer down and tossed the reins to a startled Sammy. "Watch him for me, Sam. I need to talk to your mother."

She burst into the front room without waiting for a response to her knock and found Judith rising heavily from the settee.

"Lizzie, are you all right?" Concern colored her aunt's voice. "Has something happened at home?"

"It's horrible, Aunt Judith! It's so unfair!" She began to sob out her painful story. Judith sank back onto the couch, her eyes never leaving Lizzie's face throughout her recital. When Lizzie had finished, Judith sat still, watching her carefully.

"What can I do?" Lizzie wailed. "I have to make them see they're wrong."

Judith's eyes closed briefly, as if offering up a prayer for guidance. "Lizzie," she said in a voice that was quiet yet full of strength, "I want you to listen carefully. I know how you feel about Tom Mallory. And you know how concerned Jeff and I have been about that. I've been praying that God would show us all the truth about him." She paused, holding Lizzie's gaze with her own. "I believe He has."

Lizzie's jaw dropped, and she fought to control her quivering lower lip. "You mean you're siding with them?" She saw the pain in Judith's eyes and knew the answer.

"But I've been praying, too," Lizzie countered. "And I believe God has answered my prayers. Are you telling me He will answer you, but not me?" She paced wildly across the room, unable to stand still a moment longer.

"Well, are you?" she demanded when Judith didn't answer.

Judith's face was pale, her gaze fixed on something in the far distance. "Lizzie—" she began.

"You're the one who told me He had a wonderful plan for my life," Lizzie broke in. "And you were right; He does. I believe Tom is part of that plan. And no matter what you or my parents think—"

"Lizzie." Quiet as it was, the tone of Judith's voice brought her up short. "I want you to gather the children together and take them home with you."

"What? Aunt Judith, you have to understand—"

"Do it now, Lizzie," Judith ordered. "Find Jeff, or send someone to get him. And send your mother over quickly." She offered a faltering smile at Lizzie's bewildered expression. "It's the baby, honey. He's coming. Do you understand, Lizzie? I need you to do these things. Now."

The words finally penetrated Lizzie's brain. She helped Judith to her bed and into her nightdress, then raced out the door to obey.

Chapter 13

Two hours after returning to the ranch house, Lizzie felt as if she were ready to explode. She had gathered the three children, putting Sammy and Rose together on their gentle mare and holding little Travis securely in front of her on her own horse. Leading them home as quickly as she dared, she had been relieved to find Jeff saddling his own horse. Upon hearing Lizzie's news, he had climbed into the saddle and raced off without a word. Abby had set out in the buggy after gathering up some supplies.

Lizzie read to the excited children, played tag and hide and seek with them, and now felt both her patience and her resources were exhausted. She settled the trio at the table in the kitchen and poured them tall glasses of milk.

"Why haven't we had any word?" she fretted to Vera, who was setting out a plate of molasses cookies. "How long does it take, anyway?"

Vera, imperturbable as always, cocked an amused eye at Lizzie. "It hasn't been all that long since Travis was born. Don't you remember how we waited all day long for news of him?"

"All day!" Lizzie fumed. "I'll go crazy if I have to stay cooped up much longer."

"Are you sure you don't have more on your mind than Judith's baby?" Vera asked with a knowing look.

Lizzie shot her a sharp glance but didn't reply. Somehow, Vera always seemed to know what was going on with members of the Bradley household, often before they were aware of it themselves.

"Why don't you go take some time for yourself?" Vera continued. "I'll keep an eye on these three until you work off some of that steam."

"Would you?" Lizzie rushed around the table to give the housekeeper a hug of gratitude. "Thanks, Vera. I wouldn't do this if I didn't really need the time alone. I'll make it up to you, I promise."

"Oh, get along now," Vera replied, giving Lizzie a good-natured swat on her behind. "Give that horse of yours a good workout and come back in a better frame of mind, that's all I ask."

Like a bird loosed from its cage, Lizzie flew out the door. She had Dancer saddled and was on her way in short order. Bending low over the horse's neck, she relished the feel of the wind whipping her hair. She wished the wind could blow away the turmoil in her mind as easily.

She gave Dancer his head and exulted in his response, his long stride eating up the ground. Sooner than she would have thought possible, she saw the familiar outline of the cedar grove. Their grove, hers and Tom's. The perfect place to spend some time by herself to calm her nerves. She pulled Dancer down to a trot, then a walk, to let him cool off after their wild run.

Slipping from her saddle, she was in the process of loosening Dancer's cinch when she heard hoofbeats not far away. She was startled, but not afraid. In her present mood, she wasn't afraid of anything or anyone. Just let someone try to tangle with her now!

A thought struck her and twisted her stomach into a knot. What if it was that officious Adam McKenzie, coming to spy on her? She almost hoped it was. She'd give him a piece of her mind! Peering out between the cedars, she saw not Adam's horse drawing near, but Tom's.

"Tom!" she cried joyfully. She threw her arms around his neck as soon as he dismounted.

"Whoa! Steady there," he said, trying to maintain his balance under her unexpected assault. "I saw you coming in here, but I never expected this kind of greeting." Lizzie realized just how brazen she'd been and stepped back, embarrassed. Tom's grin widened. "I'm not complaining," he continued. "In fact, I'd like to try that again." And suddenly Lizzie found herself held tightly in his arms.

She tensed, then relaxed as she warmed to the feel of his arms around her. Her own arms crept around Tom's neck again and held him fast, tightening when she felt the beat of his heart beneath her own. "Oh Tom," she breathed. "I'm so glad you came! It's been awful these last few days."

"Miss me that much?" he asked with a cocky grin. "I think I like that." Then, seeing her troubled face, his expression sobered. "What's the matter? What's been going on?"

"Everything's the matter!" Lizzie cried, waving her hands dramatically. Tom loosened his grip and she strode back and forth, unable to stand still a moment longer. "It's my family—all of them. They think you're some kind of monster. They've tried to make me believe you're a gunfighter, that you're connected somehow with Billy the Kid, and that you're leading Willie and me down the path to ruin."

Lizzie saw Tom freeze in place and watch her with a guarded expression. "Where'd they get ideas like that?" he asked slowly.

"Oh, some crazy notions Uncle Jeff and Adam McKenzie got in their heads. And then when your friend came to lunch today—"

"What friend?" Tom cut in suspiciously.

"He said his name was Henry Antrim." Lizzie's eyes glowed with pride while she recounted the fine things he had said. "It was wonderful, Tom. Perfect timing. But then my father came home, and he thinks Henry Antrim is actually Billy the Kid."

"Your father knows?"

Lizzie went on, oblivious. "He and my mother had me cornered, trying to fill my head with doubts about you. But I stuck up for you, Tom. I didn't let them sway me. Even when my father said he knew about us meeting, I didn't back down a bit." She faltered a moment, noticing his shocked expression for the first time.

"You told your father about us meeting here?" he asked, looking edgy.

"Not to start with. That is, I don't know how he found out, but when he confronted me, I didn't deny it." She laid a trembling hand on his arm. "I couldn't deny you, Tom. I wouldn't! And he'll come around in time. Don't worry about that. I'll admit he wasn't happy when I told him how we felt about each other, but once he gets used to the idea. . ."

She broke off as Tom let out a low moan and paced back and forth, raking his fingers through his hair until the dark brown strands stood on end. Lizzie watched helplessly, unable to understand.

"It's really all right," she told him. "I know we weren't ready to tell him about us yet, but. . ." Her voice trailed off at the look on Tom's face.

He stopped his pacing and took her by the shoulders. "Lizzie," he began in a husky voice. She looked at him wonderingly, trustingly. He held her gaze for a moment then averted his eyes. He cleared his throat and started over. "You're a wonderful girl, Lizzie." Her heart felt as though it would pound right through her chest. The moment had come at last—he was about to propose! "Way too good for the likes of me," he continued, and her heart melted as she watched him struggle to find the right words.

"You don't have to go through all this," she whispered, wanting to make it easier for him. "I know what you're trying to say."

"I don't think so." He laughed bitterly and drew a long breath. "Lizzie," he said, framing her face with his hands, "there is no 'us.' "

She smiled reassuringly and shook her head. "It's all right," she repeated. "No matter what they say, I believe in you, Tom. In fact," she declared boldly, carried away by a sudden idea. "I'll leave with you right now if you want. Once we're married, they'll have to—"

"Hold on there!" The alarmed note in his voice stopped her as effectively as a dousing with cold water. "Listen to me, Lizzie, and listen good." One glance at her bewildered face made him groan again.

"Look, honey, I never meant to hurt you. You're a sweet girl and we've had a lot of fun together." Lizzie felt like she had stepped off a cliff into empty space. This wasn't going at all the way it was supposed to.

Tom looked at her with pleading eyes, begging her to understand. "But that's all that it's been, fun. A good time."

"A good time?" Lizzie echoed hollowly. "But Tom, you kissed me!

You let me think—"

"Hold on." Tom held his hand up defensively. "Whatever you thought was all in your own mind, not mine." He twisted uncomfortably and rubbed his hands together, trying to explain. "I like women, Lizzie. I always have. And they've always liked me." He shrugged, and his lips curled up in a self-deprecating grin that twisted at her heart.

"You mean you've done this...with other women? It didn't mean anything special to you?"

Tom's grin faded a bit and he shifted uneasily. "Come on, Lizzie, you're making too big a thing out of this. Sure I've kissed other women. I've done a lot more than kiss some of them, too," he said, beginning to sound angry. "But you're such an innocent, I couldn't go any further with you. I do have some scruples, you know."

Lizzie couldn't answer. She just stood there looking at him with wounded eyes. Without another word, he grabbed his horse's reins and swung into the saddle.

He paused at the edge of the grove and turned to her one last time. "I'm leaving now. Knowing how your father feels, I don't think I'll be welcome here much longer." When she didn't answer, his voice grew rough with irritation. "It's time you grew up, Lizzie. Quit acting like I've done something terrible. I didn't do a thing to hurt you, not really. And you never know," he continued, the familiar heart-stopping grin beginning to tug at the corners of his mouth, "I may have done you a favor by waking you up a bit. You may wind up thanking me for this after all." He spurred his mount and loped off toward the distant hills.

Lizzie stood frozen in place. Finally she moved one stiff leg forward, then the other, until she was just inside the protective shelter of the trees. Standing with one hand braced against the trunk of a small cedar, she watched numbly as Tom's figure dwindled to a speck in the distance and then topped a low hill to disappear from her life forever.

Chapter 14

Lizzie turned and made her stumbling way back to the fallen log. Their log. She looked again at the places she had treasured. The promises she thought they held had turned out to be empty, and she felt as if their very existence mocked her.

She clung to the numbness, wrapping herself in its folds as if it were a protective cocoon. If she waited long enough, surely this would turn out to be nothing more than a bad dream. But never, never in a million years, would she have dreamed Tom would betray her trust and then ride away.

Lizzie could feel her flimsy armor cracking, and she fought against it. If she could preserve this blessed lack of feeling, she might somehow live through this moment. But the first pricks of pain skirted their way through the fragile shell and opened the way for other, stronger shafts of anguish that assured her this was no dream, but bitter reality.

Tom's words came back to dance through her mind, tormenting her thoughts. What was it he'd said? *"Quit acting like I've done something terrible. I never meant to hurt you."* If only he knew!

Lizzie's legs began to tremble so that she could barely stand. Then they gave way altogether and she pitched forward onto her knees and buried her face in her lap. How could she have been so foolish?

She pressed her hands over her eyes, trying to blot out the sight of those places she had thought so special. Despite her efforts, her mind pitilessly replayed every memory of every moment she and Tom had spent together.

Lizzie writhed with humiliation as those scenes unfolded. Looking at them with the eyes of her painful new knowledge, she could see how naive she must have seemed to Tom, whose worldly experience vastly outweighed her own. How he must have laughed, she thought miserably, seeing how easily she had been duped! She had yielded to everything he asked of her, would have run off at a single word from him, she remembered with mortification. And those moments she deemed so precious had never meant anything to him at all.

Lizzie rocked back and forth, her breath coming out in helpless little whimpers that grew into racking sobs. Knowing she was utterly alone, Lizzie gave way to her feelings and wailed aloud as she poured out her pain, her grief, her shame.

ॐ

Adam McKenzie rode in a slow loop that would bring him back to ranch headquarters soon after dark. What a whirlwind day this had turned out to be! He had thought he would be glad to see Tom Mallory's true character unmasked. But after Charles's revelation and the following confrontation between him and Lizzie, then Jeff's rapid departure to see to the birth of his fourth child, Adam had had enough emotional turmoil for one day.

He had volunteered to look over the area Charles and Jeff wanted to fence, knowing it would take him the rest of the day to finish the job, and welcoming the solitude it offered. After what he'd gone through, Adam felt he was due for some peace and quiet.

Inspecting the area had meant a fair amount of physical exertion but involved little thought, just what he'd needed to calm his spirit and clear his brain. The lengthy ride gave him plenty of time to do some serious praying, too, something Adam was grateful for.

He leaned back in his saddle, more relaxed than he had been in days, and enjoyed his horse's smooth, even gait. When the bay's ears pricked up and pointed straight ahead, it took a moment to register in Adam's mind. Then he snapped out of his reverie and looked to see what had caught the animal's attention.

In the distance, a lone rider emerged from a stand of trees. The rider halted and turned his mount slightly, as though he meant to turn back, then wheeled the horse around and headed south at a gallop.

Adam stopped and tried to puzzle it out. As far as he knew, no

Bradley riders should have been in the area, and no one else had any call to be there. Of course, it could have been a drifter who found a shady spot for an afternoon rest. But why pause and turn back, almost as if talking to someone else there? And why ride away in such a hurry?

Moreover, the outline of horse and rider bore a striking resemblance to Tom Mallory, and Adam could see no reason for him to be stopping there. No good reason, that is. But with Mallory, who could tell?

It bore checking out, Adam thought as he nudged his horse into a trot, then a lope. Adam didn't like mysteries. He preferred things to be honest and open, and there had been far too many things lately that had been anything but. He'd be glad to satisfy his curiosity on this point so easily.

He slowed again as he neared the trees, looking for tracks and any other telltale signs that might help him grasp the situation. He cut across the trail of the other horse and felt a grim satisfaction as he recognized the tracks of Mallory's mount. He had come along here, paused for a moment or two, then continued toward the trees. *Finding a quiet spot to practice his gunslinging?* Adam wondered.

The bay halted of its own accord at the same moment Adam heard the sound. An eerie wail, rising and falling, only to rise again, sounding like an animal in torment. Not daring to speculate on what he might find, he jabbed his spurs into his horse's flanks and headed into the trees at a gallop.

Adam pulled his horse to a sliding stop as he spotted another horse standing head down in the clearing. Dancer? He swung around frantically, and his heart stood still at the sight of a disheveled Lizzie crumpled in a heap in the dust, howling out her misery like a lost soul.

He froze for a moment, fearing the worst. Then he leapt toward her and gathered her in his arms. "Lizzie, sweetheart, what is it?" he murmured gently, all the while thinking, *Mallory! If he's harmed her, he'll regret the day he was born!*

He pressed her head against his chest with one hand and stroked her hair, comforting her as he would a frightened child. To his great relief, Lizzie didn't resist his embrace, but leaned against his shoulder and continued to weep.

Adam settled Lizzie into his lap, feeling the warmth of her body, feeling it quiver against him. He crooned endearments in her ear, not knowing whether she heard, but hoping the soothing sounds would calm her. The sweetness of this proximity was something Adam would have wanted to prolong had it been under happier circumstances. Now, though, it was vital to find out just what was wrong before Tom Mallory gained too much of a head start.

"Shh, honey, settle down. I need to talk to you," he whispered, smoothing moist wisps of hair away from her forehead with his fingertips. "Can you hear me, Lizzie?" Sobs continued to rack her body and her shoulders jerked convulsively, although her cries were diminishing in volume.

Adam groaned inwardly, even as he tightened his hold on her. *Lizzie, my love, I can't stand seeing you like this. I promise you, if Mallory has harmed you in any way, I'll take care of that sorry piece of trash myself!*

Finally, only a few pitiful moans escaped her lips, and while her breath continued to come in jerky gasps, it seemed to Adam that most of the tumult had passed. Breathing more easily himself, he loosened his hold on Lizzie, rocking gently as he cradled her in his arms.

The fervent wish that she were there of her own accord was immediately followed by a mental tongue-lashing. Adam berated himself for enjoying a situation that had cost Lizzie so much. And what that cost might be was something that needed to be determined quickly, he reminded himself, before the miscreant had time to complete his getaway.

Adam put a finger under Lizzie's chin and tilted her head back gently. It took a moment for her eyes, still blurred by tears, to focus on his face, and another moment before she seemed fully aware of who he was. When awareness of his presence registered on her features, she ducked her head again and laid it trustingly against his chest. Adam thrilled to the knowledge that she did this of her own volition, and his hand trembled as he tenderly wiped the tears from her sodden cheeks.

How he'd love to stay like this, enjoying her nearness and being her source of comfort! But duty reared its stern head and reminded him that he needed information, and needed it now.

How on earth do I ask her? he wondered in a momentary panic. *It ought to be her father talking to her like this, or at least Jeff. Lord,* he breathed, *You're going to have to give me the words and the strength, because I can't do this one on my own.*

"Lizzie?" he asked tentatively. "Can you hear me now?" She swiveled slightly in his lap, raising her face to meet his. Her lips still quivered, but he was relieved to see that her breathing had steadied.

She nodded slowly, her eyes dull. "Yes, Adam. I hear you."

Adam swallowed and tried to work some moisture into his suddenly dry mouth. "When I was riding up, I saw someone leaving here. It looked like—like Mallory. Was it?"

Lizzie's lips quivered even more and Adam could feel the tremor that ran through her body at the mention of Mallory's name. "Was it?" he repeated gently.

She lowered her eyes. "Yes. It was him."

Adam drew a ragged breath. "Lizzie, I have to ask you this. Lord knows I don't want to, but I need to know. Did he. . .did he hurt you?"

Lizzie buried her face in her hands, and Adam's heart sank like a stone. She heaved a great sigh and raised her face once more, still avoiding his eyes. "No, Adam," she whispered. "Not in the way you mean."

Adam tried not to let the surge of relief show in his voice. If she hadn't been harmed physically, it was obvious that something had happened to reduce her to this state, and he meant to tread softly so as not to cause her more pain.

"Then what is it?" he asked, taking advantage of the moment and daring to encircle her in his arms once more. "You don't go to pieces like this for nothing."

Her brittle laugh shocked him. "Don't I?" she asked bitterly. "You pulled me off of Willie just the other day, remember? And you saw that scene in my father's office, as I recall. The one where I made a complete fool of myself standing up for T-Tom." She managed to get the last words out just before her face crumpled and she pressed one hand against her lips.

"There's nothing wrong with standing up for what you believe in," Adam said, searching frantically for the right words to offer her.

Lizzie battled for control before she could speak again. "There is when what you believe in is based on a lie."

"You mean Mallory—"

"Tom's gone," Lizzie stated flatly. "Gone for good. I was a fool, Adam. A fool, pure and simple."

"No, Lizzie. Never that. If you had feelings for Mallory and thought they were returned, it was his doing, not yours." Her silence gave Adam the boldness to continue. "Maybe he's never met a woman like you before, someone who's loving and good. He didn't have the sense to realize what he had and treasure it." His arms tightened around her just a fraction. "If anyone's a fool, Lizzie, it's him, not you."

She tilted her head and looked him fully in the eyes as if searching the depths of his soul. She nodded slowly, apparently satisfied with what she saw. "Thank you, Adam. I believe you mean that." Her lips curved briefly in a tremulous smile. "I'm only sorry I can't agree with you."

Adam's senses reeled at the intensity of her gaze. For once he held Lizzie Bradley's attention, and held it completely.

He held Lizzie herself, for that matter, he reminded himself with wonder. The golden hair flowed across his hands in a shimmering wave, and he longed to twine his fingers through its silken strands. Her breath brushed softly against his face.

Looking at the pale pink lips mere inches from his own, Adam wanted more than anything to stop their trembling with his own firm lips, giving her a pledge that as long as he was around, she would never be hurt like that again.

The moment held, then was broken when Lizzie drew back and scrubbed her hands against her face, suddenly looking more like a lost little girl than a desirable woman.

Probably for the best, Lord, Adam thought ruefully as he pulled back himself. *If I started kissing her, it'd be awfully hard to quit.*

He helped Lizzie to her feet, and after she took a few unsteady steps, he boldly scooped her up and carried her. She lay unresisting, a welcome weight in his arms. He reluctantly set her down next to Dancer.

"I don't know what I would have done if you hadn't come along, Adam," she said softly, looking up at him through still-damp lashes while he checked the cinch and gathered the reins for her.

She laid a gentle hand on his arm and a wild thought jolted through him. After all the years of keeping his distance, to have her so near now was overwhelming. Could he dare believe she had feelings for him, too? His heart soared, feeling the first faint stirring of hope. Maybe now was the time to tell her how he felt.

"I want to thank you," she continued, as he tried to marshal his thoughts.

"Lizzie—" he began.

"Having you hold me like that. . ."

Adam's throat constricted and he could hardly believe his ears. Was she telling him she'd enjoyed being held? "I've been waiting for a long time for the chance to—"

"I can't tell you how wonderful it was."

Wonderful didn't fully describe it for Adam. He would use words like heavenly or stupendous. This was going to be easier than he'd thought.

"Lizzie, what I'm trying to say is—"

"It was just like having my father hold me when I was little."

Adam's heart, which had been spiraling into the clouds, plummeted back to the dusty earth with a resounding thud.

"Your father?" he echoed.

Lizzie nodded, her earnest gaze fixed on Adam's. "My mother was very ill when I was a little girl. A few times I got so scared at the thought of losing her that I just fell apart. My father would take me in his lap and hold me and rock me—just like you did—and somehow I knew things were going to be all right."

"Your father," Adam repeated.

"And Uncle Jeff helped, too, sometimes," she added, summoning up a brave smile. "My two favorite men. I guess that almost makes you family, doesn't it, Adam? Kind of like a big brother."

Adam stared in silence, feeling like someone had just poured ice water over him. He shook his head, trying to clear it. *You idiot!* he scolded himself. *And Lizzie thinks* she *built something up out of nothing!*

He grabbed her, none too gently, at her waist, boosted her unceremoniously into the saddle, and handed her the reins. Lizzie stared back at him uncertainly.

"You'd better head for home," he said, slapping Dancer on the rump. "I've got work to finish before dark."

Chapter 15

Lizzie neared the ranch house, flopping loosely in her saddle. Her father would have criticized her horsemanship, calling it sloppy, but right now she didn't care. Her world had turned upside down in the space of a few hours, and something as insignificant as her riding ability wasn't important at the moment.

If she were being honest with herself, nothing seemed important just now. She couldn't remember a time in her life when she'd gone through so many conflicting emotions in such a short time. The hope, the joy that filled her life so recently, had given way to an aching emptiness, and Lizzie didn't know how she was going to cope with that. She was only nineteen, she reflected. How could she exist another fifty years or so, feeling the way she did now?

How could I have been so blind? she asked herself for the hundredth time. *I thought he loved me! How can I ever trust my own judgment again?* The house and outbuildings came into sight and a wave of depression swept over her as she realized she would have to face her family soon. As if the humiliation she had just experienced weren't bad enough, the hardest part was just beginning.

After all the fine things I've said about Tom and our "love," she thought bitterly. *I'll never be able to hold up my head again.* How could any of them ever look at her without remembering what a fool she'd been? Her father would hardly be able to wait to say "I told you so."

Adam hadn't, though, she reflected. And considering that he had seen Tom's true character early on, that was surprising. But he'd only held her and comforted her and seemed more concerned about her feelings than her stupidity.

A tiny frown creased her brow. He'd been so tender and caring right up until she was ready to mount Dancer. Then he'd all but shoved her up on the saddle and sent her on her way. What happened? She'd only tried to thank him for his kindness, and it almost seemed to anger him.

She sighed. Apparently she'd misread Adam, too. More evidence, if she'd needed more, that she wasn't any judge of men.

Dancer ambled by the corrals and Lizzie braced herself, hoping against hope that she wouldn't meet anyone until she had a chance to pull herself together. That hope was dashed the moment she led Dancer into the barn and encountered Willie. With one sweeping glance he took in her distraught appearance and blurted out, "What happened to you?"

Lizzie pressed her lips together, wishing he would go away. He followed her and watched her begin to groom Dancer. "Where have you been? You missed all the excitement."

"I've had enough excitement of my own, thanks."

"Well, there'll probably be more to come tonight, with all three kids staying over here."

All three kids? What... With a start, she remembered she'd left her cousins in Vera's care, not intending to be gone very long. And here it was, almost dark. Her shoulders slumped. It was more proof of her flightiness.

She closed Dancer in his stall with a flake of hay. "Why are they staying?"

Willie stared at her as though she'd sprouted an extra head. "The baby, remember? Everyone thought Jeff and Judith would be better off spending the first night with just them and the baby, instead of having all the other kids jumping in and trying to help."

"Oh, the baby's here? That's nice." Now she'd have to spend time taking care of the children instead of hiding out in her room.

"What's with you, sis? I thought you'd be as excited as the kids are." Willie peered at her more closely in the gathering dusk. "You've got that kind of faraway look on your face, like when you've just seen Tom." He perked up, visibly excited like a hound on a scent. "Is that it? Is Tom back? You've seen him, haven't you? Hey, that's great! I've been practicing, and he's really gonna be surprised when—"

Lizzie stiffened under the onslaught of questions. "He's gone, Willie."

It took a moment for her words to sink in. "You mean he had to leave again? What for? When's he coming back?"

"He isn't." Her hands clenched and released, balling the fabric of her riding skirt into a mass of wrinkles. "He left this afternoon, and he won't be coming back. Ever." Her throat felt thick and the prick of tears stung her eyelids.

Willie threw up his hands in disgust. "For crying out loud, sis! What did you do to run him off—throw yourself at him?" The justice of that remark was more than Lizzie could bear, and she ran sobbing to the house, where she managed to evade her small cousins and barricade herself in her room.

Dropping to her knees beside her bed, she buried her face in the coverlet and gave vent to her emotions. As the sobs shook her shoulders, her heart cried out to God. *I don't understand what's happening. I prayed; You know I did. Aunt Judith says You always hear our prayers, but what happened this time? I thought I heard from You, and look how wrong I was! You're supposed to be the hope of Your people. You're supposed to work all things together for good, and I thought that's what You were doing. Now everything's falling apart, and I don't know how I'll ever know whether I'm doing the right thing again.*

She drew a shuddering breath and the question sprang forth from the depths of her soul: *What's wrong with me?*

Footsteps sounded in the hallway and a rapid tapping at the door brought her to her feet. Mindless of the damage to the coverlet, she used it to mop her face and brushed her hair back with both hands. "What is it?" she called, her voice sounding strained and unnatural.

"About time you got back," came Vera's cheery voice.

"I'm coming to take over with the children," Lizzie said, hurrying to smooth her clothing into place. She opened the door to find Vera standing there alone.

"Don't worry about them," Vera told her. "The little scamps finally wore themselves out and I put them to bed nearly an hour ago."

"I'm sorry!" Lizzie cried. "I didn't mean to go off and leave you so long."

"It's not the first time I've had to deal with rambunctious youngsters," Vera reminded her, giving her a reassuring pat on the shoulder. "I just wanted to let you know there's a cold supper waiting in the kitchen. There's been such a flurry today, I decided it would be better to let you all help yourselves when you had a chance."

"Thanks. That was a good idea," Lizzie said, thinking guiltily of the extra responsibility that had been heaped on Vera's shoulders this day. "Willie said the baby has come," she ventured, following Vera to the kitchen. "What's his name?"

" 'His' name is Susannah," Vera replied, chuckling.

"It's a girl?" The news momentarily shocked Lizzie out of her despondency. "But Aunt Judith—"

"Was mistaken," Vera finished for her. "But that's not to say she isn't thrilled. And from the way your mother described Jeff strutting around, it sounds like he's not too disappointed either. As for Rose, she's floating on air at having another girl in the family. Says it's about time things were evened up a bit."

Lizzie's mouth curved slightly, in spite of herself. "I'm glad for them." Then she frowned, remembering what Vera had said. "Do you mean Mama's back already? I thought she planned to stay for a couple of days, at least."

"That was the plan," Vera agreed. "But she said Jeff told her he'd done this with three babies already; he figured he was capable of handling things with this one, too. Your mother's getting a bite to eat right now," she said, reaching the kitchen door.

Lizzie stopped in her tracks. "Go on ahead," she said to Vera, who raised a quizzical eyebrow. "I'll be there in a minute."

She leaned against the wall for support, and Vera disappeared through the door. There would be no postponing the interview with her mother now. She inhaled deeply and squared her shoulders. She was as prepared as she'd ever be. Time to get it over with.

Lizzie found she wasn't prepared, though, when she met not only her mother's inquisitive gaze, but her father's and Willie's as well. Her step faltered, but she forced herself to move to the sideboard and begin filling her plate with a calm she didn't feel.

Abby, who had apparently been describing the new baby, barely paused to acknowledge Lizzie's entrance before resuming her narrative. "She has Judith's blond hair, and lots of it. I don't think I've ever seen so much hair on a newborn! She's quiet, too. Seems like a calm little thing."

"That'll be a nice change," Charles said, grinning.

"Isn't that the truth?" Abby agreed with a laugh. "They're about due for a break. But wait till you see her, Charles. She's such a beautiful baby!"

Charles regarded his wife with fond amusement. "I don't know that you've ever seen a baby you didn't think was absolutely beautiful," he teased. "Is there such a child?"

"I guess not," Abby admitted. "At least not to me." The look that passed between them made Lizzie's breath catch in her throat. It was a look that spoke of a relationship filled with understanding and trust. The kind she had thought she'd found with Tom.

Charles shifted his gaze to his daughter. "And what have you been up to? Vera says you were gone quite awhile."

The abrupt question caught Lizzie off guard, and she took her time answering.

"I needed to be alone for a bit," she said quietly. "So I went for a ride."

Down at the end of the table, Willie snorted. "Alone, right?" he sneered.

Charles's brows drew together. "And what does that mean?" he asked sharply.

"Nothing—" Lizzie started to reply, but Willie cut in.

"She may have left alone and come back alone," he said, "but somewhere along the way she ran into Tom and then she ran him off."

Abby's quick intake of breath was audible. She and Charles turned astonished eyes on their daughter. Charles's face looked like a thundercloud. "You saw him again? After what I told you?"

Whatever Lizzie had imagined this scene would be like, the reality was a hundred times worse. "Yes, I saw him," she answered in a voice that shook. "But it wasn't planned. He happened to see me when he was on his way back home, and he stopped to talk to me."

"Just talk?" The suspicion in her father's tone made Lizzie flinch.

"Yes." Only a few hours earlier, she would have bristled at the implication and leaped to Tom's defense. Now, she found herself barely able to meet her father's eyes. "He. . .he wanted to tell me he was leaving."

"For where? What's he up to?"

Lizzie closed her eyes. "I don't know where he's going," she said. "I only know he isn't coming back."

The silence that greeted her announcement was broken by Willie's muttered comment. "Yeah. Thanks to her."

"What are you suggesting she did?" Charles demanded, turning on his son.

Willie shrugged uncomfortably, sensing he'd pushed too far. "I don't know, but she must have done something."

Abby laid a sympathetic hand on Lizzie's arm. "Are you all right, dear?" Her tone was one of concern, but Lizzie could see the relief in her mother's eyes.

Charles opened his mouth as if to speak but fell silent at a wave of Abby's hand. Lizzie bit her lower lip, wishing she could control the quaver in her voice.

"I'll be fine," she said, knowing that it wasn't true at all. After the things she had said and done—after being totally convinced she knew God's direction for her life—she didn't see how she could ever be all right again.

Her father seemed to sense some of this, for his voice softened when he spoke. "Of course you'll be all right. You're a good girl, Lizzie, and you have a lot to look forward to."

Lizzie's eyes blurred with tears. She wasn't good at all. She was an idiot, a ninny who couldn't trust her own judgment.

If she didn't change the subject now, she knew she'd break down in front of all of them, and she couldn't bear that. "Are the children supposed to go home tomorrow? I'll take them back to meet little Susannah," she said with forced brightness.

"That's fine, dear," her mother answered. "Why don't you go to bed now and get a good night's rest; you've had a long day." Before Lizzie could answer, the kitchen door burst open and Bert stumbled inside.

Charles leaped to his feet and hurried to the cowboy's side. "What is it?" he asked. Looking at Bert's ashen face, Lizzie held her breath, knowing she was about to hear something horrible.

"It's Dan Peterson," Bert gasped, leaning against the counter for support. "He was coming out of Farley's store in town and he was shot, right there in the street. Happened about an hour ago."

Lizzie felt the color drain from her face and glanced at Willie, who looked as stricken as she felt. They had known Mr. Peterson since early childhood, and their father had often jokingly accused him of spoiling them when he had brought them candy and spent countless hours telling them stories. A kind, generous man, Lizzie knew he had never hurt a single person in his life.

"Is he. . ." She couldn't bring herself to say the word.

Bert shook his head, raking his fingers through his hair. "Doc says he thinks he'll pull through, but it'll take time. He was hurt pretty bad."

"Why Dan? How did it happen?" Charles rasped.

Bert spread his hands wide. "There wasn't any reason for it, boss. None at all. A couple of yahoos were shooting at signs. Dan walked out right smack in the middle of it." He gulped in a breath and cleared his throat. "One of 'em even had the gall to laugh and say it was Dan's own fault. Said Dan shouldn't have got in the line of fire."

"Who did it, Bert?" Willie rose from his seat, his young face grim and stern. "Do they know?"

"Yeah, they do." Bert looked down and studied the toes of his boots. "One of 'em was Billy the Kid. No one recognized his friend, but he was medium height, slim build, brown hair. About Billy's age." He looked up at Charles with somber eyes. "Looks like Lincoln County's trouble has become ours, don't it?"

"It looks like it's come all too close to home," Charles agreed, his eyes fixed on his children. Willie sank back into his chair as though his legs would no longer support him.

The room swam before Lizzie, and she left without a word, knowing she might faint if she stayed a moment longer. Once in her room, she threw her clothes off into an untidy heap and sought the sweet oblivion of sleep.

Chapter 16

Abby's birthday dawned bright and clear. The moment Lizzie opened her eyes, she knew it was going to be a perfect day. As far as the weather was concerned, anyway. Her own spirits would have been more in tune with an overcast sky filled with lowering clouds.

Time was supposed to bring healing. But the two weeks following Tom's departure hadn't done a thing to ease her pain or restore her confidence. She awoke each morning to a dull throb of hopelessness that didn't dissipate as the day wore on.

Lizzie avoided contact with the rest of the family as much as possible, unable to face either their censure or their pity. She had even gone so far as turning her mirror to the wall, so as not to have to face her own reflection.

This day, though, she knew she owed it to her mother to present as bright a face as possible, so she swiveled the mirror back around before she began dressing her hair.

Lizzie reached for her hairbrush, then halted with her hand outstretched, staring at the forlorn creature peering back at her. Hollow eyes gazed listlessly into her own. Her skin stretched tautly over her cheekbones, and her hair hung dull and limp. No wonder she had caught worried looks from her parents and Vera the past few days. But this pitiful person portrayed her true self accurately, she thought.

Lizzie drew the brush through her hair again and again, trying to restore some of its normal luster. In the end it lay neatly over her shoulders, but lacked its customary sheen. It would just have to do, she thought as she swept it back and tied it in place with a sky blue ribbon.

She slipped out of her nightdress and selected a matching blue dress with more ruffles and flounces than she ordinarily wore, hoping its cheerful hue might give her wan cheeks more life. It helped a little, but not much, Lizzie decided, surveying her appearance in the mirror once more.

I look like I've been sick for a month. She pinched her cheeks and bit her lips to bring out some color. *You'd think I was primping to go to a ball,* she thought with wry amusement before reminding herself how unlikely that would ever be.

Vera rapped on the door and stuck her head inside the room. "Well, look who's up and dressed," she said cheerfully. "I brought your breakfast on a tray, since it's a special occasion."

Lizzie felt a surge of gratitude for Vera's thoughtfulness, followed by a twinge of guilt as she remembered how she had studiously avoided Vera the past two weeks.

"Thank you," she said, attempting a smile that almost looked real. "But I'm not the birthday girl, remember?"

"Doesn't matter." Vera swept in and set down the tray with her usual efficiency, then turned to survey Lizzie with a practiced eye. "It's an improvement," she said with a satisfied nod. "It'll do a lot for your mother's peace of mind. Thanks, Lizzie. We can always count on you in a crunch." She gave Lizzie's shoulders a quick squeeze and was gone.

Lizzie stared at the closed door, openmouthed. Was it possible Vera didn't despise her after all? She picked at the fluffy scrambled eggs and discovered she had an appetite for the first time in days.

With no other plans for the day, Lizzie found herself with time on her hands. She wandered down to the barn and went directly to Dancer's stall.

"Hello, fella," she said when he pushed his head over the half door and whickered a welcome. She stroked his glossy neck lovingly, mindful of her dress and the need to keep it clean. "I haven't paid much attention to you lately, have I?"

Dancer nuzzled her hair in answer, and she pushed his head away with a gentle hand. "Not now, boy. I have to look presentable today. But tomorrow I'll wear something more suitable and give you the best rubdown you've ever had to make up for it. And we'll start going out again soon, I promise."

The scuff of boots behind her made her turn. Adam stood there, as if hesitant about whether to enter the aisle. Lizzie stared back, her eyes wary. Adam had come to her rescue when she thought her world had ended, but then he had ridden away. Apparently his solicitous concern was only commiseration for her tears. Once he had sorted through what had actually happened, he was as disgusted with her as everyone else. After all, he had left her almost as abruptly as Tom had.

Lizzie found his actions thoroughly confusing. But then, she was having trouble understanding even her own feelings. Why, for instance, should the knowledge that Adam McKenzie held her in low regard bring such a sharp pang of regret?

"Hello," she faltered. "Am I in your way?"

Adam blinked as if just waking up and a slow smile spread across his face. "Sorry," he said. "It's just that I'm not usually met by such a lovely sight when I come in to feed in the morning."

Lizzie felt the heat wash across her face and knew they must be as pink as the roses her mother had planted near the front door. The aisle seemed to have shrunk somehow, leaving barely enough room for the two of them. Was he serious, or making fun of her? Given his baffling behavior two weeks ago, how could she possibly know? Better to take the safe road and not make any rash assumptions that might embarrass her again. Hurrying to get past him, she murmured, "I'd better get back to the house."

The aisle truly had shrunk, she decided when she attempted to squeeze by Adam without brushing her dress against the wall. He turned sideways at the same time she did, and they stood face to face, mere inches apart.

Lizzie wondered if a thunderstorm was brewing. There was that same tingling feeling in the air, raising bumps all along her arms. Adam seemed to sense it, too, for his dark gaze was fixed on hers and he stood as if rooted to the spot.

Lizzie recovered first. *Here I am, about to make a fool of myself again. What must he be thinking?* Aloud, she said, "Excuse me, I need to go."

❧

Adam watched Lizzie leave and tried to get his heart to slow back down to its normal rate. *Idiot!* he told himself. *Every time you get a chance to talk to her, you freeze up like a block of ice.*

He shook his head, reliving the encounter. Every nerve in his body had reacted to her nearness, and it left him breathless. He could have sworn she had felt it, too. But, he reminded himself, he would have sworn she'd looked on him as something more than a brother when she had nestled in his arms that day two weeks earlier.

He kicked himself mentally as he went about his chores, wishing he could find someone with good, sturdy boots who could do a more thorough job of it.

❧

Jeff, Judith, and all four children arrived shortly after the noon meal. The family gathered in the living room, where they could watch Abby open her gifts and at the same time they could fuss over baby Susannah.

Lizzie looked anxiously at Judith, hoping that with all the excitement of the new baby she hadn't forgotten the precious quilt. A reassuring wink from her aunt put her mind at rest, and she settled into a wingback chair, trying to give the appearance of enjoying the festivities.

Rose, Sammy, and Travis presented their family's gift first, bearing it importantly, as befitting their mature status. Abby oohed and aahed over the job they had done on the wrapping, and carefully opened the box to reveal a delicate china tea set.

"We helped pack it," Travis volunteered. "But not Susannah. She's too little." The twins nodded in solemn agreement.

"Thank you, all," Abby said, gathering the three in a big hug. "It's wonderful." A smile over their heads was directed at Jeff and Judith, including them in her thanks as well.

Willie's offering was next, and his mother expressed delight at the tortoiseshell comb and mirror he gave her. He received her thanks with a grateful smile. The unwarranted shooting of Dan Peterson seemed to have awakened Willie. Little by little, his sunny disposition was returning, much to the relief of the entire family.

Lizzie fidgeted in her chair. Would her mother really like the quilt? She almost wished she had substituted something else for it instead, some trinket that would please her mother without making Lizzie feel so vulnerable. Maybe no one would notice if she didn't present the quilt to her mother. Or if they did, perhaps they would assume she had been too distraught this last couple of weeks to remember to get a gift. Maybe it was better to be seen as thoughtless than an object of pity.

"I guess I'm next," said Charles, glancing around and not seeing any more presents. "Here you are, dear. Many happy returns of the day." He handed Abby a small white box.

She opened it with care and stared for a moment at what lay inside. "Charles, it's beautiful," she breathed, lifting from the folds of paper a delicately crafted gold pin fashioned in the shape of an oak leaf. Crystal drops shone in the corners of her eyes as she gazed at her husband.

"I picked it up on my last trip to Santa Fe," he said proudly, obviously pleased with his gift's success. "I'm glad you like it."

"You knew I would," Abby told him as she pinned it on her dress. "Thank you so much." She gave his hand a tender squeeze and a look passed between them that made Lizzie feel the rest of the group was intruding upon a special moment meant only for them. She tried to ignore a stab of envy.

Abby gave a happy sigh. "It's been a wonderful birthday. Thank you all very much." Lizzie tried to ignore Judith's quizzical look. After seeing all those wonderful gifts, she couldn't bear it if her own was a disappointment.

"Shall we go into the dining room for some refreshment?" Abby took the arm Charles offered and prepared to lead the way. She looked questioningly at Judith, who was clearing her throat repeatedly.

Getting no response from Lizzie, Judith took it upon herself to speak. "I think you have one more present, Abby. Jeff, would you bring it in from the wagon?"

Jeff left the room with a grin on his face, and Lizzie sank further down in the chair, wishing she could pass right through the cushion, the floor, and into the earth itself.

Willie held the door open for Jeff, who maneuvered a mysterious bundle wrapped in brown paper through the doorway and held it out to Abby. She accepted it with a smile, but looked curiously at Judith. "Another one?" she asked.

"This one is from your daughter," Judith replied.

Abby's eyes shone with delight as she beamed at Lizzie. "Thank you, dear," she said.

"Better wait till you open it before you get too excited," Willie muttered, earning himself a reproving look from his father.

Lizzie held her breath as she watched her mother tear the paper away. Abby stopped with her hands in midair as the bright colors of the quilt appeared. Silence filled the room as she touched the fabric tentatively, tracing the lovingly stitched design. She looked first at Judith, then Lizzie, her eyes filled with wonder. "You made this, Lizzie?" she asked breathlessly.

Lizzie nodded, hoping against hope that she hadn't let her mother down again.

"But how? When?"

"I asked Aunt Judith to show me how," Lizzie answered. "We made it at her house, and she helped a lot," she said. "I wanted to do something special for you. . ." Her voice trailed off.

"And you have," said her mother, her eyes glowing with happiness. "Charles," she said excitedly, "just look at this!" She spread out the quilt, carefully smoothing the folds. Everyone gathered around, with Jeff and Judith keeping their eager threesome at a safe distance. Lizzie's handiwork was duly inspected and approved.

Abby slipped away from the group and came over to kneel by Lizzie's chair. "It's beautiful," she told her. "But I still don't know how you managed it. How long did it take you?"

"We've been working on it for months," Lizzie admitted. "We got it finished just before Susannah was born." She flinched inwardly, remembering what else had occurred on that fateful day.

"And you kept it a secret all this time?" Abby shook her head, smiling. "I don't know why that surprises me though. It's just the sort of thoughtful thing you'd do." She slipped her arms around her astonished daughter and held her close. "Thank you, Lizzie," she whispered. "I'll treasure it always."

"I'm glad you like it, Mama," Lizzie responded, returning her mother's embrace. She felt so good, so accepted. If only she could measure up to her mother's opinion of her!

Chapter 17

Are you ready for the picnic, Lizzie?" Rose's eyes shone with excitement, and she bounced from one foot to the other in anticipation.

Lizzie sighed and tried to summon up a smile for her cousin's benefit. She had tried to opt out of attending the annual church function but her parents had insisted they needed her help to keep an eye on Jeff's three oldest youngsters. Susannah and her parents needed some time alone together, they reasoned, and with all the excitement the picnic would bring, it would take every available person to make sure the children didn't get into too much mischief.

Lizzie wasn't sure whether the need for her help was real or a manufactured reason to get her away from the ranch and out of her doldrums. She suspected the latter, and while she appreciated her parents' concern, she wished they would leave her to her own devices. Especially when it involved a church activity. Church was one place Lizzie simply didn't belong.

Right now Lizzie didn't feel like she and God were on especially good terms. She had tried to forge ahead in spiritual knowledge. She'd read her Bible and discovered verses that she thought applied to her, and look what had happened. God might talk to others, she reasoned, but he obviously didn't communicate with Lizzie Bradley.

Rose's insistent bouncing brought Lizzie back to the moment at hand. She gathered her cousins together, feeling something like a mother hen when they followed her out to the wagon, where Vera efficiently loaded them and the baskets of food. "You're ready to go," she announced, smiling.

Lizzie's parents emerged from the house and Charles boosted Abby to the wagon seat before taking his place beside her and clucking to the horses. Lizzie sat in back with the children and waved good-bye to Vera, who had declared that her old bones weren't up to all that jouncing around anymore.

Several of the cowboys rode alongside the wagon, ready to take advantage of any opportunity to socialize with their far-flung neighbors. Lizzie glanced around, but didn't see Adam among them. Just as well, she thought, breathing a little easier. Ever since their encounter at the grove, and especially since their meeting in the barn, she had found his presence unnerving, and didn't understand why. To have to deal with him on top of the other emotions she was experiencing right now would be too much.

She leaned back against the sideboard and closed her eyes. The light breeze played with loose strands of her hair and tugged at her full skirt. The constant rocking of the wagon lulled her into a half-doze, broken only by the excited chatter of Rose, Sam, and Travis, who saw this outing as a high point of their existence.

Lizzie sighed, adrift in her own world. If only her life could be as simple as theirs! Lost in her thoughts, it seemed only a brief time until they arrived at the picnic grounds. The children scrambled over the tailgate even before the wagon came to a stop, with Abby's admonitions to stay close and behave apparently falling on deaf ears. Lizzie helped carry their baskets to the waiting table and tried to avoid conversation with the friendly but inquisitive older women who were organizing the food.

When her mother handed her a blanket and told her to find a place for them all to sit, Lizzie seized the opportunity for escape gratefully. She spread the blanket on the ground a distance away from the others, telling herself the children would need extra space to run around.

Lizzie looked up when a shadow crossed the blanket, and her mouth went dry when she recognized Brother Webster, their pastor. Wasn't it enough that God had made her painfully aware of her shortcomings? Was it necessary for Brother Webster to mention them, too?

The pastor smiled and dropped down onto the opposite end of the blanket. Lizzie tried to return the smile, but her lips felt brittle. Brother Webster's eyes crinkled, as though he was aware of her discomfort and found it amusing. "How are you, Lizzie?" he asked, compassion warming his voice.

"All right, I guess," she mumbled, wondering frantically how much he knew about her disgrace. Without thinking, she blurted out, "Did my mother send you to talk with me?"

His eyes widened and he chuckled. "Actually, I was just making the rounds and greeting everyone here. I hadn't intended to single you out. It seems like you have something on your mind though. Would you like to talk about it?"

Talking about how foolish she'd been was the last thing Lizzie wanted to do, but something in his tone softened her heart and before she knew it, she asked abruptly, "Why doesn't God keep His promises to me?"

If she thought she'd shock Brother Webster with her question, she was wrong. His face was calm as he replied, "What makes you think He doesn't?"

Lizzie hesitated for a moment, then decided to plunge ahead. The question had been burning in her heart for weeks, and if anyone could give her an answer, this man could. "The Bible says He'll direct our paths. Isn't that right?"

The minister nodded in agreement. "I can't argue with you there."

"It also says that He'll give us the desires of our hearts." When he continued to nod, she drew a deep breath and ventured. "Then why doesn't He do that for me?"

Brother Webster regarded her thoughtfully, then said, "Instead of my answering that question for you, why don't we let God speak for Himself?"

He laughed gently when Lizzie frowned and looked around as if expecting some sort of divine announcement right then and there. "I don't understand," she confessed.

"You don't have a Bible here with you, I suppose?" She shook her head, shamefaced. Things went all wrong when she read the Bible and tried to put it into practice. She had decided to leave that to people wiser than she.

Brother Webster didn't seem put off in the least. "Then let me give you a verse to look up when you get home. Can you remember the reference that long?" She nodded, hoping she wasn't overestimating her abilities. "It's Jeremiah 29:13," he told her. "Spend some time thinking about that, and if you still have a problem understanding, come back and we'll talk again, all right?" He pushed himself up off the blanket and continued circulating among the crowd.

"Jeremiah 29:13," Lizzie repeated to herself. The verse suddenly took on the importance of a lifeline, and Lizzie was determined to keep a firm hold on it.

Brother Webster hadn't sensed anything wrong with her, she remembered. It was her own guilt that made her assume her inadequacy was plainly visible. She lifted her eyes and scanned the crowd, wondering if that might hold true for the rest of the people there. Was it possible she'd be able to pick up her life and go on, in spite of making such a monumental fool of herself?

Occasionally she caught the eye of one of the picnickers, who would smile in her direction. Lizzie would force a smile and nod back, feeling a tiny flutter of hope for the first time since Tom Mallory rode out of her life and her world came crashing down around her.

When the call came to line up to eat, Lizzie abandoned the pretense of holding down the blanket and made her way to the table. Shaking her head at several offers to let her slip into the line, she took her place diffidently at the end. Being here at all was a first step, she told herself. Getting in line was another. For now, she'd take things one step at a time and see if it was possible to regain some of the normalcy of her life.

Out of the corner of her eye she could see her father rounding up the children. She supposed she ought to be helping him, but just now she wanted to savor the tiny bit of progress she had made. Her mother, helping to serve the food, beamed at her when she reached the table and handed her a plate. "Help yourself," she said gaily. "There's plenty for everyone."

Then, looking over Lizzie's head, she cried, "Why, Adam, how nice to see you! We didn't think you were going to make it."

Lizzie felt like someone had punched her in the stomach. She turned stiffly to find Adam standing right behind her, plate in hand.

"I wasn't sure I'd make it, myself," he said, answering Abby. His brown eyes, though, were focused on Lizzie, and that tingly feeling was raising goose bumps along her arms again. "But I hurried as fast as I could. I didn't want to miss this."

He looked behind him, where the line was backing up. "I guess we'd better move along," he said, smiling at Lizzie. "It looks like we're holding things up."

Lizzie came to herself with a start, and moved quickly along the table, scooping various items onto her plate without regard for what she was selecting. Her cheeks were warm and she hoped she hadn't made a spectacle of herself in front of all those people, just when she had begun to believe she might one day be able to hold her head up again.

Mercy, what was wrong with her? She had stood there, staring like a ninny at Adam McKenzie before everyone in the whole church. Maybe they hadn't noticed. Maybe they'd assumed she had been talking to her mother. *Yes, surely that would be reasonable,* she thought, breathing a sigh of relief.

But what was the effect Adam had on her? He had been a part of the ranch ever since she was a young girl, and there had never been anything about him to set him apart from the rest of the ranch hands.

Adam had always been. . .just Adam, steady and dependable and always there, but nothing more.

Lately, though, any time he was near her it seemed that every nerve in her body stood on end, and when he held her gaze with his, it was almost like a caress. Lizzie shook herself angrily, as though by doing so she could shake off that feeling. She ought to have learned by now that she couldn't be trusted to discern a man's feelings about her. She certainly couldn't decipher the look in his eyes whenever they rested on her. Was it pity? Censure? She couldn't tell, and she wasn't sure she wanted to know. Either one would be impossible to bear.

Lizzie reached the blanket and cast a furtive glance behind her. Thank goodness! Adam had waited to speak to Charles and was helping him fill plates for the children. That was supposedly what she'd come along for, she reflected, but at the moment, she needed some time to regroup.

She could be civil to Adam, she decided, but not overly friendly. There must be nothing in her demeanor to lead him to think she was throwing herself at him. After her disastrous experience with Tom, she wouldn't leave herself open to charges of improper behavior again.

Lizzie watched Abby leave the table and approach their spot with Charles, Adam, and the children, each adult carrying two plates and trying to herd their rambunctious charges toward the place Lizzie had chosen. Apparently Adam had been invited to eat with them. It was all right, Lizzie reassured herself. She'd had time to pull herself together, and she would handle the situation with grace and dignity. Beginning today, Adam and everyone else would see a new Lizzie Bradley, one who could be trusted to behave as a proper young lady.

When the children descended, giggling and squealing, on their picnic spot, Lizzie settled them firmly on the blanket near her and had them more or less subdued by the time the adults arrived. Charles and Abby sat opposite her, stifling sighs of relief, and Adam took his place next to Charles.

"How did we ever manage to keep up with Lizzie and Willie at this age?" Abby asked, shaking her head and laughing.

"I think the fact that we were a few years younger may have had something to do with it," Charles answered with a twinkle in his eye.

"Charles Bradley!" Abby's tone was ominous, although it was belied by the sparkle in her own eyes. "Are you implying I'm getting old?"

Charles gave an exaggerated sigh and looked ruefully at Adam. "You see what it's like being married? A man has to watch every word he utters."

"I'll try to remember," Adam responded with mock solemnity. His gaze rested once more on Lizzie, seeking the response he was sure he had sensed at the table only moments before.

Instead of the welcome he expected, she met his gaze serenely and included him in the conversation, although he could just as well have been one of the children, for all the attention she gave him. *Just like one of the family again,* he thought in disgust. The anticipation he had felt all week at spending the afternoon in Lizzie's company faded away like a morning glory blossom at high noon. *If I had any sense,* he told himself, *I'd have stayed with the horses.* Was he ever going to be able to make any headway with this woman?

❧

On the way home, Lizzie rejoiced in her newfound dignity. *Finally,* she thought, *I can be the person I'm supposed to be.*

She jumped out of the wagon and gathered the food baskets before her parents set off to take the children home. All three had been worn out from their frolicking and had fallen asleep on the drive.

Leaving the baskets in the kitchen, Lizzie hurried to her room, where she opened her Bible and eagerly sought the verse Brother Webster had given her.

There it was, Jeremiah 29:13: *"And ye shall seek me, and find me, when ye shall search for me with all your heart."* Lizzie blinked and read it over again, slowly. The last four words burned into her soul as if placed there by a branding iron—*"with all your heart."*

Lizzie thought back over the assumptions she had made concerning Tom. Had she sincerely sought the Lord with all her heart? The answer came swiftly, unequivocally—no.

Truth and conviction swept over Lizzie in a consuming tide, and she dropped to her knees beside her bed, tears pooling along her lower lids and spilling over to stream down her cheeks. What had she done? She tried to assess her actions ruthlessly. In all honesty, she had looked for passages that had conveniently spelled out the answers she wanted, without paying much attention to what the Lord desired. As long as He had seemed to agree with Lizzie, she had been content to assume that she had found His will.

"With all your heart..." The words pounded through her brain. Where had her heart been? With Tom Mallory and his easy, empty promises, she admitted, writhing in shame. Hadn't her parents raised her to believe that she mustn't be unequally yoked? That marriage should only be to another believer, a godly man? How had she dared to take God's Word, that sacred book, and twist it to mean that Tom was the right man for her?

She flipped back to Psalm 37, searching for the verse that promised her the desires of her heart. Yes, that's what it said; but this time, she also read the words before it: *"Delight thyself also in the Lord...."* Not a blanket promise that *"I'll give you anything you want, Lizzie,"* but *"Delight yourself in Me, and I'll fulfill your desires."*

It made sense, she thought miserably. If she was walking with the Lord, her desires would be His. Then He could give her what she wanted most, because it would be in accordance with His will. How far short of that necessary condition she had fallen!

Lizzie groaned under the weight of conviction, and the tears poured forth anew. "I'm sorry. So very, very sorry," she wept into her coverlet. "I want to listen to You. Please speak to me."

It occurred to Lizzie like a flash of lightning across a dark sky that in pointing these words out to her, God had spoken, and very clearly. "Thank You," she whispered, and the tears came again, but this time in relief and gratitude.

Chapter 18

Whap. Whap. Whap. With a final blow, Adam drove the last nail into the porch railing and stepped back to view his handiwork. The railing now stood tight and firm, where before, it had sagged slightly. Sufficient for a bachelor getting on in years, perhaps, but not good enough to set up housekeeping with a view to raising a family there. Not good enough for his Lizzie.

The porch was one of his final projects, the major structural repairs having been finished earlier. He walked slowly around the house, surveying the tight clapboards, the newly painted shutters, and—his particular pride—the addition.

There he stopped, hands on his hips, a lump of joy and pride swelling in his throat. The original house had contained one small bedroom situated next to the kitchen, with two even smaller bedrooms upstairs. After judicious planning, Adam had torn out an outer wall and revamped the design. Now the enlarged kitchen boasted a roomy pantry where the original bedroom had been. And upstairs. . .

Adam had to see it once more for himself. He entered the front door—noting with approval that it hung true and no longer caught on the floor as it swung inward—and bounded up the stairs with boyish exuberance. The landing opened onto three spacious bedrooms. Adam entered the largest one and made his way to the window. Leaning against the sill, he took in the sweeping view of plains, hills, and distant mountains. It was as beautiful as any painting he'd seen back east during his boyhood, he thought, only this scene was alive, vibrant and constantly changing. He knew he could be content to view its grandeur for the rest of his life.

Turning, he surveyed the rest of the room. It needed a woman's touch, he knew, but the basic work had been done, and done well. In his mind's eye he could picture lacy curtains framing the window and the scene beyond, a braided rug on the floor, maybe a rocking chair in one corner. Yes, he thought, it would make a fine home. A fine home to share.

He needed some time to put on the finishing touches—a coat of paint here and there—and once more he was thankful for Charles's and Jeff's generosity in allowing him time to work on the house. After all was in complete readiness, he planned to lay his vision of the future before Lizzie. Surely by then she'd be ready to hear of his love for her.

Time to head back, he reminded himself. *Better do something to earn your keep.* The prospect didn't bother him. It was a pleasant ride back to Double B headquarters, and he could fill the time with thoughts of Lizzie.

Lizzie glanced up at the ruffled curtains hanging limply at her bedroom window. Not so much as a breath of air disturbed them, though her window was wide open, inviting whatever breeze there might be to waft inside. She sighed and reluctantly closed the Bible on her lap. She had spent a wonderful time with the Lord, pouring out her heart to Him and digging deep into His Word, but now the room was growing unbearably stuffy, and she could feel the beginnings of a headache coming on.

Even though she had made halfhearted efforts over the years to learn the domestic skills expected of a young lady, Lizzie was an outdoor girl at heart. Today the house seemed more confining than ever, and she hurried outside where the wide vistas and smells of summer beckoned. Her temples throbbed slightly, and she decided the effort required to saddle Dancer was too much, so she set off languidly on foot.

Settling herself under an enormous cedar within sight of the house, she decided that today even the outdoors wasn't much less stuffy than her room. Heavy clouds had massed overhead, but instead of delivering rain, they only loomed oppressively over the landscape. No breeze stirred, yet the still air took on an almost tangible quality of its own. Lizzie loved the summer rains that brought freshness and renewed life; this sense of tension, of violence waiting to break loose, was something else altogether.

She turned her mind deliberately to the time she'd spent in Bible study. Had all those wonderful promises really been there all the time? Why had she never seen them before? Trying to be honest with herself, she admitted that she'd never done much looking before now. Even though she had become a Christian as a child, she had coasted along all these years without giving much thought to growing spiritually.

A passage about new believers being babies in Christ had sprung out at her during her reading. She had become a newborn babe in Christ the moment she had asked Him to be her Savior. More than ten years later she could still remember the feeling she'd had that night—like she'd been washed clean. And yes, it was very much like she'd been reborn.

But babies, precious as they are, are supposed to grow. She tried to imagine what it would be like ten years from now if baby Susannah still lay helpless, wrapped in her blankets. Why, if that happened, she reasoned, Jeff and Judith—all the family—would be grieved beyond measure. Susannah was supposed to grow, to learn, to become less dependent on her parents and able to take care of herself.

The comparison struck Lizzie like a physical blow, startling her into wide-eyed awareness. For all her years of being a child of God, she had stayed a spiritual infant, dependent on her parents and others for her feeding and nurture, never bothering to learn to grow on her own. In a spiritual sense, she was little older than Susannah, still waiting to be fed and diapered. She shifted uncomfortably at the thought. How much had she grieved her heavenly Father by this lack of growth? she wondered somberly.

Lizzie scanned the panorama before her, where the sense of anticipation hung heavy. Even the slender blades of grass stood motionless, waiting for the release the storm would bring. God's creation was spread out before her, vast and unending, and she felt as though God Himself was focusing His attention on the tiny speck that was Lizzie Bradley. The Creator and creation alike seemed to be waiting with breathless expectation. Waiting for what? For Lizzie to make the choice to end the years of infancy and take her first feeble steps toward growth?

Instead of bowing her head, Lizzie prayed with her eyes open, the better to fix this scene and this moment in her mind forever. "Father," she said aloud, "I've never really understood before. I know I've been Your child for years, but I never once thought about going beyond that. And I never thought about it hurting You." She paused a moment to order her thoughts, then went on. "I've been riding along on my parents' relationship with You, depending on their knowledge of You and not thinking that I needed to develop my own." She sighed, knowing the hard part was to come, but that beyond it lay forgiveness and release.

"I'm sorry for taking You for granted all this time. Please forgive me for letting You down. With Your help, I'll learn to grow like You want me to. Thank You," she said as the sweet feeling of freedom washed over her, cleansing and restoring her soul more than any number of summer rains ever could.

Lizzie rose and stretched, grateful that now the building storm was only outside and no longer in her heart. With slow steps she retraced her way toward the house, happily making plans. Just how did she go about growing? she wondered. Babies needed milk before they graduated to solid food. What did that mean in a spiritual sense? She couldn't wait to talk to Brother Webster and find out. Lizzie felt that a whole new adventure lay before her. Growth wasn't always without its pains, she knew, but it would be worth it. For the present, she would concentrate her whole being on her spiritual quest.

Adam McKenzie's face sprang into her mind, and it surprised Lizzie so that she stopped dead in her tracks. She rubbed her eyes, as if she could scrub the image away. Why was she thinking of Adam, with his unruly hair and melting brown eyes? Was this a temptation being thrown at her to stop her spiritual journey before it started?

Maybe it was time to deal with thoughts of Adam once and for all, she decided. She had known Adam since childhood, and had seen him only as a routine part of the fabric of her life. Like the background of a tapestry, she thought, where the muted colors formed a regular pattern necessary for contrast with the central part of the design, but didn't stand out on their own.

So why had this section of the background suddenly taken on brilliance enough to keep popping into her mind, unbidden and at the most surprising times?

Adam had stepped out of the background more than once recently, she had to admit. His name came up repeatedly in family conversations of late, although Lizzie had to confess she'd been so absorbed in her own thoughts that she really didn't know all that had been said about him. Papa and Uncle Jeff spoke of him with increasing respect though. She'd picked that up unconsciously, just from the tone of their voices.

And it wasn't just in conversation that Adam appeared. He had sprung out of nowhere to rescue Willie the day her brother had played his horrible trick on her. *Or did he rescue me that day. . .from myself?* she wondered wryly. Then he had come to her rescue like the most gallant knight of old when he had found her alone after Tom's desertion. Lizzie couldn't remember that episode clearly, only that she had felt safe and protected when he had cradled her in his arms.

And lately. . .Lizzie's stomach did a flip-flop at the thought of how she had felt when Adam's gaze bored into her at the picnic, in the barn, wherever they happened to meet. Even when other people were around, their glances only had to meet and hold for Lizzie to feel that only the two of them existed. It was a pleasant feeling, but unsettling. Did her presence affect Adam the same way? Was it possible that. . . ?

Lizzie shook herself, irritated. Hadn't she learned anything? Tom's sweet words had taken her breath away. The touch of his hands on her face had made her toes curl. But feelings weren't enough, as she had learned to her sorrow. The honeyed words were hollow, and by Tom's own admission, his hands had caressed other faces besides hers. What she had taken as a great love had been nothing more than a pleasant pastime for him. If that was the way men were, she determined, she would never again trust mere feelings for guidance. And Adam, she reminded herself with regret, was a man—a man just like Tom.

Wasn't he?

She wouldn't—couldn't—make the same mistake again. It was better for herself, for Adam, for everyone concerned if she devoted herself to growing in Christ. She needed to put Adam out of her mind and focus on the Lord. Maybe someday she could examine her feelings for Adam with some spiritual maturity. Until then, she would avoid contact with him. It was only fair.

Lizzie halted on the porch steps. Poor Dancer, she thought, cooped up in his stall. Even if she didn't plan to go for a ride, the least she could do was bring him outdoors for a breath of fresh air, such as it was. Her mind made up, she turned and walked to the barn. The poor horse must be as hot and miserable as she was. She would brush him down, fuss over him, and let him know he was appreciated. With Dancer, at least, she didn't have to worry about his affection being a product of her imagination.

Adam rocked along in the saddle, so much at home there that keeping rhythm with his horse's gait came without conscious effort. The horse knew the way back to headquarters as well as Adam did, leaving Adam free to daydream. As the completion of his renovation drew nearer, so did the time he would be able to tell Lizzie of the life he envisioned—and how he hoped she would share it with him.

Adam played out various scenarios in his mind, rejecting them one by one. Lizzie had gone through a lot with Tom Mallory. Adam wanted above all to make her understand that his own intentions were beyond reproach and that he would be honored to be given the responsibility of caring for her for the rest of his life. The moment would have to be perfect.

He would wait, he decided, until the final touches on the house were completed. He had previously entertained the notion that with most of the work already done, it might be finished enough to let Lizzie see. Now he discarded that idea. It would be better, he was sure, to wait until every detail had been attended to.

How would he approach Lizzie on this? If she would consent to it, he might invite her to go for a ride, then take her to his ranch and get her reaction to the place first. Then he would have a better idea of how to proceed.

If he weren't working so hard on the house, putting in so many hours there in addition to his work at the Double B, he might have time to court her properly and build the relationship gradually. As it was, though, he was so busy building the beginnings of a life for them that there was no time for that.

Adam liked to do things properly and in order. Life dealt its share of changes to the plans he made, but he still found security in starting a project with a definite goal in mind. The problem with the current situation was that he really had no idea of Lizzie's feelings toward him.

He had been in love with Lizzie Bradley for years, since way back when she was just a girl, and voicing feelings like that about his boss's daughter then would probably have gotten him thrown off the ranch, if not worse. It hadn't kept him from loving her though. Nor from following her with his gaze, memorizing every facial expression, every gesture. He could close his eyes in the dark of night and call up a picture of Lizzie without any conscious effort. After all, he'd practiced enough over the years.

Adam had sensed that Lizzie was feeling the first stirrings of womanhood before she had been aware of it herself. To Adam, it seemed like God's providence that his accumulated savings had enabled him to buy the Blair place at just that time. He had taken it on faith that God was opening his way, one step at a time. To have Charles's blessing and support in this venture was an additional encouragement.

Adam was completely certain of his own feelings, and God seemed to be making the way plain before him. The only unknown in the whole situation was Lizzie herself, and how she would react. In the past few months Adam had known the heights of joy, then plummeted to the depths of despair, as Lizzie's manner toward him had alternately warmed and cooled. The advent of Tom Mallory had appeared to set him back immeasurably—at one point, seemingly forever—but now he could see how even that could work for good. If only Lizzie could see it the same way!

Her attitude lately had puzzled him. The day he had come across her in the barn, it seemed to him that a magnetic force was drawing them inexorably together. And at the church picnic, he knew beyond a doubt that when their eyes had met and held, she was drawn to him as much as he was to her. Surely he couldn't have imagined that! Immediately afterward, though, she had chattered to her parents and the children, hardly sending a word or a glance in his direction. He had to know where he stood, and soon. The uncertainty was killing him. That was why his approach, when he made it, had to be done just right, thought out perfectly.

His horse's gait quickened, and Adam glanced up to see the ranch house and outbuildings coming into view. His heart nearly stopped when he recognized the object of his daydreams walk to the house, then pause and turn toward the barn.

Something shifted in Adam's brain. Maybe he'd been too methodical, too cautious. Maybe Lizzie needed to see a more spontaneous side of him. Without pausing to think things through in his usual way, Adam suddenly threw caution and all his careful planning to the winds and galloped down to the barn.

Exhaustion from the work he'd already put in that day rolled away as he swung from the saddle and threw his horse's reins over the hitching rail. He took a moment to run his fingers through his hair and tuck his shirt in snugly, then took a deep breath and strode into the barn.

❧

Lizzie was already halfway down the aisle with Dancer when Adam entered, blinking to accustom his eyes to the darker interior. Her eyes widened at the sight of him, and her breath caught in her throat. She willed her feet to move forward, though it felt as though she were forcing them through a molasses-filled swamp.

It was a good thing, she thought, she had just had that talk with the Lord. Knowing the way she felt around Adam, coming upon him so soon after he had once more filled her thoughts might have left her dangerously vulnerable. And she wouldn't allow that to happen. It wasn't good for her, and it was hardly fair to Adam.

Adam seemed as ill at ease as she did, she noted. Normally the model of self-assurance, today he stood shifting his weight from one foot to another like a nervous schoolboy. What was wrong with him? Well, it wouldn't matter, once she got around him.

If she got around him, she amended. Either he didn't realize he was blocking her way or didn't care. Lizzie cleared her throat. "Good afternoon," she said civilly, if coolly.

"Lizzie." Adam cleared his own throat in echo, looking distinctly uncomfortable as he twisted his hat in his hands. "I need to talk to you."

Even a good ten feet from him, Lizzie felt her breath quicken as that now-familiar tingling ran up and down her arms again. She didn't want to be rude, but it would be pointless to prolong this encounter.

"Would you excuse me, Adam? I need to get by." Adam shifted all of six inches to his right, and Lizzie sighed impatiently. There was no way she was going to try to squeeze between him and the barn wall. Not the way he affected her.

"Lizzie, please listen," Adam pleaded. "I wanted to wait to tell you this. I'd planned it all differently, but seeing you now, I can't wait any longer."

Lizzie stared, openmouthed. Where in the world was this heading? Had Adam done something he needed to apologize for? Even as the thought crossed her mind, she rejected it. If that were the case, he'd come right out and admit it like the straightforward man he was. Something in his eyes, locked on hers, entreating her to stay, touched a responsive chord deep in her soul. Warning signals flashed wildly in Lizzie's head. If she didn't watch out, her resolve would melt into a puddle right there on the barn floor, and her newborn determination to grow in the Lord along with it.

She'd better try to get past him, after all, whether he moved over any farther or not. She moved forward, edging Dancer close to Adam to increase the distance between them. Feeling a flush of relief when she was past, she led Dancer quickly toward the outside door. Surely Adam wouldn't continue this conversation outdoors where anyone could see them.

She hadn't counted on Adam moving swiftly behind Dancer and coming up on her other side. She whirled when his hand closed on her shoulder. "Adam, what. . ." Her voice trailed off as she saw the anguish in his eyes. "Are you ill?" she asked with dawning concern.

Adam dropped his hand and smiled sheepishly. "I do feel a little shaky," he admitted. "I'm doing this badly, Lizzie, and I'm sorry. I meant this to be something special, and I'm making a mess of it." He breathed deeply and began again, his voice husky with feeling. "In case you don't know it, Lizzie Bradley, you are one very special woman. I've known that for years. . ."

His voice went on, but Lizzie didn't hear any more. The voice in her ears was not Adam's, but Tom's, saying nearly the same words. *"You're a wonderful girl, Lizzie."* The words echoed inside her.

If she had needed a sign, this was it. She refused to go down that path again. With a raised hand she stopped Adam in midsentence, not knowing or caring what he was trying to say.

"Adam, I made a decision just before you came. I need to learn more about myself, and what I'm supposed to do. I don't think we should be having this conversation."

Adam started as if she had slapped him, and a red flush stained his cheek as if her hand had indeed made contact. His lips moved, but no words came forth. His gaze probed hers as though trying to read her thoughts.

"You're sure?" The words came out in a hoarse croak.

Lizzie nodded. She couldn't think about God—or anything else!—when Adam was nearby. Keeping her distance would surely be the best thing for both of them. Without another word, Adam turned on his heel and strode out of the barn. Through the doorway, Lizzie could see him mount his sweat-stained horse and gallop away. She wondered briefly where he was going in such a hurry. It wasn't like Adam to overwork an obviously tired animal.

Chapter 19

After a week of much Bible study and prayer, Lizzie had to admit that she had wasted years of her Christian life by not getting better acquainted with her Lord. Time spent with Him had become a precious part of her day, and she was steadily gaining a better sense of her identity in Him.

She also had to admit that having Adam out of her life hadn't been the relief she had thought it would be. An overheard conversation between her parents told her he was spending time at his own ranch, wherever that was. Lizzie remembered vague snippets of talk about his ranch but had not really registered the fact that Adam had another place he could call home now, a place that wasn't the Double B. While she no longer had to contend with the effect he had on her whenever he was nearby, it didn't prevent her thoughts from turning to him again and again. Even prayer didn't seem to drive his image away, and Lizzie had come to a startling conclusion—she missed Adam, missed him deeply.

In frustration, she decided to get away from the familiar surroundings for a few hours. Maybe some time spent alone with the Lord would enable her to make sense of the whole confusing situation.

Today she turned Dancer toward the northwest, deliberately choosing an area she seldom visited. She wanted to see nothing today that would evoke an emotion-laden memory. The ground grew rough, and she guided Dancer carefully around a maze of sharp rocks. *Father, I need this same kind of guidance. Show me what I'm doing wrong, and help me to know which path to take.* A depression opened up in the ground before her, apparently the mouth of a ravine.

Lizzie studied the opening. She didn't remember seeing or hearing of this place before. It was too steep and rocky for Dancer to try, but she was curious to see what lay within its walls. Tying Dancer's reins loosely to a tree trunk, she patted his neck, saying, "You stay here in the shade. I probably won't be a minute."

Lizzie picked her way carefully through the undergrowth, hanging on to the trunks of small trees to keep her balance as the floor of the ravine descended at a sharp angle. What a wild, lovely spot this was! Once inside, it seemed she was in her own private world. It would be a perfect place to come when, like today, she needed to get away.

Stopping to catch her breath, she scanned the ravine. Sheer rock walls rose on either side, and numerous trees and bushes dotted the interior. Up ahead, it appeared the ravine made a turn, and Lizzie moved on to see what lay beyond.

When she was about to round the corner, Lizzie heard a sound ahead of her and froze. Was it a voice? But who would come here? Who else even knew of this place? She pressed against the wall, cautiously eased her head around the bend, and stopped still in amazement.

Adam knelt beside a large rock, his elbows propped on its smooth surface. His back was to Lizzie, and she strained her eyes to see who he might be talking to. His voice continued, and she realized with a start that he was praying. Embarrassed by her sense of intrusion, she started to slip away, then stopped short when she heard her name. Calling herself the worst kind of eavesdropper, she leaned her back against the rock wall and inched her head closer to the corner.

". . .don't understand it," he was saying. "Have I read everything wrong, thinking I saw Your hand at work when it was my own selfish desires?" Lizzie blinked. Could someone as stable as Adam possibly have the same kind of struggle she had experienced? She tried to keep from breathing, wanting to hear every word.

"You know how I feel about Lizzie," he went on. "For years she's been all I wanted, all I hoped for. As far as I could see, You were working things out in Your timing. I've even thought lately that she felt some of the same things for me. But now. . .I tried to pour out my heart to her and she sent me away. Why, Lord? Why?" The cry sounded as though it had been wrung from the depths of his soul.

Lizzie trembled from head to foot. Adam took a shuddering breath and continued. "You ask us to sacrifice sometimes, but I never dreamed I'd have to sacrifice my love for Lizzie." He went on in a stronger, more determined voice. "If that's what you're asking of me, though, I know that You know best. Father, I lay my love for her and my hopes for our future on the altar before You. Help me to bear the loss if I have to give her up forever."

Lizzie pressed her fist against her lips to stifle a sob. She started to ease away, but stopped once more at the mention of her name. "Please look after Lizzie, Lord. Guard her and protect her, and do what's best in her life. I trust You with that, because I know You love her even more than I do."

It was too much for Lizzie, who crept back from the corner and made her unsteady way to Dancer. She gave the horse his head, not trusting herself to guide him when she couldn't see for the tears that blurred her eyes.

Adam loved her! The thought blazed across her consciousness like a comet. "Adam loves me." She said it aloud, testing the sound of the words. It still didn't seem possible. When had this happened? And why hadn't she known of it until now? Lizzie reviewed the years since Adam had come to the Double B, seeking some clue.

He had always been around when she needed him, always helpful, always polite. But a man in love? He had never once let her know of his feelings, never showed any undue familiarity. He'd never even made an attempt to kiss her. *Like Tom did,* her memory whispered.

Yes, it always came back to Tom, she thought wearily. Everything she had experienced with him was what she had always thought went along with falling in love—the special way she felt when he looked at her with his sparking eyes, her willingness to alter her own goals in deference to his. If that wasn't love—and it obviously wasn't—what was? She had good examples in her parents, also in Jeff and Judith. Their relationships contained strong feelings, she knew, but also were firmly grounded in the commitment to put the other's welfare first.

Like Adam? her relentless inner voice goaded. *Yes, like Adam.* Lizzie took another look at the years she had known him, approaching it from a different viewpoint. Looking at it from this new perspective, she realized that Adam hadn't found it necessary to pursue her physically in order to show his love. He had shown her in a hundred other ways.

When had the change come? Was there a moment when simple courtesy had become a lover's tenderness, or had it grown up gradually, rooted deep like an oak? However it had happened, it was a fact she could no longer deny. The words Tom addressed to her had been intended to deceive. Adam had poured out his heart directly to God, and she had no doubt of his sincerity. The question now was how she felt about him.

Lizzie thought about the way she reacted when Adam was near, the way a lightning bolt seemed to shoot right through her. It was similar to how she had felt with Tom, but it was different, too. This was not so much sheer excitement as it was the feeling that they were being drawn together, two halves that needed one another to make a complete whole.

She remembered the Bible stories of her childhood about creation, when God had said, *"It is not good that the man should be alone."* Did that imply that it wasn't good for a woman to be alone either? Did that explain the aching emptiness she felt when Adam was no longer around? Was it possible—even desirable—that she could serve God wholeheartedly and allow Adam a place in her life, too?

Lizzie wrestled with these questions all the way home, and long after she had gone to bed, but not to sleep.

Chapter 20

Two days later, Lizzie had found some answers but was struggling with a new set of questions. There was no question about Adam and the caliber of man he was; everything about him was upright and true. Just as she had looked for the responses she wanted from God, regardless of what He wanted from Lizzie, she had been looking for the wrong things as proof of love.

And she could no longer delude herself into believing that a life of service to God meant that He wanted her to live it alone. One honest look at her parents' godly example was enough to convince her of that. Lizzie shook her head slowly. How blind could a person be?

Now that she saw things clearly, she was plagued by the fear that in her fumbling attempts to do the right thing and protect them both, she had pushed Adam away so far that she had ruined her chance for happiness.

Even the memory of Adam's prayer didn't soothe her. She had heard him put the situation in God's hands. Did that mean he wouldn't come around again until God somehow took an active role to work things out between them? Now that she understood her feelings for Adam, Lizzie didn't think she had the patience or the courage to wait and wonder indefinitely.

But what could she do? She might be in love, but she was still so unsure of herself that she couldn't take the initiative and make the first move. It looked like an unsolvable dilemma.

Lizzie glanced outside for the hundredth time that morning. The clouds were still there, gray and threatening, promising to let loose at any moment. Apparently the rains had decided to come early today, and there would be no chance for a ride until they had gone. And just when she needed to be outdoors, to be alone and think!

Feeling that if she didn't expend some energy she'd explode,

Lizzie went out to the porch and paced from one end to the other until she was surprised she hadn't worn a groove in the wooden planks. A few light drops fell to the ground, the forerunners of more to follow. Lizzie wanted to scream in frustration. If ever she needed to work off some steam, it was now, and she seemed to be blocked at every turn.

Maybe there was something she could do in the barn. If nothing else, the presence of the horses and the soothing smells of straw, hay, and leather would provide a balm for her troubled spirit. She dashed off through the raindrops, which were already increasing in force and number by the time she reached the barn.

❧

Adam muttered to himself as he watched the sky and wondered if he should turn back. He'd picked a fine time to decide to apologize to Charles for taking off without warning. But then, he couldn't say any of his actions lately had been especially wise.

Look at the way he'd raced up to Lizzie and babbled about his feelings without any preparation, catching her completely off guard. No wonder she sent him packing! He must have looked like a wild-eyed maniac, descending upon her like that.

But running off like that. . . He'd told himself at first he was doing it for Lizzie, taking his unwanted presence away from her. In all honesty, though, he had to confess it was the blow to his ego that had done it. Initially, at least. Staying away had been nothing short of cowardice. He was afraid to meet Lizzie again, and that's all there was to it. Strong, self-reliant Adam McKenzie was afraid to face willowy Lizzie Bradley. He had faced her rejection once; he didn't think he could take it if she rebuffed him again.

It was time he faced up to that fear. If he was going to consider himself any kind of man, he had to go back. He still had responsibilities there, after all, even if he hadn't been acting like it lately. And, he admitted to himself with a rueful laugh, it would be good to sleep in a real bed again, even if it was just a bunkhouse cot.

The proud owner of his own refurbished home, Adam had been

sleeping on a pile of hay in his barn ever since running home with his tail tucked between his legs. After all the work he'd done on the house with Lizzie in mind, he hadn't been able to bring himself to take up residence there without her. *What am I going to do if she never comes around to my way of thinking? I can just see myself, twenty years down the road, with a fine house on the best horse ranch in New Mexico, spreading my bedroll out on the hay every night!*

Tiny drops of rain beaded on his saddle, and a larger one splattered across the bridge of his nose. *I should have known better than to come out when it looked like this.* He checked his location; he was about halfway between the two ranches, but slightly nearer the Double B. That decided his course, and he urged his horse into a lope as the rain pelted down in earnest.

Lizzie glared sullenly at the sheets of rain pouring down from the heavens. Coming to the barn had seemed a good idea at first. She had spent time fussing over Dancer, and had polished her tack until the leather gleamed. Seeing that the rain hadn't diminished, she straightened the rest of the tack, rearranged the tools, and organized the feed bags into neat rows. The activity had helped use up nervous energy, but the rain was still coming down in torrents and showed no sign of abating.

She supposed she might throw a saddle blanket over her head and dash for the house, but she knew she'd be soaked to the skin by the time she got there. It looked like she was stuck where she was until the downpour slackened; she might as well find something else to do. She glanced around the barn and sighed. She'd been altogether too efficient. There wasn't a thing that needed fixing, unless she scattered tools, tack, and feed around and started in all over again.

Wait. Her gaze traveled upward to the loft. She hadn't been up there in some time, but being out of the line of sight, things were usually left in disorder up there much longer than down below where they were noticed. Lizzie nodded, relieved. She would climb up and get started right away.

Halfway up the ladder, Lizzie remembered why she hadn't climbed up there for so long. Her long skirt wanted to catch under her toe every time she raised her foot to climb another rung. She grasped the irritating garment with one hand, wrenching it loose and nearly throwing herself off balance in the process. The ladder teetered slightly and Lizzie closed her eyes, waiting for it to stop before she went on. The agile cowboys had no problem here, but then, they didn't have yards of fabric wrapped around their ankles either. It wasn't fair, she thought angrily.

The ladder ceased its swaying and Lizzie climbed another step.

❧

Adam could barely see ten yards in front of him. The last time the rain had come lashing down this hard was...well, he didn't remember a time he'd ever seen it rain like this. And here he was, caught out in the open.

His horse slowed and Adam could make out dark shapes looming behind the sheets of water. He breathed a sigh of relief. They'd made it to the barn! He could hardly wait to get inside. Even if it took a while for the rain to let up and he was stuck in the barn, he'd be under shelter, and that was all that mattered at the moment.

❧

"Oh, isn't this just grand!" Lizzie groused. Now nearly at the top of the ladder, she had maneuvered her skirt out of the way long enough to put her left foot on the next rung, but as soon as she lifted the right foot, she knew she was in trouble. Somehow the fabric had gotten wrapped around her right leg, holding her foot halfway between one rung and the next.

Gripping the ladder with both hands, she looked down and sighed with exasperation when she saw the problem. The hem of her skirt had caught on a nail and was now stretched so tightly by her right leg that it wouldn't pull loose. Furthermore, it had somehow managed to wrap around her leg and held it immobile. Now what? She couldn't stay up there indefinitely. Already her legs were beginning to ache. She reached down tentatively with her right hand, but the ladder started swaying so violently that she stopped, afraid to move again.

Lizzie surveyed the barn floor, trying to pick the best place to land if she fell, which now seemed all too likely. Unable to free herself from the constraining cloth to move either up or down, she would hang there like a fly caught in a spider's web until she could hold on no longer. Then she would drop like a stone.

If only someone would come! Even as the thought raced through her mind, Lizzie realized how unlikely that was. Who in his right mind would be out in this deluge? Twelve feet didn't seem all that high when one was standing on solid ground looking up. Looking down from that height, though, gave it a totally different perspective. How high had Willie been when he fell out of that cottonwood tree and broke his arm? Only ten feet or so, wasn't it? And he'd had a thick bush below to break his fall.

Her left hand, the one with the better hold, slipped a fraction.

Over the ceaseless beat of the driving rain, Lizzie heard a steady *splash, splash, splash* and recognized the sound of a horse's hooves plodding through mud. Bert, she knew, had been out before the storm had hit. For some reason he had apparently come back home instead of holing up somewhere for the duration. It was foolish on his part, but Lizzie blessed him for it. If only he got to her before she lost her hold completely. She needed to get his attention; he'd never think to look up here when he walked in.

Twisting as far as she dared, she focused her eyes on the open door and called out as loudly as she could. "Bert! Hurry! I'm caught on the ladder and I'm about to fall!" She caught sight of a shirtsleeve as she turned back around.

The maneuver proved too unsettling for the ladder, which shifted abruptly to the right, loosening Lizzie's hold still more. Splinters dug into her hand as she made a desperate effort to regain her grip, but she was too far off balance now.

With a piercing scream, she plunged off the ladder, hearing the sound of ripping fabric as the hem of her skirt tore loose from the nail. She saw the knotholes in the wall flash by as she dropped downward—straight into a pair of muscular arms. Lizzie squeezed her eyes tight at the moment of impact, aware only that by some miracle she was alive and unharmed. Then she opened them to look up at her rescuer, and stared right into the face of Adam McKenzie.

Chapter 21

The impact of Lizzie's landing drove Adam backward, slamming him against the wall. He stood unmoving, staring back at Lizzie in astonishment. Lizzie suddenly became aware that Adam still held her, and moved to pull away. Adam loosened his hold a trifle, but kept her within the circle of his arms. Unable to continue looking into his eyes, Lizzie stared straight ahead, where she could see the pulse pounding in the hollow of Adam's throat, keeping pace with her own wild heartbeat.

"Are you all right?" he asked in a voice hoarse with worry. "What happened?"

"I'm fine," Lizzie replied, feeling anything but. "My skirt—it got caught on a nail, and I couldn't move."

Adam nodded as though it made perfect sense, then frowned in puzzlement. "What were you doing up there, anyway?"

Trying to keep myself busy so I wouldn't go crazy thinking about you, Lizzie thought. Aloud, she responded with a question of her own. "How do you always manage to be around when I need to be rescued?"

She saw the corners of his full lips tilt up ever so slightly in the beginnings of a smile. "Just lucky, I guess." Her scalp felt prickly when Adam slowly raised one hand and tenderly brushed a wisp of hair back from her forehead. Lizzie's gaze flickered up to his eyes again, where she saw her own sense of wonder reflected in their depths.

Adam's hand moved to her shoulder, slid down her arm, and clasped her fingers in his own. The tingle she always felt when he was near now seemed like a living thing shooting back and forth between them. He moistened his lips. "Lizzie, I acted like an insensitive clod the other day. Can you forgive me?"

Lizzie nodded, never taking her eyes off him. His smile grew a fraction wider. "Would it be all right if I tried to start over?" he asked softly.

She nodded again. This time she was ready to listen to every word he had to say. His grip on her hand tightened, and he swallowed nervously.

"Lizzie, I have loved you for years. I've never told you before this because I didn't have a thing to offer you. But now, God has blessed me with a place of my own, a place where I can do what I know best—raise and train the finest horses around. It'll take a while to get it into full operation, but I know I can make a go of it, and Lord willing, in a few years it'll be known throughout the territory.

"The only thing that's missing," he added bluntly, "is you. I can't guarantee what the future will bring, but I can promise you this—I will love you, protect you, and do my best to see that you're happy and cared for as long as there is breath in my body."

Without loosening his grasp on Lizzie's hand, Adam knelt in front of her. "Lizzie, will you do me the honor of becoming my wife?"

Tears welled up in Lizzie's eyes, but for the first time in a long time, they were happy ones. Joy and a sense of peace like she had never experienced rose up inside her, filling every part of her being. Only one thing remained to be settled before she could give Adam the response he wanted.

She raised a trembling hand and rested it lightly on Adam's shoulder. "Before I answer, I need to know something. Can you forgive me for the way I behaved over Tom?"

Adam's brow creased at the mention of the name and Lizzie plunged ahead before she lost her nerve. "I let him kiss me, Adam. Nothing more, but I did do that. I'm not proud of it—in fact I'm horribly ashamed—but I can't agree to marry you without knowing that you know, and that you forgive me."

Adam slowly stood and laid one hand along the contour of Lizzie's cheek. "That belongs to the past now," he said, "and we'll keep it there. It's not only forgiven, it's forgotten." He released her fingers and cupped her face with both hands, tracing her cheekbones with his thumbs and staring at her as though he'd discovered a priceless treasure.

Lizzie had thought she'd known joy a few moments before, but it was nothing compared to what she felt when Adam lowered his head and touched his lips to hers, gathering her to himself in a warm embrace. When he raised his head, he looked at her with satisfaction and declared, "There. That marks the end of that chapter of our lives, and the beginning of a new one."

Lizzie nodded her agreement, too happy to speak. Adam's lips parted in a wide grin. "I take it that means you accept my proposal?" he asked her teasingly.

"Yes. Oh yes!" Lizzie cried, hugging him tight.

Adam responded by wrapping his arms around her and whirling exuberantly around the barn. He didn't stop until he was dizzy, and they dropped onto a bale of hay, laughing giddily. "Do you think your parents will object?" he asked, his tone serious once more.

Lizzie smiled and entwined her fingers in his. "God has brought us this far," she said simply. "He'll see us through the rest of the way."

"In that case," Adam said contentedly, sliding an arm around her shoulders, "why don't we sit right here and make some plans?" He nodded at the rain sheeting down beyond the barn doors. "It doesn't look like we'll be going anywhere soon."

Chapter 22

Lizzie Bradley, soon to be Lizzie McKenzie, looked out her window upon a glorious fall day. The sky, a flawless expanse of crystal blue, formed the perfect backdrop for the golden hills. Behind her, she heard a steady thumping sound and turned to see Judith removing Rose from Lizzie's bed.

"That's enough bouncing," Judith scolded her daughter. "Go find your father and see if there's anything you can do to help."

"I did," Rose protested. "He told me to come help you."

Judith rolled her eyes. "Then check with Vera," she ordered. "If she doesn't have anything for you to do, just remember to stay indoors, stay out of trouble, and stay clean."

"Yes ma'am." Rose left the room, mumbling.

Lizzie chuckled, glad for the distraction. "Children are a blessing," she reminded her aunt impishly. "The Bible says so."

"Thank you," Judith replied with a grin. "I'll remind you of that some day."

Lizzie laughed, blushed, then laughed again. The door swung open again to admit Abby. "Are you ready?" she asked.

Lizzie nodded happily, raising her arms so her mother and Judith could slip the exquisite white dress over her head. The two women had labored long hours over the gown, fashioning a creation that took Lizzie's breath away. More wonderful than the beauty of the dress, though, was the love that had gone into its making. Carefully easing herself into the bodice, Lizzie watched the soft folds of the skirt settle around her.

Abby stooped to arrange the full skirt while Judith began fastening the long row of buttons in the back. "I'll get it," Abby said when someone rapped at the door.

It was Sam, wanting to know what he should do. "Go see what

Travis is doing, and keep him out of mischief," Judith told him, rocking Susannah's cradle with one foot while her hands maneuvered the tiny buttons. "Honestly," she said as the door closed behind Sam, "I thought I raised them better. Is everyone else in this family completely helpless?"

Once more came the sound of knocking. "What now?" Abby exclaimed in exasperation. This time Jeff stuck his head into the room. He pursed his lips in a silent whistle at the sight of Lizzie, encased in the flowing gown. "Honey, you look gorgeous," he said, and in the same breath added, "Have any of you seen Willie? He took off after lunch and I haven't seen him since."

"Do you mean to tell me that boy's run off, today of all days?" Abby cried, her patience clearly slipping.

Lizzie's stomach knotted in panic. Willie was supposed to be Adam's best man. Surely he wouldn't take a chance on ruining her wedding!

"I'm sure he'll be back soon," Judith said soothingly, fastening the last button and giving Lizzie's shoulder an affectionate squeeze. She cast a stern look at Jeff and mouthed, *Find him. Now!* Jeff scuttled off obediently.

Abby lifted a garland of fall wildflowers and fastened it onto Lizzie's head, then turned the mirror so Lizzie could see. "Oh!" was all that she could say. She felt the sting of tears. "Thank you, Mama. Thank you, Aunt Judith. It's beautiful."

"You're beautiful," her mother said gently.

"I'll second that," Charles said as he peeked cautiously around the door, then entered the room. "Would you ladies mind giving me a few minutes alone with my daughter?" Judith gave Lizzie a warm hug and an encouraging smile. Abby checked the dress, the garland, and Lizzie one last time, then enfolded her daughter in a wordless embrace before leaving the room with Judith.

"What do you think?" Lizzie asked, indicating her attire with a lighthearted gesture meant to mask the sudden nervousness fluttering inside her like a host of butterflies.

Charles regarded her with immeasurable pride shining in his eyes. "I think Adam McKenzie is one blessed man." Taking her hands in his, he looked down at her tenderly. "I can't believe this day has come so quickly," he admitted. "You are sure, aren't you?"

Lizzie nodded decisively. "More sure than I've ever been about anything, Papa."

Charles smiled. "You're getting a fine man. I'm happy for both of you."

Lizzie hugged him tight, heedless of her lovely dress. "Thank you, Papa. I love you."

The door opened one more time and Willie entered, his hair slicked down and clothes in perfect order. Lizzie felt lightheaded with relief. Willie hadn't let her down; how could she have doubted him?

"Ma says to tell you it's time," he said, and Lizzie's butterflies returned, wings whirling madly. Willie cocked one eyebrow upward and a slow smile spread across his face. "Not bad, sis. Not bad at all." He gave her a wink and was gone.

Lizzie drew a tremulous breath and picked up the bouquet of fall flowers. Charles leaned near, offering his arm. She nestled her hand in the crook of his elbow and closed her eyes for a moment. *Thank You, Lord, for what You've done in my life. Thank You for the husband You're giving me. Help us both to grow in You for the rest of our lives.* She opened her eyes, squared her shoulders, and looked up at her father with a smile. "I'm ready," she said.

Rose waited for them at the end of the corridor, where Charles leaned far enough around the corner to catch the pianist's eye. As the strains of music filled the air, Charles gave Lizzie an encouraging nod and they stepped through the double doors of the living room. Rose preceded them, solemnly scattering flower petals on her way.

The living room had been transformed for the occasion. Candles cast a soft glow over banks of flowers covering every available surface, and rows of chairs had been set up to accommodate the many guests, who now rose from their seats at Lizzie's entrance. Vera stood next to the aisle, beaming and wiping her streaming eyes with a handkerchief. Bert, looking uncomfortably stiff in his best clothes, stood next to her, and beside him Hank leaned on a cane, grinning for all he was worth.

Lizzie looked toward the front of the room and the guests and decorations faded away. Her gaze was fixed on Adam, and Adam alone. He stood waiting, tall and trim in his frock coat, watching her approach. When she reached him, she barely noticed Charles's kiss on her cheek as he placed her hand in Adam's and sat down next to her mother.

Lizzie heard Brother Webster's voice through a joyous haze as she repeated the vows to love, honor, and obey. But she and Adam, hands joined as they made their pledge before God, seemed to exist in a world apart.

Brother Webster stopped talking, but Adam and Lizzie stood staring into each other's eyes. The pastor cleared his throat and tapped Adam on the shoulder. "I said, you may kiss the bride," he told him above the ripple of laughter from the guests.

Any embarrassment Lizzie might have felt was forgotten as Adam embraced her for the first time as his wife, and his kiss blotted out everything but him and the certainty of their love.

The reception passed in a happy blur, with Lizzie and Adam accepting the congratulations of their friends and neighbors. Hank brought up the end of the line, nudging Adam in the ribs and saying, "I guess those pretty gray eyes will just be looking at you from now on." Adam flushed a dark red, but managed to grin back and say, "You're a pretty sharp old codger, all right." He bent toward Lizzie and whispered, "Isn't it about time for us to leave?" Lizzie, glowing with happiness, nodded her agreement and hurried off to change while Adam went to hitch the horses to the buggy Charles had loaned them for the occasion.

When she emerged a short time later, Adam was waiting for her, fending off good-natured wisecracks from Jeff and the cowboys.

"Better hurry," he told her with a laugh. "I can't take too much more of this!"

The children crowded around, demanding to say their goodbyes. Then Jeff shook Adam's hand and kissed Lizzie on the cheek, and Judith hugged them both. "God does have good things in store for you," she said with a smile.

"I know," Lizzie replied, her eyes alight with joy. "And I'm willing to let Him show me what they are...all in His timing!"

The others moved back, allowing Lizzie's parents to be alone with their daughter and new son-in-law. "Thank you for everything, Mama," Lizzie whispered, giving her mother a fierce hug. "Not just for today, but for always." Abby, close to tears, returned the hug and nodded without speaking.

Charles stood in front of Adam, hands on his hips and a stern expression on his face. "Take good care of her, son. You hear?" Adam nodded, eyeing him steadily, and Charles's face broke into a broad smile. "I know you will, Adam. Welcome to the family!"

Adam helped Lizzie to her seat in the buggy, and she turned for one more look at her family and her childhood home. The buggy rocked and settled again when Adam climbed to his place and took up the reins. "Are you ready to go to your own home, Mrs. McKenzie?" he asked.

Lizzie started to nod, but stopped at the sight of Willie coming out of the house. Crossing the porch at a run, he made a flying leap down the steps and came loping toward them. "Wait up!" he cried, waving frantically.

"It's about time," Lizzie teased him. "I didn't think I was going to get to tell you goodbye."

"You're running late for everything today," Adam said. "You had me plenty worried, not showing up for the wedding until the last minute." He studied Willie, who had climbed onto the buggy step and was dutifully hugging Lizzie. "Where were you then, anyway?"

Willie looked up with innocent blue eyes. "Why, I figured with all the hullabaloo today, you might not have had a chance to tend to your stock," he said virtuously. "So I rode over to your place to make sure everything was taken care of." Lizzie shifted on the seat and eyed Willie uneasily.

Adam assumed a deadpan expression. "And was everything 'taken care of' to your satisfaction?"

Willie jumped down off the buggy. "It is now." He grinned and gave them a jaunty wave. "Have a happy homecoming."

Adam clucked to the horses and they moved away. "What all do you suppose he has lying in wait for us?" he asked with a rueful smile.

"With Willie, there's no telling," Lizzie responded. She looked up at her new husband and tried unsuccessfully to stifle a giggle. "I guess this makes you a full-fledged member of the family."

With the buggy cover shielding them from the view of the wedding guests, Adam gave her a kiss that told her how glad he was that it was true.

Carol Cox is the bestselling author of 30 novels and novellas. A third-generation Arizonan, Carol has a lifelong fascination with the Old West and hopes to make it live again in the hearts of her readers. She makes her home in northern Arizona, where the deer and the antelope really do play—often within view of the family's front porch.

You can find Carol on the Web at: AuthorCarolCox.com and Facebook.com/carol.cox.

If You Liked This Book, You'll Also Like...

Love's Story
by Dianne Christner

Venture into this classic historical romance set in California from bestselling author Dianne Christner. As a female journalist, Meredith has something to prove with her big story on forest conservation. But when her heart becomes entangled, will she risk her career? Also includes a bonus story, *Strong as the Redwood* by Kristin Billerbeck.
Paperback / 978-1-63409-901-1 / $9.99

The Lilac Year
by Janet Spaeth

Travel to the northern prairie wilderness where this historical romance from author Janet Spaeth is set. Mariah is searching for her nephew and a quick way to leave the frontier when she meets homesteader Ben Harris. Also includes the bonus sequel, *Rose Kelly*.
Paperback / 978-1-63409-908-0 / $9.99

Wildflower Harvest
by Colleen L. Reece

Enjoy an inspiring historical romance set in Wyoming territory from author Colleen L. Reece. Dr. Adam Birchfield risks losing love in order to keep searching for his brother. Also includes the bonus story, *Desert Rose* in which a woman falls in love with a man through his letters.
Paperback / 978-1-63409-907-3 / $9.99